CAPTIVITY & KINGS

BOOK ONE OF OF CAPTIVITY & KINGS

BY
E.Y. LASTER

COPYRIGHTED MATERIAL

OF CAPTIVITY & KINGS

DEDICATION

Until the lions have their own historians, the history of the hunt will always glorify the hunter.

~African Proverb

For the love of my heritage and history: To my grandmothers, queens in their own right, my grandfathers, who made me believe in angels, my mother, a saint, my father, my hero, and my sister, my first friend. This book is dedicated to my family who enchanted me as a child with stories from centuries past, to my friends who encouraged me to chase my dreams, and my readers who may still be struggling to learn how. Have the courage to pursue your passion without restraint.

ILLUSTRATIONS

Ms. Crystal D. Turner designed the cover image as well as the drawings below.

GIRL ANKOLE-WATUSI

For questions regarding designs, illustrations, or the commission of Ms. Turner as an illustrator, please send all inquiries to c1times7@gmail.com.

TABLE OF CONTENTS

MAP

Cuicul 🏛

Ghadamis 🏛

Cairo 🏛

† Sertes Desert

Ghana Empire

🐪

Beja Kingdoms

Niger River

Makouria 🏛

Kingdom of Kush

🏛 Gao

Dhenne 🏛

Sao Kingdom

Aksum Kingdom

🦁 Igbo

Chad

Nile River

Kibera River

Kibera Kingdom

Mount Kilimanjara

Bridge of Martyrs

Scorpion Kingdom

Essi Kingdom

Exile Island

Skeleton Coast

Namib Desert

Kalahari Desert

Ice Mountains

Sotho Kingdom

River Nub

Nabara Kingdom

Torrent

† Desert Fathers

🏛 Gold

⋮ Salt

💎 Diamonds

6

PROLOGUE

MEROË – 4TH CENTURY A.D.

"Don't be scared. You can trust me," her neighbor repeated softly, the blood dripping from the edge of his blade creating a scarlet pool around his feet as he moved the scimitar behind his back and out of sight.

The ten feet of space between them in her sandstone home had become a canyon. Her father on his back in the middle, gutted from navel to throat as his blood created a sea around them. And she, his eldest daughter, an unwitting witness who had stumbled upon this crime. *What has he done to my father?* Frozen, Nekili pointed the farming scythe at him, arm shaking violently from the weight of the steel in her eight-year-old hands. Her sister's small arms suddenly wrapped themselves around her waist, squeezing tighter as though she held fast to the only tree for miles in the midst of a sandstorm in Meroë. Looking at her neighbor, Nekili hesitated.

Voices shouted outside in the darkness and her chest heaved as she struggled to breathe from the weight of what might happen next. Ezana's soldiers forced their way in, filling the room like fire as she cowered with her sister in the corner. Left, right, up, and down the blades met over and over again as blood sprayed across her face. When it grew quiet she looked up. Pointing the scimitar at her, her neighbor gritted his teeth, nostrils flaring as he narrowed his eyes. A *khopesh* protruded from his back, the blade covered in blood and entrails as he smiled apologetically at her, opening his mouth slowly.

"Run."

Grabbing Naima's hand, she leapt over the dead bodies on the ground and past the door, not looking back once as she fled the carnage. They were being hunted. Leaves and branches whipped at her face, clawing at her skin and tangling in her thick, black hair as she ran blindly through the dark away from Meroë, dragging her sister along behind her as her heart hammered in her chest. Snatching branches out of her way she did her best to keep quiet, even as they left long, red scratches on her brown skin. She didn't cry out. If she did the slavers would hear and they would find them all. They needed to cross the Nile and reach the desert. Pressing on, the sand sucked at her feet as she pushed huge leaves aside, the wood snapping like the sound of her father's fingers when her *papo* cracked his knuckles. *My dead father.* As much as she wanted to grieve she had no time. His face arose in her mind and kept her pressing on. Black blood seeping from his mouth, fog colored eyes staring at the ceiling, neck twisted like the vines wrapped around the acacia trees which grew in her family's sorghum fields. She didn't have time to wonder where her mother was. Or her older brother. There'd been no sign of them. It wouldn't be her fate. Or her sister's. The last memories of her brother and father working in their sorghum fields just outside of Meroë seemed so long ago. The ragged breathing of her sister brought her back, Naima squeezing her hand as though she meant to break it, trying to keep running as a lion would if the cheetah hunted him. The mongrels' faint barking was the only sound that warned how close the slavers were. If they weren't fast enough they would soon be slaves. And slaves were property, and property was money and power.

Slowing down as she reached a clearing, her eyes widened. There were so many of them. Farmers, blacksmiths, herders, fisherman, many she recognized. They were standing there, still as stone, and the hairs rose on the back of her neck and arms. A scream cut through the air, high, and shrill, and terrified, as everything seemed to happen at once. Arrows flew from the trees to her right and she grabbed her sister and began to run again. Their lives depended on it. All around them men and women fell like stones to the ground, screaming in the darkness like the lambs her father slaughtered for meat.

Her arm wrenched behind her and she looked back in time to see her sister crumple to the ground. Kneeling quickly, she pressed her hand over Naima's heart. She wasn't dead, only hurt and stunned. Without a beat she gripped Naima around her waist, dragging her towards a tiny sandstone structure meant for holding cattle at the edge of the clearing, the sound of steel tipped arrows hitting trees and flesh filling her ears.

Tears ran down her face as she pushed her sister inside, squeezing in behind her. Pulling her sister into her lap she held her close, rocking her against her body. Blood ran from a cut on her leg. With a small sigh of relief she looked up. Eleven pairs of eyes stared back at her, wide and scared in the moonlight shining through the top air hole as arrows continued raining against the shelter. The smell of sweat and fear hung in the air. Suddenly a man, tall and brown shouldered inside, grabbing her sister's leg to drag her out and get inside himself.

Nekili screamed and reached for his leg, sinking her teeth into his ankle as the arrows continued hitting the walls like so many bees zipping by her ears. When he stumbled she pushed him roughly, the arrows hitting his body and ripping through his clothing as she pulled her sister close again. She wiped the tears from her sister's face and looked back up at the eleven pairs of unblinking eyes. None of them judged her. *Apedemak save us.*

A moment later, the assault stopped, and silence fell over the clearing. She reached for her sister's leg tenderly. It had only been grazed.

"Can you walk?" she whispered.

Naima nodded, resting her head on Nekili's shoulder as the smell of shit and blood filled the air. She tried to push the thoughts from her head in the silence, but it didn't work. Her family had been torn apart in a second. Squeezing her eyes shut she could still remember the feel of the breeze against her cheeks earlier that morning as she ran through her family's sorghum fields just outside of Meroë. The tall, stepped sandstone pyramids just in sight in the distance as she ran. Stalks slapping at her legs and knees as she searched for her father.

"Papo!" Running through the stalks Nekili had made a beeline to her father, Naqyrin, cutting through the tall stalks towards him, her shoulder length, coal curls bouncing as she came, hopping over the burrows in the earth. When she reached him she lifted her hands towards him and he laughed, picking her up as she tried to catch her breath. Turning her head from left to right wordlessly she spotted her brother Neka from his yells. After a moment she sighed and put her head against his shoulder. Her heart beat furiously like a hummingbird's wings as it settled from her sprint, the hot sun against her face. She was over a mile away from their home.

"Papo," she began slowly, "Mother wants to know what you and Neka want for dinner. Can I climb the tree with Neka? I'm big enough now and I can run faster than him, Papo."

"Yes you can-"

Her gasp interrupted him. "I can?" she asked excitedly, her head lifting immediately.

"Run faster than him. You know I don't want you up there. Use the ground. There is nowhere to fall."

"Hmmph," came her reply. She laid her head back down on his shoulder again, wrapping her arm around his neck as she rested.

"Ahhhhhhhhh!"

The piercing scream made her father turn quickly, scanning the fields around him as he searched for the source of the sound. When he found it he chuckled. She twisted in his arms to follow his gaze. A flock of red-beaked birds swarmed in the air above her brother's head. Palm sized feathered birds that obsessively devoured the sorghum if they weren't careful. She'd seen them terrorize elephants in huge numbers. They were ruthless.

"Neka!" her father called to her brother. Neka stood atop a young acacia tree, sticks and pebbles in his hand, waving them wildly, the tree shaking slightly under his weight. The birds cawed back at him as some flew away, others, disinterested until his stones got close enough. Hopping back and forth they teased him mercilessly as he continued wildly shaking the branches and throwing pebbles.

"Papo, I'm keeping the sorghum safe!" Neka yelled, legs shaking as he moved the acacia tree with his weight.

"Tch tch, do it quietly," her father called back, his deep voice full of amusement.

"Papo, how? The birds are not scared of me."

"That is because they can fly away and you cannot follow. They are not scared of anything. They are flying locusts!"

"Papo, make me a bird," her brother cried back.

Her father had laughed, throwing his head back, shoulders shaking. "You want the world."

"Not the world," Neka said. "Just wings!"

"It's time to come down soon, we are almost done. I want you to help draw water with Nekili."

"Naima went to draw water already, Papo," Nekili told him, squirming in his arms to let him know to put her down. Quickly seating herself on the ground among the sorghum, she began to tie the stalks into small figures next to her. "She'll be back in time for dinner."

"Excellent."

Stretching as he picked up his rake, her father looked across at the bright red fields, eyes straining against the dying sun. Nekili squinted as she looked up at him. His shoulders were strong from his farming as well as his support of other farms by picking that grown from the adjacent fields when they were shorthanded. It was a strong grain regardless of the rainfall. Neka continued hollering at the top of his lungs, shaking the acacia tree with his legs as he gripped a branch with his right hand, his left waving wildly about as he tried to disperse the birds and prevent them from landing among the sorghum. Nekili shook her head as her brother continued, determined, undaunted.

"Brother Naqyrin!" a voice called. "May Apedemak keep you!" Their neighbor was making tracks around the stalks, careful not to tread on the sorghum, his head bobbing between the red seeds as he moved.

"Brother," his greeting came with an outstretched hand.

Her father grabbed it once before releasing it to grip his forearm where his elbow connected tightly.

"How have you been, Kedjeh?" he asked him.

"Well. Truly. Well," came their neighbor's reply. "The flooding season is almost here. Will you have all you need?"

"With the gods pleasure. Half of our food we have bundled into sacks for the market. Some I hope to send south to my cousins in Nabara for trade during their Festival of Kings next month. I think it will be a very productive grain." Her father's dark eyes were excited and lively as he thought about the prospect of the sale.

"Have you any word from Nudolla? From the Kingdom of Nabara?" neighbor Kedjeh asked. "Or the Sao?" he asked suddenly.

Her father shook his head. "Only what some have told me when they passed through heading south."

"It is not a good time to be without friends or neighbors. They are moving closer, Naqyrin. King Roktami should have asked Kashta for help! From the Kingdom of Nabara I'm told High King Kashta *still* commands over a *thousand Medjay* and holds alliances with neighboring kingdoms. More than enough to aid us. The slavers are finding ways to move to the interior. Creating garrisons in Berber cities just like Cuicul. And even here, outside of Meroë, there are problems with raiders and thieves who seek to usurp trade routes."

"They will not survive here. The desert will kill them faster than we can." Turning his head towards her, her father smiled brightly and she grinned back before twisting the stalks into dolls again with her fingers as she continued listening. "It is too far and King Roktami of Kush does all he can to ensure there are still trade routes left for us," her father had emphasized, continuing to cut the stalks.

"Not anymore, Naqyrin," neighbor Kedjeh whispered, stepping closer to her father. She made sure not to look up as she continued eavesdropping on their conversation lest her father send her away. "They have Berber guides, they marry them, and they trade with them. And the rest they sell and send across the sea for their gladiator games. This Ethiopian King Ezana does not care except to trade with the Romans and usurp the trade routes of Kush. Our resources are too tempting for him to leave us alone. He trades whatever he is able to. Even his *own*. Our Kushite King of Meroë will not last much longer. The only place we will be safe will be the desert and then we must live like the Christian hermits I hear rumors of. Drowning in the sand. Always running with our tails between our legs like hunted *beasts*. Ezana will eat our hearts and that of King Roktami if he so chooses! My cousin has seen it with his own two eyes," their neighbor pointed at her father, his second and third finger aimed at him. Shaking his head their neighbor tapped his right fist against his left before spreading his right fingers wide, quickly bringing them up to eye level. "You must *open* yours!"

Nekili bit her lip at the tone he took and looked back and forth between him and her father. Fear ran through every word he uttered.

After a moment their neighbor spotted her on the ground, catching her eye before she was able to look away.

"Hello little one," neighbor Kedjeh smiled at her and she waved back. Their neighbor finally touched her father on the shoulder. Until tomorrow morning?"

Her father nodded, watching as he left. "We will have some of this with dinner." He planted a wet kiss on her cheek as he shook her slightly, throwing her into the air as she giggled happily before setting her down.

"I did not forget, Papo. I want to climb. I will remember," she warned him, pouting as she looked at him.

"I know, Nekili, I know," he replied reaching down with his scythe to cut the leaves and bed seeds from the sorghum cane at his feet.

"One day I'll be as tall as a hippopotamus, you know."

"Hippos are not tall, Nekili. You will be fat."

"Ah! Papo, no. I will be tall. You will see." He tweaked her pug nose as her cheeks puffed out. Smiling he leaned down to cut the sorghum cane and separate the seeds and leaves.

Watching him closely she worked next to him, helping move the freed leaves and seeds a little further from him and out of his way as they were cut. The workers would return to help in the morning.

"After you see your mother take your sister with you to the *manas*." The pools were a distance, but she and her sister loved to play in them. And at this time, with such little water her father never worried about dangerous animals. The water was drying with the hot dry winds blowing harder and the rain was not as abundant as before this season. He handed her the bundle of sorghum and a piece of sorghum cane the length of her forearm. She began chewing on it immediately, her little fingers tightly wrapped around the middle of the cane for a firm grip. At eight she ate more than her sister and brother combined yet she was as slim as a stalk. Her father had lifted her up one time and turned her upside down as she laughed and screamed to see if anything would come out.

"She's your daughter," her mother always told him, "it is no wonder she eats like a hippopotamus. It is all she sees."

Coming to stand next to her, her father put one hand atop her head, looking around him. Laughter sounded in the distance and Nekili frowned, looking up at him as he met her eyes. It was most likely hyenas. They came too close sometimes. Closer than she expected. Closer than her family wanted. Leaning against her father's leg she wondered if she would ever see one. From the stories her brother told her, she never wanted to.

A hand touched her cheek and she looked up at her father's worried eyes as she sucked at the cane. "Papo?" she asked, her big brown eyes full of concern. He pulled her closer to his side.

"It is nothing, Kili," he smiled and waited until the smile came back to her face. "Go. Take this to your mother and then to the river and find Naima, my little cheetah." She had smiled, nodding and lifting the sorghum bundle before taking off through the field as fast as her legs would carry her.

Faint barking met her ears and the memory faded from her mind as the darkness pressed against her eyes and the smell of blood reached her nose.

"We have to move before they come," she whispered to Naima, her eyes wide in the darkness as she put her mouth closer to her sister's ear. "Or they'll find us and take us to King Ezana."

The others started moving too, running outside quickly, tentatively as the familiar song began. Barking. Grabbing Naima's hand she pulled her outside and towards the oasis near the Nile, tears running down her face, blurring her vision she ran. They could swim across the Nile if they reached it. She had to try. Mud sucked at her feet as the slavers closed in on them and she looked down in confusion. The oasis was bordered by sand. Nothing but sand and a short distance away sat the Nile. But not anymore. Now the oasis was a wide stretch of mud and refuse and rank water that was filled with the leavings of animal bones and waste. But if they reached it they could hide. If they reached it they might live. Screams cut the air as the dogs found runners. They would be next. Dragging her sister, she pulled her into the swamp, up to her chin.

"Nekili," Naima sobbed, terrified. "I want *papo," she protested between sobs.* I can't-"

"When I tell you to, you go under. And don't come back up until I say," she whispered back.

"I can't…"

The dogs broke through the brush and she grabbed a hollow stick floating on the water. She sank back into the water next to Naima, putting the stick into her sister's mouth and ignoring her eyes as they widened.

"Breathe through your mouth. Only your mouth. And don't come back up until I squeeze your hand twice."

She pushed her sister under slowly until her shoulders disappeared and then the top of her head and only the stick remained. It was the hardest thing she'd ever done. She waited until the dogs' barking was loudest and sank up to her mouth and then her nose. It was an eternity. The mud was thick and the water covered her ears. The barking was faint and she began to tremble as cold seeped into her bones. She counted to forty before she began to panic, releasing her breath slowly every ten seconds after that as she ran out of air. Praying Naima had done what she told her to. Rolling to expose an ear, her heartbeat quickened. Nothing, only silence. She squeezed her sister's hand and Naima's little fingers clawed at her arms, clutching at her clothes as she pulled herself from the mud next to her. Pushing at the bottom of the swamp floor with her feet, she rose slowly, only letting her nose up, her head tilted back. When she rose, she covered Naima's mouth with her hand, forcing her to breathe through her nose.

The warning growl was soft yet frightening. One pair of eyes stared at her and the dog's lips pulled back in a snarl, growling softly. He opened his mouth to bark as Nekili drew back her fist and punched the mongrel as hard as she could in the muzzle. He whined and turned, his tail between his legs as he ran back through the trees. *They didn't see us. They don't realize we are here.* All of her panic gave way as she clutched her sister's hand, slowly turning to look at the water. She thought the oasis was filled with logs, clogging the base of the river along with refuse in the swamp. But there were more than logs around them. She gasped as her eyes landed on at least thirty corpses. Most bloated and decaying rapidly. The open mouthed surprise on her father's face as he lay in his own blood in the doorway of their home flashed before her eyes as she looked at the slaver's victims. Her vision blurred and she angrily wiped at her tears.

Next to her, Naima retched into the swamp again and again, her whole body shaking. "I want *papo,*" her sobs cut Nekili's skin, closing her throat. "King Roktami…maybe... we can get to Nabara to see High King Amkarqa Kashta. He can help-"

Nekili turned and grabbed her sister by the shoulders.

"You heard what Ezana's men said as well as I before he killed our neighbor. You *saw.*" Her piercing gaze bore into her sister's. "We are *everywhere.*" Naima's shoulders began to tremble and she pulled her into her arms hugging her tightly. "There's one place I know they're not. The Scetes. That's where we'll go. No one will find us in the desert. That's where we'll be safe."

"It's too *far,*" Naima cried. "It's too *hot.* We'll never make it. We are not hermits they will never take us in!" Naima's face began to crumple as she finished. "I don't want to go, I want *Papo,*" Naima sobbed.

Looking up into the trees she spotted an owl landing on a branch above them. It spun its head to the right as it ruffled its feathers, huge eyes looking down on her before hooting softly. A warning. Before Naima could start crying again, she grabbed her sister's hand.

"*Papo's dead.*" Pulling Naima behind her and out of the swamp she pushed the bodies out of the way gingerly. *They are at rest now.* She was not. Their journey had just begun.

IMANI

Waking with a start, she nearly fell from her bed as her coughing echoed throughout the chamber. Her bright, amber eyes wide and full of shock. *It was just a dream.* She was still inside the palace walls, the sea of dead bodies nowhere near. Raking her fingers through her black curls she inhaled deeply, out of breath and shaking from the vividness of her dream. A flush spread over her deep brown cheeks. The water seemed to have filled her lungs too. After a pause, she moved from her bed, grabbing her black lambswool cloak and slipping it around her body. The heat was stifling during the day, but it was always colder at night in Nabara. As soon as the sun disappeared the cold crept into her body, making her ears tingle as the hairs on her neck rose. Seeping into her bones. Pulling the cloak's hood high, she pushed open the stone door, careful not to wake Ama from where she slept on her bed. Ama had arrived well in advance of the Festival of Kings. Two years older and fearful of Imani's High King father, the two were close. Her father was brother to Imani's mother, the High Queen. But Ama's parents were long dead. They had both taken ill on a trip back from Kibera and passed. Her cousin would beg her not to go. Imani had been in trouble more times than she cared to count.

Creeping slowly down the stairs, she walked toward the secret meeting of the council members of the Empire of Nudolla. Hidden tunnels ran underneath the palace, and she followed them as quickly as she could until she reached the lion-shaped *deffufa*, a temple reserved for ceremonies, prayer, and as a memorial for the dead members of her royal family. The voices grew louder as she descended into the underground chamber, the hood covering her maple face, almond-shaped eyes darting from crevice to corner as she descended the steps, fearful should any guards catch her. She'd been forbidden to attend. Her father was the High King of the Nudollan Empire, holding sway over an alliance of a number of independent Kings from his seat in the Kingdom of Nabara, each with their own territories in Nudolla: the Kibera Kingdom, the

Kingdom of the Sao, the Scorpion Kingdom, the Essi Kingdom, and the Kingdom of the Sotho. As High King, her father alone commanded the Medjay and Adamantine warriors as well as ruling on foreign matters and threats to Nudolla such as slavery and trade. All of the kings were descendants of ancient civilizations, fierce warriors, brilliant philosophers, great builders, and mighty kings. Most called it an empire, others a collective. Whatever they chose to call it, it was an alliance built on loyalty, courage, and justice. Each of them were sworn to protect these secrets.

Even as a child she knew not to ask her father again once the word *forbidden* came from his mouth. When she was young they'd been returning from a visit to the Kingdom of the Kibera, their large caravan snaking over mountains and down valleys into the Kalahari Desert and away from the jungle as they returned to the Nudollan Empire's seat in Nabara, Kingdom of Gold. Shouting and yelling caused her to gasp from her seat in the litter, pushing the shade aside as her sister tried to pull her back in. When they came to a stop, she shook Nema's hand off her shoulder and jumped to the ground.

"He is dying," her Uncle Shaharqa told her father. "There's no saving him."

She crept up quietly, watching her uncle's hand as it rested against the lion's neck. Somewhere, laughter sounded and she looked over her shoulder, frowning. Nabaran archers still had their arrows drawn, eyes looking into the distance, wary.

"The hyenas were too many. And he was alone. He might have been driven out by his pride. Or simply traveling by himself. There's no way to tell," her father replied.

Holding her breath, she finally got close enough to see the lion's shredded hind legs and ripped throat. Blood poured from it onto the ground, the grass a deep scarlet around him. His chest rose and fell softly as he breathed, her father squatting down in his raiment to gently put one hand on his dark red mane. When his chest stilled, tears filled her eyes like the River Nub, and she gritted her teeth to keep from letting her father see her cry. Next to her the grass swayed suddenly and she looked down, gasping as she took two steps in her gown and fell to the ground to scoop up her prize.

18

"Imanishakheto!"

She barely heard her father as she slipped her fingers under the soft fur of the lion cub and pulled him from the log he was under into her excited arms. He took one swipe at her face, and she leaned back quickly, tickling her fingers under his chin. The sound he made was nowhere near a growl though he'd opened his mouth wide enough for it to be. Squirming in her arms, he caught her finger in his mouth and she gasped, fear and excitement running through her at the same time as she struggled to hold his tiny body. But he only nipped it before releasing it, using his paws to try to climb up her chest toward her shoulders.

"Imanishakheto, release him." Her father stood behind her with her uncle and Medjay, who were looking over their shoulders cautiously.

"It's Apedemak, Father!" Her eyes lit up as she grinned down at the cub.

"The Lion-God will be fine on his own. He needs no help. We have enough lions at the palace for you to play with." Her father looked to her uncles Asim and Shaharqa, raising his eyebrows briefly.

"Father, he doesn't have anyone." Looking up at him with hesitation, she lifted the lion cub back up as he slid down in her arms.

"Still. You must let him go." Her father was unrelenting.

"But he will die!" She looked back and forth from her father to her uncles, her eyes pleading with them to understand. "You said so yourself," she reminded him. "The hyenas may come back." Even now she could still remember the determination in her heart to change his mind.

"That is life, Imanishakheto." Her father looked down at her with sympathetic eyes that told her she wouldn't win this argument. She never did. "He may die, as everything does. Even the acacia trees will die and new trees replace it. He may die, or he may survive. One day, he may even eat *us*. The longer you hold on, the harder it will be to let go. He must learn to survive on his own. That is life."

Looking down at the cub in her arms, she kissed the top of its head, looking one last time into its golden eyes as its tiny ears flicked back and forth. When her father put a hand on her shoulder, she set him down, watching him play at her feet, circling her, his tail batting at her ankles as he tried to use his paws to climb up her gown and back into her arms.

"But—"

"I forbid it."

Biting her lip, she looked down at the ground, kneeling to let the cub nip at her fingers again.

"Come, Imanishakheto." Her father had moved back toward the litter swiftly. "It will be dark soon."

She turned around one more time before feeling a hand on her shoulder. Her uncle held out a large chunk of salted meat to her, nodding to the cub. Smiling, she'd taken it and held it out to the cub, which pounced on it immediately. He only took one bite before mewling again, rolling onto his back to let her rub his stomach. When her uncle put his hand on her shoulder once again, she rose and turned around. Oblivious to the dirt and grass on her gown, she looked back again, and again as she stepped through the high grass, watching the lion cub softly trying to hop through the grass after her, the meat held tightly in its mouth. *He'll survive,* she told herself. *That* is also life.

Smiling at the memory, she let her fingers trail over the sandstone walls of the *deffufa* as she descended, the soft glow from her torch illuminating the figures drawn on them from long ago. The drawings were as familiar to her as her own face. A Nubian archer stood tall, one brown arm outstretched as his other pulled the string of his bow taut. Her eyes followed his gaze, a herd of antelope a foot away, standing, eating in the tall grass. Her hands moved up the wall to let her fingers feather over the cattle of kings, ankole-watusi, the pride of Nabara. Their unmistakably tall horns were magically uniform as they grouped together to adorn the wall. A lake full of fishermen sailed just below them, their reed boats sitting among the curved lines that made the waves. To their left a parade of dancers, some mid-air, swirling against the rock with their black hair caught in the wind above them. Alive. A history. Her history.

Moving her eyes farther down, a soft murmur greeted her ears. She shrank back. Her father had forbidden her attendance, and she'd known after the first time not to ask again. She moved closer to the balcony, carefully looking down as the voices grew louder.

"Our response must be swift and sure. They dare come into Nudolla to steal our people? The arrogance of thinking they can get away with—"

"Yes, but they have gotten away with it, haven't they? And make no mistake they will do it again as often as they can. There is no telling how much they know of Nudolla as yet. Some have never heard the name before. Each of us are known by our own kingdoms, but few know of the strength, the alliance that is Nudolla."

A sharp intake of breath followed, and she tried her best to make out the faces down below, but it seemed impossible, save her father. He sat above them on the High King's seat, fire glinting off his *khepresh* crown as he watched and listened. His gold and blue collar covered his shoulders, heavy and strong. She'd tried to lift it as a child before falling with it to the ground as one of her handmaids found her and rushed to help her.

"Are we quite certain this is not the work of pawnship? I see no reason to become excited if not. Pawnship has been a part of the nomadic families for years."

"Save in pawnship one reaches an agreement," one of the lower kings cut in, "an understanding with mutual benefits if not some profit. An agreement is made whereby goods or something of value is given to the borrower, and the borrower provides the lender with a member of his family as assurance of repayment. At other times a member of one's family is seized to force payment of some prior debt. Upon repayment, their kin are returned. Here, there is none of this. No agreement, no warning, no exchange of value, not even a face or name to the thief. The slavers are using these customs to their advantage."

Silence fell in the hall, and Imani stepped up onto the stones in front of her, so that her chest was level with the top of the wall she struggled to lean over. Her father had outlawed pawnship in Nudolla, but many of the nomadic and independent nations fought to keep the practice as part of their traditions. At times they would ask her father for support during drought, but because of his stance on pawnship, it came with conditions. Some had too much pride to take it. And they rarely asked. But from living in Nabara and watching her father's hand shape the kingdom she had learned an important lesson. One could be desperate and another could be proud. But it was a difficult thing to be both. She wrapped her right arm around the cracked stone lotus shaped pillar to her right, slipping her hand inside the crevice for a better grip as she bent her left arm in front of her, pressing against the wall. Gasping as her grip slipped, she pressed her lips together and braced herself against the pillar, closing her eyes at the sound of the pillar's crumbling rocks hitting the floor. Imani held her breath as it came to a stop, looking over the top of the wall again.

"...Asim, tell me what you know of the nomadic families' involvement in this?" Her father motioned to his right, and Asim stood. She knew the captain of the guards by the mark on his shoulder in the shape of an X and the white breastplate covering his chest. He was her father's captain, and held rank over Medjay, guardians of the High King in service to the royal family.

"Your Grace. The Nomadin owe no allegiance to any in the Kingdom of Nabara or the alliance of Nudolla for that matter. They trade with us, true, but most of them settle near necessary resources—water, cattle, and farmland when they can find it untouched and unclaimed. If they met with any foreigners, it is likely they would be killed on sight. The Nomadin have long been known to raid among competing families in the desert as well as any who have valuables on their person. Their women are sometimes slaves, stolen from other territories. Of those accused of trading with slavers, the Nomadin would be most susceptible. The most...willing. The Berbers of the Sahara have and continue to hunt those south of their lands. As nomads they cross the desert as one would a bridge, easily and without hesitation. And Cuicul is now a Roman garrison. The Romans drove the Berbers out and made many of their people slaves. Or martyrs. Noubadia gained the trust of Rome after helping them rid their land of invaders to the South. We believe the Mandé assisted them with weaponry and possibly men, though they deny it. As long as there is a supply, and willing traders, slaves will continue to be sold along the north and eastern coasts at ports in Adulis, Opone, Malao, possibly Rhapta, and more."

"Are there so many? Are other areas compromised?" the Sotho King asked.

"And more, Your Grace," Asim confirmed. "It is also possible that prisoners from Exile Island may know of this. Often, thieves and raiders exiled there spread information among the captives. The island may be home to dead trees made of stone, but there are plenty men yet living. And men talk." Then he nodded once to her father and was silent.

Next, Kandake Bamanirenas rose, the symbol of an elephant on her headdress, ivory around her neck. She was the ruling Kandake, Queen of the Kiberan Kingdom.

"My forest lands are far-flung and hard to reach. Even the sun has a difficult time getting through our rain forests. Yet these stories have reached my ears as well. The leaves and forests of my lands are young and green, as are the hanging gardens we cultivate in my city. Like anything of the land, it flourishes when one tends to them, protects them from weeds, serpents and beetles. These slavers will overrun us just as the weeds and beetles of the earth consume every leaf and turn it brown with death. We cannot leave this to chance. The longer we wait, the larger they grow, the tighter their hold, the farther their reach."

Imani slipped again and caught herself, biting her bottom lip as rocks slid from the pillar once more. When she looked over the edge this time, Asim's eyes caught hers and she froze. He raised one eyebrow before turning his attention back to the council assembly, crossing his arms about his chest in the same motion.

Please don't let him tell Father.

Imani bit her lip, worrying at the thought even as she pushed it from her mind. She narrowed her eyes as she tried to make out the current speaker's facial features from her vantage point. A lock of her tightly coiled onyx hair fell in front of her eyes, and she released her grip on the pillar to push it back underneath the hood of her cloak.

"The Scorpion Kingdom has no reason to set foot on Torrent, but we've word that trade may be at risk. If the Essi can't protect the high seas, it puts all of us in danger. What of it?" The Scorpion King's tone was nothing if not condescending. The tension rose. She could feel it even from where she stood.

"The Essi have been weathering storms for hundreds of years…and that includes you," the Essi King stated firmly.

A soft chuckle followed his statement, and he continued. "We are not yet overrun. But what you hear is true. Twice they have attempted to take our ships by sea, and twice they have been rewarded. They will try to take us again. The Empire of Nudolla must mount an offense."

"Agreed." The deffufa echoed with the voices of the lesser kings' concurrence.

Her father stood again, walking to the center of the chamber as Imani's heart beat faster. What would he say?

"Nudolla will send Medjay to the coast. North, south, east, and west are to scout and bring what news they can. Until then, we will move forward with the Festival of Kings. Now more than ever, we must band together. Tradition will keep us that way. I expect every leader to take precautions within their kingdom to protect their trade routes and their people. Should you have any difficulties, make your requests known."

In turn, each of the lower kings bowed before the High King and waited as he took his leave, flanked by the Royal Guard. All watched as he exited before gathering into smaller groups to speak amongst themselves. Imani leaned back from the edge of her precipice and slid to the floor before fixing her hood for the third time. *Slaves. Are we at war?*

Her father had fought long and hard for peace through a bloody campaign before she was even born. He would not want to risk it if it could be avoided in some way. But how? She could not see how this would end, but now she knew how it had begun.

KOMORO

"Must we attend the Festival of Kings this year? Missing one won't matter. Send Ketemin if you wish one of us to go," Komoro said simply, stretching on his hammock.

"It will," King Kwasi replied. "All of the families attend to show their strength, the skill of their warriors, and to speak of our alliances. Further, as we are a patrilineal kingdom, your sister is not my immediate heir," his uncle finished, frowning.

"Even the fake alliances?"

"Hold your tongue," his uncle commanded. "I still hold the throne of the Kingdom of the Sun and will until I die and not before!" His uncle's voice echoed across the great hall. The servants took no notice, continuing with their duties as before.

His uncle lectured him constantly. He would rule the Sao Kingdom someday true, but not until his uncle took leave of him or stepped down. Both were unlikely to happen in the near future. The people loved his uncle far too much, and he was in excellent shape for his age despite nearing three quarters of a century. The king continued to supervise sparring among the soldiers, his red cloak flying in the wind. At his back the sun shone brightly against the desert, and he looked as if he were aflame. The snakehead of his staff seemed even more menacing, its jaws open, lifelike as his uncle's fist gripped it, the falcon head of Ra inscribed on an amulet on his chest.

Komoro gritted his teeth, holding back his retort. His ebony skin shone in the light of the sun. The Sao Kingdom worshipped the sun. And the women worshipped him. Women loved his skin. They told him he was blessed with the blood of the old ones to be so loved by Ra, the Sun God. A true son of Ra. His brilliant white teeth seemed a row of perfect ivory when he spoke. His eyes were almost black as he closed them to gather his words. Completely shaven, he preferred to keep his hair cut close, smooth, loving how women would stroke his head when they spoke to him, begging his favor. Tall yet slim, he avoided hard labor; his narrow frame often frequented the bathing pools and wine farmers of the city. He wore a white shendyt and red overlay, his headdress falling low on his brow; gold chains, bracelets, and earrings decorated his person so much that one could hear him coming. The more lavish, the better.

His uncle was growing harder to reason with. Why must he wait for his inheritance? He was the firstborn. Komoro's father had died when he was only ten, and before he'd done so, he'd taken care to appoint his uncle as successor before his son took the throne. Succession by appointment of another bloodline was rare, but legal. And limited. He'd resented his uncle's rule ever since. Though he'd hidden it well.

"Yes, Uncle. You know best. I merely meant that it is such a great distance, at your age. I only meant to spare you," he said contritely. "But it's such an old tradition. Why not bring new ways? Faster? Better? The only great thing of the past was the Red Summer. Would that we could still use it to collect additional taxes. With the long drought, food will grow scarce."

"You are not to mention such measures in my presence again. Collecting additional taxes in a drought is tantamount to ordering the deaths of our people. With the increasing drought, there will be less food from the farmers of the Sao Kingdom. The Red Summer brought more than wealth, Nephew. The people began to starve, growing anxious as they watched their children's bellies enlarge while their ribs began to protrude. We could not feed them all. Some took measures into their own hands and began to eat...any one they could find. Old and young alike died in this manner. Class was of no import. Many were openly attacked in the streets without cause. Each person caught was put to death. Family turned against their own. You were too young to remember; though you heard the stories, you did not feel the pain. To be a witness to such a thing is to remember the whole and not the part. One must never shade their history in order to rewrite the past. No matter how ugly a commentary it may be." His uncle sighed. "Nephew," King Kwasi started, "you aren't an only child, and I fear I've spoiled you. Would that your late father left you more brothers and sisters. It's best that we continue this tradition. The High King began it to honor progress, trade, and peace among the kingdoms. Each year we solve problems and spark development; our ambassadors make new discoveries and foster relationships and *trade.*"

Rolling his eyes he shook his head as his uncle finished. *More blathering.*

"Come with me, nephew."

"What?" Komoro turned his head sharply to look at his uncle.

"Come with me," his uncle repeated firmly, not bothering to wait as he turned swiftly away from the balcony and moved towards the steps that would take him outside of the palace.

Confusion spread across his face, but he followed the old man, moving quickly to keep up with his uncle's long strides. The litter was already waiting for them, six stunning chocolate mares, brushed until they shone, stood fast. The guards bowed as his uncle approached. One kneeled quickly, his thigh parallel to the ground as his uncle put one foot on the guard's thigh and stepped up, barely allowing his weight to settle into his heel. Komoro followed, sitting opposite his Uncle as they pulled off quickly.

The wheels rolled swiftly over the sand as their driver kept a tight pace, his initial whip of the rains encouraging the mares to a rapid trot. Like smoke, the sand drifted behind them, stirred by the litter which angrily woke each tiny brother and sister from their gentle slumber, before settling again into a sea of desert, the rising wind helping to conceal their tracks. Moving swiftly, they passed large green lakes and lush greenery surrounding them. A private oasis for the weary traveler or a retreat for the citizens of the Sao Empire, many were known to frequent their shores.

"Where are we going?" He couldn't conceal the boredom in his voice as he finally relaxed in the litter, his gaze falling on the ten warrior escorts following behind them on horseback.

"You'll see," his Uncle replied, lazily relaxing in his seat, a satisfied smile on his face.

Komoro nodded. *Toying with me like one of his pets.* It annoyed him to be at the end of one of his uncle's games. And now, here he was in the middle of the desert, waiting to see where this journey would bring him. Sighing, he stretched out on the seat, tilting his head back as he yawned, allowing the sun to sink into his skin. At least he could sleep until they arrived wherever his uncle's whims took them.

"Komoro. Komoro."

"Hmm?" Lifting his head slowly he let out a long yawn, not bothering to cover his mouth as he tried to focus on his Uncle. Blinking slowly, he tried to shake off the heaviness in his body as the sun and the heat encouraged him to return to sleep.

"We've arrived."

His eyes narrowed as his Uncle stepped from the litter, moving across the sand as though he was floating. Shaking his head again, he followed, eyes moving up towards the sandstone bulwark that loomed in front of them, its rocky countenance at once awe inspiring and menacing. It stood the height of four giraffes, stacked one on top of the other, some ending in stiff unyielding daggers, and others flat plateaus that taunted those from the ground to try and reach them. His sandals were ill-equipped to aid him on this climb. Grasping at the narrow walls on either side of him for support he followed behind his uncle, following the strong legs and shoulders, which easily twisted and turned up the rocky paths.

"Ahh!" Pulling his hand back quickly he jumped back, cursing Ra as he watched the green-bellied snake slide down the rocks and disappear into a crevice. His uncle hadn't turned around once, his bald head still moving upwards without a pause.

When they were almost at the top his uncle finally turned around to face him.

"Wait here," his uncle commanded, nodding at the escorts at Komoro's back.

"Yes, Your Grace." Two of the guards took up their positions, one facing the bottom of the rocky bulwark from which they came and the other facing Komoro. *There's really no need*, he thought, continuing the climb. *No one in their right mind would climb these cliffs.* Besides, it would be dark soon. Rocks moved under his feet as pebbles pressed into the tender parts of his heels and arches. They might as well have been made of dough. Gritting his teeth as he attempted to find even ground, he finally crested the top, his uncle already there, waiting for him with his hands on his waist as he looked out beyond the horizon.

Komoro stood beside him, looking at his uncle slowly before moving his eyes downward over the edge of the cliff. At least a hundred camels milled below, a quarter of them immersed in the shallow blue-green waters running between the towering sandstone walls. Others drank at the edge, their long necks stretched out in front of them like wilting flowers as they lapped at the water, ears twitching ever so often to keep the flies from landing for too long. Archways that sank into deep valleys ran to their left and right as the narrow oasis rested comfortably in the middle. From here, he was sure he could even seen the edges of their kingdom. Each Sao resident likely winding down. Their thoughts turning to dinner. He never quite bothered to think about it, but with the falling sun and the shadows turning the sharp, jutting rock towers a light purple and pink among its orange brethren, one might even call it beautiful. One day, he would call it *his*.

"The caravans travel through these canyons seeking Sao trade. Go too far, without the proper protection and the unlucky ones may fall victim to caravan robbers. Thieves that will steal anything to sell. Including *salt*," his uncle finished, looking at him gravely.

"Uncle…" Komoro sighed. *So this is why he brought me here.*

"It's important that−"

"I know, Uncle. I asked to oversee the salt mines for a reason. I wouldn't jeopardize it now. Don't you trust me?" Komoro finished incredulously.

When his uncle turned to look back down into the canyon, silent as a tomb, Komoro pursed his lips. *Of course not.* Who could run the Sao Empire as well as the great Kwasi of the Kingdom of the Sun, the Son of Ra? A title he hadn't even earned.

"One day, you'll understand everything," his Uncle said softly, interrupting his thoughts. Looking down he found his Uncle's hand resting on his shoulder. "I know you'll be a great king one day. I hope to live to see it."

You've lived far too long already. He regretted the thought immediately, gritting his teeth as he tried to quell the irritation rising in his chest. Here he was looking over what should be his kingdom. The kingdom his father meant him to have, meant him to claim, meant him to rule. Instead all he had were his uncle's promises that he would rule when he was ready. *Ready how?* he wanted to yell. What must he say? What must he do to show his uncle that he was ready? What did it take to be king? Curling his hands into fists he lifted his gaze from below.

29

A gentle squeeze answered his thoughts and Komoro looked back down at the hand on his shoulder, smiling at his uncle to show he understood, before crossing his own arms over his chest as he looked back down the rock-face. *What did it take?* His gaze moved swiftly to the right as he surveyed his uncle from the corner of his eye. *It would be so easy...*

So easy. And who would dare question him on the matter? It was growing darker already, the sun just a heartbeat away from beginning its slow descent behind the sand in the distance as it set. And they were so high up, having climbed until his legs felt as though they would give like a newborn colt; even he had questioned why they were going so far up. Perhaps he could explain how his uncle was senile and accidentally fell on his own, not paying attention to where he tread on the plateau? Or maybe his uncle did it on purpose, just after telling Komoro of the beauty of the spot, his wishes for his burial, and his certainty that his nephew would be a great ruler. Even a gust a wind would do it. It would be an easy explanation to Sao officials who often came across winds stronger than an elephant pressing a young sapling aside. Winds that stole heavy blankets, pushed chariots speeding along the sand, and lifted heavy pottery from the ground. The way his uncle stood so close to the edge with not a care in the world...made it so tempting. Even the guards wouldn't be able to prove it, one way or the other.

But his sister. Ketemin was so fond of their uncle. She'd shared his love for science and metallurgy, entering the good graces of every tutor he and his sister ever met. She was the ideal pupil. Every answer she received was followed by another question, desperate to know exactly *how* and *why* each thing *was*. Lessons about their trade became something she thrived on, creating new methods for the Kingdom of the Sun to gain ground with their neighbors and establish alliances. And their uncle sometimes taught them himself, though Ketemin never allowed their lessons to end while Komoro escaped before his uncle called him back to continue. His eyes always stayed on the water clock. Ketemin's eyes stayed on their uncle. Ever since their father died she treated their uncle as though he was their father. But he wasn't. And he never would be. She would never forgive him if she found out. But then, he could always make sure she didn't.

"Komoro," his uncle said gently, interrupting his thoughts. "I love you as a son. I always have." His uncle was looking at him now with an earnestness he'd never worn before. "I know you've taken your father's death harder than anyone and I know I am no replacement for him. But I hope to be there when you need me. Whenever you need me. Even when you become king. I'll help you make decisions if you need my counsel. There may come a time when I am no longer...here. And I hope you will remember everything I taught you. You will have to make hard decisions at times. But they are necessary. And the outcome will always be worth it."

Komoro nodded, finally placing his right hand on his uncle's shoulder. "You're right. I will have to make hard decisions, uncle." Squeezing his uncle's shoulder gently, he allowed his eyes to travel over the old man's face, memorizing the strong jaw and clear eyes that sat within smooth, rich, earthen skin. "I understand now." He made sure his grip was firm and squeezed it one last time. *Decisions are always hard.*

"Your Grace!"

Komoro jumped, turning with his uncle towards the guard as he pulled his hand back in alarm, heart racing in his chest.

"Your Grace, forgive me, I thought you heard me. A sandstorm is coming."

At that, the escort turned and pointed behind them. In the distance, thick clouds of sand mushroomed towards the sky, stretching across the land as though it needed more room. A herd of oryx ran from it, their curved horns like branches of scimitars sprouting from their white coats, birds circling above them as though to land at the earliest convenience. More than one vulture would have food soon if the storm grew bolder.

"Come, Komoro. I have seen all I need to today." His uncle smiled and followed the guard.

Komoro turned back towards the edge as the winds began to whip at his shendyt, the camels clearing away from the oasis as though they sensed what was coming from the growing winds. His uncle's retreating back dipped lower and lower as he descended. Animals could always tell when danger was near. But could his uncle?

When they arrived back at the palace he walked up the steps with his uncle.

"Remember, Komoro, if kingdoms wish to move quickly, they must go alone. If we wish to go far, we must go together."

Komoro stroked the stubble of his beard, thinking for a moment. *He still treats me like a child who only wants for a playmate,* he thought. *Yes, would that my father was alive to see how you've grown old and useless, clinging to ancient customs while pretending to embrace progress.*

"Uncle, forgive me," he replied slowly, kneeling near the old man's hand. "We will go. I should not be so hasty to flout tradition."

His uncle smiled proudly, placing a hand on his shoulder. "Rise, Komoro. It is already forgotten. I don't think you will be so disappointed when we arrive. Princess Imani is the picture of beauty, with the eyes of a lioness and bewitching. I dare say she will tempt you to change your mind."

"I doubt she's so beautiful as to tempt me. I'm sure there are better options." *Regardless, whatever would the harem think should I return with a bride, wedded and bedded without one last farewell,* he thought smiling.

"Reckless. The man who does all his thinking below will soon lose what he should have cherished more above." His uncle shook one finger at him as a warning. "Women are fickle."

"And doubtless, so is the Princess—"

"No. She is a bright star in a time of uncertainty; beautiful, intelligent, a virgin bride for whomever would win her hand. Take care you don't take up with the local harems, Komoro. Talk spoken in darkness always comes to light."

So you spy on me too old man. "Yes, Uncle," he replied. "Sleep well."

Komoro took his leave, his robe sweeping across the limestone floors as he went to his bedchamber. He threw his headdress on the ground, pulling a black cloak over his head and placing a pouch full of gold in his pocket, rushing into the night as the sun dipped low, barely peeking out behind the hills in the distance.

The guard nodded to him when he placed gold in his

outstretched hand. He could hear the drums and the sand rattles making a soft tune. Laughter drifted through the quarters. The noble who lived here was celebrating his youngest's birthday. He wouldn't miss his wife too soon. He didn't need much time. Incense was burning, tickling his nose gently, and causing his mouth to water.

"Welcome, my Prince. She's through here," a veiled woman whispered in his ear.

When he turned, his eyes met those of a familiar acquaintance. The handmaid's dark eyes smiled at him even as his eyes traveled to the tips of her dark nipples, her breasts clearly visible against the yellow silk dress she wore, a slit opened to reveal her right upper thigh. She smelled of lavender.

She offered him water, holding a silver gourd up, "*Aman,* Your Grace?"

"No." He shook his head and moved past her.

"Saai awaits your pleasure," she said gesturing down the candlelit hall. Nodding to her, he turned towards where she pointed.

He pulled back a thick black veil in anticipation. She was waiting for him in the depths of the bath, her hair pulled atop her head. Seeing him, she rose, water trickling down her full breasts to her navel, gathering at the opening of her thighs. She walked to the red-dyed furs in the room, sinking to her knees before turning back to him. *Her husband has never known her like I've known her.*

"My Prince, my Prince. It's been too long," she said softly, her hair tumbling down her shoulders as he raked his fingers through the dampness.

Running his hands along her spine, he knelt behind her, his cloak and robe falling away in one fluid motion. She gasped as he gripped her hair tightly closing his eyes at the same time.

He knew what would happen if he was discovered. Well. *She* was discovered. He couldn't be touched. But he so enjoyed touching her. And she wasn't the only one. Was it his fault if married women enjoyed the pleasure of his company? He stood, dressing quickly while she was still asleep. If he woke her, she would beg him to stay. Married woman were supposed to be the easiest to let go of, but she clung to him like sap to a tree.

Pushing a back door open, he left quickly, moving through the winding streets of the city. The door to his chambers had barely closed before he heard a heavy knock and turned quickly. *Had someone seen him?*

"Your Grace, if I may have a word?"

Komoro sighed. All he wanted was a bath. He walked to the door, intent on railing at the lateness of the hour. *What does he want now?*

"You realize that—"

"Your Grace, I think she knows." The Chief Treasurer said gravely.

"What? What are you talking about?" he asked, closing the door behind him. *The man is unhinged.* He watched the treasurer pace up and down his chambers like a nervous baboon, his fists clenching and unclenching as he talked.

"Princess Ketemin. She asked to see me earlier today about *the state of affairs* and I could not say no!"

"What did you tell her?" Komoro grabbed the man to stop him from moving.

"I could not say no! I – I told her of course we could speak; I was however wanted on business and would not be back until late. She said tomorrow would do just as well."

Komoro released him. "Well then, it's not urgent. Find your manhood, Odwulfe." The man was losing it, and quickly. He realized he needed to reassure the man and give him a plausible story.

"Tell her I ordered you to divert extra money to some of the farmers to compliment their drought. If she says there is in fact more money, then tell her we renegotiated agreements with some of the traders. She won't ask you too many questions."

"Yes, but which ones? Your sister is highly capable, and she's smart. She'll know which ones to ask about."

"Smarter than me, is she?"

Odwulfe gasped as he realized his mistake and took a step back. "I did not mean *that*, Prince Komoro. I only meant, she never gives up; she may try to catch me in a lie."

"Don't worry. I will deal with my sister. If she asks more questions, tell her only that she is to speak with me."

"Yes, Your Grace. And what of the morning's caravan? We are sending one north in the morning with the salt gathered this week."

"And…"

"We need guards to see it north."

"How does that concern me at this time?" Komoro was growing irritated. It had been a long night and he needed his rest. Sitting in the chair on the dais near his bed he yawned. The carvers built it so that he could take meetings in the comfort of his own room, but still let others know his position. It would not do for them to become too comfortable with him.

"You…we…removed a number of guards from the salt mines for other…purposes…so we don't have that same number to see it north. Shall I divert some from the other guards around the palace?"

"No. Leave it. It's always been safe before. Who would have a mind to steal salt deep in the desert? And in the heat of the desert I have no idea who would even attempt to make that journey. I can barely stand to be outside for more than three hours at a time. It will be fine with the number we have, which is..." He raised his eyebrows questioningly when he didn't receive an answer from the treasurer.

"Four, Your Grace. For two hundred camels…" The treasurer's voice trailed off hopefully as he held the scroll in front of him.

"Four it is then. I'm sure you will take care of it. Arm them with extra weapons if it comforts you. Make sure they send a report when they reach Timbuktu or Gao. Whichever one it is." Waving Odwulfe away as he spoke, he rose, walking towards his bed.

"Yes, Your Grace. Sleep well, Your Grace."

Stretching onto the bed as the door closed, he reminded himself he needed to go see the salt mine in the morning as well. Soon, he would be king. Soon, he would be as the Sao were, giants among men. Yawning he relaxed further to sleep. He needed his rest. *It will be difficult work being King.*

IMANI

"You can follow me, or you can run and tell my father. I have no feelings on the matter," she told him.

Shaharqa looked at her in exasperation, his face contorting with a mixture of fury and desperation as he tried to work out the best course of action, knowing she might disobey him regardless. He was built like a rhinoceros, his broad shoulders supporting massive arms and a tapered waist, a trunk that people knew better to go around than attempt to cut down. He crossed his arms over his chest, dark eyes narrowing at her.

Imani smiled as he glared at her. *He'll do no such thing, and I'll be halfway towards the coast before he finishes the conversation with my father.*

She'd followed them at a short clip from the time they'd left the palace. Now she stood toe to toe with Shaharqa as he towered over her, his shadow blocking the sun from her face. She pulled the comb from her hair before snatching the tight black curls back into three thick braids that hung down her back, using three bands to hold them tightly at the ends. Taking the gold-plated half circle crown from the top of her horse as he pushed his nose into the small of her back, she pressed it backwards into the top of her hair. Fitting snugly to the shape of her forehead it would protect her from temple to temple and from her crown to the bridge of her nose. Stroking the stallion gently she admired his gleaming kohl coat and ivory legs. Powerful and strong, his muscles flexed underneath her fingers as he nudged her side.

"Imanishakheto...He ordered you to stay at the palace. Once he sees you it will not go well for you."

"Don't worry, Uncle. I'll tell him myself," she assured him as she dropped the reins on her stallion. "You have my word. But the longer we wait..."

Shaharqa's jaw flexed as she watched him, eyebrows raised. "Promise me you will stay out of sight."

"Am I meant to keep it? You once said I had the fastest draw you'd ever seen. *You* said it rivaled father's."

There is something they are not telling me, and I need to find out what. After a moment she turned quickly, one hand on her horse's neck and the other on the reins as she lifted herself up without assistance, turning to nod at him, the black stallion at a gallop before she was even seated. Shaharqa watched in dismay as the distance increased between them, and Imani laughed as she sat, turning around to squeeze her knees into her horse harder, the horse gaining more speed as she hurried to reach Nabara's forces.

They shall not leave our land with free men at their feet.

The roar of waves crashing against the shore sounded in her ears as they rode in closer to the coast. A broken mast tipped to the side met her eyes, sitting on the other side of the mountain in front of them that silenced their approach. They dotted the coast like ants around a hole in the ground, at least two hundred by her count.

"Shhh." She put one hand to her horse's neck, her restlessness causing him the same uneasy wait as he shifted from foot to foot. Stroking his neck, she surveyed the shoreline.

And well armed. They may not have been expecting us, but they expected someone.

Turning to her left, she finally spotted her father. Raising one hand, his fingers splayed before closing it into a fist. The moment he did he kicked his horse and the forces of Nabara rained down the mountain, charging towards the shoreline. The first yells came from her right, and she ducked from her hiding place as her heart raced, watching the battle. Her father slipped his right hand into the sleeve at his mount's right flank and pulled out one long, slim spear, eyes narrowing as he launched it forward. A grunt of surprise followed as it slammed through a slaver's body and pinned him to the ground, both arms splayed out as the blood streamed over the rocks. *A sentinel. If only he'd been doing his job.*

The cries grew louder as those on the shore looked up, realizing their trap. Few were on horseback, but most grabbed swords at their waists or on the ground, dropping their work as they turned to face the army before them. A moment later the sound of swords hit her ears and the sharp sound of arrows flying past made her lower herself closer to her horse's back, pressing him further into the deep alcove and safe from harm.

Her father ducked quickly from horseback, dodging an arrow before slipping his hand back into the sleeve. Hurling the spear forward once again, it punched through the slaver's eye. Quickening his pace as the man fell backward, he reached down and gripped the end of the spear, yanking it upward and out, the eyeball popping off and disappearing in the brush. All around him his men fought, those no longer on horseback using their throwing spears generously; the quick soft thuds letting her know they'd met their mark. Even on foot they were a force to be reckoned with, but it was Nabara's cavalry that their neighbors both feared and attempted to persuade into their own battles to no avail. It was his cavalry that those who survived remembered. Nubians were renowned horse masters. Assyrians had sought horses from Kushites since before Pharaoh Piye's reign. For the Kushite, there was only one way to ride a horse: bareback or not at all. It made both horse and rider faster. The horses were freed from the repeated chaffing and friction caused by the leather or metal against their backs, allowing them to cool themselves faster as the wind moved under their bellies and over their backs. The difference was plain, even in the riders, improving balance, coordination, and skill. Little wonder every Nubian was expected to master the art of the bow on horseback, heralded for his ability to turn astride and rain arrows upon the enemy even from a distance while in motion.

Raising her head over the rock, she turned to her left in time to see Shaharqa's *khopesh* pull backwards and punch forward into a slaver's belly, spilling his insides as Shaharqa put one foot to the man's chest and kicked him backward to release his weapon, riding forward for more. The terrain changed from rocks and grass to sand as her father moved down the mountain. She left her horse to follow him, stealing down the shoreline towards her father's soldiers before a sudden movement to her left caught her attention. Her father fell to the ground, slapping his horse hard so that he ran from him to safety. Gasping, she watched him, fear clutching at her heart.

A moment later, a hand snatched her head back by her hair, slamming her to the ground as she grunted in surprise, his sword hand drawn back. As he brought it down she rolled to her right, punching her short *khopesh* into his stomach, twisting it as his mouth fell open and stayed that way. Blood dribbled from his mouth, wide blue eyes frozen on hers. The *khopesh* was a popular weapon of soldiers and Medjay. Shaped like the long leg of a horse and hooked at the end like a calf, it could slice an opponent or bludgeon him in an instant. Pulling it from his stomach, she pushed him to the ground unceremoniously, standing and stepping over the dying man as he clutched at his waist in a fetal position before his body relaxed in death. Chest heaving, she looked down at him without remorse.

The sound of shifting rocks caught her attention, and her eyes narrowed as three slavers ran toward the mountain, one injured at the shoulder, his flailing arm likely broken as his figure swung from left to right as he struggled to the top.

Imani reached behind her shoulders, the pack running from her shoulder to the small of her back securely held there. Pulling one long, slim, silver-tipped arrow from it along with her bow, she leaned back and fired it high into the sky, not waiting to watch it arc high above her in the sky. Drawing back a second time, she aimed straight, the top of one's head visible above a tall boulder as one scream told her the first met its mark. Again, she released her finger and watched the boulder behind the man spray with blood, the top of his scalp attached to the arrow.

And three. She paused, eyes dancing from boulder to boulder for some sign of him, her shoulders tense as she realized he may have gotten away, and she moved closer.

"Bitch!" she turned and slid her *khopesh* across his throat as the man raised his to hack her down, wiping the blood on his shirt as she moved past.

"Imanishakheto!"

Ignoring the sound of her name she pressed closer toward the mountain.

"Imanishakheto!" Her father's voice followed her, and she resisted the urge to turn around.

She shook her head and continued forward, beads of sweat rolling down her back as she pursed her lips, the sound of grunts and groans making her look around, just to be careful. Softening her footsteps, she moved swiftly up as a lizard ran down and towards her, stopping her in her tracks. *They prefer the shadows.*

"Imani!"

Her fingers clutched her last arrow.

"Imani, to me!"

Tightening her grip on her bow she advanced, the string taut as her right hand pressed close against her face. Cowering before her, he raised his hands in defeat as she moved her eyes over his body, leather and armor mixing with his sweat. She could smell him.

"He's here!" she called back as she waited for her father and Shaharqa, string still taut, the arrow aimed at his heart. His eyes moved up and down her body and toward the coast.

"Leave him alive," her father told her as he walked up. Imani turned her head towards him. "We need—"

A sharp crack and a *thrum* sounded at the same time and the two soldiers to his right looked at the man in shock.

A sword, hidden under his body, had been brought forward and was clanging back to the ground as her arrow pinned him back against the rocks. His defiance faded as he gripped at the arrow as if to pull it back out.

"How dare you disobey my orders." The fury on his face did nothing to break her courage. "You could have been killed. I ordered you to stay at the palace." The soldiers nearest them fell silent as they surrounded them as a shield, Medjay circling them protectively to ensure there were no other slavers nearby. The remainder began to sink their spears into the rest of the dying slavers to ensure they met their end.

"Father…" She tried to steady her thoughts as she looked at the anger writ across his face.

"You put Medjay at risk to protect you. How dare you follow our armies into battle without my knowledge?"

Imani looked back in disgust at the slaver as she bent down, pulling her arrow from his chest. Turning quickly, she whistled for her horse. "There. Now you can ask him what his plans are." She pointed at the dead man. "*They* only understand one thing."

"We will speak of this later," he warned her. Imani gritted her teeth as she nodded.

She gathered the arrows she could as the soldiers began to pile up the bodies, stripping them of their weapons as they did.

"What shall we do with them, Your Grace?" Her uncle looked toward the growing pile of bodies, the sand stained with blood around them as he waited for his brother's orders. A pyramid of slavers with no more secrets to hide.

"The hyenas can have them if they're lucky. There's no need to deny the animals so much meat. Though the type may spoil their digestion," her father responded, turning to consider the ship a moment.

"We need to search the ship." He nodded to Shaharqa as they walked towards the ship, which listed to the side. *They must have wrecked in some fashion.* Imani watched them for a moment before walking quickly towards it herself.

"I'm coming with you." Her father turned at the sound of her voice and her uncle's eyes narrowed. *He'll likely have words with me later too.*

"Medjay will watch her, brother. She'll be fine." Shaharqa signaled to his seconds as they flanked her and her father nodded grudgingly, his eyebrow warning her not to step out of line. They waded through the water to reach the ship, a party of thirty strong to ensure there were no surprises. Shaharqa rose first with twenty Medjay before pulling her up beside him and letting the ladder down for the others. Water barrels dotted the corners of the deck.

"They certainly had enough to drink," her father noted, walking towards the back on sure feet as the ship bobbed slightly under them, the waves moving it just so.

"And to eat." Shaharqa nodded to a drum he'd opened, full of salted fish.

"Continue searching the ship. Make sure none of them are hiding here," her father commanded, his head turning this way and that as he looked about the deck. The soldiers nodded and moved to the back. She could hear them moving from door to door as she followed her father into the captain's room, pulling out a map in front of her. The writing was Latin, but there was no denying the mark in the lower right corner. *Gold.* The Roman number for five sat next to it.

"Your Grace." Both she and her father turned at the call and moved onto the deck before the soldier caught her eye and motioned for them to go down as he stayed to guard the entrance to the chamber below. Pocketing the map, her father descended slowly. The smell caught in her nose as she followed him, and her stomach roiled as she put her forearm to her mouth to help cover the smell. She removed it after a moment, her attention turning to the deep grooves on the walls of the ship as she went further down. *Claw marks.* They lined the walls like a deadly inscription on either side of her.

Shaharqa stood with her father and the soldiers in a small circle, their gazes directed at the floor. She walked closer still.

"Ethiopians, Your Grace. A few Greeks and Judeans and one Syrian slave. The Jewish that refuse to combine their faith with elements of Greek and Roman culture are made slaves. They were likely transporting them back to Roman territory when they wrecked."

"Imani." Her father's voice was tinged with doubt and warning.

He cannot shield me forever. She came forward, and they parted for her as she too looked at the floor before her. Too well she remembered the fall of the Judeans at the hands of Rome from her lessons. The Judeans had once sought the Kushite Pharaoh Taharqa's aid against the Assyrian Emperor Sennacherib. And still the Judeans fought, though now, many Hellenized Judeans were now enemies of Kush. *How far they have fallen.* What she saw on the ground of the ship only stoked her anger further, hands curling into fists as she looked down at the sight. A small pile of bodies, chained and rotting from disease, lay before her. A child to their right curled dead on the ground, his small protruding bones a testament to the starvation slaves endured before reaching their destination if food ran scarce. The skin around his eyes seemed hollowed, as if someone had reached in with a knife and shaved them down, eyes sunken and staring in shock as though he'd seen a ghost the moment before his heart stopped beating. Imani saw no windows down here. It was likely the reason the vultures hadn't been able to pluck them out.

Kneeling down next to the dead boy's small, brown body, she covered his eyes with her hands, closing his eyelids and running her finger along his long, feather-soft eyelashes. His skin had turned a slight gray, almost as if ash covered it. The fingers on his right hand were stretched and curled like an acacia branch in the winter, clinging to hope that its leaves, like fallen soldiers, would return to protect it. Pulling her blade out, she hacked at the chain that bound the boy's ankle to the ship. She slipped her arms underneath him carefully, lifting him in her arms and walking with him back towards the stairs and up towards the deck as the soldiers followed. Even with his sagging skin and bones, he felt as light as a paperweight. Wading through the water now, he seemed to grow heavier in her hands. *Or is it my mind playing tricks on me*? She pulled her legs through the waves as they lapped at her knees, both hands clutching him firmly to her breast, making sure his head and feet didn't touch the water. When she rose on the shore, the soldiers stared at him. His small lifeless body needed no explanation.

When she reached dry sand, a soldier came over and laid his cloak down before her, standing as she began to wrap the child in it. Over and under, securing it around his shoulders and covering his feet. Like swaddling a baby. She memorized his face one more time before she pulled the cloth over his black curls, wrapping his head gently, lifting it and wrapping, lifting and wrapping. When she finished, she secured it as tightly as she could, knotting it at his small hands as she knelt next to him.

Lifting him in her arms, she stood again and looked to the pile of slavers before catching her father's eyes. It was always hard to tell what he was thinking. But somehow she knew what he would say next.

"Sever their heads," he commanded. "Then burn the bodies."

"Your Grace," Shaharqa acknowledged.

"And Brother," her father continued, putting his right hand on Shaharqa's left shoulder, "make sure we haven't missed any of the slavers. Send sweepers along the coast and as a tail to return after dark. I want to be sure none make it into the city."

"It is done." Shaharqa turned swiftly, giving orders as he did, his men moving toward him to listen.

Turning to her quickly, her father pointed at her. "We will speak later." Moving away from her, he signaled to his men, and they made ready for their return back to the palace. Biting her lip, she looked back down at the boy in her arms and walked carefully back to her horse. *I will pay him the respect he deserves.*

Later that night she left as discreetly as she could, only taking two Medjay with her toward one of the many Nabaran pyramids at the edge of the Kalahari and on either side of the River Nub. They had insisted. The Temple of Mysteries was even further than the Temple of Peace, which she sought. Entry to the Temple of Mysteries was severely limited and no one gained entry without answering riddles written in Meroitic script on the outer walls. It was fitting. Meroitic had been used for years among the people of Kush, having developed separately from the hieroglyphs used in Kemet and among her ancestors, the black pharaohs of the twenty-fifth dynasty. It was over two thousand years old. The uncial letters were used to hide discoveries, locations of gold mines, burial chambers, and government affairs. Given Kemet's susceptibility to attack because of its rich resources and perfect location for trade, defending it had become second nature, and precautions had to be taken. Now though, the Romans ruled over Kemet, calling it Egypt instead.

There were many entrances to the temple, her father once told her, but only a few people could answer the questions posed. Her father promised to show her the temples and the sphinx along the Nile one day. Perhaps when the chaos of Rome and the threat to Meroë no longer existed she would see it again. *They were built to last ten thousand years,* he told her as child, regaling her with stories at night. Four large stone sphinxes twice her size lined the approach to the pyramid known as the Temple of Peace, a symbol of protection in Kushite culture. With the body of a lion and the head of her late grandfather she felt a calm come over her as she walked toward the entrance.

She hadn't wanted to at first but she forced herself to go. She owed it to the boy. Taking the stairs slowly she descended to the underground chamber of the pyramid. The Temple of Peace. With its high vaulted ceilings, the artisans and engravers had outdone themselves. Meroitic inscriptions and beautiful hieroglyphs decorated the walls from ceiling to floor with ancient prayers meant to guard whomever sought refuge here from harm. Most were dedicated to Nephthys, goddess, and protector of the dead. Her father once told her the scribes were often commissioned to leave coded messages whose answers would only be revealed to those with a pure heart and a sharp mind. That, and walls that were ten meters deep with iron encasing the middle-most layers. Her mother rarely stepped inside, save to light candles and take her leave. As a daughter of Christian Makouria her mother worshipped only one God. Though her father adhered to the Old Religion of Kemet and Kush, she had never seen him pray to any of the gods and goddesses of Amun or Apedemak. And she'd never seen him cry. After her grandfather died, it became even more clear he did not believe in the multiple gods and goddesses thought to protect them. Foolish, he called them. She often wondered how her mother and father reconciled their beliefs and were able to live such a happy marriage. Regardless of her mother's beliefs, Nabarans practicing both religions loved her more all the same. Her kindness, grace, strength, and support of the commoners matched none. *And what must the High Priests think?*

All of Nabara was aware that the High Priests held not only to ma'at but also in their personal lives worshipped Amun, Anubis, and more, preferring the Old Religion. Charged with carrying out justice and order, her father, as High King, broke the tie when they were deadlocked. Even with nine, some often needed to recuse themselves. The High Priests held great power in Nabara. As protector of both the mortuary and offering temples, they received gifts from all over the territory that they would dedicate on behalf of the giver to the gods. The nine longest standing members of the High Priests sat on a council known as the *Kenbet*, a court of justice that adjudicated minor offenses in Nabara. As all of the High Priests were taken from among the most pious nobility, province chiefs, and scribes, they alone represented Nabara in its entirety, ruling as they should under ma'at to ensure justice and order. However, their jurisdiction was limited. The nine High Priests of the *Kenbet* oversaw minor offenses such as theft, property disputes, and marriage contracts. Major crimes were referred to the *Great Kenbet,* the sole adjudicator being the Vizier or her father, as High King. Tomb robbers, accused murderers, and major land transactions were all heard at the *Great Kenbet*, though anyone might petition for a hearing in front of the Vizier or High King. It was well known that the *Great Kenbet*'s discretion leaned toward hearing foreign matters and punishment for involvement with the slave trade. Anyone could serve as a witness or be called forward to give further information for the court. It was a grievous error to refuse the summons or lie after taking the oath of truthfulness under ma'at. Witnesses had been tortured for less. The legal system was a delicate balance between the superiority of the old gods, and the logic of using the court to resolve disputes. Regardless of the outcome, the scribes recorded each inquiry, complaint, ruling, and sentence on their papyri for future reference. High Priests could create laws, and expected the High King to enforce them. Though the High King sat above it all, the High Priests alone held sway over the length of his rein, and could dethrone him or order to him to suicide if they deemed him unable to ensure justice and order. But this had never happened, he'd constantly reassured her as a child. *Like any great deterrent,* he whispered to her, *the threat alone is sufficient.*

Candles lit each visitor's way inside the temple, giving off a hypnotizing fragrance that calmed the mind. Many sought refuge and prayer here, but the lower chambers were only open to a few. The entrance level of the temple held a large, wide room that stood empty save for a cream palm and papyrus reed basket filled with sandals, sitting lonely and unclaimed just inside the door. A single door loomed at the back wall with a Meroitic inscription that read; *when you are ready, you may enter*.

The door sprang open as she neared, revealing a man older than her late grandfather smiling at her. Without a word he nodded and stepped aside. A narrow well-lit ramp with small torches along the bottom of the wall urged her to follow it down. The second level held hundreds of candles on the back wall and one large one in front of them all, which was never put out. It flamed bright, whipping back and forth as though blown by some unknown wind. She lit four of them herself before she sought what she was looking for now - the priest who would prepare the dead boy's body for burial.

Priests walked by her in long white robes, each of them bowing lightly to her and she nodding in reply. Though she was robed in a long-sleeved white gown the heat did not reach her here. Moving down the narrow passageways, she found the door the priest instructed her to come to. *This one if you please, Princess, and no other*, he had asked of her. She couldn't help wondering what lay behind each closed door she passed and whether those on the other side were looking at her. Like the walls in the first chamber, this door held inscriptions and prayers. Lifting her hand to knock, the stone door slid open before she could. Priest Hameht smiled at her and stood back for her to enter. Letting the stone door close behind her, he welcomed her inside.

"If you are going to stay, Princess, why stare at the wall?" Smiling at her kindly, he ushered her towards the table at the back of the small room. Like the others, this room too held scented candles, no doubt meant to mask the smell of death.

"Remember," he told her softly, "he is already at peace. This is merely a tribute to him out of respect for the life he lived. So that he can let go of this world and to ensure his journey is an easy one." Touching her shoulder gently, he moved away, robes sweeping the ground softly.

Squeezing her eyes shut and opening them again, rapidly she turned around. Breathing was difficult when she looked at him. His bones protruded from his waist and knees, making his head look like a boulder atop a branch from the starvation he'd endured. The priest began by picking up a long, thin iron instrument, hooked at the end and smoking from the kiln he removed it from. Sliding it carefully up the boy's nose, he moved it back and forth carefully, blocking her view momentarily before doing the same with his right nostril, pulling it out and pushing it back in. Several minutes passed before he turned the boy's head to the right and slid a bowl underneath his nose. Brains drained into the bowl like mashed rotten grapes, and her heart squeezed as she watched. She'd been warned, but her stomach still tightened in protest. The priest set each bowl aside as it emptied, and she could only imagine what crimes the boy had endured before he came here. When her mouth began to tremble, she covered it with her hand, refusing to let any tears fall. The priest must have heard her slight inhale, for he turned around, dropping the cloth he had picked up.

"You must not cry, child. The boy's spirit will stay to grieve with you," he told her gently. When she nodded he turned back around towards the table picking up a new cloth this time. "I know you asked me to wait, but I already removed his internal organs save for the heart. It is a much slower process. Though it is not standard to prepare others besides the royal family and nobles in this manner here, it is necessary to preserve the body for burial."

"Thank you for showing him this kindness."

Rinsing the body slowly, the priest poured water from a gourd over him, starting from his neck and working down towards his feet. Picking up an ivory linen cloth, he dipped it into a coconut-sized bowl and began to wash the pads of the boy's feet, ankles, and toes until the dirt and debris on them disappeared, turning the cloth a dark brown. Heavy, black splotches on his legs became more visible as the dirt was gently smoothed away. His stomach curved sharply, the ribs so tight against his skin they reminded her of elephant bones in the Kalahari Desert. Dipping into a separate tiny bowl filled with what smelled like rosewater, he cleansed his face and forehead, wrapping two fingers in the cloth to wipe under his eyes and across his mouth. Next he picked up a comb and began to rake through his brown curls starting at his temple.

"Please," she said, placing her left hand on top of his right one to stop him, "let me."

Nodding, the priest moved back a step to allow her room.

Sand and grime fell to the table and through the round holes of the tray beneath his head as she worked. Putting one hand to the left side of the boy's head, she turned it gently, combing the right starting at the ends of his curls and working to the root. Dipping her hand in the olive oil next to her she smoothed it onto his hair and continued detangling, noting how smooth his hair became under her fingers. She wondered if his mother had ever done the same. When she finished, she ran the pad of her thumb across his long, kohl-colored eyelashes, softer than feathers. Moving back, she nodded to the priest, and he stepped forward to massage oils into the boy's body. By the time he finished he smelled of palm wine and myrrh. The Noble Bimbola had been kind to deliver the wine a day earlier at her request. Sprinkling a mixture of natron over him from head to toe, he used a feather duster to evenly distribute it across his body.

"The boy was severely dehydrated, Princess. He will not require a lengthy waiting period before we clothe him." His face was kind as he looked at her. Accepting his comment, they began to wrap the body slowly, winding it over and over again, lifting his legs together once it reached his knees. Softly, he began to recite prayers from the *Book of the Dead,* a gentle rhythm that matched his movements. Keeping the cloth smooth, he stretched it tightly over the cloth that covered him from hip to thigh. After each wrap he smoothed liquid resin over the linen to help hold them together. She stepped forward again when it reached his chest, putting one hand there. The priest turned to her, eyes questioning. Reaching towards her waist she turned to remove a tiny, gold, lion-shaped *ushabti* from a hidden pocket inside her gown. Smoothing her fingers over the lion's head of the funerary figurine, she turned to the priest.

"I did not..." she trailed off slightly, "I did not know his name to inscribe—"

The priest stopped her, placing both hands over her own and stopping her voice from shaking, though her eyes shone.

Looking down at the *ushabti,* she started again. "I did not know his name. So instead I wrote...'my brother'." Swallowing she looked back into kind eyes.

"The gods will understand. It will protect him well." The priest removed his hands from hers, touching her cheek softly.

Imani placed the lion *ushabti* on the boy's chest, the funerary figurine tiny on top of his body. When they were almost finished wrapping, she stroked his hair gently one last time and kissed his forehead. The priest walked her up the stairs, past the prayer hall, and up to the top back chamber to see her out.

"May the gods protect you, Princess."

"And you," she told him. When she walked away she held her head high, at peace now, knowing this was as much for the boy as it was for her. And she also knew one more thing. *I'll find out who killed you one way or another.*

AMKAR

Watching his daughter carefully, he took note of how she met his eyes without a hint of regret or fear. *Defiant to the last.* He tried hard to calm his anger before he spoke. He was renowned for his temperament, and he would not change that for his youngest daughter. He could walk into chaos, full of angry High Priests and controversial disagreements about the law, and military commanders threatening the use of force, and silence them all without raising his voice. The lower he talked, the more they listened, his face like a still lake that swallows the ripple. The tree that merely bends in the storm. He carried out sentences without one trace of anger or excitement for revenge. And the people respected him for it.

His gold *khepresh* shone in the light cast from the great golden torches hanging from the stone walls of the room. Great curved bronze plates held pits of fire from the ceiling, lighting the room with their glow. The head of a lion was carved into the front of his crown. Wearing a loosely draped and folded ivory linen shendyt, which fell to his knees, he sat on his throne, watching her carefully. His shoulders held a lion's fur, signaling the authority of his reign. Staring down at his daughter, he shook his head with frustration. *She ignores me at every turn.*

"If my memory serves me well, I do believe I told you to *stay away* from the coast. Let Shaharqa exercise his authority over the newest soldiers and never to ride with the soldiers into battle unless I am by your side."

"I did not ride with the soldiers into battle. The soldiers followed me."

He'd been told at least ten untested soldiers in training followed his daughter to the coast. The soft shuffles in the room made him look to Shaharqa now, who met his eyes apologetically. Only his closest advisors and two handmaids were present, but he saw from their faces a few felt as Shaharqa did. Though there was something else in the curve of his brother's mouth. *Pride.*

"Then you are a poor leader," he snapped at his daughter. The affront that appeared in her eyes did not please him, but he knew the insult would be well placed. She had much to learn.

"You took men with you to confront an unknown threat. Men with a ship who might have captured you, killed the soldiers, and taken you and the remaining into slavery and across the sea where I may not have known where to follow."

"But they did not."

"Today they did not. *Tomorrow* is another day." His anger filled the room and ricocheted off the walls.

"Father—,"

"Do not speak," he growled, rising from the throne and looking down at his daughter. The servants seemed to bow lower, cringing as they listened in the hopes of avoiding his wrath.

"Leave us," he said suddenly, quietly, throwing his arm out toward the door. The servants quickly made their exit at his command, and Imani watched them go, a flush rising in her cheeks.

"Imanishakheto," his wife's voice sounded from his right.

"I know what you would say. I am a warrior, after my father," Imani replied, the golden pools of her eyes full of reproach.

"And warriors have leaders too. Leaders they follow. Leaders they listen to. The threat on the high sea is growing, and we do not yet know the force of it. As does the danger of our trade routes by land. You must be careful." Samya was doing her best to make their daughter understand.

"And why not my brother?"

He raised his hand, gesturing to their surroundings. "You were born a daughter of the pyramids, Daughter of the Desert. Not a son. I will hear no more of this. I forbid it." *She must remain protected.*

"I am not a son, that is true. But I am a daughter of Kush. Queens have ruled Kush solely for many years. How many other empires can say this? *None.* Today, I held a boy no older than five in my arms. His skin sagged from his bones like old and well-worn leather. His ribs so devoid of meat I could play them as an instrument. Chains held him to the ship that carried him across the sea. And I helped kill the men that rode that ship. I would do it again."

"We only ask that you take care with your own life so that you do not shorten ours," Samya pleaded. "I would die if anything were to happen to you. The time may come when you have to fight. When you have no other choice. Your father and I recognize that. But we will delay that day for as long as we can. The Festival of Kings is tradition and approaches us with each day. God forbid something should happen to you.

Imani stared at the floor before turning to look up at him, her eyes full of reproach.

"I know...everything." She stood at the bottom of the dais, her luminous eyes full of anger and disappointment as she looked up at him. Even from the great distance he could see that clearly.

"The slavers are increasing in number. The royals despise each other, some for cowardice; foreigners multiply on coasts to the east and merchants are losing cargo. Not to mention the drought. I should *know* these things. I don't want to rule another Kingdom or this one to sit as some *war prize* I want to help our people. I want to fight for-"

"Fight? You are *a Princess*. You are *my daughter!*" he bellowed down at her.

"*I am my father's daughter!*" Imani's fists were clenched at her sides. Ama stood near the door, shifting uncomfortably as she listened to the exchange.

He stood suddenly from his seat on the dais, "And until that changes or one of us should die that will remain your reality and you will never fight! "

She tried another path, her desperation to make him listen growing. "If you had but been honest with me..."

"You don't *listen* to me..."

"I listen to you..." she pleaded.

"You don't do what you're *told!*" he snapped.

"Not when I ask for and need answers!"

"Answers that I will give you in time if you would only heed my instruction."

"I have tutors for my *instruction*," she said spitting the word out vehemently. "*You* are my father and honesty is what I expect—"

"Your expectations are none of my concern! The truths which I impart are meant to keep you safe."

"*Truths?*" Imani replied incredulously. "You *withhold* the truth, forbid me to attend the war councils, and expect me to do as you *command. In everything.*"

"And this is one more thing which I have asked you to do to ensure the continuance and stability of the Kingdom." He waved his hand dismissively, missing the expression of shock on his wife's face. "*I* will fight for our people. It is not your concern. If you would but listen to me."

"Listen? I am not eager or willing to be more desirable to men I detest and would not trust to tell me the source of water should Amun decide to make it rain." Her hands curled into fists as she stared at him. "I speak more than ten languages, I can draw you a map of this entire Kingdom and every river in it, I know the history of every family and royal house, and have helped make Nabara wealthy from its investments in our local citizens and none of this you would know or care to take note of because you only look at me to find something I can change."

"Is *this* what you think of me? You always miss the point. You're missing the point now!"

"NO!" Her reply was sharp and rang throughout the chamber as her chest heaved. "I have *never missed the point.* I understand the point very well, and all the possible repercussions." Her voice dropped. "I just don't care."

He watched her turn on her heel, her hair swinging as she turned and left his presence, throwing the hall doors open with Ama close behind as the servants bent their knees gently as she passed, too quickly to allow them to bow.

Shaking his head, he turned to Asim and Shaharqa. "Make sure there are Medjay at the market and patrolling areas closer to the coast for now. We cannot risk this threat so close to the Festival of Kings. I do not believe in taking chances. There may be slavers yet that escaped from the ship."

"Yes, Your Grace." Each of them nodded before quickly leaving the throne room.

"Was she meant to be my third son?" Amkar murmured quietly when he and Samya were alone.

"No, she was meant to bring you joy," his wife said, smiling.

"Joy? She has the power to stop my heart. How should I treat someone so intent on killing me without a hint of remorse?"

"You may be a soldier, my love, but you cannot win every battle."

"Are we at war?" he replied incredulously.

Samya laughed lightly, her smile brightening his mood with ease. "Tell me, my great and powerful King. When have you ever known a child to fight against the wishes of their father when they come of age? Yes, you won my heart while yet you fought against the Nomadin of the west. None could match you with spear nor *khopesh*. How your battle cry struck fear into the hearts of the bravest of warriors. And yet, my High King," she said softly, lowering her voice, "the cry of your children when they leapt from my womb undid you just the same." She took his hand then.

"This does not make you weak my love, it means you care for the lineage of your loins, your heirs, your blood. It is said that a woman becomes a mother at the moment of conception. A man, a High King even, becomes a father at the moment of birth."

He gazed into her eyes. "After all these years, still you move me. You clever witch." They laughed together and he touched her cheek. "I do wonder my love, as a leader, is it better to be feared or loved?"

"It is better that your queen love you, your children fear your disappointment, and your people admire you. To be loved is to bear a kind and caring heart. To be feared an obedient child. To be admired is to retain the respect and command the loyalty of your people."

IMANI

Leaning on her balcony she grinned as the sun shimmered on the waters of the River Nub. Hundreds of columns on either side of it leading to the sandstone homes, pillars, temples, and pyramids beyond. Her chambers were on the outer walls of the palace on the tallest level. The pinkish-blue hues of the sky blended purple and glowed with fire from the sun. Dawn. No one was awake and she could safely wander about the pyramid, down to the kitchens or take a morning ride. Most of all, it was time to visit the market. A daily gathering of merchants from the city as they sold their wares. Locals and merchants from other kingdoms alike participated as long as they gained permission first, paying tax to the vizier and registering with his scribe. She could almost smell the fresh fish caught from the rivers; the cinnamon and nutmeg used in the sweetest of desserts, the milk sweetened with honey from beehives, the top burnt slightly and crusted with sugar. Mangoes, lemons, nara, plantains, coconuts. Sometimes the traders would split a coconut with a *khopesh* for her if she wanted and let her drink the sweet milk from the inside.

"Ama!" she called softly to her cousin. "It's dawn!"

"Hmmm?" Ama murmured sleepily from her bed.

Imani threw the heavy green and gold silks that covered her cousin aside and swung out of her reach as Ama tried to pinch her, moving around one of the four thick golden pillars at its edge.

"You sneak!" Ama cried, clutching her arms around her body. "It's so cold."

"I'm sorry, Ama," she said as she ran to her. "I don't want to miss it. We'll be late!"

"Imanishakheto, your father would not—"

"I know what the High King would not. Still, he can't have risen yet and you know how I love the market."

Ama rose, smiling, and walked naked to the western corner of the room. She disappeared for a moment, slipping her green and white gown over her shoulders. Ama's hair was in dozens of small twists, swinging about her shoulders in a mesmerizing display. The tiny cowrie decorations at the tip of each all the decoration she needed. The dimple in her left cheek winked at Imani every time she spoke. Though she had a matching one on her right cheek, she'd often stuck her finger into Ama's when they were children, as if it was a hole through which she could pass. When she emerged, Imani stood smiling in the middle of the bedchamber, her smile matching the ivory gown she'd chosen. Its only strap sitting on her right shoulder, its heart shape stopping just above her breast and hugging her ribs until it reached the golden band around her waist and fell in loose waves down her hips to the floor. A soft slit showing the glow of one bare thigh in the soft torchlight.

Ama went to her, adjusting her gold, diamond-studded crown around her ears and forehead before undoing the braid the handmaids had created the night before, allowing the thick tight curls free, watching them immediately spring up Imani's back as they shrunk slightly, absorbing the moisture in the air. Still, her onyx curls hung low to her waist, smelling of coconut and honey. Her crown.

"Come! We'll miss it," Imani cried, tugging Ama's hand before running quickly to the door. She pulled the stone latch free from its hold, holding her breath before exhaling, worried the sound might wake the palace.

They ran quickly through the halls on soft sandaled feet. *Swift as a cheetah*, Imani reminded herself as she slipped down the narrow passages of the pyramid, nodding to the guards as they smiled at her briefly. This was not her first time sneaking out.

"Princesses!" Asim called softly.

"Uncle," she whispered.

"You did not think to leave without me, did you?'

"Never, you always know where we'll be," Imani said laughing.

"And so I do."

Asim was as an uncle to her even if her grandmother had adopted him. Even her father treated Asim as he did her uncles Shaharqa, Yemi, and Semi. Theirs was a long relationship built on trust, shared battles, and loyalty. Imani felt her heart jump as they walked toward the market. Her father had asked her not to leave the palace without her guards, but he wasn't always there. And it was safe regardless. Asim was her father's most trusted Medjay. As young boys, Medjay, as Royal Guards, were taken into the Kiberan jungle and the desert, returning only after they'd learned to kill lions with their bare hands, ran as swiftly as the gazelle, and found water where no lakes formed. Those that did not return were unworthy of servicing the High King's family. She always felt safe when Asim was by her side. But this was Nabara. And she had never feared anything with their land under her feet. Asim's cousin Ram followed quickly, his black braid swinging. Ama's bracelets tinkled softly as the group went.

A herder went past with at least twenty ankole-watusi cattle, likely having brought them to market for their milk. Over two hundred called the palace home, groomed and decorated with paint and more on behalf of the royal family. The watusi were well loved and only used for their milk when their calves were weaned. Often, they were named as members of the owner's family. They were frequently gifted as part of the bride price paid to a bride's family upon her marriage or sold as a part of the large trading market along the coast and even towards the Sao Kingdom. A man's wealth could be counted in terms of the number of cattle he owned. In Nabara, it was forbidden to kill them. Only when an old one had died was the meat portioned for the city at a festival in his honor. Imani walked over to one, white and black splotches of color overlaid its silken coat. She ran her hand over its back and toward its neck, opening her fingers as it pressed its wet nose against her palm. His horns were well over three feet from root to tip, smooth and curved, forming a U-shaped crown that could be neither ignored, nor mistaken for anything other, than the Cattle of Kings.

A few minutes later they heard the soft cries of the market growing louder. Imani's mouth watered as she smelled meat roasting. The carver would cut thick slices each morning for his patrons.

"Princess!" one woman called. "Try some seared bananas." Sometimes patrons would crowd to eat what the royal family tasted each day, and in the mornings, it was the same.

The merchant cut the bananas into small slices and Imani and Ama shared them with the guards. Tasting of honey and coconut, her mouth watered at the flavor.

"Thank you," she said, dropping coins into the woman's bowl as the woman bowed low to her.

"Princess! Here!" others called as she and Ama turned back towards the market. She watched a little boy running to his father, handing him fresh fish, the lines still in their mouths and bloody as they piled them high for the day. The ice that surrounded them was just beginning to melt as the temperature rose with the sun. She knew that the traders took care to freeze water at night by placing clay trays filled with water atop their roofs and flat surfaces, allowing the cool night air to freeze it. They must sell their fare quickly the same day or risk losing its freshness.

She and Ama continued along, passing a stand filled with terracotta figurines. Each of the figures held varying positions; sitting, standing, waving, bent at the waist, one knee to the chin. Carefully molded beads decorated their necks in collar form to closely resemble those they only imitated in life. Many of them were on horseback, the head of both the animal and rider of identical shapes. The one thing they all had in common was the face—large triangular eyes and nose beset by a long and prominent chin. She picked one up from where it sat and studied it carefully.

"Benue," Asim told her.

"What?"

"Benue. It is the art of a people who live near the river Benue. Once, I met a man from there who told me his home was a plateau that was the mother of many rivers. He gave me a figurine like these as a gift for my daughter, Azima. It is a part of their culture."

"Benue," she repeated as she turned to look at the rest. Life-sized representations were just behind them with hairstyles as detailed as any living person. One contained the round knots the women in the village sometimes wore. As did the farming families migrating south away from the Sahara. She touched them lightly, enchanted with their detail.

"Cousin, look!" Ama said, pointing to a brightly colored stand with a royal blue silk canvass. "Jewelry!"

"Haven't you enough, Princess Ama?" Asim's eyebrow rose as

he watched Ama try each piece on.

"A woman can never have enough!" Ama's eyes sparkled as she continued.

Imani laughed at her excitement. She had no real interest in buying jewels and baubles, but her cousin loved to trade whatever she could for them. No matter how many precious stones and golden bracelets she had in the palace. A woman next to her cousin picked up a bracelet and tried it on, the bright blue beautiful against her dark skin. Imani stared in awe as she watched her. It was the baskets that caught her eye. Piled one on top of the other on her head. *They could almost be a crown.* Her balance was spectacular; even as she looked at the table of bracelets in front of her, she only moved her eyes and her neck, never bending her chin down as was the natural tendency for most. All at once she turned to Imani and smiled, startling her. Blushing at having been caught staring at her for so long, Imani smiled back. The woman bowed out of respect, carefully bending only at the knees, her back straight as she lowered herself, her eyes on the ground. Imani's eyes never left the baskets on her head, wondering if they would fall. When the woman rose again, Imani's eyes met hers and she nodded to her in answer, admiration in her eyes.

"May you live a thousand years," the woman said.

The woman was still smiling as Imani turned and walked back toward Asim, this time passing a snaking line of girls. The oldest was no more than ten, and all four followed carefully behind their mother. All four with baskets filled with fruit and grain. The littlest one kept reaching her hand above the bowl to pop tiny pieces of what appeared to be sugared sorghum into her mouth. Imani laughed as she watched her. *It certainly is one way to lighten the load.*

"Ama, look at the scrolls! They must be a hundred years old," she cried in wonder as she stopped at a nearby merchant's stand.

She stepped inside slowly, her hands touching the date palm pillars holding the black and yellow silk roof together. It billowed up like a mushroom whenever the breeze swept in and Imani's eyes danced with pleasure at the sight it created.

"You honor me, Princess Ama. Princess Imani," the proprietor said, bowing low. His hair was black and peppered with salt, standing only an inch high. His long face gave way to a strong jaw and chin with the whitest teeth she'd seen in such an old one. He wore black robes with sleeves that billowed out, growing longer toward his hands and falling slightly over his wrists.

What caught Imani were the white painted symbols across his brow and cheek, standing starkly against his brown skin.

"May the sun shine upon you today, elder," she said respectfully. "May I see your scrolls?"

"As you wish, Princess," he said reaching for the nearest one. "We have many that may be of interest to you. Tales of far-and-away places. The history of Nubian archers. How to create magic and wonder. The secrets of the pyramids. The architects of the Deffufas. The Nile and her wonders. What pleases you?"

Asim, Ram, and Ama stood at her back, waiting patiently, their eyes moving over all the room contained.

"The secrets of the pyramids, elder. I should like to buy that one." Reaching quickly inside the belt of her gown, she drew forth a gold coin with a bow on one side and a crown, the *khepresh,* on the other.

"That is too much, Princess. I could not—"

"Please, take it. I love to read. I hate to argue," she said smiling.

He bowed low again, his sleeves sweeping the ground. "Karim, prepare the scroll for our Princess," he called without turning, the corners of his eyes crinkling as he smiled at her.

A young man stepped forward quickly, gently rolling the scroll in his hands. He bound it with twine and placed it in a feather-filled box. Imani watched silently. Karim had thick black, coily hair, shorter than his master. He moved gracefully, with the sure step of a man though he seemed to be no more than twelve. He was tall and his brown skin was pleasing against his wide-set brown eyes. Imani noted how his teeth shone white as he smiled, handing her the scroll before lowering his head slightly in respect.

"Thank you, Karim," she said. "And you, elder. I will enjoy this very much."

"The honor is ours," the elder replied. "Please come again."

"I will," she promised as she turned to leave.

The sun was higher now, throwing its light across the fields, flowers, and desert, though they still stood in shade. Imani felt her skin begin to warm under the light gown she'd chosen. She took Ama's hand and led her to a long row of fruits and vegetables. The trader created juices and desserts with the flick of his knife as they watched, a bowl of sweetened milk or a light pinch of cinnamon and sugar picked from rows and rows of baskets filled with different spices. Dipping sweet bread inside it, Ama threw back her head and sighed with pleasure, looking up sneakily when Imani pinched her arm.

"Come," Ama said, smiling as she led Imani towards the gourd maker. Sometimes he filled his gourds with treats and wine. His patrons always came for a taste and left with a gourd, unable to resist the beautiful decorations his wife designed around the rims. They were legend. Stepping inside, she looked around as Ama began peeking inside to see where the wine was, giggling as she did.

"Where is he?" Her cousin looked around impatiently. It was unusual for the gourdmaker to be missing at this time of day.

Imani's nose wrinkled as she moved towards the back. "It smells—"

"Awful!" Ama covered her nose and mouth, frowning as she stepped toward the back of the tent.

Asim moved past her towards Ama. "Princess—"

"Are these the little kittens then? So far from home?" she heard someone say.

Her eyes widened as she recognized his vulgar Latin. She'd had many lessons in it. Her father and mother made sure of that.

"She is a comely one; they told it true," the man said roughly. Lifting a ladle to his mouth, the Roman gulped greedily. His hair was yellow, his skin pale and burnt red from the sun, dirty with sand and black as if he'd stood too close to a fire and not yet bathed. His clothing was rumpled and stained. She could smell his sour odor from where she stood.

Asim's *khopesh* was in his hand in an instant. "Watch your tongue," Asim demanded, stretching out the blade of his *khopesh* as Ram stepped up beside him. The surprise on the slaver's face was palpable. He did not expect to hear Latin come from her uncle's mouth.

"I meant no harm. I'd rather bed her than beat her—"

"You are from the ship are you not? Who are you?" Imani said, stepping in front of Ram, touching his wrist lightly in reassurance. She had no doubt they were from the slave ship that wrecked at the coast. He'd escaped and run, like the coward he was.

"Well, my friends call me Decimus." He smiled lecherously.

"I am not your *friend*. I am a Princess of the Pyramids. Daughter of the Desert. And you shall address me as such."

"I meant no harm...Princess." Smiling at Ama now he set the ladle back down and into the gourd on the table.

"What have you done with the calabash maker and his wife?"

The man inhaled softly before exhaling as he shrugged his shoulders. Imani gritted her teeth, ignoring Ama's soft gasp as she stepped backward and toward the door.

"We need horses, Princess. And you have plenty. Just four. And we'll be on our way. We don't want to kill anyone," he told her, glancing at Asim, the same satisfied look in his eye. "I promise you——"

It seemed to all happen at once. The foreigner's words were unintelligible, yet four men sprang in front of her. The same dull, stringy hair, blonde, and brown falling about their shoulders. Leather plates covered their chests with heavy, long pants. They knew nothing of the climate of the deserts. Sweat fell profusely from their faces. They smelled as if they hadn't bathed in days. The daggers in their hands glinted softly as one lashed out toward her.

Turning quickly she pulled a dagger from her sleeve, driving it upwards just below a man's breast. The satisfaction she felt at the surprise on his face was short-lived. Unable to free the blade from bone she struggled, gasping as another reached for her. Asim pushed her back just in time, his *khopesh* slicing easily through the brown-haired ones throat, spraying her gown with blood. A soft splatter rang in her ears, and Ama screamed as Ram pushed them both behind him roughly. The merchants cried out in fear and shock all around her as Ram's blade swept down again, singing as it hit the blade of the blonde one's dagger. It barely missed his thigh as he dropped low to his knees, his shoulder digging into the stomach of the second as he sliced through the knees of the third, sending a cascade of blood across the sand. A moment later, her uncle pulled her to her feet, and Ama beside her, running his hands lightly over her face as he touched her gown where the blood had spread to make sure she wasn't hurt.

"We must make for the palace," Asim said, looking to the ground briefly at the slaughtered men. The only concern that could be found settling in the crease between his eyebrows.

"Your arm..." she pointed at the blood running down Asim's forearm, alarmed at the amount of blood gushing from it as she looked at it.

"It's only been nicked," he told her softly, touching her chin gently to reassure her. "The rest is his."

She glanced behind her momentarily and saw the yellow-haired foreigner's head crushed in, his bowels spreading across the desert sand. Asim had taken no mercy.

"Bring him," Asim told Ram, pointing to the last foreigner standing there alive. His bowels had loosened without his command, the stench of urine filling the air as it pooled at his feet, his body shaking in fear.

"Please!" he begged.

Rather than walk, her uncle commanded a city chariot to take them home, binding their prisoner to the back with heavy chains. The sun stood higher in the sky, and a sea of white clouds sped across the sky. The sand seemed to note their urgency, blowing roughly across the desert floor at their backs, faster until the storm blotted out the sun. Imani held her arm across her face as the desert sand blew across the open chariot, buffeting it this way and that. The storm broke just as they reached the walls around the pyramid, wheels rolling swiftly towards the steps. Imani's eyes hit the ground in shame as she took note of the stunned faces of the Royal Guard and the Medjay as they ran to assist them. Her father would not be pleased.

CASSIUS

"Kill them," he commanded. Cassius's back was soaked with sweat from the heat of the desert. He'd come too bloody far to worry about getting caught now. It didn't matter where the money came from as long as he received payment.

It had been two days since he crossed *Mare Nostrum. Our sea.* The tribune had agreed to pay half his weight in gold if he delivered one thousand slaves from the desert lands. Young and old, he planned to sell them to Master Petronius for use in Rome. The nobles had become fat and greedy, seeking to use warm bodies to perform the labor they required. Mining from the mountains, serving in their homes, reaping in their fields. Cheap labor was hard to find and trading in slaves was nothing if not profitable. It was of no consequence to him. However, the number and transport posed the greatest problem of all.

One thousand slaves, he thought. *How in the world will I move one thousand slaves across the desert each month without more men? Fucking cowards, the lot of them.* Most of the Berbers from the North had cut and run, scared off by the prophecies of death that followed at each city or the massive beasts that had eaten one or two in the night. Some had been loath to enslave those from neighboring populations, but others he'd learned, saw no likeness and treated none as brothers or sisters. And even Romans were slaves. Most of the Greek slaves believed they were philosophers, begging their masters for their freedom. The Assyrians were just unlucky. Having failed to maintain their hold on Egypt they were even more bitter when they fell into Roman hands. To him it mattered little once they were in chains. *Then, they all look alike.* And it was most important that he find ones with skills or a trade. Blacksmiths garnered the most profit, and the black farmers were always wanted given their ability to nurture a crop through drought and the ease and speed with which they picked it. Some of their techniques were fascinating, and unknown to those in Constantinople. He would find more catchers soon. To replace the ones he'd lost.

Two of his men had been eaten in the night. He'd tripped across one of their lifeless carcasses at dawn. Or what was left of him. They'd even eaten half of his bones. The other had disappeared entirely. A trail of blood and a ripped sandal the only trace of him besides large paw prints leading into the bush. The locals mentioned hearing the cackle of spotted hyenas late in the night, but dared not venture out. Hyenas would drag men from their beds by the throat, easily pulling four times their weight out into the open, before their pack rushed in. Young babies, they told him, hyenas shook by the throat, while larger prey would be eaten alive. Their sculpted, heavily muscled upper bodies were twice the size of their lower bodies and hind legs. The Berbers claimed these were no hyenas, but a new breed of monster feeding on the living and bringing terror to hunters and farmers. Where there was one, many would gather. *And I'd rather not be part of that bloody feast.*

"What are you doing!" he bellowed at the mercenary. The mercenary had been put in charge of each slave they caught, keeping track of their class, status, height, weight, and trade. The tall man had reached for a chain to re-shackle the slaves kneeling before him.

"I—"

Get up!" he said to the five slaves, motioning upwards with his hand and pointing outside the tent. Cassius felt the anger rising as the mercenary turned to look at him. *He can't be serious.* They understood his gesture, but not his words. Rising shakily, they moved as quickly as they could, the iron chains clanging with each footfall. The fear in their eyes as they knelt did nothing to move him. He pushed the first roughly to the ground by the shoulder, his dagger flashing out quickly, arcing toward the slave's throat, blood spraying from the cut. A sigh escaped his mouth as he clutched his throat, eyes rolling inside his head as he fell to the ground. The last four struggled against their chains in fear.

"They're runners, and they're diseased now thanks to you! Marching them through the desert to an auction would be a waste. Do it quickly. Think you can handle the rest?" he mocked, looking at the man, eyes narrowed in disgust.

"I'll take care of it," a voice said behind him. Cassius looked up to see Sicarius moving towards him. He was pleased that the catcher had arrived. In charge of supervising the mercenaries they had hired to aid him in capturing slaves to sell at the coastal markets and to transport to Roman territories, Sicarius had been invaluable. He navigated the desert almost as well as a Berber. To the Berbers of the desert, this was home. Fierce camel riders, they spent their days in this fiery grave, wrapped in black and blue cloaks, all but their eyes often covered to guard against sun and sand. Their skills were invaluable. And Sicarius seemed to have them in his blood. It helped that he was familiar with a number of their languages. *And looked like them too.* Understanding the slaves helped them to determine whether they were worth a ransom. At times, weapons and tools were needed before they could carry out their trade, and iron was in great supply here. With Sicarius's help, Cassius had quickly learned which commodities were scarce and which carried heavier prices than most, such as salt. But it was the slaves he was after.

Now he watched as Sicarius did what he did best. The slave catcher walked over to the four who were still trembling as Sicarius held out one hand and lowered it palm-down towards the ground. The slaves complied, moving to their knees and trying their best not to look at the one bleeding on the ground in front of them, the sand staining fast. Two of them raised their hands, wrists together as they began to mumble words he could not understand. Sicarius pulled his sword and swiped right as he stood in front of them. In one broad stroke, he slit all four throats at once, the surprise still on their faces as each of them in turn realized their predicament. The first fell to the ground, mouth gaping open and pressed into the sand as though he only desired one last meal. The second's hands rose to his throat, pressing against the opening spurting blood like a well, panic growing as he grimaced and fell backwards. The third blinked rapidly over and over before his head dropped backward and took him with it. The fourth was the only one to stay on his knees until the end, reaching one arm out toward Sicarius as though to ask for a hand up. But then, Cassius realized he was pointing at him, his eyes filled with rage, the last remnants of life focused on communicating his hatred. His whole body began to shake as he struggled to stay upright.

But Sicarius didn't wait for him to fall. He looked at him once and turned his back to him, walking towards Cassius.

"Nicolae will not be happy with you." Cassius couldn't hold back the pleasure in his voice, but he suppressed his smile.

"I'm happy to speak with him," Sicarius replied. "When they ran, they cut their feet. Two tried eating at their wrists in order to slip them through the chains and the first had snakebite. It was the reason his ankle was swollen. Treatable, but not worth the trouble. The mercenary is new to this and lied to you about his experience. Next time I'll watch them myself. As I should have."

Cassius's jaw tightened as he took in this information. The bastard Roman mercenary had lied. *I suspected as much.* Most saw the slave trade as a way to get money as quickly as possible. And it was. Turn a slave here, capture another there, and sell them to the highest bidder. But few had the knowledge and tools necessary when it counted. Like experience in the interior and the ability to not only navigate the desert, but find water. Or chains to keep the slaves in line and under control. Even a novice in the slave trade knew a young child could do that as easily as iron anklets would. Sicarius had taught him that. He rarely needed chains as long as their mother or other family was under control. The younger they were the more they would bounce and skip along with a reckless curiosity for adventure, slightly confused, but unable to resist youthful desires. But Sicarius had warned him in the city to take care with certain mercenaries. The former gladiator had fought enough of them to know what to watch for. And even now he put the blame on himself, offering to watch them more carefully despite the fact that Cassius had insisted the mercenary should do fine with a simple task.

Cassius nodded. "Thank you for your candor. We'll continue into the interior with only the Berbers. I'll see you shortly."

The catcher nodded, and Cassius turned and left. Sheathing his dagger, he didn't bother to wipe the blood from its edge as he turned back towards the tent. Running a hand over his short red hair, he smoothed it back from his forehead. His face was hard as marble and set in a permanent scowl. Taking a swig from the beer on the makeshift table, he frowned at the realization that it had grown warm in the heat.

His employer had given him four weeks to come up with the number, discreetly and quickly. The resources he'd been given would soon dwindle to nothing. And if he failed to pay that would be his head. He would be paid double the price per head if he captured any who looked to be of high birth. He wiped the blood from his hands slowly, his face hardening into a scowl. The ship he sent out had not returned, and he had no idea what had become of it. *If I want it done right, I'll have to do it myself.* He did not plan on disappointing.

Footsteps sounded behind him in the tent, and he leaned onto the tables, his palms flat as he took a deep breath. He didn't have to turn around to know who it was.

"Nicolae," he sighed.

"Why did the catcher kill the slaves?" Nicolae moved further inside, pulling a chair toward him to sit as he watched his brother. He had been brought here to learn from him, gain his knowledge so that he could one day venture out on his own, and begin to trade. As a former captain in the Roman Navy, Cassius's expertise was far greater than his brother's, and came with the respect of a multitude of men.

"They were runners, Nicolae," Cassius took a swig of beer. The sweat was pouring from his temples in the heat, his clothes sticking to him like Nicolae's disappointment. "They tried to escape. Two of them were damaged goods and we cannot use slaves that have wounds like that. They would never sell. When those wounds become diseased, it is better to kill them off. In this heat it wouldn't take long."

"And where did the cattle come from?" Nicolae looked at the roasted meat sitting on the table. Cassius watched him swallow as his brother stared at it. *He's hungry.*

"Eat." Cassius pushed the platter toward him, spearing a piece for himself.

"Where did the meat come from?" Nicolae persisted, his eyes narrowing.

"I told you before, taking the cattle here is not stealing. The people go to these...*debt* courts for the claim, and we will pay them. It is their rule for pawnship with agreements and otherwise."

"And how will they find us, Brother?" Nicolae looked at him, accusation growing in his eyes.

"That's not my problem. It is their custom, Brother." Cassisus put his feet up. "And quite to our advantage I might add. But as Ambrose would say, 'When in Rome'..." Smiling he waved at the food again. "Eat."

Cassius looked at his brother as Nicolae reached for the meat, his eyes moving over the face that closely resembled his own. Younger by ten years, Nicolae's youth alone could propel him to success in a field where older men died each day. His dark blue eyes were exactly like their dead mother's, earnest and kind. Flame red hair that held none of the brown that Cassius's did fell over his eyes when he failed to cut it like their father. Even with all of this it wasn't their looks that set them apart. It was their temperament. As a boy, Nicolae would follow Cassius everywhere, stealing pies from open windows in Rome or raiding docked naval ships at night to see what goods may have been left behind. Always his lookout. Not much had changed. Except for Nicolae's conscience. Cassius frowned as he remembered listening to his mother's last words to her youngest son, her bony fingers cupping Nicolae's cheek as she lay dying, intent on him hearing what she had to say. "*He will lead you to ruin*," she told him. "*Follow your heart*." He held his mother no ill will. It was no secret Cassius had been trouble as a boy. But that had changed after his mother died. He'd married and become a captain and a trader. The profits were endless. If only Nicolae could stop thinking like a man of medicine and begin to learn the trade in slaves like him. Cassius looked at him. Thick red hair fell to his shoulders, earnest eyes begging him to reason. At twenty-two, his brother stood of a height with him, over six feet and growing stronger every day. Nicolae had been in his medical books for too long, coddled by their mother who likely died because of the way their father treated her. This would be good for him. There was no money for him to become a physician, and he needed to learn that. He needed to learn the way of the world. He needed to prepare for disappointment.

"I could have healed them for you," Nicolae offered, interrupting his thoughts.

Cassius laughed. "And waste your talent on them?" he scoffed. "No. They were rotten. It was for the best. Better than risking them trying to kill us in our sleep."

"I thought the catcher was to make sure they didn't try it. Keep them from escaping."

"He was, but I sent him on an errand, and these mercenaries from the coast were to act in his stead. You can't trust a man who only does a thing for the money."

"And Sicarius? The catcher? It seems you trust him well enough. And he did warn you about the mercenaries," Nicolae reminded him, tearing at the last bit of meat before crossing his arms in front of him as he looked at Cassius, his mouth tight with concern and disappointment.

"Sicarius is different. He's one of us. A citizen of Rome." Cassius leaned back against the table, his arms crossed about his chest. His brother and the catcher were as thick as thieves. It was a wonder his brother hadn't just asked him his thoughts on the matter outright. *He still gives me the courtesy of trust. As he should.* Deserved or not.

"Sicarius is Nubian. Rome is not his original…home. He's receiving payment."

"And so are you. But he doesn't need it. And he's been in Rome longer than he has any of the lands of Aethiopia. All he really wants is his freedom, and he has it. And he's killed plenty of men to get it. That is recommendation enough."

"Aren't you worried he'll kill you?"

Cassius laughed. "Kill me? What for?" He shook his head. "Sometimes I wonder about you, Brother." He pulled his own chair closer to his brother's, leaning his elbows on his knees as he spoke. "You see, Sicarius, he may only be a product of Rome, but the last years of his life, he was a *citizen* of Rome. He has political freedom now, the right to vote."

"He was a gladiator. Traders *sold* him to Rome," Nicolae challenged him.

"And the people loved him. It is why they offered him his freedom if he agreed to become a trader." Cassius took another swig of beer. "When you kill as many people as he has. The only color that matters is *red.* I suspect he has grown quite used to it. He may even enjoy it. And we allow him to continue doing what he's grown to love. It's just that now…now…it's in his nature."

SAMYA

"Who did this?" **her husband demanded**, looking at the Royal Guards, fury playing over his face. "Bring him forward!" Amkar commanded.

Her daughter hadn't had time to change into another gown. The blood had dried and darkened on her daughter's hands. Dark red stains were smeared across her forehead. Her niece stood shaking next to her. Ama's eyes were full of fear as she looked at the only Roman left standing. Samya resisted the urge to run to them and hold them tight. They had business to concern themselves with first. She motioned with one eyebrow and tipped her head to her right, waiting as Imani and Ama came to stand by her. Ama's hands shook as she stood there, and she watched as her niece clasped her hands behind her back, raising her head higher as she exhaled. She rested one hand on the back of Ama's head briefly and felt her niece relax somewhat. *She's such a gentle thing.*

Samya never missed a thing. She could read her people like a book. The deep inhale they took right before they told a lie; the way women would smooth their hands over their gowns which told her they were with child; the clenched jaw of her soldiers as they contemplated revenge, a fingernail or two eaten to the quick with worry. Her piercing, dark brown eyes unsettled most, made them want to confess all. A mother's eyes. As High Queen she sat back on her throne next to her husband, her blue and gold funnel-shaped cap crown sparkling in the great hall. It covered her hair completely, setting off the luster of her deep mahogany-toned skin, her long neck and generous lips, her graceful movements. Her gold and diamond necklace sat on her collarbone, intricate and falling to the top of her breasts and just over the edge of her shoulders. The gown underneath hugging her body close as though she'd been dipped in cream, curvaceous hips making her waist seem even tinier as she sat, ankles crossed in front of her. Her oversized sleeves loose and long, hands resting on either side of the arms of

71

her seat as the iridescent tint of her white robe lit her from head to toe. She almost glowed.

"Your Grace. This poor excuse for a man we kept alive to answer your questions. He refuses to give his name or that of his master. We found this among his belongings."

Asim held out a yellow parchment with writing upon it. The scribe to his left took it, reading it quickly before walking to hand it to Amkar.

"A promissory note in return for murder," Amkar said thoughtfully, turning the note over in his hands before handing it to her. "Who gave you this?" Amkar demanded quietly as Samya read the Greek words.

The captive glared back; having regained some composure he refused to speak. Yet the sweat upon his forehead betrayed him.

"I'll tell you if you promise to let me go," the prisoner replied. Samya's eyes narrowed at his response. She couldn't believe he had the gall to require a promise after having made an attempt on her daughter's life.

Amkar looked calmly back at the prisoner. "You are in no position to make requests. I am the High King of the Empire of Nudolla. King Amkarqa Arkamani-qo Kashta of the Kingdom of Nabara. Descendant of the ancient line of rulers of Kemet and Kush. Bloodline of Meroitic kings. Now, tell me your name."

The captive stayed silent, but something changed in the look in his eyes. The surprise he'd shown as he stood looking around in the Great Hall was amusing. *He's not used to gold like this.* Amkar raised an eyebrow and the Royal Guards stepped forward, pulling the captive's head back swiftly by his hair, bringing their *khopesh* up to his throat at the same time.

"Julius, my name is Julius!" His body began to shake, and the man's pants darkened. A river of his courage ran down his leg and became a puddle on the floor. "They said there were no Kushites here. In the south. I never…He never. He *promised*. Ezana told him they were the last of their kind…" Looking back up at them a realization stretched across his face. "Please, please I won't say anything!"

Amkar's head tilted slightly as disgust stretched across his face. A moment later he turned his gaze back towards the parchment in

Samya's hands.

"Where do you come from?" he asked quietly, his voice softening slightly.

"North of Rome. I have plenty of money to pay for my freedom. I won't return to the desert lands if you just let me—"

"Plenty of money? I doubt you'd come so far south, on a promise no less, had you any amount of money. And the starving slaves from your ship mean that either you are as you seem with no conscience at all, or you had nothing with which to buy the food to feed them. Now, tell me who sent you, and I might grant you your life."

"That's not fair —"

Amkar's laughter rang throughout the chamber's halls. "How large are the serpent's in Rome? You've seen ones fangs no doubt? One bite will render a victim immobile. Our most dangerous ones wear a hood, disguising its true intentions, a distraction, like your rambling words with no answers. You stand in the great hall of judgment. We don't often have use for this room. You will see something many of my people only ever hear as legend. I'll make you a gift."

He nodded to Asim, and her husband's brother signaled to the guard posted near a large stone wheel. The muscles of the guard stood taught as he pulled the levers counterclockwise. The prisoner's eyes searched Amkar's face before landing on her own in desperation. He struggled against the guards, kicking, before the butt of a spear caught him between his shoulders, forcing him to his knees.

"Please, please, please, I can pay, I didn't mean it, I can, I can."

His body trembled as the hiss of a number of pythons grew louder. The great wheel opened a slab of stone covering a hole in the great room's floor. The torchlight reflected off the eyes of each, making them appear like so many jeweled stones.

"You can't—They call him the Roman Merchant! The Enslaver! I do not know his name. I told you! You promised! I gave his name! This is not justice. Savages!" he screamed, spittle flying from his mouth.

"I said…*might* grant you your life. Sometimes, the things we say are even more important than the actions we take. I've heard much of the justice of Rome. You throw men of different religions into a pit. To fight with animals that haven't been fed for days. They say a man sits for weeks, months, being fed off the riches of a city. That these same systems allow for confession. Yes, a man may confess to a crime and receive a lesser punishment. A murderer may thus become simply a kinslayer, moved by passion. That a rapist may become one who simply acted with lewdness. We have heard much of your…justice. The Kushite Empire of Nabara did not become the greatest lands that ever were by denying justice and allowing their victims to suffer. Your law is slow. Ours is not." Amkar looked at her then, holding her eyes as she sat there. "Unless you are granted a reprieve." Samya held his gaze before turning to Asim and nodding once.

The Roman gasped in surprise, relief washing over his bloodstained face. "Thank you," he said softly.

Amkar walked down the steps of the dais towards the prisoner.

"Thank you, thank you. I won't come back," he promised.

Reaching toward him, Amkar placed one hand on the Roman's shoulder. "I believe you," he told him as they stood facing each other. "But I like to be sure."

The Roman's mouth fell open as he realized his predicament. "You said, she, she promised, she gave me leave to go, mercy!" He looked up at her, his face a mixture of fear and surprise.

"You expected mercy, after having shown none?" Amkar questioned the man.

"I needed the money. He said…you were not supposed to be here. He said they had erased all Kushites from the land! I would not have attempted – I would not…" The man's face crumpled.

"Erased all the Kushites? The pyramids were built to last ten thousand years. They touch the sun. The shadow of our likeness towers over the waters of the Nile, the very air itself is filled with the cries of joy of the Kushite people, and the mark of our sun kissed skin and hair is a testament to the god's love of our dark beauty. In what world could *you* have ever erased *me*?"

Amkar slammed his foot into the man's chest, the Roman's arms flailing as he fell backward into the pit, screaming as he did.

Screams echoed off the stone walls as he clawed at the walls of the pit, snakes biting his flesh at every turn as he struggled to climb. The thick body of the largest python moved toward him. The prisoner's hand reached the top of the pit, and he began screaming louder as he looked behind him, seeing the body of the snake as large as himself. In one fluid movement, the python sunk its teeth in his neck, wrapping its body slowly around the man like a lover, squeezing and squeezing before falling with him back to the pile of snakes.

The guard turned the wheel again, and the huge python opened its mouth, using its muscles to slide its victim down its throat. Paralyzed, but alive, the Roman's skin dissolved as acid ate through his flesh, the stone slab slamming shut behind them.

Samya turned towards Imani with concern.

"Come, Ama," she said softly. "Come Imanishakheto," she said, using her given name.

Imani descended the throne steps with barely a sound. Asim and Ramos waited at the foot. Their *khopesh* sheathed at their hips.

"You were very brave. But you should not have been there," she admonished her daughter before narrowing her eyes at her niece.

"Aunt S—"Ama started.

"Please, Ama. As her cousin, I know what it is you would say. If your parents were yet alive, I trust they would say the same. Yet, a daughter of the desert would not lie, nor would she fail to take responsibility for her actions." And she waited.

"I am sorry," Imani said softly. "Uncle Asim and Ram protected Ama and I, and we are both thankful to have had them there. I asked them to accompany me to the market. They should not be punished."

"Nor will they be," Amkar interrupted her. "However, you will remain inside the pyramid walls until the new moon. Should you be required to leave, you *will* be accompanied by no less than ten Royal Guards."

"Father, I—"

"Shall no longer leave the pyramid before dawn," the fury in her husband's voice was apparent. Even without yelling, he had the power to strike fear in the hearts of men. "You may be able to fight when you take someone by surprise, Imanishakheto, but today you were unprepared. A warrior and leader would never make this mistake. Your presence at the market until such time as I choose is forbidden. I expect Asim and Ram to do the same, no matter how persuasively you may ask them."

Asim and Ram bowed low, their heads uncharacteristically kept towards the floor in silent assent and disgrace.

"Brother. What did the other men say before you killed him?" Samya asked, turning to Asim.

Asim spoke first. "He called himself Decimus. The liar told us he meant no harm, Your Grace. He spoke to the princess with too much familiarity before we bid him hold his tongue. He told us he required horses and nothing more. The gourdmaker and his wife were unharmed." Ram nodded his head briefly in agreement.

"Decimus, Julius, The Roman Merchant. We must find this *Enslaver* and deal with him. A reward shall be given to any having information on his whereabouts. I want this coward found. Immediately. Before the festival. We have thousands coming to attend the Festival of Kings. Peace is crucial to our alliances. I do not mean to be worried by such filth. If he was aided by the Northern nations, I wish to know," Amkar commanded, his voice echoing through the great hall.

"It shall be done," Asim replied.

"Imani, you must be very careful. You are an important key to the future throne. You must take care my love," Samya said softly.

"Yes, mother," Imani replied, bowing her head slightly.

She watched her daughter carefully, studying her mouth and her intelligent eyes. Imani did not realize the danger she was in. The North bled for riches daily, and lately there had been tales that many chiefs and noblemen's daughters had been captured and ransomed in the outlying lands. The Silk Road had many dangers they often avoided if they only traded inside of Nabara, but that was foolish. Rich resources and the wealth of their allies helped others prosper. Slavers saw the desert as an opportunity and the disturbing reports had not failed to reach the High King's ears and the seat of Nudolla - Nabara, the Kingdom of Gold. Imani was no nomad's daughter. They must keep her close at all costs.

Imani turned to look at her father, her face strained, eyes pleading as she started, "Father—"

"Go," Amkar commanded, interrupting her. "Change before

supper, Imanishakheto Aminata Kashta. And you, Ama."

Samya turned to her husband sharply, noting how he addressed their daughter. Her husband was worried. He never blamed Ama. Amkar only called their daughter by her full name when he was angry, and she knew it served to remind her of her duty.

Ama and Imani disappeared through the heavy golden doors of the great room and she moved to follow. Not without throwing one last glance at Amkar in reproach. Touching the smooth surface of the walls as she went, her eyes lifted to the paintings decorating each side of the hall, the carved faces of Amkar's gods following her. Not long ago, she was a stranger here. In just a short time she went from being a Christian Nubian daughter to a newly reigning High Queen of Nudolla and Great Wife of Nabara, married to a Kushite High King. They had allowed her to take the throne as a Christian, but it had still been quite an adjustment. She was no longer the timid new bride watching from her seat on the throne. How quickly things changed.

Her heart squeezed as she pushed open the thick white stone door, her gaze falling immediately upon the blood stained gown shed on the floor. Imani looked up as she entered, her body half hidden in the great ivory-lined bath cut into the stone floors of her room. The great bast-shaped faucet streaming water down into the same was heated from the water passing through the narrow tunnel system. Water flowed into the bast as it was heated and came steaming out of the great golden teeth. Imani reclined opposite, her knees tucked tight to her chest despite the great size of the ivory pool. Her hair was still filled with sand and matted with dried blood. Ama turned as she entered, lifting Imani's gown from the floor, and folding it quickly to hide the blood stained garment from her.

"Ama-ka, leave us sweet one," she spoke softly before giving instructions to the handmaids as they walked behind Ama towards the door and out of her room. Ama's steps were slow, her face a mask of fright. Samya reached for her quickly. Placing her hands on Ama's shoulders she kissed her forehead, squeezing her tightly before nodding to the hall.

"Imani-qo," she started, using the *qo* form as a term of endearment. Kushites used the Meroitic term to convey love. At

77

other times it signified this one, spirit, or soul and were written on stelae. She often greeted Imani with *malu* when she was a child, meaning good, beautiful, or precious one. Now, she only hoped it would let Imani know both that she loved her, and that she was serious.

"He's furious." Imani finally looked into her eyes when Ama had gone. "Father expects more of me and now I've angered him. And placed Ama in danger as well. My dagger was stuck inside the bone...I couldn't pull it free..."

Samya knelt beside the tub, removing her ivory cape from her shoulders and placing her crown beside her feet. *Yes*, she wanted to say, *you have. You never should have gone. You're a princess, an heir to the Pyramids of the Kingdom, Daughter of the Desert, and a Princess of the Great High King.* Nabara was safe and always had been. But things were changing now. She worried for the kingdoms closer to Meroë, including her home of Makouria. Caution was paramount.

Samya couldn't say any of this. Not yet. Instead she picked up the ivory comb from a small shelf and gently combed the tangles from her daughter's hair. Filling the black clay pot at her elbow with water, she blew on it to cool before pouring it on Imani's hair, lathering it with rose-watered soap and coconut oil.

"Listen carefully, my little flower. We've received word that slavers have ventured further south than they first dared. They leave the comforts of their northern homes in search of gold, however they may receive it, searching for precious stones and metals. Our Nomadin allies and nobility in the west and east have sent messengers, warning us of the same, for their people have suffered losses at their hands. They have plenty of land, and too few people to farm it. Laziness and greed will breed an enemy faster than quicksand will choke the careless.

"The lucky ones are ransomed," she continued, "under pawnship for some." However, families cannot always pay. Even the many noble families bearing proud names have been unfortunate, some so deep in debt that they have been unable to provide the sums requested. Some retaliate. Many have lost. Soon you'll be a woman. I shouldn't have to tell you the dangers," she finished quietly.

Imani's fingers tightened around her knees, her jaw tightening in anger. "Why didn't father tell me of this? I'm not a child. I know there is something he's hiding."

"You will always be our child. No matter your age. A father will protect his child's innocence until his dying breath," she replied calmly. "Once, I was a stranger here. Given to your father as a gift from my own. To serve the High King. To be his queen and please him in every way. I know your father can be severe at times. Loyalty comes easy, but he has a hard time showing his love. I did not always love him."

"What?" Imani's face fell as she listened to her mother.

"Love takes time. Even those who choose each other enter marriages born of passion and not love. Passion is what moves you to marriage. Love keeps you together. Women are often slaves to the games of men, bartered and exchanged for gold, alliances, and council seats. Your father was determined. He never gave up."

"Determined? How?"

She smiled. "My father refused him. More than once."

"He refused father?" Imani was incredulous.

"He refused a *king*, Imani-qo." Imani turned towards her, amber eyes widening in surprise. "He offered your grandfather one thousand ankole-watusi, their weight in salt and fifty baskets filled with gold dust, mined and ground to the finest powder. But my father refused. A man will what you allow. But there are some things that are to a woman's greatest advantage."

"Like what?"

"Her mystery. Things that lie in her heart and mind. How a woman moves, thinks, loves, protects, rises to a challenge, and endures. And you too have inherited this. You are of Kush. It's in your blood."

"Mother. You believe in God. As a Christian," Imani said slowly, "did your father have no concern for marrying you to father given that he practiced a different religion? The Old Religion of Amun?"

"Your grandfather lived at a time when it was difficult to believe in God and stay alive at the same time. He sought to protect me from the fickleness of Rome. He still worried about their hatred of Christians despite the Edict of Milan. Many refugees passed through Kushite and Nubian lands to escape persecution. And Kush was ever battered by Roman greed and the threat of Aksum."

Samya stroked her hair as she thought of the gods and goddesses—Apedemak, Amun, Seth, Isis—the gods of her husband's family. And the single God and father of Jesus Christ, whom she believed in. She was a daughter of the Christian kingdom of Makouria. Married to a king of Kush and ruling his kingdom jointly as her own. Even she had wondered at Nabara's acceptance of the practice of both the Old Religion and Christianity among its people without bloodshed. Amkar loved her and would not be swayed.

"Have you never considered how similar the two religions are in terms of how our world came to be? Christians believe God is the father of us all and that he created the first man and later the first woman from man's rib. Worshippers of the Old Religion believe that Amun was the first God and father of us all, creating the first man, the god Shu, and the first woman, the goddess Tefnut." Cupping her face gently she softened her voice as she spoke to her. "My flower. I pray to God for you each and every day. He will protect you no matter what. When you are older you can choose who you believe in and who you want to be, and I will love you no matter which path you take."

Lifting Imani's comb she began to move it gently through her tangled raven hair, starting from the ends. "When your father tripled the gift your grandfather brought him into our house and asked him to stay until the next moon. He treated him as a guest. You will want for nothing here, my father told him. He built a guesthouse at the back of our land and stocked it with scrolls and fine pillows with servants to tend to his needs. He gave your father one silver coin and told him he must turn it in thirty days. He sent your father the most beautiful women." Pulling Imani's head back carefully she looked into her eyes. "Even my own handmaids. And they were lovely." Laughing at the look on Imani's face she smiled at the memory as she tilted Imani's head so that she could look into her eyes. "One after the other, night after night. He gave your father reign over the punishment of our people to deal with as he chose, from the lowest thief to the highest noble. Of course, they had no idea who your father was. He made him remove his raiment, of course, while in Makouria and his brothers ruled during his absence from Nabara. Only my father, your father and I, and his brothers and my sister know the whole story."

"Mother?" Imani interrupted her thoughts. "Did father…what happened?" Imani's curiosity was getting the better of her. The excitement sparkling in her daughter's eyes made her smile.

"I was fortunate, Imani-qo. One day I will tell you the rest of this story. But your father was beautiful, brave, and fierce and love comes easy to such as that. His mind proved greater than his skills as a warrior and he won me with his spirit, compassion, and devotion. You are fortunate in that you are not born to Kemet's rule. The games were set up long ago, so that the blood of the great kings and queens chose whom they wished. One may even adopt a successor under the laws of the Kushite of Nabara. But you must take care. Heavy is the head that wears the crown. For many are the fingers that seek to steal it away. Men will forget their gods, sell their children, and spread the blood of the innocent for power. And every day it becomes more tempting to do so."

"If someone should kill me—"

"Or marry you…"

"Against my will?"

"It doesn't matter. There are those who would recognize the marriage and rally behind a pretender. The royal line flows through the queen."

"I understand." Imani stood and Samya wrapped a lion's fur loosely over her daughter's shoulders to dry and warm her, wishing she could stop her from getting older for a few more years. Her daughter's amber eyes searched her own, hungry for the truth. She wanted to tell her everything, but it could wait. There was time yet.

"What aren't you telling me? What are you keeping from me?" her daughter asked as she walked towards the door.

"Soon you will attend at audience." She closed the door behind her, ignoring the question posed. She could not bring herself to answer her yet. *Life will come hard, my daughter*, she thought. *And quickly.*

JELANI

He refused to wait. He'd only been back for a mere hour, but it seemed like a month to him. He'd heard more than he needed to from his Uncle Asim. And his Uncle Shaharqa. His mother had advised him to give her time. Jelani clenched his jaw, his dark eyes narrowing at the thought. He shrugged his broad shoulders, placing his hands on his narrow waist in defeat. Leaning his tall frame against the balcony wall he looked out towards Nabara. He wore white cotton long pants, with a golden belt secured around them. His stomach and waist were bare, gleaming from the oil freshly rubbed on them. Jelani's hair was shaved close, in the style of the High King. A gold and emerald crusted minted cap crown, thin and shaped to hug the outside of his head sat on his dresser like a discarded, half-eaten apple, the reflection he saw there still, unmoving. He squinted as he looked at it, trying to make out his eyes or his face through the high shine, but he couldn't. The only thing he could see were his arms crossed on one another, stiff, unyielding.

Snatching his crown from the dresser he strode out of his chambers, feet moving quickly over the stone floors of the pyramid as he rushed towards his sister's door. Throwing it open as he did when they were children, he spied her on the balcony, her long, white bed gown around her feet.

"Brother!" Imani called, breathless, her black curls bouncing slightly as she rushed into his arms, smelling of coconut and jasmine. Lifting her off her feet he held her tightly, crushing her in his arms as her heart beat against his own. *May Anubis take me if something happens to her.*

A sharp growl sounded at their feet and his sister gasped, looking down as her pet cheetah pawed at his feet, struggling valiantly to bite at his ankles.

"You are a poor guard," he told it scornfully before turning to smile at his sister. Setting her down gently he looked into her eyes.

"Troublemaker," he said softly. "I'm glad you're safe. Father warned you, did he not?" He stroked her hair. "And Ama?"

Imani sighed with relief. "She's fine."

"Thank the gods."

"And probably hates me."

"Don't entertain those thoughts."

"My dagger, Brother. It...I...I couldn't free it." The helplessness in her eyes softened his next words as he stood in front of her, taking her hand.

"It happens to soldiers all the time. Battles, wars even, are always subject to one thing men can never plan for. Surprise." Taking her chin in his hands he looked into her eyes. "Next time, you form your hands into one fist and bring it down as hard as you can on the hilt. It will free itself," he promised her.

"I will. But there is something they're not telling me," she returned, frowning as she closed the door.

"I'm glad you're safe. Still, you must be careful. First the slave ship and now *this?*"

"I'm not a child. And I *always* attend the morning market."

"You're a princess. You must be careful."

"I will," she murmured, squeezing him tightly before releasing him. "Father wants you now. It is your turn to face the lion."

"Yes, I expected as much."

"What did you do?"

He laughed, watching his sister curl her legs underneath her as she picked up the cheetah cub and walked to sit on her bed, a vulnerability in her eyes he rarely saw. Briefly he wondered how much Ama might have told her and if his sister knew his lover, or pretended not to.

"I did nothing."

"Is it the farmer's daughter?" The soft question took him by surprise. "I see the way you look at her. She is very pretty."

Jelani sighed, "You're too smart for your own good."

"I know," a grin spread across his sister's face. "Will father let you?"

"Imani-qa," he said sharply. "Speak of this to no one."

"I wasn't—"

"I know," he interrupted. "But father would be very angry. I have no need of his anger as yet. He has much to deal with."

"I was only curious, but I understand. I would never hurt you."

"I know." He kissed Imani's forehead, knitting his eyebrows as he pointed to a spot below her chin with mock curiosity. When she looked down to see what was there he brushed the back of his fingers up her chin and over her nose quickly, causing her to laugh. Imani slapped his hand away.

"Don't change the subject." Her amber eyes narrowed as she watched him.

Sighing, he thought quietly for a moment. The memory of warm palms resting against his chest as the feel of cotton-like curls brushed against his cheek rose in his mind. His chest tightened as he remembered the promise he'd made to her, kissing the inside of her wrists as he told her no one would make her their slave. *No one*. Her trusting dark brown eyes had begged him to stay away, let time run its course so that her little brother might have a chance to study and learn while she worked off her father's debt. Jelani did not like the look he'd seen in the master's eyes when he was with her. Impatient, hungry, pleased. The way he forced her to follow behind him like his shadow.

He felt Imani's hand slip inside his and he looked up, his attention returning.

"Tell him," she said firmly.

"In some ways you're braver than I. I have to be careful. She would be in danger should we be discovered. And not just from the wrath of our father. You have more to worry about just now than who I may or may not be seeing."

Imani's eyes widened, meeting his in surprise, "I don't have to choose anyone! The people of Kush have allowed women to become scribes, priestesses, and warriors for hundreds of years. We are singular in our successive lines of ruling queens. Why should I be made to suffer?"

He laughed. "Suffer? You are a princess, sister. Daughter of the Desert. You should never suffer. It is an honor to celebrate your coming of age at the Festival of Kings. You may find a man worthy of your hand."

"My crown." She scowled at him. "Even if he pays the bride price, there's only one thing he could possibly want. And everyone knows succession flows through the queen. What's worth more than a seat at the High King's table?"

"Your love."

"And when should that come?" Imani asked fiercely, her fists clenched at her sides.

"Little sister," he said softly, taking her hand, "go to the festival. Attend them with perfect attention. Speak highly of them to our mother and father and watch. The games are not just to celebrate your coming of age. It is tradition. Resources, gold, iron, strengthening of alliances, and discussing important matters of each kingdom. They would never force your hand, but they expect you to act as a princess, a future ruler. You were born to bring unity to the realm and peace to the people, as was I. I know you would rather fight as one of the men than watch them, but do this and I promise to speak with Father regarding the matter."

"Truly?"

"Truly," he said solemnly, cupping her chin. "Your spirit cannot be tamed, and I fear your skills would put the men to shame. Would that I hadn't aided you in the lessons you asked for."

Jelani smiled as he remembered the first time he'd seen her hold a spear in her hand, wielding it as any child would. He'd laughed and asked their Uncle Shaharqa to train her in spear and whip, to teach her how to light a fire, to show her direction by following streams and reading the sun, and to ride camels and horses as fast as the wind. Their High King father had not been pleased. Especially to learn that one of his brothers had aided her.

"Yet you did, dear brother. And I love you for it," she said, throwing her arms around him again before releasing him. "And I would bring no one shame," she said reproachfully. "Why should not men have to fight against me before winning my hand? I would not respect the one who could not kill me with ease."

"Kill you he might try and lose his own head for it."

"And save me the trouble of marriage."

"Imani-qa, stop. You are too much trouble," he said smiling affectionately.

Sighing she looked down at her hands then back up from where she sat on her bed. "Nema's letters are no better. She keeps telling me no man will have the security enough to allow his wife to remain a warrior after marriage and the courage to let her rule independently in her own right rather than expecting her to breed. Our history is a history of ruling queens. Yet she still says I'm searching for a sphinx. She's wrong on both counts. I'm not *searching* at all and I refuse to. What am I supposed to do about that?"

He took her chin in his hand. "You'll just have to wait until you find one that can do both."

Nodding she looked out to his balcony.

"Here, I made this for you."

She looked down at his hands. A sparkling amber stone glittered against diamonds encrusted around a chain. She gasped as the torches lit them one by one. They matched the color of her eyes. Jelani raised it to her neck and secured it around her throat. "Take care, lion cub." She was too busy looking at the stones in shock to correct him for using the term. "To come of age in the land is a wonderful thing. Don't grow up so soon."

"You know I don't wear jewelry," she said softly, though her eyes were still studying the jewel.

"And these." He slipped a forked comb with edges as sharp as any dagger into her hair. "And these." Lifting her wrists, he clasped bright gold bracelets around each, running from the bottom of her wrist, to the middle of her forearm.

"What…" Her voice trailed off.

"This is not any jewelry. The bracelets are made from the finest metal. The metallurgists took special care that they were as light as any feather, but as strong as the Adamantine warriors. They are unbreakable."

Her smile was infectious.

"The comb in your hair is sharper than a lion's tooth. Take care," he said softly.

"And the necklace?" she asked, curiosity and wonder in her voice.

"Is to remind you of home. The sun. The earth. Nabara."

"I love you." Her eyes shone as she looked at him.

"And I you."

Holding Imani tightly, he kissed her forehead before taking his leave, looking back as she closed the door smiling, an impish look on her face.

"Stay, Isis," he commanded the cheetah cub, who growled at him in reply and sat just inside the door.

Eyes sparkling, Imani puckered her lips and crinkled her nose at him. He shook his head as it closed, walking slowly back to his room. When he reached it he went immediately to his bed, arms crossing beneath his head.

I should tell father. Perhaps he'll listen this time. He'd done away with pawnship under his reign save a few of the outlying nomadic nations where tradition was strongest, ensuring slavery was held at bay and protecting Nudolla. But some were not to be trusted and Jelani knew it. And this man was among the worst of them. The man would carry the debt for as long as possible, using her brother as the excuse for what he claimed was his generosity. And her *wages.* They weren't sufficient to feed a dog, let alone her family. He'd speak with his father soon. He had to. It made his heart ache thinking of what she had to endure. He turned on his stomach and returned to his back as he tried to fall asleep, but the thought of her safety worried him, and rest didn't come easy.

The next morning he dressed quickly. Taking one last bite before licking the juice sliding down the side, he threw the nara fruit away, heading toward the first-floor weapons room at the back of the palace. *It's unusually quiet this morning,* he thought. Passing the great hall and waiting chambers, he watched a handmaid walk past with a stack of colored linen on her head and a quartz gourd in her hand. The realization struck him that it was almost midday. *I've overslept.*

"Prince Jelani."

When she dipped her knees gently he nodded in return, watching her continue on before walking past the engraved walls of the outer entrance to the weapons room depicting battles from years past. Nodding to the guards outside the entrance, they opened the doors and stepped aside as he entered. Turning his head upwards to look at the light thrown across the weapons chamber from the single side opening admitting light into the room, he surveyed it slowly. The walls were stacked with iron-bladed scimitars and golden daggers. A sapphire-inlaid battle-axe sat on the east side of the room just above a gold-headed mace fitted with a leather handle. Thousands of bows and arrows sat gently on top of protruding nails, while others hung from tiny holes in the ends just above their quills. Their iron tipped heads shone in the light.

Moving towards the western wall he touched a spear the height of an elephant but no thicker than a garden snake, spiral engravings decorating it from top to bottom. Ruby colored acacia bars were stacked to the right and he lifted two now, reading the Meroitic inscriptions drawn along the middle before swinging them upwards. Wrists spinning rhythmically he swung them in circles, huge gusts of air sweeping past his face and ears. Smiling in satisfaction, he set them back, noting the perfection of the balance as he held them in his palms.

Armor sat in three of the four corners of the room in dyed golden jars reaching his hip. A small blast furnace sat in the other. His father often used it to mold and sharpen any weapon he was using at the time. *Father knows everything.* And it helped to have some of the most advanced metallurgists from Meroë at hand. From weapons to art, chisels, saws, and tools for skin grafting and surgery they created it all. Glancing inside one of the jars of armor, he walked towards the northern wall of the room and lightly put his palm inside an opening. Sliding left, the stone opened rapidly and he put one arm up to shield his eyes as the sunlight spilled through. Squinting he stepped forward onto the balcony, cheers reaching his ears as he leaned over the side.

She's training. Smiling, he stepped back, closing the stone door with the same movement that opened it before walking quickly towards the outdoor training grounds.

His twin uncles stood watch with Medjay along with one of the caracals that ran wild outside the palace. Too young yet for the guards to bother killing before it began to hunt the livestock. Only his sister had bothered to name him. *Little Terror because he's harmless,* he could hear her saying. She teased the guards with him sometimes, holding him in her arms and making growling sounds, her laughter infectious as they did their best to keep a straight face. *It will eat the cattle*, they told her. *But not yet*, she always replied. And they watched her now. It was better to train here, rather than in the weapons hall inside the palace. Filled with everything from spears, arrows, and *khopesh* to ropes and whips, it provided an arsenal for training. Outside, one had to learn to do with only one weapon.

Beads of sweat pooled at Imani's back, a thick leather breastplate protecting her chest and shoulders while the shin and ankle guards protected her legs. Sunlight glinted off her bare stomach as her ivory harem pants blew in the slight wind. His sister's eyes shone with determination on either side of the metal that covered the bridge of her nose.

Crouching low, she wielded her spear in front of her, moving forward, preparing to strike.

"Ah!" she yelled, thrusting her spear at the man's temple.

"Hay!" she delivered her thrust with another yell, grunting with the effort. Her opponent moved so swiftly out of her way it unbalanced her, and she stumbled in her attempt to right herself.

"Oomph!" Her opponent's spear slammed into her back, and the sound it made upon impact made Jelani cringe. His sister's chin slammed into the sand so hard he knew her teeth must have rattled. He winced as he watched her wipe blood from her lip, likely having bitten the inside of it.

She leapt off the ground with such speed Jelani's eyes widened as she vaulted over her opponent; spinning deftly, she rammed her spear into his shoulder, knocking him sideways. She landed low, using her *khopesh* in her right hand to cut his spear in half. She smiled softly, watching the bottom half of her opponent's spear spin away and fall to the ground.

She turned back, the smile still on her face when his steel-tipped boot slammed into her chest. She gasped in surprise even as she fell, reaching for her dagger.

He landed on top of her, one knee on her breastplate, crushing the air from her lungs. Imani's eyes took in the *duat* he held to her throat. Jelani winced as he watched her. *That will cause a bruise.*

"Never take your eyes from your enemy, Imanishakheto. Never underestimate them. When you think you've won, they will show you their true colors and their strength. You must be ready."

The High King stood, removing his knee from Imani's chest and offering her his hand to pull her up from the ground.

"You're fast, but you talk too much," their father said.

"I—" she started.

"Grunt and yell with every move. You must be silent as the grave, or your enemies will always see you coming. Shaharqa, Asim," he said, turning to a tall, broad shouldered master of arms. "You've done well. My daughter grows confident and skillful in weaponry."

Father smiled gently, cupping Imani's chin in one hand and turning her head from side to side. "You have the blood of a great warrior. To lead, you must also learn to follow."

Imani grinned and Jelani knew she was pleased from the look on her face. Their father's praise was few and far between. Behind him, his uncles smiled.

"Little one, we knew you were our blood. We had our doubts," Uncle Semi jested as his Uncle Yemi began laughing.

Jelani jabbed him in the ribs with his elbow. "What he meant was, you're a better fighter than he was at your age." He smiled at her.

Asim moved forward to take her armor off. "She smiles even as she bleeds," Asim noted incredulously, rolling his eyes. The captain pulled Imani's helmet off, using his sleeve to wipe the blood running down her lips and chin. "There now, lion cub." Asim shook his head. Asim had trained each of them in the use of the spear, bow and arrow, shortsword and *khopesh* since they were five years of age. When he and his uncles had gone on their journey to train without Imani he'd heard she had wept for two days, claiming her father did not love her, begging to be taken too and wondering aloud why she must be treated differently when she was the High King's offspring too. Jelani had returned and learned of her despair, swiftly taking her to his side upon their return, asking her, *Was she not a lion? Did lions cry?*

He'd dried her tears and promised to train her in their ways and she'd cried no more. Any guilt Asim and their uncle felt at her having been a girl left when Asim saw her fight. Asim had gone to their father on her behalf.

Their father had walked down the steps of his throne and put his fingers under her chin until she met his eyes. Jelani still remembered her dark eyes darting to his for reassurance. *I would never leave you,* his eyes promised as she turned back to their father.

"A man should never hide behind another for fear of punishment," their father told her. *"You are no man, but you've never feared my wrath before. You shall continue your training under Asim and Shaharqa. He tells me you have much promise and believes your agility will be of great use. As do I."*

Imani had leapt up in shock, throwing her arms around their father's neck and kissing his cheek, holding him tightly in thanks as he patted her head gently and sighed.

"Go now, come back when you've learned to kill ten men with your little finger." At the time, Imani had asked him how she would accomplish such a task. Until Jelani had shown her the bow. He still remembered how violently her eight-year-old hands shook the first time she held it.

Jelani still remembered the lessons their father taught them years ago. A vision of his father standing at a distance, pride in his very shoulders as he moved towards his children with an easy grace, the tall grass seemed to bow at his approach. Jelani's chest rose and fell rapidly as he caught his breath. He looked down at the bull that lay dying at his feet, triumphant. At seven, it was his first kill. The High King reached him at last and he parted the last stalks, peering down at the creature whose throat was pierced with a long spear. "Remember, Jelani. The spear is only a tool. This," he tapped Jelani's forehead, "and these," he lifted his hands, "make you strong. The hands of your body caress the face of a lover, changing their mood. Mold and build great houses to shelter a family, even a tomb for a dying king. They wipe the tears from the face of a child, lifting his spirit, or hold the hand of an elder giving her peace as she takes her last breath. They can tie knots to hold a captive or give a command to set one free. They impart trust and give honor and respect to an agreement, or strike a blow to one who deserves it. Treat them with care. There is power in even the smallest of hands. Your mind will tell you how to use them."

Now their uncles helped her remove her breastplate, teasing her at the muscles she'd gained, her arms lithe and strong as his father turned back towards the palace, his escort following him inside.

"Why can't I compete at the Festival?"

Jelani sighed. "Imani-qa, you have much to learn and Father

would go to an early grave should you appear," he said.

"But he needn't know." Imani bit her lip, her eyes imploring her uncles' help.

"No," their uncles said together. "It's tradition, Imani. Members of the royal family do not compete. You will enjoy it I promise little one," his Uncle Yemi finished.

"I'm not little anymore."

"No," Semi replied. "Soon you will meet the great families of the lower Kings and other nomadic families. All of the mountain, forest, and desert families will be in attendance to witness your coming of age. It's an important time for all of us."

Yemi and Semi were leaders of the Royal Guard in their own right, leading great hosts of the kingdom's armies and protecting the people. Jelani would become vizier and advisor to the High King though his heart pulled him in another direction. Even his sister Nema had her own choice. She *wanted* to be married to the Prince of the Sotho Kingdom, a mountain region where snow fell regularly and the plateaus were numerous. She had teased him mercilessly about his own future wedding since, her letters peppered with hints and questions of whom he loved and which princess he believed to be the most beautiful. She asked the same questions of Imani. Imani never answered. *"Who cares if they are handsome?"* she had asked him one day. *"Looks will only get one so far."* He had laughed at her and hugged her tightly. The only thing his mother seemed to care about was preserving her face and the number of scars she turned up with. Her handmaids always managed to fade the scars from her legs within days. Her smooth brown skin was proof of that. But he knew she loved every scar.

Jelani put a hand on her shoulder and she looked up at him, having been pulled from her thoughts. He laughed as the slight pout returned to her mouth. "You always grow quiet when you're angry, little one," he said softly. "Don't think of your part at the Festival of Kings as a sentence. You are no prisoner. Think of it as a learning exercise— not to strengthen your muscles, but your mind. You grow brighter each day and soon you will be expected to lead elsewhere. Learn as much as you can about the families that we will meet tomorrow, their history, their guards, the renowned fighters, and their skill. I trust it will be as interesting to you as reading from your scrolls on war and justice or *The Book of the Divine Cow*. True knowledge comes from experience."

Imani exhaled sharply, looking up into his amber eyes, which matched hers. He always knew what she was thinking. He knew she'd listen.

"I will," she replied. He hugged her.

"Are you hungry?" He smiled as she started at his question.

"Always." The smile on her face warmed him.

"I'll see you in the gardens." She nodded and left, walking back towards the palace to change.

Jelani took the long way, his feet taking him past the courtyard where Asim was now speaking with the Royal Guard. He had a feeling he knew what it was about. His father had asked him to sit at the coming council so that he would be apprised of their army's movements and future plans. Asim and the guards stopped as he passed, placing a fist to their chests and nodding in respect. He returned with a nod in kind.

The slave traders were coming further south. *And growing bolder*, he thought, his jaw tightening. If anything had happened to his sister it would have killed him. They were only four years apart, and he had been close to her since she came into the world. He remembered holding her on the day she was born, her tiny dark brown fingers wiggling as he did. She had the darkest of eyes, like pools of ink, and he'd smiled when he realized he could see his reflection in them. When he looked closer he noticed her irises. They weren't black at all. Her large pupils were surrounded by dark gold, branching out from her pupils like fire. He'd been shocked when he saw it. The color had only deepened, as she grew older. Born with a head full of tight, black curls that had covered her head like a crown, soft and thick. Her lips were shaped like the bow his father used during training with his commanders, only smaller, and pink like the sunset on the water. She'd been so small, and she looked so helpless. He'd told his mother and father as much as he pulled at the tight layer of curls on her head. But then she'd grabbed his finger, and the harder she squeezed the more surprised he became until he finally screamed because she was bending it backwards. And when he'd screamed she'd smiled and let go and he and his father and mother had laughed and laughed.

She's always been stronger than she looks.

When he reached the gardens, he sat down on one of the stone seats underneath the pavilion. Surrounded by flowers taller than his own head and huge fruit trees, it provided shade and had the most calming effect on whomever chose to sit. Hundreds of king flowers surrounded them, their sweet smell permeating the air. Pink and white and deep red the youngest buds sat, cone-shaped on young tree limbs, still closed in their infancy with their petals pointing towards the sky. The others were open, large white sun beds surrounded by tiny, pink triangular petals, like dozens of fingers circling an open palm. Some of them were larger than his own hand. A sugarbird landed on one and it easily supported the bird's weight as it balanced carefully, sticking its bill into the white and yellow fluorescent center to eat the sugary nectar inside. His sister loved the king flowers and the lotus that filled the garden.

Reaching for one, he smiled as a honeyguide flew just in front of his face, flapping its wings gently before landing on a nearby branch. Its light brown and grey feathers were accented by bright yellow plumage on its chest; its striped white tail hung calmly down as it walked the length of the branch before remaining still, watching him. They loved honey more than bees and would lead people to hives to make sure they got it. It was bad luck not to follow them if they fluttered and chattered around you in circles. It was their way of telling you their greatest secret. That a honey hive was nearby. If a person did not follow, it was rumored he would never find another honey hive again. Though the relationship was of mutual benefit, like ma'at, everything followed a natural order. Their sweet side matched the sour. Honeyguides were known to lay its eggs in other bird's nests, allowing the baby honeyguide to hatch and kill the other babies inside with its hooked beak.

"*Where* are my grandchildren?" a voice called.

"Here," his sister was walking quickly towards him, but he turned now to take in his grandmother. *The Kingmaker.*

Ever since he was a child she'd been called by that name. From his uncles, to the guards, to his father, the High King. When he was young they'd said it was a term of endearment amid laughter and knowing smiles. As he grew older he learned the truth. *From her, kingdoms rise and fall,* his mother told him. Succession flowed through the queen and to her firstborn before the remainder of the heirs. The political influence his grandmother wielded gave end to wars, birthed his father, the High King, and cemented his power in order to move forward with the eradication of trading in slaves. He prayed it would not be short-lived.

"Aren't you lovely," his grandmother wrapped her arms around him and Imani. "But then, you take after me."

His sister laughed, and he grinned at them both, shaking his head. His grandmother and mother were sometimes at odds, but their greatest argument lay with his sisters and whom they took after. *Women.* They should know better by now; his sister could easily live happily without donning another gown.

His sister turned in her gown before sitting, the top layers fell across her body from her right shoulder to the left of her waist, her left shoulder and waist bare. The skirt trailed slightly, simple and white, the golden bracelets on her upper arms and wrists were her only accent.

"Mother thought you might like it." Imani held back a smile.

"Oh, did she?" his grandmother responded. Jelani didn't fail to miss the tiny uptick in his grandmother's eyebrow before she raised a hand and motioned for the handmaids to come forward.

"Your father tells me you two are having a hard time...listening." She took a mango half from the platter and began to eat. Imani reached for the roasted bananas, sprinkling cinnamon on top of them before she ate.

"Communication isn't his strongest trait, either." Imani crossed one arm about her waist and leaned back as she looked at her grandmother.

She looked at them both carefully, squinting her eyes at Jelani before she began, "My great grandfather was a *jeli.* Did you know that?"

"No. But everyone has heard of them. The word *jeli* comes from the Mandé people. It means blood. Their stories are legendary," Jelani finished, popping a grape into his mouth.

She laughed. "Stories? No, child," she replied. She always had a way about her that made everyone in the room feel like a child around her. Her knowledge was endless. He was positive she would still call him child when he grew old and gray. "A *jeli* tells *your* story." She pointed two fingers at the both of them before wiping her mouth with the napkin at her plate even though there seemed to be nothing there.

"A *jeli* is the memory of your people. His song is truth. Births, celebrations, marriages, inheritance, bride price, suicide, deaths. It's all in his mind. In his song. It is his purpose. To record each life, each story, and *to remember.* Just like the Temple of Mysteries in Nabara as in Kemet and even when Kush ruled over Kemet before the Assyrians and Romans, none of the history he keeps is written. Like the neophytes of the School of Mysteries the history is kept hidden, secret, safe. It passes down from generation to generation. A *jeli* can take you on a thousand-year journey in one hour though your feet will never move. He paints a picture without a brush. A *jeli* can communicate well. Like your father, a *jeli* must tell the listener the truth, and he does so in return for very little. Your father, like the *jeli*, may not tell you what you want to hear, but he tells no lies. And only a fool would ignore what he had to say." She looked back and forth between them both.

The School of Mysteries. His grandmother may as well have told them she'd seen a live sphinx. No one was allowed in the temple save those who earned the right through a series of tests and trials, answering riddles and proving that they were learned enough to study under the masters there. Kemet held the first school, and Nabara had followed the tradition, creating a royal library not far from the Temple of Mysteries, which housed the school. It was said that the Temple itself was built of a labyrinth of over two thousand rooms holding ceramic artwork and made with brick, sand, and limestone.

"I don't mean to be rude or unkind," his grandmother interrupted his thoughts, looking between them, "but...are you fools?" she asked them.

They didn't respond, but they didn't have to. Imani worried at the bottom of her lip with her teeth.

"Then remember the *jeli*, and you will live forever."

KETEMIN

"We must bring your brother to heel. It is time Komoro married. He will be King soon and we must be prepared. A lovely, virgin bride I should think. From an excellent family."

"Why?" Ketemin asked him, her eyebrows raised as she turned her attention from her book to look at her uncle. "He's a whore."

"And whores are married every day."

"The *men* you mean."

"Yes, the men. Your brother is of the male line."

"What favor smiles upon him that he is so blessed? For a whore, if you are to be one, must surely benefit more if of the male line. A female thus titled would be shamed, thrown out of her home, and stoned in the courtyard."

"As she should be."

"I said thus *titled.* I suppose perception is reality? And even the whisper of a liar can condemn a virtuous woman without cause?"

"If she was truly virtuous, none would have cause to *whisper* about her in the first place," her uncle shot back, his impatience growing.

"Because women are never jealous of other women, and men always take rejection well."

Her uncle looked at her, exasperation playing over his face as she closed the book she'd been reading and sat up slowly. "Forgive me, Uncle. My love for my dead father does not automatically extend to my brother. No matter how closely he resembles him."

"It should," King Kwasi told her. "In time he will become more worthy as he learns, more knowledgeable about ruling."

"Are you ill, Uncle? The only thing Komoro has ever been eager to learn was of any addition to the harem."

"With you by his side he would learn faster. He's young."

"As am I."

"Kemi-qo. He's a good brother," he added after a pause. The certainty in his voice made her want to laugh.

"How would you know?" Doubt was stark on Ketemin's face as she tipped her head slightly to watch the uncertainty play over her uncle's face. She smiled inwardly. She hadn't expected an answer. You can't force love or affection. Even between those of the same bloodline.

Walking over to him, she placed her hands on his shoulders and kissed his cheek before turning and leaving the balcony in her chambers where he'd found her. Eyra pranced on the ledge of the stone steps, her black tail whipping back and forth. Shaking her head she scooped the little daredevil from her perch, massaging her ears as Eyra purred in her arms, enjoying the attention. Well known around the palace as Ketemin's pet, Eyra followed her everywhere. It was why Ketemin had decided to name her of all the other cats that ran wild in the Sao Empire. She *was* the Eye of Ra. Sneaking into bathhouses and council meetings, teasing the hunting dogs. Most called her 'Shadow.'

The beaded collar around Ketemin's throat glinted in the sun, red stones embedded in it sparkling as she walked. She pursed her lips in frustration as she remembered the conversation with her uncle, her high cheekbones home to smooth, dark sable skin the color of the coats of the sable antelope that ran wild near the palace. She needed no kohl around her eyes, her dead mother having endowed her with the darkest of eyes cloaked with smooth black shading. The dress she wore fell to the ground, dragging behind her as she went. Her long sleeves billowed out behind her as she passed through the doors of the hall, nodding to two handmaids as she did. The young girls rose quickly from where they sat on their heels, hands on their knees, lifting a large palm leaf from a vase to her right. Moving behind Ketemin, they held it high above her head, matching her pace as they left the palace. Hasea was small but strong, and both she and Essivi were bright. She could see the intelligence hidden in their eyes. She was teaching Essivi how to read and hoped she might raise her to become a scribe when she grew older. It would be a waste not to. This world needed more educated women—if only to keep the men from eliminating themselves from the face of it.

Within minutes she was standing in the guard's tower housed at the front of the palace and looking down on the people of the Sao

Kingdom below. Leaving both girls outside she set Eyra at their feet. Pressing the door open she found the commander seated at a large smooth table made of limestone, his head bent over a map, one hand in the upper-right corner, the other stroking his chin. The shadow of a beard covered the commander's strong jawline.

"Princess Ketemin." He stood at attention when he heard her footsteps, eyebrows rising quickly in surprise at the unexpected visit.

"Commander Tesir, please, be seated."

The Commander sat as she took the seat across from him, the table between them. The papyrus rustled softly as he slid it sideways and set it aside. A large sundial sat in the window, an hourglass on a low desk to his left. The sun cast a shadow on the blade sitting in the center of the sundial, slanting across the numbers around the circular perimeter of the clock. The hourglass slowly spilled sand; the amount indicating at least half an hour had passed since he turned it last. He kept time like most people kept track of gold. It was the reason he was never late. *How long has he been studying the same map?* She would ask him later. Smoothing the folds of her ginger-colored robe she began.

"I have need of your services."

Uncertainty settled in the slight crease between his eyes before he touched a hand to his *khopesh* quickly. "Anything you require."

"I need you to follow my brother."

"Princess...I," the Commander faltered.

"I know. I realize the implication and the concern for your reputation, but quite frankly, this is far more important. I want to know where he goes and with whom he visits."

The commander's eyes widened and she raised a hand to calm the panic growing behind his eyes.

"Spare me the details of his visits to the harems, Tesir. Bring me information of everything else."

"As you require, Princess."

She nodded to him and rose, taking leave of the commander without further orders for him. Ketemin knew what he would think of the implication and she would not sully his character by asking him to be discrete. He always was.

It was only mid-afternoon, but she walked quickly from the

tower with Hasea and Essivi following close behind, their small sandaled feet making not a sound as they did. Walking towards the gates and stopping just outside, the guards turned toward her, waiting her command. She turned toward Hasea first, the young girl's large dark eyes warm and eager to please as the palm leaf waved gently in the soft breeze as Ketemin leaned towards her.

"Thank you, Hasea," she told the girl. "Thank you, Essivi. Now, run back inside and find your parents. They will likely have need of you." She watched the light falter in Essivi's eyes as her mouth became a pout, covering it with her free hand as she was want to do. The girl loved spending time with her.

She leaned down further and whispered, "Or, you may run to the temple and find the High Priest's scribe. Make sure you tell him I sent you and thank him for his kindness."

Hassea nodded quickly and Essivi kissed her cheek, her tiny frame bouncing slightly as she jumped from foot to foot with excitement, the smile that stole over her face brighter than the sun.

"Go!" Ketemin laughed, waving them away as they turned on their heels, speeding towards the temple outside of the palace walls. The temple was home to thousands of scrolls that Essivi had only begun to read at Father Komil's urging. The girl had sped through his teaching of Nubian history and the Sao's place in it, slowly deciphering each letter before he moved on to the Old Tongue and taught the hieroglyphs of Kemet and Meroitic script. The temple's sacred walls were home to orphans, many of whom scrubbed the floors and drew water from the wells each day. She hoped to teach Hasea one day too. Sand flew around their feet as they sped away and through the gates, drawing Ketemin's attention to the giant terracotta statue of a Sao warrior standing in the middle of the city. His bold lips protruded from his face as he stood proudly at attention. Next to him a giant hourglass equal in size stood, its two glass chambers filled with salt that spilled from top to bottom. Markings on the glass kept track of the time.

When Hasea became a distant speck on the horizon, melting into the sea of merchants and villagers, Ketemin turned to the guards on either side of her and nodded to two nearest her, two long iron-tipped spears in each of their hands. They followed her as she walked back towards the stables, helping her to horse as she pulled her long dress and tied it in a knot so that her dress became harem pants in an instant. *And better for riding,* she thought smiling as she took off with her guards flanking her on either side. Reaching the center of the city they moved to her front and she pulled her veil over her mouth and nose as they crossed the lands, the sand and rock creating a fine mist that stung her eyes as a child when she'd been fool enough not to cover them. It would blind others on the worst of days.

Soon, the horses slowed even further, their hooves moving carefully among the rocky terrain. The acacia trees told her they were close. Their round, yellow flowers reminded her of the fumaroles of long barren fire vents for the northern volcano that her uncle's land sat upon. Even the Toubou people, a mountain nation of herders and miners, avoided the volcanoes to some extent. Their yellow color seemed like so many tall flowers from afar, but Ketemin knew better. The smell of the fumaroles alone was warning enough, a sharp, cloying smell like rotten eggs, the sulphur permeated one's nose, sitting upon the senses like a blanket even after you remembered to close your mouth. As thick as tree trunks or as narrow as reeds they peppered the landscape around them. And they were dangerous. Her brother had chased a gazelle from an oasis towards the center of the sulphur springs once, narrowly avoiding the fumaroles as he did. Foam appeared on his horse and the gazelle both as they tired in the heat. The poor beast had become desperate, and one false step found him sinking into the sulphur pits, his braying cutting through the quiet of the hot desert as Ketemin had covered her ears in horror. She'd cried out as she watched Komoro urge his horse back, but it knocked away a fumarole, crumbling at the touch of its hoof and melting away, his hind quarters sinking so fast Ketemin could only look on in shock as her uncle bellowed commands behind her. They saved Komoro, but not his horse. The animal was dead long before it's braying screams faded, long before its neck melted and turned yellow, long before the last of its ears flickered and disappeared beneath the spring. She had watched as her brother turned from the sight and walked over to one of the guard's who'd helped save him, his hand outstretched. "I'll need a new horse," her brother told him, his voice expectant. Her uncle had bellowed at him from afar and sent all but one royal escort back to the palace, assuring them he would follow. "If you want a new horse, then you will find your own way back to the palace and remember the value of things before you destroy them."

Her uncle had turned quickly, grabbing his reigns and moving with the royal escort back through the hot springs, calling for Ketemin when he reached the other side. She had moved her horse slowly away from her brother, but looked back once when she heard him crying softly. Without a word she'd drawn her horse up next to him and allowed him to climb on behind her, slowly making their way back towards the center of the city. He'd alighted just before they'd reached they gates and she went forward alone. She'd never left her brother. Komoro would always come to her later, bringing her salt candy or some terracotta figurine for her collection in thanks or in apology for something he had done. She'd always been there for him. No matter how foolish his errors had been. She couldn't share in his ways. Having dedicated herself as a Daughter of Ra, she had taken a vow of chastity and virtue.

"Princess, take care." Her escort pointed just in front of her and she thanked him, moving sideways to avoid a small hole. Sometimes the small ones were the strongest, but they had not spewn fire in decades her uncle assured her. They were almost to the lake. A source whose shores held salt and natron deposits their people had mined for years.

Komoro should be here, she thought. *But it is my home too,* she reminded herself as she reached the top of rock hills near the lake, with its pure white gold that had made her father's Kingdom a fortune, made greater by her uncle's rule and that which would likely spoil in her brother's hand. The workers were spread out meters apart, their dark red and black skin glistening in the heat as they chipped away at the crust of the salt lake, pulling away a large quantity of the salt carefully before sharpening and shaping them down to perfect rectangular blocks half a meter long and two inches thick. They were paid well as the salt was valuable, a resource hard to find and difficult to mine. She watched them work a minute longer before sliding from her horse, the three moving towards the well on the far side of the workers' area. Four young children rose at their approach, their chests puffed out in imitation of the soldiers they saw on occasion. Their eyes roved over her escorts and bounced to Ketemin, too in shock to bow.

She slipped her fingers into her pocket, pulling out four gold coins. "Is that your water?" she asked them, her eyes sparkling mischievously.

"N-no-no," the tallest answered, confused. "Your Grace."

"Are you guarding it?" she asked, still smiling.

He swallowed before taking a step away from the well as his companions followed.

"No."

"We were resting!" the smallest shouted, undaunted.

She laughed. "Were you?" She heard footsteps and she turned to her right to see a middle-aged man moving quickly towards them, his hands outstretched, shooing the children even as he dropped to his knees before her.

"Forgive them, Princess. They were bringing water for the others." He kept his head bowed in supplication.

"Rise. What is your name?"

"They call me Deemat, Your Grace."

"And which one is yours?" she asked him, turning back to the children, who were too rooted to move.

"The tallest and the smallest, Your Grace." He bowed his head slightly as if embarrassed, and she knew he was wondering if they'd done something wrong.

"Perfect. Your children are beautiful. I was just about to ask them if they would help water the horses while I bring water to the workers." She smiled at them and the children stood there looking at their father, the remaining two looking at his children, and the father, open mouthed and at a lost for words. "Would you help me?" Ketemin smiled reassuringly.

"Yes!" the youngest squealed delighted. "I'm Deema. Your Graaaace," she said, drawing out her address to sound like her father. Despite the short crop of curls she was in fact a girl, Ketemin saw, with the most beautiful light brown eyes above a small, pink, wide-set mouth, her saffron skin shining in the sun, a white headdress wrapped loosely around her head. "This is Duumel, my brother." She set about acquainting Ketemin with everyone before asking the names of her escorts to which Ketemin obliged, rare smiles coming to the soldier's faces as they watched her. Ketemin offered the four a gold coin before untying the knot of her dress to let it trail behind her and looping her arm into Deemat's as he walked her about the salt preserves, explaining the daily workings of the mine.

When she asked him where the guards and the Master of Salt were, he bowed his head slightly and told her they were indisposed in a manner so polite and unaffected by blame as to drive her mad. *I know what this is about.*

"How long have they been indisposed?" she questioned the miner quietly.

"No longer than…" his voice trailed off as he looked into her eyes and he continued, "two moons, Princess."

"Two moons," she echoed, "How…"

The words would not come to her. Her brother had control of the salt mining and was tasked by her uncle with overseeing the packing, weighing, counting, and selling of each block. Salt was too important to be this careless. They used it to clean both body and teeth. It removed oil and grease. As an anti-septic it was invaluable to physicians in cleaning wounds sustained by soldiers. Families needed it to preserve meat and fish. *And Uncle entrusted my brother with the task.* Komoro had begged for the position and received it despite her uncle's misgivings that Komoro was far too lazy to trust with its oversight.

"Show me your trade, if you would be so kind, Deemat."

"Of course, Princess. Of course." He led her to the top of a rock hill and pointed down towards the salt lakes and workers below. "It's better that you see it from here. Do you see?"

Ketemin stood in awe as she gazed down below. The saltpans were below her and the lake just ahead as she faced south. Men were slowly bending towards the water as they filled their baskets with rock salt, towards the ground, a long line just an arms width apart created a team of workers that carried each piece from the lakes to the dry beds where another team chopped and picked and shaped the pieces carefully for sorting and counting. As she watched, a young boy of no more than four tottered over to one block and squatted beside it, fully licking the side, his hands holding onto each side to make sure there was no escape. He licked his lips as he stepped back before making a face and shaking his head, running back towards his mother she presumed, who scooped him up and onto her shoulders.

"We don't...generally...taste the salt, Your Grace." Deemat cringed.

"He's young." Putting a hand on his arm she smiled warmly at him.

"Yes." He nodded back, pleased. "After the salt is shaped, sorted and counted, we bind them, three strong, and place them on the camels to carry to market. The rest-"

"The palace keeps and distributes as it will. Yes."

She realized a large number of workers no higher than her waist seemed to be working. *In this heat*, she realized alarmed.

"Tell me, why are they so many children mining for salt?" Squinting slightly she saw a guard further down the lake taking water from one of the women. *He must not have noticed my arrival.* Only *one?*

"Your Grace, we..." he stopped, glancing first at her escort.

"Tell me," she said sharply her eyes piercing his own.

"It — our wages. They have been cut in half."

"*Half?*" she whispered incredulous.

"They said if we wanted more, then they needed more bodies. More salt."

He cannot be certain...can he? Deemat did not strike her as a liar. The treasury though. They had brought in more gold from the salt trade in the last month than any time before. How was it that the soldiers asked for more labor? Ketemin looked down towards the soldier as he gave the water gourd back to the woman. He grasped her wrist when she tried to move away from him and pulled her down beside him, the water spilling to the ground. Anger burned in her chest, and she turned to her escorts.

"With me," she commanded.

Moving quickly down the rock hill into the basin with the men on her heels she descended quickly. The workers saw her coming and moved aside as she strode through their numbers, most of their gazes lowered, but some too curious not to stare as she passed. The soldier's hand was inside the woman's robe now, grasping at her breast as she tried to push him away. Ketemin was on him before he realized what was happening, using one foot to push into his stomach, forcing him partially onto his back as he opened his mouth to scream at her.

"You dare—!" Springing to his feet when he caught his breath he raised a hand to her. "Woman—!"

Her hand flashed out in the next second, the resounding backhand slap cracking across his skin and echoing off the rock walls of the basin, the force jerking his body back towards the ground.

Gasping he looked up, realizing his mistake as he took in the escorts flanking her back. She held her hand out to them to arrest their movement as they stepped forward to help her, spears raised and pointed at the guard.

"Your Highness...I—"

"Yes?" She stepped closer, forcing him backwards.

He threw himself to the ground at her feet. "I did not...I did not realize we had the honor of your presence. No one warned me of your coming."

"I can see that." The fury in her eyes burned even as she turned to the woman. "Have you a husband?" she asked her. The woman nodded, a nervousness and fear in her eyes as she pointed at her husband. He stood, shirtless, three meters from her and came to pull her back towards the rest of the workers as she cried into his neck, his arms about her waist. When she looked back down at her feet, the guard's head was tilted slightly, watching the woman walk away.

"You raised your hand to me. I shall have it struck off. Look at her again and I will scoop your eyes from your skull. I dislike the look in your eye. I detest your actions. Your actions show your character. Your character is not fit for your station." Even at her feet she could feel the anger burning from him; he could barely hide his disgust and resentment. "Gather your things."

"Shall we dispatch him, Princess?"

She watched him for a moment before turning to her escorts.

"No. I leave him for my uncle, but he will return with us. Tie his wrists to my horses. He can walk back." They nodded in understanding as they moved to him, dragging him to his feet.

"Deemat," she called. He stepped forward quickly, the people watching him. "You shall have command here. The children are not to work unless they bring water or have reached the age of maturity, with your consent. Replacements shall be here within the hour. Until that time, bring any grievances you may have to the palace and ask for me."

"Yes, Princess. You are a true Daughter of Ra, Your Grace." Bowing his head the other miners behind him followed suit. She swallowed slowly as she took in the relief on their faces before putting one hand on his shoulder and taking her leave.

After waving to the children who ran to keep up with her, she turned to watch the soldier struggling to keep up as he ran behind her escorts' horses, each wrist tied as he fought to avoid being dragged underneath their hooves.

"Whore of Ra! Bitch!" he began screaming at her when they were halfway back to the palace. One of her escorts lifted his spear, butting the man in the back once, sharply. Grunting with the impact he tried to catch his breath.

Stopping her horse momentarily she turned to face him.

"I have that effect on people." Swiveling back around on her stallion she squeezed her thighs for him to move. "I'll let you know when it bothers me."

His feet would be bleeding by the time they reached the gates. *My brother and his underlings have much to answer for.* She smiled behind her veil. *But this is a start.*

AMKAR

I trust your intelligence on the lands in the North is complete?"

Amkar turned to his brother, knowing Shaharqa was commander of his armies for a reason. Shaharqa never overlooked a detail. And he would not raise a village when an ambush or the capture of a chief would serve the same purpose.

"Very, Your Grace," Shaharqa responded. He paused a beat before continuing. "The Eastern shore is Kushite territory, and the Northeast is inhabited by much of the Kingdom of Aksum. Ezana trades with the Roman Empire. It is a...*very lucrative* trade." Shaharqa stopped short, not needing to say out loud what he already knew. *Slaves. They trade in slaves.* "While the Northern desert is an excellent barrier to invasion, the Berbers use the camel to their advantage. They divert them for salt caravans and use their trade routes to transport slaves to various markets on the coast. They cannot be trusted. The majority of them side with the Romans now. There is more profit in it. Some of the Tuareg may have useful sources of information, but we need to be careful with those we trust. As you know, the Sao Kingdom and Khoekhoe populate to the south. To the center just over the mountains and desert pass are more Nomadin and skilled hunters. Allies," Shaharqa finished.

"Yes, but will they listen to reason? The desert territories are vast, and many believe the Sahara will protect them from the threat of the slave trade. They concern themselves with drought above all else. I can not fault them for that." Amkar looked down at the map in front of him. He knew Shaharqa understood the question without it being asked. How far would their allies travel to aid Nudolla? If their information was true, piracy had given way to slave trading in Kushite and Aksum territory in the North, a result of bowing to the northern Roman empire's unending desire for ebony, ivory, and slaves. And their usurpation of well-known trade routes towards the Red Sea. The problem was that now, they were indiscriminate. Ruling families had given them information on kidnapping near Zanzibar and Pemba Island by Arab traders. The Luba and Gokomere had asked for assistance as well. Nudolla had answered their request for aid, helping them to beat back the slavers further north and deal crushingly with those involved in the slave-trading practice. *And somehow, they've found my kingdom and want to send my people to their fields for production and arenas for bloodsport.*

"It may be to our advantage to station a portion of our armies with the Sao, if they have no worthwhile objection to it. To aid them as well as to provide a force that can gain more information on slavers. And as a token of good faith."

"One hundred, Your Grace?"

"Send two hundred. There is no need to overwhelm our allies, or overstay the welcome, though I am in agreement with you. Send word to King Kwasi and the Kingdom of the Sao. They own some of the largest salt mines in the North. They should be more than able to provide assistance. They are an old family and well trusted. I doubt an extra force would not be welcome. But we must respond to the Roman and Berber slavers who think to cross the desert and make us all slaves. We must speak with the Khoekhoe and the !Kung people. The !Kung may aid us in locating the Servants of Cagn and other Sons of Prishiboro. All great hunters in the desert. The Nomadin disappear like smoke when water is scarce, but they are nomads, not ghosts. Unite them as allies and show them that we will not desert them. I will send the High Queen. Samya has the gift of tongue and more. Even the cattle herders must listen to reason. We have a common enemy now." Standing from his seat he turned towards the door.

"Adum, Shaharqa, with me." His vizier and brother rose at once, walking on either side of him as Medjay fell in line behind them at a short distance, walking with them towards the training grounds. *We must be ready.* He heard the sounds of his armies training before he saw them. Dull thuds told him they were deep into body-intensive close-combat training. Looking down from the wide staircase he noted a small pile of neatly stacked cowhide shields, their color retained from the animals they'd been taken from. Black and brown spots stretched into oblong splashes of color against their stone white background. Chosen for their durability, the weight of the shield allowed the wearer greater ease of movement. None of the power of a soldier's thrusting arm was weakened by the weight of metal. Most of the Romans he'd come into contact with as a young soldier had been well armed with heavy metal. Heavy metal swords, heavy metal breastplates, heavy metal helmets, heavy metal shields. Heavy metal that baked in the hot sun, burning their skin and making fallen shields too hot to touch to pick up from the ground. *Small mistakes lead to huge losses.* Nubians were born under the sun. They were well prepared for it.

The archers were situated on the border of the training camps. He could see a number of them headed into the fields. It was better to learn the bow by aiming at a moving target. Sometimes they used young trainees who had attained a height of no more than five feet. Holding up long wooden poles with wide leather targets at the top for archers to aim for the young soldiers were excellent practice. The boys were well protected, their faces, necks and chests covered to prevent injury as they zigzagged through the tall grass. At advance stages they trained using the animals of the savannah, staining their targets rather than injuring them as they practiced. They practiced until they no longer missed. It was the reason ancient Kemet had referred to Nubian and Kushite land as Ta-Seti, the Land of the Bow. And as their descendants, the people of Nabara had retained their excellence in it. A well-placed arrow should penetrate the eye of an enemy each time. And Amkar had never missed. When they reached the bottom he stood close to the new trainees over whom Shaharqa had charge, watching as he took over from his assistant commander.

"The thumb ring will aid in your accuracy, and reduce the injury to your thumb on the draw," Shaharqa told them, his deep voice sounding in the silence.

"Rhaka!" Shaharqa pointed at one soldier. "Draw!"

Rhaka did, the arrow meeting its mark fifty meters away. Shaharqa walked over to him, reaching for his drawing hand. He held it up so that the others could see the thumb ring on it. "Our bow strings are sharp for a reason. You will all use the thumb ring in battle when you draw and keep a backup with you at all times. The stronger your fingers, the further back you can pull the bow, the further your arrow will go." His brother turned then and nodded to him as he stepped forward, walking down along the ranks of archers.

"Ta-Seti, Land of the Bow." Amkar took his time as he walked down row upon row of his warriors in training, future scouts and defenders of his Empire. "We Kushites are well known for our skill in archery. From our ancestors of ancient Kemet to the imperial army of Persia, the Nubian archer is sought after for their mastery of the bow. It is not learned from practicing on a silent target, as your commander will soon show you. The only silent target on a battlefield is a dead one. You may shoot from your horse, or from the ground, but you can be assured that the sound of swords will be in your ears, the screams of those who wish to kill you will fill the air, the groans and pleas of the dying will become nothing more than a distraction you must ignore. Your target will run, and swiftly, your target will try to kill you, quickly. His brothers will try to protect him, he will dodge your arrows, and he will try to chase you. You must learn to aim not only for where he is standing, but based upon his movements, where you expect him to be. Notch, draw, anticipate, release."

"Notch, draw!" Shaharqa commanded. As one they executed his orders, standing at the ready.

Amkar looked each of them up and down as he surveyed their posture holding the bow, moving an arm here, pushing a shoulder down there. "The tighter your posture, the easier it will be to draw. It will decrease the pressure on your shoulders and prevent your arms from tiring."

A few rows over one arm shook heavily and he moved towards it, standing directly in front of the boy—older than Jelani but with the face of a child. Sweat poured from his temple as he pressed his chest against the boy's arrow.

"You may be the only thing standing between our enemies and this Kingdom. Be brave. Be ready. You have the heart of a lion." Amkar stared into the soldier's eyes until he stopped shaking before moving away.

"How soon can they be ready?"

"Within a week, Your Grace."

Amkar nodded. His brother would never disappoint. "We need to fortify the watchtowers, especially on the coast."

"Most of them are built into the mountains. Shall we build more?"

"Yes. I leave the details to you. Double the forces on patrol. Make sure the watchtowers drop cover at night. Moss is thick enough to do the trick. I don't want the fires seen from the water or anywhere else. Surprise is to our advantage. Make sure they stay well hidden."

"Your Grace."

"Brother. The Festival of Kings is crucial to our alliances. Double the protection around my family when they leave the palace. I want them safe. Go door to door. Make sure none of the people have seen anything suspicious. See if any have knowledge of the ship on the coast or the slave traders at the market who were killed. Someone knows something."

Shaharqa put a hand to his shoulder and Amkar mirrored the gesture, touching his forehead to his brother's.

"It is done."

Amkar moved away, walking back towards the palace with his escort.

Adum walked quickly down the steps ahead of him, having left them in the training yard to answer a messenger. His fists were held tightly at his sides as he rushed down them, his robe whipping behind him as he came. The nervousness on his most trusted advisor's face, even from such a distance, made Amkar purse his lips.

"Please," he held up one hand to his vizier to arrest his movement. Adum stopped at the top of the stairs to wait as Amkar met him at the top, his escorts close behind.

Turning, Adum fell in step with him towards the Great Hall.

"What news?"

"Your Grace. I realize this matter comes at an inopportune time, but if I may have only *your* ear."

Looking his vizier in the eyes briefly as they entered the Great Hall he turned to his guard detail.

"Wait here," he commanded the escort. They stood at attention as he and Adum entered a smaller room just inside the chamber, sized to admit no more than four.

"Speak."

"The High Priests have agreed to attend when you hold court in the morning. The full *Kenbet* will be at audience."

"Excellent. As they should."

"Your Grace." Adum was leaning on the table between them, wariness in his eyes overshadowing his youthful face. "There is a rumor that some of the nobles are watching you closely. That at least one of the eight High Priests questions our ability to meet this new threat."

"This threat is not new, Adum. Rome, the Assyrians, Noubadia. All of them have sought the gold, ivory, gemstones, and other resources abundant inside of Nubia and the interior. And we will continue to beat them back. If the High Priests took the time to step down from their lofty comforts of judgment they might understand that. "

"The only thing the High Priests understand is ma'at."

"Ahh ma'at. Justice and Order. And yet we co-exist together in our kingdom."

"Yes, ma'at through justice and order is an ancient tradition. Even the Christians allow the importance of it to Nabara. And yet the King's law exists above them all. You know it as well as I do. The High King exists to provide justice. The High King exists to provide order. And the High King must have an heir. If he fails in this he may be dethroned by the High Priests, challenged by another kingdom, or forced to suicide."

"Is that what concerns you, Adum?" he scoffed. " The King's law? It has been over a hundred—"

"Years I know," he interrupted. Surprise grew in Amkar's eyes. "Years since the priests have posted such an order to suicide, Your Grace." Adum's eyebrows pushed together in the middle of his forehead in earnest, his lips tightened in concern as though they refused to open lest their wearer know exactly the right words to say.

"You are as a brother to me, Your Grace. And one of my oldest friends. I would remind you of King Arkamani-qo, your namesake. An order to suicide is not to be taken lightly."

"I have not forgotten him, nor will I. It has not been ordered… I'm taking steps to ensure justice…and order. And as far as I am made aware, I have plenty of children to succeed to the throne. The High Priests are excellent in ruling on matters through the *Kenbet's* high court. I know each of them. I know their families. They are good men."

"Men are flawed. And rumors too often become reality."

Amkar chuckled quietly at hearing his own words quoted back to him. "What do you suggest?"

"Investigate this threat. Ask the Priests for their impression of our movements, and keep them appraised of our efforts."

The earnestness on Adum's face caused him to pause as he considered a moment. "No. We need to investigate the stench of slavery that edges into our lands. And the raids on our trade routes by sea and caravan. Begin there. Go. Apprise the High Priests of our efforts and ask them to send us an emissary of their own to keep us apprised of theirs, including any sentencing of those who are not of Nabara. They may attend audience at their leisure and hear the same requests I have for over thirty years. And find one of our most loyal, not the son of a noble if possible to speak with me immediately."

"My King?"

"We need information and we need him to get it quickly, and quietly. He is to evaluate each priest for weaknesses and give us his findings as he gains his intelligence. I don't mean to influence the priests, Adum. I want to find out if one of them has been compromised without our knowledge."

Adum was holding back a smile now. "A spy, Your Grace."

"No." He pondered a moment. "We don't need a spy. We need discretion. Someone innocuous…but natural to their environment. Someone who is supposed to be there."

"As you wish."

He finally smiled. "They are welcome to my head if they succeed, old friend. The priests have never forced a sitting king to suicide under the ancient orders of ma'at. And I care only for the safety of Nabara."

"The High Queen worries. The High Priests will not be denied the use of their traditions."

"My wife is strong. Our coming battles are more pressing."

"Your Grace, if I may…" Adum began. "We should cancel the Festival of Kings, delay it a week until we can ensure the safety of Nudolla and everyone who will come to Nabara. The city will be at risk. At least move the final day inside the walls of Nabara. We are less exposed that way as only members of Nabara may attend. Having it at the crossing between Nabara and Tharbis is too dangerous, especially in the desert. King Tharbis does not keep as watchful an eye on the desert trade as we do."

Amkar shook his head in disbelief. Adum's conviction was one of the reasons he remained his closest advisor and loyal friend. Some of the Nomadin had been at war for years, without bloodshed spilling into the kingdom. As High King he had brokered peace between them just shy of thirty years ago, yet the peace sometimes seemed as thin as a veil, the greed and warmongering threatening at a moment's notice. And still he had not been able to rid all of the Nomadin of pawnship. The council of elders among the Luba, though made of a variety of different cultures and chiefdoms, remained stronger than ever. And resolute in their customs. But others refused any alliance though trading and living within the protection of the empire. Slavery though…*it might eradicate them all if I am unable to convince them to leave their ways.* The festival would bring many a great alliance, trade, and fertility. It was another chance to see that the outlying Nomadin who attended for trade also saw the strength in the empire's seat of Nabara. The advantages of unity through Nudolla despite their differences.

"The Festival will continue," he finally replied. He could not afford to delay the opportunity and Imani must learn the significance of the Kingdom of Nabara within the Nudollan alliance. It was as the foundation of every pyramid. "We are doubling our patrols and setting aside as much grain as we can to aid the kingdoms at risk of drought. Drought brings a price worse than any harm a slaver may do. The desert continues to press upon us. Make sure the metallurgists and blacksmiths increase production of weapons as well as scythes for the harvest. The very reason for the Festival of Kings is to welcome those that normally do not sit inside of the alliance of the Nudollan Empire. I appreciate your counsel, but this tradition must hold, old friend."

"Your Grace, it may be a risk to divert our attentions—"

"The festival must continue while we root out potential trouble in Nabara itself. Asim will soon be sent on an errand for me. I know you will be on hand to see that there are no surprises." *I have faith in you.*

"Yes, Your Grace."

Adum nodded and rose, bowing low before exiting. Amkar returned to his chambers, taking note of each handmaid and errand boy as he did. Each soldier he acknowledged, nodding as they bowed. They were counting on him. They relied on him. *I must not fail.*

ADURA

The smoke burned her eyes. Tears ran unchecked down her face. Rivers of fire she struggled to wipe away. A haze of smoke and embers had filled the cave more times than she could count. Her brothers and sisters looked unconcerned.

Twenty of her family sat in a triangle, ranging in age from five to fifteen. Adura was the youngest. Her curly brown hair formed a cloud around her face. She rubbed her palms across her light brown eyes for the hundredth time, trying to hold back her tears. She dropped her eyes to the white drawings etched across her ebony skin.

"The bones of our fathers speak to us from the grave. From dust we were molded, and dust will we become again. Kneel."

One by one her sisters and brothers knelt as the chanting grew louder. The drums beat upon her ears as thunder before a storm. One by one they were cut, each cheek was allowed to bleed freely into the fire. When Adura knelt she felt the White Witch's eyes upon her. Zaxasha they called her. Her hair fell long and white over one shoulder, her light brown eyes almost seemed red now. Her black skin reminded Adura of the great panther that roamed their land. *Why do they respect her when she's so young?* They didn't treat anyone else that way. Only Zaxasha.

All at once Zaxasha's eyes fell on her, and the weight of her gaze made Adura shiver.

"Do you frighten so easily, child?" Her voice was a whisper. Adura frowned. *She's no older than me,* she thought defiantly, raising her chin higher.

"No," she said instead.

"Liar!" Zaxasha hissed back. "I know what the children call me. Why do you frown, little mouse?"

Adura was scared, but her pride made her step forward, "I'm as old as you," she replied.

Zaxasha's sudden laughter made Adura step back a pace. The old woman next to Zaxasha smiled. "How old do you imagine she is, child?"

From the way she'd asked the question, she knew her answer had been wrong. Her frown deepened. *They're laughing at me.* Their eyes and lips smiled at her patiently. *They're laughing at me.* She stared back at Zaxasha, defiant as she looked into her brown eyes. Zaxasha's hair was thick and full, flowing past her shoulders down her back. The heat from the fire seemed not to affect her. Her eyes were not watering like the rest. And Adura couldn't see a trace of sweat from the heat on her forehead. Her ears were so small they almost disappeared behind her hair. She wore a black garment much like the rest of them, which covered her from shoulders to ankle. Her eyes were bright and clear, but it was the crinkles that Adura noticed now. They feathered around the outside corners of her eyes, so tiny they were like veins in a leaf. *Why must I respect someone who is barely older than I am?* She lowered her eyes in humiliation and anger, her gaze falling to Zaxasha's feet. Her toenails were long and curved. Her heels were black, cracked, and split as if she'd walked a thousand miles. Only the elder's feet looked like that.

She drew back suddenly, and saw red eyes gazing into her own. "I've walked the earth for hundreds of years, little mouse," she whispered.

"That's not possible," Adura was stunned. Her eyes were as big as saucers in her face. *She's the liar.* Yet she watched Zaxasha's eyes glow brighter and brighter as the shadow of the flames climbed the walls.

"It's true, child," the old woman replied, her brown eyes grave.

"I've seen many things, child, many, many things. And you, you have a gift that we need only tap into once you're ready."

She means to confuse me. What gift is she talking about? What does she mean by ready? "What kinds of things? No one gave me any gift," she answered.

Zaxasha smiled. "I may seem as a child, but I was given a gift, a long time ago, when I was your age, and by sight I will remain a youth. I've seen great kings rise and fall, I've seen the world turn black as night for ten years. I've seen giants felled by ants, I've seen young men scream for death, and wombless women spring aged children from their life's blood. I know why young men thirst for glory and why the ground drinks their blood. I know how to make old women young again and why the lioness lost her mane. I know, I know, I know…" she whispered.

She pointed at Adura's breast with one long, slender finger. "And I know what it is you *dream…*"

As Adura's heart hammered in her chest the sky grew grey and claps of thunder rang out in the cave. The chanting stopped, and Adura stepped backwards, never breaking her gaze with the red eyes of the witch. Her breast heaved against her chest, and the thunder grew louder, closer, rolling again and again to the tune of her heartbeat while the White Witch smiled at her before turning to look upwards to the sky.

"See, child?" Zaxasha smiled at her. "Look how the thunder hears your cry."

Zaxasha stepped closer, placing a hand under Adura's chin.

"You must learn to control it, child. Or you will die young."

Her hands shook as she accepted the cup Zaxasha offered to her. She drank deeply from it, the smooth taste of goat's milk and honey calming her nerves. The witch had to be lying. Storms were natural to these lands. *It wasn't me.* She bit her lip hard, not knowing what to say, scared to ask for the truth. The others might avoid her because of what the White Witch said.

"It wasn't me," she said out loud this time, defiant, eyes shimmering with unshed tears. She refused to cry. *I won't.*

"Don't be afraid, little mouse. Does being different scare you? Is conformity so precious?"

Adura's lips twisted angrily, "I'm not *deformed!*" she yelled. The sudden silence made her look up. Up at the faces above her, leaning from their positions between the cracks and crevices of the cave. They were all staring at her now. Her sisters and brothers, their brown faces surprised and curious, afraid.

"No child," the White Witch said sharply. "You're not deformed. But you're not ready, either."

It was too much. Everyone staring at her. The White Witch telling her she was deformed, different, special. It all meant the same thing. Freak. She leapt up quick as a snake from her seat, darting to the entrance of the cave.

"Stop!" she heard the White Witch yell, and Adura ran, her

heart beating wildly, her feet scraping against rock and weed and stone as she climbed and climbed, heaving herself over the mountain's peak. She lost her footing and fell, hitting her head on a jagged rock jutting out, but lightly. Dazed, she stood, her hands clutching the narrow rockways on either side of her for balance before resuming her climb, faster and faster, until she slid down the other side, green grass beneath her feet, five feet tall—taller than her and swaying dangerously against the wind which had picked up suddenly.

Her brown hair flew behind her, a wild tangle as she flew to her favorite spot, ignoring the tears running down her face, legs pumping furiously until she found herself at the edge of Panther's Cliff, the waters below churning furiously as if waiting for her. She knelt down picking up a stone and throwing it roughly over the edge in anger. Again and again she watched them fall until her tears flowed freely, eyes burning with anger, until she realized the rain beat at her face, not her tears. Thunder sounded suddenly above, and Adura watched lightning break across the sky, her fury matching its pace.

I'm not a freak! Adura's nails bit into her palms, and she tasted blood on her tongue as she bit her lip, furious. Her scream broke through the silence as the wind and rain whipped her hair about her face, the lightning striking closer, and closer. Her lips were wet. Touching her fingertips to them, the rain washed the blood from her fingers as she held them in front of her face. She tried to stem the flow of blood from her nose when her eyes rolled upward suddenly, and she felt no pain as she pitched over the edge. *I'm flying*, she thought as the ground rose up to meet her, the scream of her own name in her ears.

"It was too soon," someone was saying.

"We should have waited…"

"All children must grow up. It was time. Her eyes told me."

"She's my *daughter*. I won't have—"

"She's *our* daughter, Aiona," Zaxasha interrupted firmly.

Their voices were muffled, but she could hear them faintly as if she were underwater. *I'm here*, she wanted to cry. *Stop talking about me like I'm not here!* Their voices grew louder and she could hear the calmness in them, the desperation in her mother's.

Attempting to open her eyes she saw nothing. Panic filled her. It was as though she were blind. She tried to remember what had happened but her head felt cloudy and the left side of her scalp throbbed every time she took a breath. Coughing violently, her throat burned and tears ran down her face as she swallowed.

"Be still, little mouse," Zaxasha's hands were on her leg.

"Breathe. Breathe, Adura. My little lamb, mother is here," her mother said, taking her hands into her own and stroking them gently. "Look at me. Yes. I'm right here, you're safe now."

Her mother's voice was like lambswool against her cheek. The candlelight hurt her eyes and she saw her mother's face smiling at her, tears running down her brown face, her light brown hair disheveled.

"I told you to stay away from that cliff." Her mother's voice shook.

"I'm sorry," her throat burned when she tried to speak. "I'm a freak."

"*NO.*" Her mother's voice was firm. "Don't ever use that word again. You're special. You've always been special, my little lamb. In a good way. You're not the first and you won't be the last. Only the pure of heart may wield the power you have," she finished, her voice catching in her throat.

Zaxasha continued, "It's a gift, child. From God. He has blessed you in ways you cannot yet understand. You will. In time. You must. And soon. For evil comes this way."

Evil. Adura shivered under the fur blanket, her light grey eyes wide.

"We will teach you. All of us," her mother said softly, stroking her cheek.

None of what the witch said made sense. How could she believe something she couldn't prove? How could she use something she didn't know she had? *They're all mad.*

Zaxasha's eyes burned through her. "It was you, little mouse. When you're better, we'll show you everything."

"Show me...show me how to control the weather?" she murmured weakly, looking from face to face.

"The weather?" Her mother's face was wrought with confusion and she looked to Zaxasha for an answer.

But Zaxasha didn't give her one. Zaxasha's hair covered her face where she sat, obscuring her features. Everything but her eyes. And she was laughing. It reverberated off the rock walls, sending a chill up Adura's spine as she looked at her, terror in her eyes. Zaxasha's shoulders shook, her body rocking as her laughter grew louder, uncontrollable. Throwing her head back as she did. She means to kill me. *She's gone mad.*

Adura's eyes widened even as her body became heavy. Her arms would barely rise at her command and her legs wouldn't move to run. Fighting against the weariness, her vision darkened, and she could almost feel the rain washing over her again.

All at once Zaxasha's laughter stopped. Straightening her head, she looked directly at Adura.

"No, little mouse. I'm not mad. And I do not wish to kill you. First, I'll teach you how to see the future."

ASIM

"Papo! Papo's home!"

Asim smiled as he walked through the courtyard of his home, the sweet smell of vanilla tickling his nose. His youngest was sliding down the limestone pillar in the center of the courtyard. His daughter always used it as her private watchtower. His wife would be displeased.

"You'll break your neck Azima-ka!" he heard his wife yell, her voice part anger and part fear.

Spreading his arms wide, Azima's breathless gasps rounded the corner before she did, the quick slap of her sandals against the ground growing louder as she came. She threw herself into his arms, and he lifted her high above his head, twirling her around twice before he sat her on his hip, giggling.

"I'm an eagle, I'm an eagle! Again!" she demanded, her maple-green eyes shining with delight. Her thick hair whirled in the air as he shook his head. His wife had the patience he did not. How she sat for so long taking care of their daughter's hair was beyond him. But it showed. It had grown the length of his hand in the past month, and Azima had taken to requesting certain styles now, begging for twists here, braids there, three mushroom-shaped sculptures like her friends, or all of it surrounding her face, like a lion. He knew the style by the sounds she made, the sound of a high-pitched roar sounding at various times when he was home before she sprang out from her favorite hiding place of the week, hair fanning out like a mane. Today, her shoulder-length hair was styled in multiple thumb-sized twists, at least fifty by his count.

"Put her down before you spoil her. That girl never listens to me," Marava complained, swatting at their daughter's backside.

Kissing him on the cheek, her hand cupped his face, briefly.

"I missed you."

"And I you. I'm here now." The Medjay guarded the High King's family day and night. And he was in charge of them all. Pulling at the straps on his white breastplate that signaled his allegiance to the kingdom, he removed it carefully, sighing with relief as it slid down from his chest. His dagger and sword he unsheathed and placed inside the doorway. Marava knelt before him as he sat on a stool just outside the entryway, unlacing the leather sandals that covered him from toe to calf and up his shins to guard against injury. Azima waited patiently next to him while his wife helped him, stroking his limbs gently as she did each time he arrived home. Slim fingers tracing the dark brand on his arms. Two swords crossed upon each other in the shape of an X, and under them, a bow and arrow, the mark of Medjay.

For a brief moment, he spent time with his family. A Medjay's duty was never done.

"Yes, papo, you are! How's Princess Imanishakheto? She's not hurt is she? Is she more beautiful than ever? Will she be at market tomorrow? When will I see Uncle Amkar? Who is coming to the festival? Did you rescue her by yourself? How much blood was there?"

"Azima..." he said sharply, "whom have you been listening to?"

Looking up at his wife, his forehead wrinkled with concern. He expected the city to be alive with news of the princess after the attempt on her life. He hadn't expected his only daughter to have news of it, and especially not the details of the blood spilled.

"We couldn't avoid it Asim-qo," she spoke softly, her eyes towards the ground. "I took Azima with me to the market and we were told of what happened. By then the blood had been cleared, but everyone had seen it, heard it, or had little whisperings, and I spoke with the women while I told her to go play."

He considered a moment. Azima was only seven and the smartest in her class. "There was much blood, that is true." Turning to his daughter, he set her upon her feet.

"The High King plans to continue with the games. It is a great tradition that must continue for the kingdom. You will attend the festival with your mother, Azima, but not all of the displays. The dancing you shall see." He smiled as his daughter held her breath as if to forestall him making more conditions. "That is all, run along now and find Akim while I speak with your mother. I'll take you to see the *jeli* tomorrow. He's performing in the city tomorrow night."

Azima flew away, her feet kicking up dirt and sand as she went, screaming her brother's name at the top of her lungs.

"Is it safe, husband?" Marava asked him.

He looked at her, pulling her to him. "It will be. These human leeches think to feed off of the backs of those who work hard. Use them as slaves, fighters, and miners. Much has been said of it among the Medjay, and word has spread from the outlying villages. One that I spoke with told such tales I knew not what to make of them."

"What kind of tales?"

"Tales of Meroë possibly trading in slaves along with Makouria and this...*King* of Aksum. Giving away daughters and sons for gold, furs, and riches. To Rome and any other foreigners on the Silk Road. It makes no sense. That the villages grow hungry as the desert closes in. That some elders failed to plan and harvest during the months of plenty to guard against a long drought. I don't know what to believe."

"The High King does not believe them, then?

"No. He does. He has taken precautions against it to procure the safety of the kingdom, but the Festival of Kings will continue."

She put her palm on his right cheek, lifting his face to meet her eyes.

"Why do you call them tales?"

He sighed as he looked into her eyes. He could not escape her piercing gaze. "Because I don't want to believe them."

"I believe them."

"Marava..."

"Many of the merchants I visit at the market tell the same tales. The people change, but the substance is much the same."

"I don't want you to worry." He slid a hand to the tiniest curls at the back of her neck.

"I worry because you worry."

"I'm not—"

"It's all over your face. And in your shoulders." She squeezed his left one, kneading it gently with her fingers. Her own hair was set with five rows braided close on the left side, with the right pulled down and gathered together at her neck, her tight brown coils springing outwards from it and down her back. He touched them now, watching them bounce and pull away from him whenever he let go. He ran his hands over her bare right shoulder, the red linen wrap covering her left shoulder and crossing down towards the right side of her waist. Her quiet composure calmed him.

Even as he squeezed the bridge of his nose between his fingers momentarily, she brought his hand up to her mouth, kissing his palm in reassurance before placing it against her cheek.

"Come home," she whispered softly. He smiled. She didn't mean it literally, of course. She never did. It was his mind she wanted, his thoughts. It was always difficult to leave them at the palace, but she made it easier to bury them. He lost himself in her voice, her lips, her fingers, and left the battleground behind. His beautiful wife.

"I need to do some digging for Amkar. I'll be speaking with quite a few people to get information from them, to find out more about the goods being stolen. And the disappearances."

"Are all of the disappearances from inside Nabara?"

He shook his head. "I don't understand it, but they've taken at least ten that we know of from the interior among our allies in the North. The rest are closer to the coast. The Luba, Goko, the Khoekhoe, even some friends and family of others in Ethiopia and the north. *They* trade in it, but others, like the Luba, have become victims of the trade themselves."

"Is it possible that those taken owed some debt and could not pay? Or had done some wrong?"

"Yes. It is. But it seems that the slavers need no reason at all. And their number is immeasurable." His face darkened as he continued. "They're also given as gifts and concubines, many times to lands in the east by way of the Silk Road. Rome controls a number of the northern territories, and all their citizens seem to lust for is blood. Cuicul was overtaken from the Berbers and is now a garrison. What they want, they take. One of the Tuareg, a nomad from the desert, came this way and told me of what he'd seen. He described a great pit, with lions and tigers…and men. Men of all ages and sizes, women, sometimes children. Even Romans deep in debt! All fighting to be the last one standing." He wrapped his hand around hers. "From what he told me, that occurrence was not rare. A display purely for sport on which wagers were placed, criminals punished. You should have seen his face when he described the bodies ripped apart. And the mob. Screaming for more. I could see it in his eyes. It haunted him."

"Why was he so far south?"

"He wanted to stay hidden. He couldn't trust his people anymore. And I need to find him. It's possible he may have more information that could help us fight this trade. He left a way to reach him should we meet again. I saved him once and Kashta showed him mercy. There is a raider who may also help, of the Igbo. It may be that he will help me this time. Even if he there is a price on his head." He turned to look at Marava.

"If you hear anything at the markets, I want to know. Be careful. It is a lucrative trade, Marava. And I have no idea how far it has spread or who may be involved. It seems every man has a price." He stopped short of telling her about the shipwreck on the coast.

She nodded. "I understand. And give Imanishakheto and Ama my love. They are dear to us both. Promise me you'll be careful? I don't want to think what would happen if you didn't come home." Her face was a mask of uncertainty.

Asim kissed her gently, wrapping his arms around her.

"Not to worry, Marava. All will be well."

Looking up at the sky, the blue-black starlit blanket stared back at him as he wondered what would come of the Empire of Nabara and her allies. The moon was hiding from her many shining suitors, preferring instead to run from them, peeping shyly from behind dark clouds as she waited for the sun.

The next morning he moved through the city with Shaharqa at his side. His brother could get a mute to talk. And he needed that now. At almost seven feet tall, Shaharqa was taller than most men, and his huge bulk and shoulders came naturally. Even as a child he scared those older than him. And he knew it. His whole hand could wrap completely around a man's neck with ease. Which is why most of them stayed out of his way.

"Why do you need me again?" Shaharqa had questioned him nonstop since they left the palace.

"I told you. We need to get as much information as we can, and I need your help. The High King asked that I survey everyone in Nabara, and I'd like to start with him. The Tuareg I met will be harder to track, so I'll start at home." Asim cast a sideways glance at his younger brother.

"If you'd grown up like you were supposed to, you wouldn't need me." He put one hand above Asim's head and held it there, a smile turning at the corners of his mouth.

"Please," Asim slapped his hand away and continued on, ignoring Shaharqa's laughter.

"What? There comes a time when a man must fight his own battles."

"There won't be a battle." Asim stopped quickly, turning to look his brother in the eyes. "We must keep this quiet. People like to talk, but not when they know other's are listening."

"I can be quiet."

"You could if you were under water."

Shaharqa laughed. "Is that what you think of me?"

"I grew up with you. I don't think, I know."

"Well. It's no wonder our mother loves me best. She only adopted you out of pity, you know. Who better to protect the Kingmaker?"

"She tells you that so that you can maintain your confidence," Asim snorted. He knew full well he was like a fifth son to the Kingmaker, and he called her alone mother. It warmed his heart to think of her now. She had never made him feel any less than her son despite having not been born of her. "We all know larger men sometimes have anxiety in one area that…spills over to another." He was smiling now.

"If you weren't the High King's—"

"You'd do—" Asim was in a headlock before he could finish his sentence, wrestling with Shaharqa before he released him.

"I'm sorry. I'm sorry." Shaharqa's laughter quieted as they looked behind them. The sun would rise in two hours, and they could use the darkness.

They moved quickly as they approached the scribe's home. Each profession kept a record of business. Farmers, merchants, artisans, architects, and more. The origins of each could be found by tracking their scribe. This one would be able to tell them about the merchants who weren't citizens of Nabara. Foreigners of Nabara such as the Sao were allowed to sell their goods here, but paid a tax at a higher rate. That tax flowed down to orphans, the High Priests for their service to the villages, weapon making, and other needs of the city. It provided a balance. He would be able to tell them of any new merchants desiring to trade and sell in Nabara. There had to be one who wakened his suspicions.

The sound of cicadas softened at their approach, their rhythmic chirping like a hundred rattlesnakes. Asim climbed the sandstone steps and went through the window, lifting the latch to open the stone door for Shaharqa. *He'd done this before as a child, but he couldn't afford to be concerned with it now.* One corner of the front room held a number of scrolls as high as Asim's hip. Glancing at his brother, they exchanged a look. *How does he find anything in here?*

Shaharqa lifted a cup from the table and moved it towards his nose before looking to Asim. He shook his head. They moved towards the back slowly and found the scribe snoring deeply on his bed, a naked woman at his side. Not his wife. Shaharqa lifted his *khopesh* slowly before running the edge across the pad of the sleeping man's foot. The scribe awoke with a start, jerking his foot back as he sat up, looking at them with wide eyes.

"How dare you!" A moment later his eyes filled with recognition as they looked at him.

"Get dressed. We need to talk." Asim and Shaharqa waited a moment to make sure he rose from the bed before moving back to the front room, the woman still sleeping like a rock.

In less than a minute, the man was sitting at the table across from Asim. Shaharqa stood to the man's left, just enough so that he could see him out of the corner of his eye.

"I suppose I should be honored. Even the black pharaohs suffered from tomb raids after being laid to rest in the chambers of their pyramids. To what do I owe the…pleasure of this visit?" He didn't bother to hide his resentment at having been woken.

"We need to know about your new traders."

"That's what this is about?" The scribe glanced at Shaharqa, who stood rigid in one corner like a human pyramid, unsmiling.

"Would you like it to be about something else?" Asim raised one eyebrow.

The scribe sighed. "I have eight from the last month. None of

129

them selling anything unusual or illegal."

"Any foreign to Nabara?"

"No."

"Any of them engaging in new trade? Commodities they haven't sold before?"

"Nothing that comes to mind."

"How many of them are late making payments? Refusing to pay taxes? Asking for back channels or lower rates in any way?"

"I should think you would be aware of that already." He tipped his head to the side.

Shaharqa moved so quickly Asim's head snapped towards him, bringing his fist down onto the table with such force it jumped. The scribe jerked away, flinching as though the blow were meant for him.

"Answer the question," Shaharqa ordered.

"A few, but nothing unusual," the scribe answered hurriedly. "A farmer or two suffering from lands that have experienced more dryness than usual. Nothing they cannot make up with the next harvest."

"And you, so generous," Asim smiled.

"Everyone has to make a living." The scribe's eyes flicked at Shaharqa again.

"Anything strange about your customers recently? Not turning in product to move across caravans? Not coming to market? Appearing with new partners?"

"If by strange you mean how close one of the most popular male artisans is to the son of a certain trader, then no. We all have our desires."

Shaharqa smirked, "He thinks he's funny."

"I think *you're* funny. I'm not engaging in illegal trade, I merely keep record for Nabara. The crown reviews my records, quite thoroughly I might add." Asim ignored the scowl on the trader's face.

"And who would engage in illegal trade? You see merchants and traders day in and day out. You must be aware of some way to cheat."

"And you. But I don't."

Asim waited a beat. "This is not about you. We aren't

questioning your integrity."

"Yet," Shaharqa warned.

"We're questioning your instinct." Asim knew he needed to be more direct. "We have cause to believe the trade may have more than one problem, and we need to find out what it is. I know you have a sister, a brother by law, and a niece. I see you with her. We want everyone to be safe." He leaned forward. "Now remove your hand from between your thighs. We don't plan to cut it off. Is there anything unusual you can tell us?"

The scribe looked from him to Shaharqa again before standing and moving to a back room. He returned with three scrolls in hand.

"This is all I have."

"What is this?"

"You can take these. I have copies of everything. Three farmers that I know of have sold excellent quality salt, sorghum, and wheat of late."

"What's unusual about this?"

"Two of them told me they'd been suffering from drought—not all of their crop but some.

"And?" He was anxious for him to get to the point.

"I inspect all of the goods for trade to record them. They've never brought me product of this quality before. I mean…they sell less, as one would expect for someone experiencing a drought. But somehow the quality has also improved. They're able to sell it for much more than their old product and make a profit." The scribe crossed his arms over his chest. "It can't be from their fields."

"It's not illegal to trade or sell in something you've not farmed yourself." Shaharqa's voice was full of doubt.

"No, it's not. But the ties—"

"Those that bind the wheat and sorghum? What about them?" Asim's eyes were narrowed now.

"The ties were made of animal hair. Only one farmer I know of ever used that, and *he* is from Meroë. His cousin is of Nabara."

"Naqyrin."

The scribe nodded. "A wife, a son, and two girls. One was named Nekili. I met her once. Sweet child." He shook his head now. "But he and his family have not sent word of any trade since last month."

SAMYA

The sand seemed to fill her lungs. It surrounded her. She could feel it settling about her headdress and the heat pressed in on her as the sands shifted under their small caravan. The sand was the color of blood, shifting and moving before her very eyes. *The Kingdom of Bones.* She may have been the High Queen, but the stories had not failed to reach her own ears. Punishment here was as severe as the climate and some said much worse than the nomadic families. Her father, chief and warlord of Makouria, had warned her and her sister when they were young. She had not forgotten. As queen she had helped strengthen relationships with the Nomadin, knowing their traditions and values. An ambassador for Nabara, she was well aware of their contributions and earnings throughout the land, regardless of the fact that they paid no tax. Many of the Nomadin outside of the Scorpion Kingdom traded at Nudollan markets though their laws were different. She still remembered the nomad's words born from pawnship: *Be careful of the debts you incur.* It was no wonder Tharbis found common ground with them. He loved gold more than anyone and never entered an agreement that did not benefit him.

By midday she was sitting on the veranda in a guest room looking down upon the Scorpion Kingdom in the city of Tharbis situated in the Namib Desert. And named for him. *No doubt as a point of pride for the king.* Removing her cap crown she set it on the table. Her handmaid wrung a cloth in her hands, dipping it in the clean, cool water and placing it on the back of her neck carefully.

"Thank you, Jala." She smiled at her handmaid.

"My Queen," Jala replied, smiling. "Do you think we'll be long?" she asked.

"I have no idea, Jala. But you know as well as I do that kings can be hard to reason with," she replied.

"And queens," Jala replied grinning. "If we stay too long he may try to make you his eighth wife. The Kingdom of Bones is not somewhere I would like to find myself, even with a thousand guards to protect me." Scowling Jala dipped the cloth back into the water and pressed it to her neck.

"Jala." Samya shook her head. "We needn't worry about that."

"No, I think not. The High King would crawl from Nabara to the Skeleton Coast to bring you home if he had to."

Smiling, Samya cupped Jala's cheek gently. "I can finish here. Please, rest. Wait for me."

Jala nodded before going to sit in the chair beside the bed, watching her from a distance.

Samya dipped her hands into the water, letting the cold saturate her fingers before cupping them together, her head leaning just over the edge. Splashing her face, she let her fingertips trail down her face. Her sister used to do it to her often before they slept. And Samya had done it to Imani and Nema as children. She dried her hands and replaced her crown before standing. "Come."

Jala followed her out with the Medjay close behind.

When she entered the audience hall, Queen Cima, his second wife, rose to greet her, a small hint of surprise on her face.

"My Queen." Cima bowed quickly and walked over to her. "I do not expect my husband back for some time—"

"We have much to discuss. I have waited an hour."

"Yes, and I assure you he—"

"Was notified well in advance of my visit by your Ambassador." She let her words sit in the silence, watching Cima cringe slightly as she searched for the right words.

"Samya."

"Cima." She cut her off. "You and I were friends as children, and it is the only reason I pay you this courtesy. You and I both know your husband must listen to reason. Even the smallest crimes on the high seas must be rooted out."

"Rooted out?" She turned at the sound of his voice, her lips pursing and relaxing as she hid her annoyance.

"What are you rooting out? My Queen." The Scorpion King took her hands between his, kissing them as he bowed before her.

"Traitors." Samya watched as his eyes shifted briefly to his wife and back.

"You've never been one to mince words, Samya."

"I've never been as gifted at crafting exactly what people want to hear as you."

Smiling, King Tharbis walked over to his wife, placing one hand on her elbow as he guided her towards the door. Smiling at two young handmaids just inside the entryway he touched their cheeks gently and nodded towards the hallway. They left immediately, without a word.

"Please, let us sit." He walked her over to the long table in the middle of the room, nodding for his wife to take her leave. She did it immediately without question. "Tell me why you've come."

Watching Cima go made it difficult to hold back the disappointment she felt.

"We require five hundred warriors from you. Your High King intends to send them north as a weapon against the enemies of Nudolla. It is believed that the slave traders will continue further south in search of their supply."

"Supply of what?"

Her eyes darkened at his feigned ignorance. "Slaves. Gold. Ivory. Whatever supply they can find."

"My Queen, we trade with Northern families and Nomadin."

"And Rome?"

"You know full well we trade with anyone with the right goods, but not Rome. You misunderstand me."

"I do not misunderstand you. You trade in goods and you trade with Northern families. But *some* of the Northern families and western kingdoms trade in slaves, and to trade with them is to condone their violence and massacre of our own. Meroë is caught between the threat of Ethiopia and the false friendship of Rome. It no longer has the power it should to have defended against its enemies.

"Is that what you long for? More power?"

"I long for nothing but peace."

"As you say. Beautiful women like you…and Cima…should long for nothing."

"Men though. Men will always long for something. What of your five hundred warriors?"

He looked at her a moment. "The High King will have his five hundred at your request. I would deny *you* nothing. As perilous as it may be. They come at great cost to myself, you should know."

"It is noted. I would remind you that trading with Rome is forbidden. In case anyone under your kingdom has forgotten, laws are handled quite a deal differently among the outlying Nomadin."

"I have not forgotten." He stood with her as she rose, walking towards the door, his arm briefly brushing against her elbow. "Neither have I forgotten your sister. She was just as lovely as you. And gentle. And kind. Her disappearance torments me every day."

Pursing her lips as the anger rose within her, she calmed herself before turning to meet his eyes. *He dared speak of her sister.* "I thank you. Please, don't trouble yourself. Years may pass and storms may come, but justice will always be done. I pray for it."

He smiled. "Are you any closer?" The sincerity in his voice sickened her. His brow furrowed in concern mocked her to the core, and she forced herself to smile back.

"A hawk in the sky may not be close to a scorpion in the sand, but…he will always have him in his sights."

Nodding in respect, his slight smile was replaced by a sober and thoughtful calmness that settled in his mouth and shoulders.

"Your presence alone would be an asset no matter what kingdom you ruled over, Your Grace."

"I wish you well. And you, Cima." She kissed Cima on each cheek just outside of the doors of the hall, and the two of them followed her out as she climbed into her caravan, giving a slight nod before she reclined back into her seat.

She felt drained from just that single conversation. Placing a hand to her forehead, she looked down at the papyrus as she pulled it from her sleeve. She still needed to visit the pastoralists, made up of an immeasurable number of distinct farming nations that shared similar root words in their language. She would start with the Luba and the Goko before traveling towards the Kalanga and the Zulu. That left the hunter-gatherers such as the Sons of Prishiboro, the Servants of Cagn, and the Nomadin. The Khoekhoe had readily received their messages and sent messengers of their own to Nabara to represent the Daman and Namaqua pastoralists. Several nations claimed ancestry under each of them, with varying languages of common lineage. Herders, farmers, hunter-gatherers, and nomadic people, they all called this land home. It held a wide stretch of sand and desert, mountain, valleys, jungle, swamplands, lakes, animals of every shape and size, lions and gazelles, zebras and snakes. And the endless resources that were mined inside each. Shared. Traded. All of it would come to an end if they did not listen to reason. She prayed her words would be persuasive enough.

A cacophony of sounds met her ears as they approached the beehive-shaped structure in the middle of the village holding the Council of Elders, growing louder like a lion's warning when another predator approaches his territory. The council was one in any number of councils among the Luba, but it was the only one in this area that combined them all for effectiveness, efficiency, and trade.

Medjay followed her closely, each armed with spears, *khopesh* blades, and *mambele* throwing knives. She'd told Jala to make sure she stayed close in case there was trouble. Attending the Council of Elders was not a risk lightly taken. Though village chiefs or kings led the Luba farmers, it was the Council of Elders that made decisions here. Some called it the Council of Wisdom, others the Council of the Dead, mocking the grey-haired grandfathers of the Council of Elders. It was true; some could often be seen nodding gently, eyes closed as their shoulders sagged, bodies leaning like storm-tossed trees as they fell asleep. Others quickly forgot the conversation that took place only an hour ago. Still more had trouble remembering the names of all of their children. Withered hands curled around earlobes in an attempt to hear the conversation better. Regardless of all this, their strength lay in the wisdom of the many. And the minds of the many were sharper than any blade she'd ever touched. There was no question. The elders solved disputes, divided land, and portioned resources when other families' crops failed. It was their knowledge that was essential to a thriving community and each passed down his knowledge from generation to generation.

Nodding to her Medjay who took their places outside of the beehive and mountain-shaped structure made of sandstone and set among straw and earth built homes of a similar shape. Medjay surrounded it quickly, while others stood directly at the entrance to guard her exit and screen those entering. A wide dirt floor with stone seats in varying sized circles greeted her, and she surveyed the area from where she stood for a moment where no one could see her. Yelling and shouting filled her ears as the elders argued back and forth. One elder raised a fist to his own face and made a circular motion, a veiled threat meant to let the elder with whom he was engaged know not to test him. *It is well that weapons are not allowed at the Council*, she thought shaking her head. It would be the end of them.

The Chief motioned her forward, having informed her that his Council was expecting her. Moving forward, her Medjay slammed their spears into the ground in quick succession, alerting the elders to her presence as she stepped into view.

"You now stand in the presence of the High Queen of Nudolla, Great Wife of High King Amkarqa Arkamani-qo Kashta, His Beloved, Lady of Nabara, Her Majesty Kandake Samya Nasala Kashta," Jala introduced her.

"I realize you have matters that are increasingly important to you to resolve. That your villages require your attention. That your crops are in need of tending. It is not my intention to keep you from them."

Quiet whispers reached her despite the cupped hands surrounding ears that sought to mask them.

"You will by now have heard of threats facing the families south of the Great Desert, the nomadic nations to the east, and even some of my own people in Nabara and other kingdoms not under the Kashta rule," she continued.

Their muttered acknowledgement urged her on.

"Drought is increasing among outlying nomads in the Sao Kingdom and in the hunters in the Namib."

"Why should we care about these desert dwellers, Kandake?" one of the elders cut in. They *choose* to drown in the sand."

"I recognize that it is not easy to understand why you should, except to warn you. What affects one will affect us all. Ignoring the problem until it is at your door is not a solution. And apathy too is a choice. As the largest producers of salt and natron in the south and of diamonds in the Namib, we should all be concerned. Many of you trade with them. Salt for root crops, iron, and timber. Nomadic hunters often supply you large game. It is a relationship

137

of mutual gain. It is a relationship built on fair trade."

The elders nodded, some of them leaning in closer to hear as she turned around in the middle of the room.

"The slave trade is not. Women for wine. Men for silks. Children for weapons. Who profits?"

"Kandake, your pretty speech is lost here. We do not trade in slaves." A Nguni elder looked at her, his mouth turning up and down at the same time as though he smelled something foul. Or was looking at it. His village was known as the largest holders of Nguni cattle in the area, and the third richest among them all.

"But you have considered it," she cut in sharply, eyes narrowing as she silenced him with a look. "I am aware of the offer the Akan of the western kingdoms made to the Luba. Made to you. It was a tempting offer, no doubt."

The other elders' heads snapped sharply towards him, some of them only just learning the information she shared freely. Fighting to control the smile tugging at the corners of her mouth she waited to see what he would say.

"And what of it? We are cattle raisers and farmers of the savannah. We are not under the kingship of Nabara. We call none of the kingdoms home. We may deal with whom we please. And certainly all have a right to request an audience with us. Even a queen."

Silence descended as the elder finished, leaning back in his seat, the short staff next to him held tightly in his hand as he glared at her.

"I fear your new wife has given you over to a rather fast tongue," she replied. "And possibly tainted your view of the opposite sex."

"The fairer sex," the chief offered from where he stood, arms crossed over his chest smiling at her now as he watched her.

"The more intelligent sex."

The other elders laughed together at her statement, some clapping the elder on the back, knowing she'd gotten the better of him. Looking up she watched his chest rise and fall rapidly like an old lion that lost his prey in the chase. *Yes. I know all about your new wife.* Of course, he wondered how. Far be it for her to reveal the friendships she and Amkar shared with the Nomadin in the east. Their intelligence had been more than welcome and clearly necessary. She knew before her journey the matters that plagued the farm raisers and what they valued. But knowing them more personally had never failed.

The elder started again, rising as though he meant to leap from his seat to the ground. "The Luba and Goko clear the trees to make way for savannah. For farming. Soon you'll tell us even this is an affront to your delicate sensibilities."

The other elders were silent, some of them likely agreeing with him.

Calmly she stepped forward. "I am Samya Nasala Kashta, High Queen of Nudolla and the Kingdom of Nabara. And I have seen plenty of men killed in my short life. I can assure you, elder, none would describe my sensibilities as delicate."

"What they give you now they will use against you when you have given them what they want," she continued. "A snake and a frog may both have a common interest in crossing a river, but you cannot blame the snake for biting the frog once they reach the middle. It's in his nature. It is my hope that our leaders can discuss this more in Nabara. At the Festival of Kings. Your neighbors, the Kibera, to the north, will be in attendance. My husband and I give you an open invitation, which I hope you will take to heart. We have left a number of gifts for you at the edge of your village. With the fairer sex." She smiled as the elders laughed again, nodding to her. "Thank you for lending me your ear."

Chief Nkole smiled as he walked with her briefly on her way out. "Be careful with Elder Andikan. His reach is long," he told her stroking his chin as he leaned closer to her. "His son is to marry my cousin. She finds him delightful. Soon I will call him family."

"You have my sympathies."

Inclining her head in respect, she turned to exit, gesturing to her handmaid and Medjay as she did. Rising as one, the elders on either side of her watched her exit, nodding to her as she passed, others smiling in approval. All but one. The elder who'd interrupted her stayed seated as she left, gripping his staff in his fist as though it were her neck he meant to crush.

Smiling softly as she stepped inside her litter, her eyes began to drift closed, her head gently bobbing on soft pillows with Jala wide awake and alert across from where she lay.

"My Queen?"

She blinked her eyes slowly as she lifted her head.

"Your Grace?"

"Yes, Jala."

"We've reached the !Kung nation, Your Grace. The Sons of Prishiboro have sent two to receive us. One of their scouts has agreed to take us further into their territory, but not until he sees you."

"Thank you, Jala."

Samya straightened her cap crown and stepped from the closed shade of the caravan, her guards assisting her. When her feet touched the sand, she let go of her gown, the wind catching the stark white material as she stood there.

With a series of clicks, the !Kung scouts spoke to one another as they looked at her before turning to each other. One seemed to be concerned about taking them the rest of the way. A spear in his left hand was gripped tightly, his eyes narrowed in suspicion. A moment later the slimmer of the two turned to her and inclined his head respectfully before turning west and walking with his companion.

"Wait here," she told the head of the caravan. Nodding to her escort he lifted her to a horse and Jala and ten of her Medjay followed. "Follow them," she commanded. An hour later they came to a stop, and this time she stepped out with Jala, who carried a straw basket containing a large ewer that was half black and half brown, it's substance of the finest quality, the finish smooth. The remaining gifts she hoped would endear her to the chief of the !Kung here.

Additional scouts surrounded their party, and she walked with them towards their encampment. Situated near a small lake, the water provided the refreshment they needed in the desert. The sun wasn't gone yet, but two large fires burned brightly.

A small group of men sat close to one, with young boys near each, arrowheads in their hands. Using the rocks on the ground before them, they sharpened them carefully. The boys were grinning with pride at their work, practicing their throwing technique as they sat, the men laughing and sternly correcting their efforts. The !Kung were great hunters and were a match for any of the large meat eaters in the desert. Their arrowheads were often tipped with poison to ensure the kill. Even a slight grazing of their prey's skin would slow it down, killing it slowly as the hunting party tracked its movements through the desert.

They were Sons of Prishiboro, a god who married an elephant, but all of them believed that the earth itself was their mother. She alone received the !Kung children at birth after pregnant mothers went a distance from the village camp to give birth alone. Any number of the families of the Sons of Prishiboro lived on the plains of the Kalahari, the Namib Desert, and the Sotho territories, moving as water sources willed them to. A force to be reckoned with, they were known for the ability to bring down the largest animals without force, and track water as the lion stalks the gazelle.

A child ran by her carrying an ostrich egg, water spilling from what seemed to be a small hole in the top as other children chased behind him, screaming and laughing as they tried to catch him. *It's at least twice the size of his head,* she noted, smiling. Ten more ostrich eggs were in a small pit nearby, unbroken and unbothered. They were excellent water containers in the Kalahari Desert, though it supported more animals than most. The name of the Kalahari itself meant "the great thirst." Its inhabitants knew the significance and took care to collect water at any chance, storing it during the rainy season. Suddenly, the boy was tackled by his faster friend, dust flying as they fought to keep the container upright. A moment later they began to laugh and pass the ostrich egg around with the others as she continued on with their guides.

They passed at least fifty huts as they walked, some of the !Kung sitting just inside the doorways, some watching her.

When she finally stood before Chief Kumsa, he smiled at her and stood from his seat.

"Come. We've been expecting you." A shock of white hair and the calmest eyes she'd ever seen set off his unlined brown face.

Following him into the center of their village, a circle of !Kung watched their approach.

"The !Kung's wealth is shared among the whole. You will have to sway the people, not simply myself."

"I understand."

"It is well that you understand our language. Who taught you?"

"My father. I taught my children. There are many barriers to knowing a person, he used to tell me, but language should never be one."

He put a hand on her shoulder. "Please. Sit here, by me."

"Thank you."

After a moment she realized they were all looking to her, waiting for her to speak. Collecting herself before looking around her, she stood. Just behind her, Jala rose to announce her, but she shook her head and her handmaid sat back down.

"Many of you know me. Some of you do not. I am Samya Kashta, of the Kingdom of Nabara. Wife of High King Amkarqa Arkamani-qo Kashta, head of Nudolla. My words are the words of my Kingdom of Nabara and the alliance that is Nudolla. I ask you to join us. I ask you to fight. Men foreign to these lands are kidnapping and enslaving desert people. Soon, they may find you. Us. I have come to ask more of you than you can bear, but less than these murderers would take by force. We must present a united front. I have gone to the Scorpion King, Tharbis of the Namib. We have joined forces with the Kibera Kingdom and kingdoms of the Luba."

"The Luba? The farmers?" a young woman stopped her.

"Many of these migrating farmers treat us as their enemies. They force us further south," an older man cut in.

"We need to remain united if we are to fight what threatens these lands. The threat is not just in Nabara," she replied.

An older man to her left scoffed. "The Luba would sooner sell us than fight with us. They accuse us of stealing their cattle as if our way of life is nothing to theirs. No matter how much we trade with them, they believe we would steal our meat rather than hunt it. Theirs they purchased from cattle herders."

"I realize—"

"Do you realize that they have *never*—"

"Please. I realize you are angry. I have come from quite a long way and showed you the greatest respect. I cannot speak for those who have wronged you, but I ask you not to lay the blame at my feet. Nudolla has always welcomed any who need our aid and we have fought to maintain peace among all who ask of it. That comes at a price."

"Are you saying you require payment from the !Kung?" Their faces were stark with astonishment and resentment before she even answered.

"I'm saying what my father taught me a very long time ago. Whenever he asked for anything in lieu of a gift, he would ask for peace. As a child I wondered how I could give that to him. I came to understand soon though. There is no such thing as peace. We are always at war. You can fight for peace and come close to it, but it is as a bird that will never reach the sun. There will always be someone who wants...more. More food, more jewels, more clothing, more land...more wives." Their laughter split the silence and even the chief chuckled. "A fourth husband." Giggles met her ears this time and she winked at a girl nearby whose smile was contagious. The !Kung were notorious for enjoying multiple lovers and husbands. They did so very often with peaceful outcomes.

"Help me fight for it," she finished.

In the silence that followed, she motioned to Jala and the girl came forward.

"The Empire of Nudolla asks for however many men you can spare, to advise or to fight. These gifts I bring as thanks for your kindness and for sharing your water."

Jala began pulling out beautifully decorated ostrich eggs for the !Kung, and they clapped as they watched each gift appear from the basket sitting in front of her. Pulling out ten *karosses* weaved of animal skin and smooth besides, she handed them over carefully. The !Kung shaped them into clothing or slings meant to hold their babies and wrap snugly around their backs as they continued their chores for the day, their young ones warm and secure in the *kaross* just behind them. The jewelry came next, the women to her right receiving it as they in turn handed it to the elders near them.

Samya turned to the chief. "I thank you again, for your kindness."

"If it was only up to me, you should have all you need."

Nodding she walked back towards her party with Jala and her escorts just behind.

"You do not take all of the ostrich eggs?" she noted as she

watched an ostrich in the distance, settling on top of at least half a dozen of them, but smaller in size.

"No. We only take what we need. If we took every egg, one day, there would be no ostrich."

Samya stared a moment longer at the animal. It was as tall as her, with a neck the length of her arm and slightly pink. It stared at her, unafraid as it settled further into its nest.

When they reached her caravan, she took both his hands and kissed him on each cheek. "I pray I find you in good health the next time we meet."

"And you. Though we do not pray to the same gods. The Sons of Prishiboro preserve themselves by keeping away from others and living a simple life. The desert is our shield. The earth is our mother."

He thinks that should make a difference.

"I did not forget. But my God values every life under his care. Even those of non-believers. And the Kingdom of Nabara well knows the power of many, united, against a common enemy."

"The !Kung will send our reply with haste and we will speak with the other Sons of Prishiboro that we meet. Regardless of the answer, we will see you at the Festival of Kings."

"I look forward to it."

Jala and Samya stepped into the cover of their caravan, and Chief Kumsa watched them go, his arms crossed about his chest.

Sighing heavily, she realized what they were up against, but she knew it was better to have a plan of attack than to be forced to defend against one. *Even Imani seemed to know that.* Her father certainly did, but it was hard for him to let her go as his daughter. As his youngest. And Jelani's thoughts always seemed to be elsewhere of late. She would have taken them with her had she not been concerned about her safety. The worry was eating at her, and she knew the desert Nomadin and other kingdoms would need to come together to defeat this new threat. Or pride might kill them all.

AMKAR

Imani walked slowly up the dais to sit beside him. The dress she wore was made of a white leather bodice with capped sleeves, the light gold silk of the gown beginning at her waist and hugging her ankles. Smiling inwardly, he wondered who made it for her. His warrior princess. He couldn't help it that his heart swelled with pride at the sight of her. Her black hair hung down her shoulders, four long braids on either side of her head ringed with golden combs. *She's as beautiful as her mother at that age.*

"You stand in the presence of the High King of the Empire of Nudolla. High King Amkar Arkamani-qo Kashta of the Kingdom of Nabara. Descendant of the ancient lines of the Kushite rulers of Kemet and Nubia. Bloodline of Meroitic Kings. His Grace will hear each of you in turn. State your name, trade, and business before the High King as you come forward, quickly and without delay." As vizier, Adum had warned him audience would include the brewer and a woman who'd traveled a great distance to see him.

One by one, they stepped forward. There were at least fifty today, a line of Nabarans trailing out of the audience hall doors. Their problems ranged from stolen cattle to requests for food, an extension on taxes, permits for trade. Many only wanted to give their harvest tax, and before long the granaries would be filled with sacks of salted lamb, fish, and grain. He'd ordered the tax a year ago after learning of the increasing press of the desert-causing drought in many areas. More and more elephant bones were turning up in the Namib and Kalahari Desert. A small oasis at the edge had completely dried up, and a fire had overtaken a stretch of the Kalahari. Ignoring the suggestions of the High Priests of the *Kenbet*, he had ordered the people to provide a tenth of their harvest. Some had been unwilling, but Samya, Jelani, and Imani had gone among the people to explain its necessity. His wife was his greatest ambassador. It was the reason he sent her to treat with the other kingdoms in advance of the Festival of Kings and to personally invite the farmers, nomads, and hunters to the celebration. Pushing his worry aside was difficult, but he did. Samya was well protected.

The chief treasurer moved to sit with his scribe, who carefully recorded and tallied each of the goods in turn before directing them back out of the Great Hall to collect and leave the tax in carefully protected storage locations. *Adum can handle most of this on his own as he sees fit.* The vizier had done an excellent job of increasing their storage and providing the excess to those who needed it most, earning his trust long ago. Nothing had changed since.

Towards the back of the audience hall sitting on a high dais reserved strictly for their use, sat the Nine. Nine High Priests were tasked with hearing cases among the people of Nabara and sending any matters to the High King should they reach an impasse and require the High King to resolve the matter. The High Priests were required to recuse themselves from matters involving their family members or matters in which their own interests were at play, and eight were required to issue judgment. In the event that they were evenly split, he, as High King, could appoint a special commission to investigate the matter or rule on the matter after a public hearing. Their ivory robes flowed downward towards the floor, covering their feet as they sat ramrod straight in their seats. It was their purview whether or not to attend audience to listen to the entreaties and petitions of the people. More often than not, it helped inform their decision on contractual agreements and other legal matters that came before the court. While they had vehemently opposed the harvest tax on behalf of the people, he knew better than to count on the land in a drought. He made it known that he preferred their attendance and they had always obliged. Knowing one's public should always be a requirement of those who ruled over them.

The next in line to step forward was an old woman, well past the age of bearing children. Her long, silver hair was wild and strewn about her shoulders. Shaking it from her face, she began her tale, her gnarled, bony fingers pointing to emphasize her point.

"Your Grace. My name is Serram. I am Khoekhoe. My family is an old one, skilled in raising cattle, goats, and sheep. Our children will follow in our footsteps. We are an independent people, but I request your ear."

The High King knew well of the Khoekhoe. A people born into husbandry, having talents in the raising of livestock. Unlike the hunter-gatherers of the Kalahari, the Khoekhoe succeeded as herders and had both rich and poor members of their communities, numbering their wealth by the number of cattle. Many of them preferred Nguni cattle to any other. A breed with thick, curved horns of medium size, they were well known for their coats. Their skin a work of art to even the untrained eye, a mix of black and white and brown, spotted and multicolored, they could easily be mistaken even from a distance. They blended well against black mountains, earth-colored hills, and savannah. Despite their coats, their noses were always black, from the oldest to the newborns.

"You have it. Please, continue."

"Our cattle are being stolen. They are our livelihood."

"By whom?" Imani sat up straighter in her seat and he knew by her posture her curiosity was piqued.

"We believe it to be the work of those who eat from the ground." Voice tinged with disgust she raised her chin as if to show her superiority, and what she thought of that. Animal fat glistened on her skin, a sign of status. As lofty as she believed herself her mouth turned down in a frown, the disdain coating her face.

"What do you mean by 'eat from the ground,' elder?" Imani was frowning next to him, but he continued watching the Khoekhoe woman.

"The gatherers. These !Kung and more! They eat any plants they can find and pick from the ground and steal our cattle because they have none," she replied. Her distaste was apparent and she didn't try to hide it.

"How do you come to believe this?" Amkar was losing his patience with her answers. "Have you proof?"

"Your Grace...I..." she hesitated.

"Before you speak I am sure you are aware that these...gatherers, as you call them, are hunters and have been for many years. Their survival relies on their ability to find, track, and kill a great number of animals."

"Your Grace, I was told-"

"And I am sure you have not come so far without more proof of your accusations."

When she didn't answer he settled back into his seat.

"I saw you eating grain and fruit while you waited for my ear. Grain and fruit. It, too, comes from the ground. Take ten cattle from our stores and go."

Serram pursed her lips. "Thank you, Your Grace. My coming was…a mistake. Thank you for your attention." She turned quickly and left the room, a number of heads turning to watch her leave. From the back of the Great Hall, he saw Jelani watching her go as well, leaning against the wall next to his Uncle Shaharqa.

They will both need to learn. Turning to Imani she leaned towards him instinctively.

"What proof could she have offered, Father?"

"She needs more than the word of her neighbor. Had he but been here. Nabara does its best to resolve disputes between neighbors, but the Khoekhoe and the people of the !Kung have long been enemies at varying times in the past. As those who farm and raise cattle move further south, the ability to hunt on that land is diminished. And many of those become the target for accusations of theft. This woman was given information she does not know to be completely true. The first report is always wrong. Imagine if she sought retaliation rather than coming to audience. And a man's lack of one resource should not mean that the only way he possesses it is by stealing it." Understanding dawned in Imani's eyes, and she nodded as he turned back towards the audience.

Two men stepped forward this time, a young girl close to Jelani's age stood between them. Her hair was back and away from her face, six long braids close to her scalp that reminded him of rows of unharvested grain. Her light brown features filled with unease as she looked to the man to her left and held the hand of the one to her right. The man's fingers gripped hers tightly as they came.

"State your business," he commanded, watching them closely.

"Your Grace. Thank you for your attention," the first answered smoothly and calmly. Much like the rest of him. Older and clothed in green robes, his hair was well oiled, black coils barely half an inch, but shining with the ointment he'd likely coated on it. His posture was impeccable, shoulders pulled back as he kneeled in front of the throne. The rings on his fingers shone from where he stood.

"My name is Bimbola."

"And I am Akachi," the other man finally spoke. His well-worn robes were caked with dirt at the bottom and fraying at his sleeves. "This is my daughter, Kachima."

He nodded, wondering what the problem may be. A marriage proposal declined? An insufficient bride price? The man was a great deal older than her and her father. He forced himself not to glance at Imani though he felt his chest tightening. *That will not be her future.*

"Your Grace," Bimbola spoke first again. "This man refuses to pay a debt owed me for almost two seasons now. I kindly offered him my assistance. Granting him the sums he asked for in order that he might educate his youngest and support him in becoming a scribe. I bear him no ill will for wanting this for his child. But he granted his daughter's service until the debt could be repaid. And now he refuses to pay it."

"I did not refuse to pay it, Magnificence," Akachi spoke up in the silence that followed. His daughter's head hung low next to him. "I...I just can't."

"Can't or won't?" Bimbola responded, looking at the girl's father as he spoke.

"You know I have tried. I made attempts, Your Grace, but with the drought...my wife is long dead. I am all that is left to provide for my children."

He held up a hand, interrupting the man. "Why is it you are here? Is what you lack for repayment of the debt, more time?"

"I gave him six months already, Your Grace. My pockets have suffered greatly from the redistribution of my wealth."

"And so it is that you have denied him more time?" His eyes bore into Bimbola, who shifted under his gaze. "What is the outcome you seek?"

"Your Grace, I...she is as my own handmaid now for a period as I rightly interpret the agreement. It was orally made." Bimbola seemed uneasy now, and he knew it.

"Slavery...is forbidden." The hall quieted as he spoke. "Pawnship in Nudolla, is forbidden. I realize you did not seize her as in pawnship. I also remind you that pawnship is widespread among the nomadic families, using a pawn as an assurance of payment, as collateral for the debt. But your actions come dangerously close to it. I despise it." He turned to Akachi now. "You would do well to remember that before you use your blood...as you would cattle."

Imani shifted in her seat, and slight murmurs sounded in the room. He would make an example of them both, that neither escaped his judgment nor his opinion on the practice. Long had he known that Nudolla was at risk from the impact that pawnship may have on the kingdom and her people.

A tear rolled down the girl's face where she stood next to her father.

"I would not act the same if I had the chance, Your Grace. My regret fills my heart," Akachi's voice broke as he spoke.

"You have two weeks to make full payment or reach a settlement. Sell your belongings, part with your jewels. If not, your daughter is to be in his service for a time certain. And she shall return to her home every single night that she is in this man's service. She is to sleep there every night and return to your brewery each morning. Service shall not last more than two months depending upon the amount of the debt." Looking at Bimbola now he narrowed his eyes. "And no longer."

Jelani was no longer leaning against the wall. Standing in the back of the room, his jaw tightened and his eyes were full of anger. He could not miss the way his son's chest rose and fell as he watched. *Does he know this girl?* They were of an age. At any rate, it was nice to see him taking an interest in Nabara's affairs.

"Thank you, Your Grace." Bimbola bowed, taking the girl's elbow he moved her away from her father.

"Make sure you see the scribe before you go. He will record the guarantee. And the new agreement you reach today with the time certain." Bimbola started as he listened, but inclined his head respectfully as he left.

"He's not very pleased," Imani said next to him.

"No, he's not. It's quite possible he wants the girl for marriage and her father refuses. His advanced age an impediment, no doubt. But as the agreement will be recorded, I can make sure the vizier follows the matter. I want no tricks or excuses." Looking to the back of the room, he no longer saw Jelani. He sighed heavily. *My son will never learn if he continues to disappear and refuses to even concern himself with these affairs.*

"You dismantled a number of pawnship courts when I was younger. I still remember." Imani was looking at him with the unmistakable look of pride in her eyes.

"Audience has ended. You may state your claims in seven days. Go in peace."

Amkar watched as the Great Hall emptied save for Asim's Medjay and the Royal Guards. His scribe, treasurer, and vizier stayed knowing they had more to discuss. The Games were a week away, and his twin brothers, Semi and Yemi had gathered guards and soldiers, training them as well as dispatching some to scout the kingdom and make sure no further slavers from the shipwreck were in Nabara. No word had reached them in two days and precautions must be taken.

He leaned back, relaxing on the throne, one hand leaning on his *khepresh*. Placing his arms upon the armrest, he began. "In seven days the Games will commence, and we will host a great many noblemen, families, and spectators from throughout the kingdom. What preparations have been made to announce their arrival?"

Before the treasurer answered the Royal Guards opened the door to the Great Hall and his Queen walked through, her handmaiden, Jala, at her side.

"Husband, forgive me for missing audience." She was radiant. Her ivory robes were beautiful against her brown skin. Her *khat* hung down her shoulders, hair covered underneath it. It bore similarities to the khat of old, save the lack of the snake. His wife didn't need the adornment. He smiled.

"Just in time, my love." Rising to give her his hand as she climbed the steps to the dais he kissed her cheek. "How was your journey?"

"Long. Most of the families will arrive at sunset and will be greeted by Medjay. A spread will be prepared for the feast, two long-tables covered with Nabara's finest dishes and a serving girl for each. Houses have been cleared for the nobleman's use and their families. We have plenty of room for all." She turned to the Vizier. "Will the competition begin at the height of the first morning of the festival?"

He smiled. *Trust my Queen to ride for half a moon only to return ready for the next battle.*

"The first morning shall convene a meeting of the Council of Kings, Your Grace," the vizier replied. "Each member will list whom he has entered into the Games. A register will be prepared the night before, as council is merely a courtesy. The High Priests will give their blessing to each and conclude the business. The Council of Kings will meet at the conclusion of the Games to go over the business of the realm, new trade, boundaries, weapons, taxes, and more."

Nodding as the vizier finished, he waved him on. "And what of the substance of the Games? What new events have been added to this tradition?"

"The bow and arrow, the sword, the ropes course, and the maze. Of course the dancers of Nabara will perform and *Tahtib* combat will occur. The last day will feature the gifts and a surprise for the High King and Queen's family."

"The maze?" Imani interrupted, excitement in her voice. "What kind of maze?'

"You will see soon, Princess." The vizier chuckled, trying his best to hide his smile. "Your brother has seen to it that it is a challenge meant to test the bravery of the boldest men. And he told me not to tell you," he sighed regretfully.

"Jelani? Jelani's seen it and he didn't tell me?" she replied.

"Where is your brother? He should have been here this morning." Amkar turned to his daughter, eyes narrowed.

"I haven't seen him since audience ended. He was here throughout, Father." Imani bit her lip quickly before looking to her mother.

"I'll find him after our meeting. I know he's been working hard on preparations. He's never far from us." Samya put a hand on his arm.

Never far, but never where I expect him to be. How can he be expected to lead if he cannot first follow? Jelani's difficulty of late had not been lost on him, and he needed to speak with him about his whereabouts soon. Young men were so eager to lead, to be respected. But respect was earned. And one who shows no care for the trials of his kingdom will soon find himself without one.

"Vizier. Make sure the *kol* is finished before the games." The well needed to be ready by the next rainfall. "The Kalahari Desert is unforgiving, and the Festival of Kings will no doubt require that the reservoir provide water for many of our travelers."

The vizier nodded. "It is done, Your Grace."

"When the plans are finished, brief me before the arrival of the Nudollan kings. You all have much business to conclude. You are dismissed."

They rose in unison, save the queen and Imani, his beautiful, wild daughter. They made quite a pair sitting opposite one another. He shook his head as Imani stuck her tongue out at him like a lizard, the smile that came to her mouth puffing her cheeks up like a giraffe eating his fill.

"I trust you will ensure your daughter is ready for the festival, Samya?"

He watched the smile fall from Imani's face at his words.

"Of course. Your daughter is just as wild as you once were, Amkar-qo."

"Would that she took after her mother."

"Oh, but she does," Samya replied smiling.

"I'm sitting right here." Imani's eyes flickered with annoyance.

"Yes, you are. And you've also chosen to dress yourself in the style of Medjay. I know you don't intend to wear this during the festival. Who made this for you?" His eyes narrowed as he looked at her.

"A very skilled craftsman, Father. There is none like it in Nabara."

"You're not Medjay," he replied sharply. "You look part warrior."

"I *am* a warrior. Nabara is a Kushite kingdom. And the people of Kush are warriors. I know it would please them to see their princess dressed as such."

"Amkar-qo," his wife replied, touching his arm again. "The style suits her. It brings out her eyes, and she is right. She has the blood of a warrior. The people see their daughter as beautiful and fierce. They toast to her health every day. She may be young still, but all birds must one day leave the nest. Those that don't die young, weak, and afraid."

Clenching his jaw, he looked at them both. He wasn't sure what bothered him more. The fact that his daughter would have more suitors than he could kill at one time or that she was wild and sometimes refused to listen. *She is my blood. I can't deny it.* She would make a fierce queen one day. He was loath to part with her for some young, nubile devil thinking to break her into compliance.

"And any man who fears a woman is no man at all."

She even speaks like a king.

He pointed at her. "Imanishakheto, see to the festival. I'm sure Jamal requires assistance with some of the details for the harvest. It's almost dark, so be careful."

Imani's head snapped up in surprise. He'd told her not to leave the palace walls, and her sentence was not yet up. Still, she jumped from her chair quickly, hair flying as she kissed his cheek and flew down the stairs. Wincing as he watched her go, he shook his head. The way she ran she was like to break her neck on the dais one day.

Extending his arm to Samya they rose from the hall, the fading sun at their backs as they walked back to their chambers.

"This could be a disaster."

Laughing softly Samya tilted her head and pressed it against his gently. "My love, she's young and full of spirit. She means well, I'm sure. Besides, none can resist her beauty. Half the kingdom is in love with her on that alone. And everyone in Nabara speaks well of her generosity. The orphans at the temples are mesmerized by her and beg her to stay. And the young men—"

"Will be castrated should they look at her the wrong way."

"Amkar," she began again, holding back her smile. "Many young men were in love with me when we first met. Our courtship lasted three years. It torments me that you did not keep that same promise when we wed."

Frowning as they reached their bedchamber, he nodded to the guards as they pushed open the stone door, raising their fists to their hearts and bowing their heads slightly as they closed it behind him.

"Must you test my patience?" he replied, holding her against the back of the closed door.

She gasped slightly as he did before the corner of her mouth broke into a soft grin. "It's not your patience I wish to test, Arkamani-qo."

"No?" Lowering his head towards her neck, he brushed his lips against her skin as she sighed.

"No. I have no use for your patience. Don't start what you aren't able to finish." She placed her palms flat against his chest. "What news from Tharbis? And the Floating City?" Her eyebrows knit together as she questioned him.

"They will attend. As will the Kingdom of the Sao. I fear for the old man's safety during travel. King Kwasi has seen too many harvests."

"He has a son. He will come too, will he not?"

He sighed. "A nephew. But I fear Komoro is not half the man his uncle is. He's young, ambitious, and undisciplined. I must speak with Kwasi, but temper my words. His hopes do not align with my beliefs on this union."

"He still believes Komoro will wed Imani? She'll never have him if he is what you say."

"We shall see. Ama may be a match. Time may have changed him."

"I've had word from Bamanirenas. Her family will attend the games. They are of noble blood."

"And the swordfish?" he asked, one eyebrow raised.

"The Essi build ships, command and train fleet crews. Saltwater runs in their blood. Who better to treat with our daughter? And King Tharbis of the Scorpion Kingdom will attend. With all of his sons. I would sooner invite the Romans to attend."

The chamber echoed with his laughter. "Samya, be serious."

"I am. The man is a different story from his children. Five boys, and not one to speak well of? A son is meant to be a blessing upon the family, not a reign of terror upon all whom cross his path. And what of his sixth wife? I hear rumors of which I know not what to make. He is too lenient with them."

"And it is too late to advise him on that matter. They are well grown."

"And a beating at any age will put sense into a person. I could arrange—"

"Stop!" Amkar shook his head, laughing at her outrageousness. "The slavers still raid outlying villages, Samya. And these slavers they speak of will cause problems we don't yet know of. We have more than a few bad sons to worry about just now."

"I know. I warned the !Kung and a number of other outlying Nomadin. All of the chiefs were willing to listen, but I'm afraid they believe their position is one of safety." Her face filled with concern.

Amkar nodded. "They confuse the difficulty of reaching their location in the interior with safety."

"Yes. I warned them that nomads coming by camel and by foot had begun to lead others further into the interior. I'm not sure they listened, but many promised to attend the Festival of Kings. And all accepted our gifts."

He kissed her hand. "Of course they did."

"Has Nema responded to your message?

His oldest daughter would be here before long. Her small family had begun the journey a few days ago. "Not yet. We should hear something by the morning."

IMANI

Her right leg swung back and forth from where it hung over the edge of the massive arm of the statue of Apedemak, the lion-headed, warrior god of Kush. His sandstone image was over thirty feet tall, sitting opposite the goddess Sekhmet, his equal in war, and sought for her powers of healing and life. The High Priest's lessons had run much longer than usual today. Ten of them had marched into the pavilion at dawn, armed with scrolls as though they were prepared to go to war, using only their knowledge of what lay within as their weapons. She hadn't minded the rapid-fire questions they asked of her on the new iron technology being used for the soldiers and archers of Nabara. Nor had she minded their lesson on the foundation of gold processing which allowed an increase in trade and sale to the artisans. Nor had she shied from the hour-long practice of the Greek and Igbo tongue. It was the sounds of the city that kept trying to steal her attention away. Like the beauty of the moon still trying to compete for a flower's love as the burning rays of the sun cut through the night like a sword. The Festival of Kings was upon them. Hoards of cattle were being decorated just outside the palace walls, their mooing a gentle rhythm in the calm of mid-morning. The horses had been fed and let out to roam free, only half of them painted as of yet. Even from her perch there was no mistaking the black bodies and ivory legs of the Kushite stallions as they pranced and galloped through the grasses. There was no need to worry that they wouldn't return. Treated as precious treasures by the owners, nobility, and royalty alike, they always did. Traders would come from far away to purchase them. She would see to her own soon.

Chisels and axes fell rapidly over and over, the sharp *clink clink* of the metal sounding repeatedly. The workers seemed not to have rested as they ground away at the replica of her father, a gift from the people of Nabara. Jelani had told her that a small number from Exile Island were rumored to be working to complete the sculpture. *What was the purpose of Exile if you were allowed to return?* he'd asked her, laughing. Smiling as she remembered his playfulness, she inhaled deeply before exhaling, leaning her head back against Apedemak's stone waist. Even the air itself was alive, the sweet smell of fresh lotus flowers lingering in her nose were mixed with cinnamon and honey.

Looking back down at the papyri she held she realized how much the physiology of the body interested her. The priests were masters in the art of healing, but even they were believers in the body's ability to heal itself through proper diet and care. The embalming of the dead child from the Roman slave ship haunted her. *He could have been my little brother.* After a moment she realized a horn was sounding and looked up. The black and gold colors of her brother-by-law's kingdom rose from beyond the valley. *Nema!* Her sister had arrived! *She's so early. Why didn't they tell me she was coming this early?*

Grateful for the one-piece, ivory harem pants she wore, she gently pulled the leather top of them up her chest slightly before climbing down the sandstone, the balls of her feet slipping inside any curve she could find as her bare arms skidded against the side. Jumping the rest of the way she reached for the sheer overlay she had left on the ground, shaking the sand from it before slipping it up her arms and over her shoulders.

"Really?" Ama asked, a deep edge of disbelief in her voice.

Imani turned around quickly, cheeks warming as she continued to dust herself off. Ama wore a white sheath with her hair in a long braid down her back, her hair covered by a thin gold crown circling the top of her head. Kohl ran down her eyelids and into the crease of her eyes, perfectly applied.

"I'm ready!" Imani assured her. "Don't worry."

Her cousin stepped forward and placed a crown on Imani's head, the golden crown fitted with a lion crest containing one sparkling diamond in the center. Running down the palace halls as quickly as they could, the Royal Guards laughed as they sped by. They only slowed when they reached the Great Hall. Ama grabbed her arm suddenly, reaching for the top of her head. Her crown dangled precariously, having slid to one side in her haste. She fixed it, smiling before the guards pulled the doors open for them.

She's more beautiful than ever. Imani rushed to her sister, throwing herself in her arms. Nema hugged her close while Imani greedily inhaled the scent of her sister's perfume. *She smells of jasmine.* The scent filled her nose and made her smile at the familiar notes.

Nema had been greatly loved by the people as firstborn. As a child she had been reckless, and had even been caught stealing from the market on occasion. When the High King learned of it, he had Nema brought directly to him and forced her to endure the *Kenbet's* sentence. Imani remembered how Nema's head remained bowed, looking at the floor. She'd been so surprised her sister had stolen something and was in awe of her older sister's audacity. Her mother had been relieved her oldest daughter was finally married off; as wild as she'd been, Nema could always make her father laugh, and had his gift for words as well. *Pity she's such a bore now*, Imani thought, grinning. And seemed to have conveniently forgotten any of her errors as a child.

Her dark brown hair held looser curls than Imani's. A slim nose and high cheekbones identical to their mother's adorned her face. A complete contrast to Imani's pug, lion-like nose with a tiny dent just between it and her lips. Nema always teased her that she looked like a lion with her large eyes and wide mouth. Nema's skin was a light brown, only highlighted more so by the gold and black gown she wore on her petite frame to represent her husband's house. Her sister had filled out some, and had womanly hips. Two rows of perfect white teeth were smiling at her.

"Little sister, how you've grown," Nema said, leaning back to look at her. "You are stunning."

"Cousin!" Ama moved forward smiling and Nema opened her arms to take Ama in, running a hand over the smooth braid atop Ama's head.

"Aren't you a pretty picture?" Jelani smiled as he hugged Ama. Ama blushed furiously, closing her eyes as her brother squeezed her tightly, holding their cousin against his bare chest. When he released her Ama seemed positively breathless, staring up at him in adoration. She had always wondered if her cousin favored Jelani, but Ama had always denied it.

"Where's Noli?" Imani asked. "I don't hear him." Noli was always underfoot. He was a wild thing, a mountain dog generally used for herding. Imani loved him.

"Underfoot, I suspect, or sniffing his way to the kitchens." Her sister shrugged.

"You mean licking his way there," she laughed. He was always hungry. "Keep him away from Little Terror!"

She looked up when her father walked in.

"You gave no word you'd be arriving today." Her father was pleased. "Where is your husband? Has Yuri sent you alone?"

"Here, father," Yuri answered from his seat, standing to greet his father by law. They embraced before her father placed his hand on Yuri's shoulder, looking at him with pride.

"You look well," her father told him.

Imani knew her father regarded his son-in-law in high esteem. Yuri was intelligent and treated Nema well. His skin was the color of desert sand, much lighter than Nema's, and his hair, when not cut short, had loose curls. He was tall, and his deep booming voice held a ring of authority. His hands were soft, though he worked hard. As prince of the Sotho, he stood to inherit the kingdom from his father. Their caves held diamonds and coal, which kept them warm during the winters.

After a moment, Yuri smiled at Imani, embracing her tightly.

When she released him, the sound of high-pitched laughter met her ears. Her mother was coming from the balcony with Imani's nephew, Tamayis, on her hip and one of her fingers gently tapping his nose. His golden head was covered with a fine set of dark brown curls. With eyes as large as eggs, he'd stolen their heart.

"Will you let no one else hold him?" Imani mocked, laughing at the dirty look her mother gave her before turning back to Tamayis, who was now focused solely on trying to bite his grandmother's finger. A moment later he knocked her bracelet loose and watched the gold jewel fall towards the ground.

"How is my little Destroyer?" she asked her nephew, walking over to where her mother held him and tickling Tamayis's feet, capturing his fingers in her mouth as he giggled. Picking up her mother's bracelet she reattached it before pinching Tamayis's exposed belly softly.

Behind her she heard a sigh. "You always have a new name for him every time you see him. He'll never remember them," her sister admonished.

160

"Of course he won't. But all of them make sense. He has a different personality every time I see him." Imani tickled his stomach to his laughter before turning expectantly to her father.

"Come." Her father motioned for them to follow. "We have much to discuss. The Festival of Kings will begin in two days and we must be ready. I would speak with you before our guests arrive."

"Of course, Father," Nema said softly.

They walked to their litter, headed towards the eastern *Deffufa* that sat at the northeast edge of the city closer to the River Nub. Construction on the *Deffufa* had begun five months after she was born. Her father had tasked the royal architects with building the structure in celebration of their two girls, their births two years apart. Their closeness was a symbol of pride, a healthy queen, and a good omen bestowed upon the Kushite Kingdom of Nabara. Imani could see its high, mud-brick walls even as they left the palace. Its profile was that of a lion resting on its stomach, its carved eyes open and alert. Years ago the chief architect had placed large gold stones in the middle of the eyes to make them lifelike. Now, they shone in the morning sun, and as always, the lion's eyes appeared to be moving on their own, watching over Nabara from its perch. A close boundary wall over ten feet high surrounded its base, and it was this that they entered now, the *Deffufa* guards pushing on the doors to allow them entry. The litter moved forward, passing under the jutting mouth of the lion, its shadow created from the sun shining over more than three stories, putting them in the shade.

Two life-size pillars of her mother and father sat on either side of the entrance as they walked inside. Nema spoke quietly with her mother and father, her mother cupping her face briefly as Yuri walked behind them quietly, one hand sitting on her father's shoulder with affection. It was rare they were able to see their oldest daughter in the months since their grandson was born, but whenever Nema needed them they would make the journey.

Imani's head turned left and right as she looked at the walls of the long hallway on either side of her. A mixture of black, red, blue, and yellow, the colored engravings painted a picture and told stories of Nudolla, some of which she was familiar with herself.

Even here, the cattle of kings were prominent on the wall, their elephantine, u-shaped horns unambiguous and distinct to their kind. As descendants of Nubia and Kush, Nabara had attempted to record their ancient lineage so as not to forget it. The Kingmaker had been right though, much of their history was oral, an ancient tradition that flowed through the memories of the *jeli*. Imani touched an engraving on the right side of the wall featuring an old man standing in front of a massive crowd with two symbols above him. *May you live a thousand years.* A blessing spoken to royalty and *jeli's* alike. A blessing that touched on the importance of educating the next generation and making sure that one's family success, beliefs, histories, victories, and secrets of their civilization were passed to their children.

The wall behind her held the scene of a great battle for Meroë. The former Kushite Queen Amanishakheto for whom she was named stood in the center, twice the size of the soldiers depicted around her, a bow and arrow in her hands. Her rule began in 10 B.C. at a time of peace, brought about after a five-year war that ended when her predecessor, Queen Amanirenas, successfully brokered a peace treaty with Rome in which they agreed not to attempt any further invasions of Nubia. She was a warrior and a great builder, commissioning a number of pyramids along the Nile. However, Rome broke the agreement, and Kandake Amanishakheto led her soldiers against those of Augustus, beating back his forces yet again in a humiliating defeat.

"Imani?" her sister was looking back at her. Hurrying to catch up she walked quickly into the center chamber. Stelae dedicated to her grandfather and her earliest ancestors lay in the lower chambers, but they would not go there today.

Moving upwards until they stood at the top, Imani shielded her eyes momentarily from the morning sun. They stood on the lion's shoulders now; the back of his head had been carved into a half circle pavilion, like a bowl on its side, the opening facing the tail and overlooking the city.

Her Uncle Yemi, Uncle Semi, and Jelani rose from the steps as her father waited for them.

"It's not often that I have all of you here, together as today," he told them. He turned to face the city, holding his arms out as he

162

stood. "One day, you will rule over all you see and more. Together, alone…only time will tell. People will come from outlying lands to seek your guidance, advice, alliance, and help. A good leader will listen to each one, in turn and with objectivity. You must be a servant to the people. You are here to serve them, to make them better, to bring growth and progress while remembering our traditions. But these choices are your own."

"There are things which your mother and I cannot tell you as yet, but trust me when I say, our only thoughts are of keeping you and the people of the city safe. I am so very proud of all of you. Always remember that."

Jelani's eyes narrowed across from her. Her uncles nodded at her father, their eyes slightly curious. Father rarely expressed his affection. It worried her.

"Father, is everything all right? Does this have to do with the slavers?" She couldn't help voicing what was on all of their minds. She always asked the tough questions. Even one elephant in the room was far too many.

"Some," he nodded. "I sent Medjay to patrol our territories and have tasked Shaharqa with ensuring the reinforcement of our watchtowers near Torrent. The Mountains of Apedemak are a great barrier between Torrent and the kingdom but they are not impassable. Your mother has already taken it upon herself to visit neighboring nations and chiefs. A number of our allies in the kingdom are already aware of this threat. Even at audience there is a hint of the trade."

"You think the stolen cattle may not be the work of the !Kung but of the slavers? Is this also to do with the slave ship?" Her curiosity was peaked. The Khoekhoe woman had been so sure to the point of defiance.

"It's possible. Pawnship is an ancient custom for some, but its tenets are loose and changing. The chiefs decide many of the disputes, though the rules and requirements are left to parties. Kinship ties secure any pawnship agreement and protect those seized from harm. The slavers have no such ties and adhere to no such rules. They are lawless, greedy, and immoral. And as for the masters of the slave ship, they have not yet felt our wrath, but they will. Our trade routes over land are also becoming more dangerous. Raiders have found it prosperous and I mean to end it."

"Father, how can we help?" Nema held Tamayis close, her eyes full of worry.

"Is there anything we can do?" Yuri asked. "How safe are the trade routes north? On my father's borders, we often trade on the coast. It may be worthwhile to determine the danger of the seas." Yuri was at the edge of his seat now, hands clasped in front of him.

"For now, I have ordered extra guards on trade routes as a precaution. I know of no other threat this far south, but no one will ever regret being prepared. Keeping our distance and being hidden behind the danger of the shores, mountains, and vast desert is to our advantage. But when you aren't able to stay hidden, the best place to hide is in plain sight. What do you see just beyond the city, Imani?" Her father waited patiently for a response.

"Mountains," she looked towards them as she answered.

"Pyramids." He corrected her.

"But we have pyramids all along the River Nub." Imani's eyebrows knit together as she turned to look at her mother.

"Pyramids," her father confirmed as he looked at them all. "In plain sight. Some of those mountains hide the most valuable stones you will ever see."

Her mother continued, "Stelae, art, sculptures, pottery, and even burial chambers. All in plain sight. Some of them were built and then covered with sand or dirt and spread with seeds of shrubs and flowers and trees. Too often our ancestors history was erased because it was easy to find, steal, ransack. So we hid it in plain sight. The mountain. Others we dug tunnels into, fortified and erected them inside. It is what we leave behind when we are gone. Things even the *jeli* may forget. We may wish it every day, but I have never met one who has lived a thousand years."

"Do you understand?" Her father was looking at them now.

"I understand brother, but," Yemi started.

"I just can't believe it," Semi finished, both of them looking towards the mountains, eyes squinted as they raised their hands to shield them from the sun.

"Is it so hard to believe? The Kushite pharaoh's of Kemet's twenty-fifth dynasty reignited the construction of pyramids. Nubia's High Kings passed that knowledge down and improved it.

Even now hundreds of pyramids lay near Meroë with underground chambers that rivaled Kemet's treasures. Kemet may be the province of Rome now, but it wasn't always. Their *Egypt* was once called Kemet, ruled by a thriving dynasty of pharaohs. Your ancestors. One day I'll show you all. Our pyramids along the River Nub are identical to those in Meroë, and hidden ones are heavily stocked with food and weapons. A fortress in a mountain."

Imani smiled at Nema and Yuri. Even Jelani was impressed and couldn't hide his excitement.

Yuri nodded as he took Nema's hand.

"Children," her mother was looking at all of them, her face calm and reassuring. "Go, enjoy yourselves. We will see you this evening to walk through the market for the Festival of Kings. It has grown quite a bit since you saw it last, Nema. Your father and I will discuss more with you then."

Why wouldn't they discuss it now? The market could wait as far as she was concerned, but they all rose and rode back to the palace in their litter. Nema spoke excitedly about Tamayis's first words while Imani sat silent, thinking on what she'd learned. When she felt fingers against her wrist, she turned, looking up at Jelani as he met her eyes, slipping her hand into his. He was thinking the same things she was. They needed answers her father wasn't yet willing to give.

Jumping from the litter before it came to a stop, her cape floated behind her as she moved up the steps. Something else was at the back of her memory, but she couldn't recall what it was. The archives would be the perfect place to search, but then she could also visit...*the scribe!* Trying to slow herself from running down the halls, she moved quickly, her mind racing. When she reached the scribe's chambers, she pushed the door open. He didn't always sleep here, but copies of his records were here, and she'd been here enough to know how they were organized. He was as meticulous as a squirrel storing food for the winter. Every scroll had its place, and his memory was excellent when he needed to recall information. She found the date she wanted and unrolled the papyrus.

One gold cup. With a gladiator engraved on the bottom. She'd once thought it to be a warrior, but she knew now that wasn't the case. *Who had the audacity to gift this?* And how would she find them? It had been part of a number of gifts to the High King on his birthday, carefully recorded. And the inside had been in the shape of a coliseum. Turning towards the door, Imani rolled the papyrus closed.

When she reached her chambers, she went immediately to the cube shaped alabaster chest in the corner of the room, kneeling in front of it as she ran her hands over the lid. Painted a dark gold, each side featured scenes of Kush in Nabara. From left to right cattle of kings were featured grazing, their horns decorated beautifully. Another depicted a series of nine portraits, each woman in varying shades and differing hairstyles such as knots, closely braided rows, locs, twists, and more. The third side featured a leopard and a lion facing off, both mouths open wide, teeth bared. On the fourth was a pyramid, the symbol of strength. Removing the flat lid, she placed it on the floor. Inside were some of her most treasured possessions. A story of Meroë in a series of tiny pictures, gifted by her parents and written on a slim stela the size of her hand. Lines of Meroitic script sat along the outer edges. A map depicted on papyrus drawn by her. The second created by the architects of the pyramids. Her mother's combs. She'd loved to comb her mother's hair as a child rather than have her own done. It had made her mother laugh, but she often acquiesced. Her father's thumb ring to his oldest bow and her sister's letters were bundled tightly together at the bottom.

It was the second map she pulled out now, trying to remember the last time it had been revised. There were thousands of maps in their archives, and her father kept hundreds of maps in his royal vault where he retreated to go over his plans for the empire. Once he had shown her a map from the twentieth dynasty of Kemet. It was a copy, he told her, of a map created by a scribe serving Heqamaatre Ramesses IV, the third pharaoh of the twentieth dynasty. The map was made of papyrus, light brown and containing hieratic script in the upper-right corner. She could still remember tracing the letters with her fingers. *Here*, he'd said, *is the valley*, pointing to the middle of the map and moving his finger in a horizontal line to the other side. *These*, he'd continued, *are the surrounding hills, quarries, and the gold mine along with notations indicating the locations of other gold deposits in the surrounding mountains.* The papyrus was colored pink and black in order to denote the types of stones recovered from the hill deposits, detailing the sizes of the stones and the distance between the stone quarry and the gold mine. *You'll never be lost without one,* he'd warned her, *but your mind, your ability to remember in your head, is even more important.*

Her tutor had explained the importance of maps such as these. The Romans had used what they found to steal resources before inviting the Noubadian into Roman territory. It was a false friendship. One only meant to aid them in ridding themselves of the nomadic families in the area and use them as a buffer to the Kingdom of Kush. When the Ethiopian King Ezana had risen to power, Rome had turned a blind eye to the Noubadians, their supporters. It was to Rome's advantage not to provide aid. What better way to ensure a willing and docile trading partner than to invite your enemy in and use another to wipe them out? Her uncle told her as much during training. *Letting your neighbors kill one another was as good a war plan as any,* he often said. He worried as much as her father about Meroë's position. It was precarious.

Biting her lip, she looked back down at the papyrus map, tracing one finger along the coast. *If the trade routes are affected, that would mean food as well. But what better way to grab luxuries and resources if not by ambushing caravans along the roads?* And making those along it slaves. *Slavers couldn't make the journey without help.* Not in the interior. Kiberans were notorious for their reclusiveness, keeping to their jungle territories like whales in water. *They had to have someone who traveled by both.*

"Imani!"

Nema was calling her.

"Imani, we're going to the market!"

She'd have to meet them there.

It took her some time to put things back in place, but when she did, she knew there was more she'd need to learn. Like who'd given the gift and where he'd received it. *Who is trading and selling Roman goods so far south? And which kingdom with access to the interior and the high sea would risk so much by befriending slavers? Without becoming slaves themselves.*

She walked from the palace with her escort, sliding into the chariot and nodding for its departure. It took off for the market located not far from the River Nub, at the border of Nabara and the Kingdom of Bones, the black horse decorated in a headdress that billowed out behind him as they rode. She found her family near the boat makers, the river craft stacked in high piles on the ground. Banana shaped carriers carefully crafted from papyrus reeds growing near the water. The reeds grew tall and long, bright green stalks in massive quantities that were regularly cut to make the boats. The most recently made ones were still green, the others now firm and dried from the sun, a cream and yellow color all the way around. And they were popular with fishermen. Even a child could create smaller, simpler boats from the reeds if he was willing and patient. Imani smiled remembering how Nema and she had done just that as children, getting lost before their father came and found them himself, the guards pulling them from the water. Even now the River Nub with its golden tinted reeds was populated with women cleaning their skins and rugs in the river. Beating the dust from them before letting them soak in the waters while their children played near them, splashing sounds ringing out close to the river's edge.

Her father was speaking with a goat herder who was offering samples of the milk, cheese, and meat his goats produced. The baby goats were being picked up and petted by many of the children. Their dark copper coats were so clean they shone. *He's an excellent trader,* Imani thought. The children would force their parents to stop and wait, giving the merchant time to speak with them and offer them refreshment in the heat. He knew exactly what each of his patrons valued most.

"The season has been kind to us, Your Grace. Some of our land is still healthy, green. Enough for our goats to eat. Your contribution was a prayer answered."

"Please, it was nothing. I would like you to send…"

Imani turned in time to see her mother lightly kiss each cheek of the woman standing in front of her in greeting. She was a popular artisan, and both of her forearms were covered in black henna. Even Nema stood next to her in awe, bent over beautifully composed designs spiraling around her wrists, admiring her work.

Nema looked up, motioning for Imani to join her.

First gowns, now this, she thought, her frown deepening.

"It's tradition. Don't let mother see your face like that." Nema swatted her gently.

"Yes," her mother was saying, "she loves to read, but I don't want writing on her arm. Besides, the *Book of the Coming Forth by Day* will not fit. It must be a design." She took Imani's face in her hands and turned it from side to side. "On her back, neck, and arms I think. Her sister will make sure she's here tomorrow night." Nema was grinning at her mother with excitement that Imani did not share.

"Imani!" a voice called. Now it was Imani's turn to smile. Her close friend had appeared from behind the shade, grinning at her, her hands decorated with henna. She looked radiant, her black hair in three thick scalp braids that ran down her back.

"Sanaa." Hugging her friend tightly, she kissed both cheeks before pulling back to look at her. "You look lovely."

"And you in…something close to a gown!" Sanaa teased her, laughing at the expression on her face.

"What were you doing back there?" Imani nodded to where she had come from.

"A bride is to be married tomorrow. I've started her designs for her, but I heard your voice." Sanaa pinched her and grinned again, gesturing to the Medjay surrounding the henna stands like a wall. "And here you are, scaring away patrons," she teased, pointing just behind her. Imani followed her finger, looking past her Medjay to the other side of the market. She smiled when her eyes found a young family with children standing in the shade of a mango merchant. Two boys hid shyly behind their mother as a young girl of no more than five beamed back at Imani, holding her father's hand. Lifting a hand, Imani waved gently, a smile on her face as she did. Their reactions were priceless. All three children gasped in shock before looking up towards their parents, squealing in amazement.

"See?" Sanaa's voice made her turn back.

"I'll be with your mother soon, the night before the festival. The bride's family was close to my mother's as a child in Makouria," Imani replied.

The surprise on her face made Imani smile. "With all of us? I can't wait to paint you!"

"Please, stop. How am I supposed to do anything without getting the henna everywhere?"

"It *dries,* Imani. It is the smoking that will probably annoy you most. But how else to set it!" She looked over at her mother quickly, her voice dropping to a whisper. "Did I tell you Tuma had an accident? He broke his arm lifting the slab for the stele he made for his brother. The mother's of the village helped pay for his recovery."

"I'm sorry to hear that."

"*He's* not! Tuma asked about you." Imani's eyes widened as she tried to free her arm from Sanaa who was laughing now. "He wanted to know when I would see you again so he could be there. He thought you might have more sympathy for him if he was wounded. *Battle scars,* you know?"

Shaking her head, she freed her arm, kissing her friend on each cheek. "Tomorrow," she said, giving her a pointed look before walking away.

"Say hello to your brother for me, Imani-qa!" she whispered as Imani laughed, walking towards her family.

Jelani wrapped his arm around her shoulders. "Did she ask you about Tuma again?"

She blushed. "Yes," she told him as they walked to the edge of the market. "And she told me to tell *you* hello," she smirked, as Jelani averted his eyes quickly.

Sliding her arm inside of her brother's, she leaned against him as they continued on. At the sound of a trumpet, she looked to her left and Jelani stopped with her. One of the merchants led a large bush elephant, a light stick broom tapping gently in front of him as his right hand rested against the animal's side. A moment later a line of children and parents stepped onto the stacked block at the elephant's side, grasping tightly to the rope as they seated themselves on the rug spread across the giant's back. When ten were aboard, the merchant's assistant held the others back as those on the ground looked on with disappointment at having to wait their turn. Another trumpet sounded, and the grey king of the bush began to move, following slowly behind his human friend, trunk wrapped around the branch the merchant held as he fed it bark, nara, and other fruits in the basket dangling from his arm as a child skipped along next to him. The elephant flapped its grey ears like some great flightless bird as it walked, its enormous curved ivory tusks scooping towards the ground and rising upwards again. His riders pointed and waved from their seats-the small ones anyway. Some of the parents gripped their children uncertainly, knees pressed tightly to the animals hide. *That's one way to travel.*

Jelani trumpeted at her to get her attention and she smiled, allowing him to pull her along, noting the wandering eyes of the women as they cast their hopeful eyes at him in excitement.

"Stop!"

"Ooof!"

"Princess!"

Stumbling against Jelani, he caught her to keep her from falling as she looked down to see what had slammed into the backs of her legs. A girl lay flat on her back, trying to sit up, tight brown curls with a red sun-colored streak on the right side covering her face as she shook her head, dazed from her fall. She was no more than eleven. The shift she wore was a smaller fit than she needed, rising past her knees. Her skin was riddled with fresh pink cuts and bruises. And some old ones.

"Princess," her Medjay guards walked toward the child, *khopesh* drawn.

"I'm fine," she told them. Jelani looked down at the girl, frowning in sympathy.

"Are you alright?" She reached down for the child, brushing sand from her arms with her palm as the girl looked up at her with wide eyes, mouth slack as Imani and Jelani pulled her to her feet.

"Stop!"

The girl gasped and bent towards the ground. Jelani made a sound behind her as the child picked up nara fruit and what smelled like cinnamon plantains wrapped in linen.

"Stop her!" The city soldiers sprinted towards the girl, and she took off down the market towards the blacksmiths.

Jelani laughed as the soldiers came towards them, stopping in front of them and their Medjay escort.

"Leave her!" Imani commanded. "I think she's too fast for you anyway. We'll pay the debt." The soldiers nodded, bowing as Jelani held out five gold coins and dropped them into their palm.

"Prince Jelani, Princess," the soldiers nodded and turned back the way they had come. The people at the market were smiling around them, bowing gently as they passed.

"She thought you were going to turn her in!" Jelani laughed when they were out of earshot.

"She was just a child. And probably hungry." Imani felt heat rising at her neck.

"The nara merchant will be pleased," he teased.

A while later both of them stopped to observe a silent trade, the Royal Guards standing at a distance, alert. An ankole-watusi was being sold, lying on the ground next to a tall man carrying a spear, the cattle's horns almost as tall as him. The owner stood on an elevated platform, surrounded by a number of men on stone seats sitting with tables in front of them, each holding their preferred choice of payment. One had a small stack of salt bars on the mat, each one as thick as his wrist and the length of his hand. Another sat behind a large quantity of cowrie shell necklaces. A third was placing a tenth sickle on his mat, each of the blades curving out from the handle in the shape of a crescent moon or ear. The man to her left was sprinkling the small pieces of gold onto a small mound, another man standing behind him. All of the men noticed their approach and turned, nodding in respect, smiling, before turning back to the trade. It might take an hour before the cattle sold, but the silent trade was a way for each trader to avoid misunderstandings and bypass problems caused by any language barriers from those who came from distant lands. For them, going to the market was a much more rare occurrence given the journey.

"Which will he choose, do you think?" Jelani asked her.

"Everyone has something they value." Their father stood next to them, Medjay a pace behind. "And they pay well for it."

"You mean something they desire." Jelani looked at their father.

"Desire can be another word for it."

"Then it's better to make sure you don't put such a high value on such things." Imani turned back to the auction.

"It would be. If it were possible." Her father's eyes moved over the sale.

Exchanging a look with her brother, they both waited for their father to continue. "To a man begging for mercy, his life is the most valuable thing to him. To a man lost in the desert, water."

Jelani considered, "So desire is temporary and so might be the value you put on it."

"For the same man might continue eating to excess, stealing, putting his life at risk despite being granted mercy," their father replied. "And as soon as a lost wanderer finds water, his priorities change."

"Value depends on your present condition and your future desires then?" Imani was intent on getting to the answer.

Her father looked at her, his crown shining in the falling sunlight. "And everyone places a different value on certain things. Cattle, jewels, water." He turned to her brother. "A bride price." Jelani blushed, and Imani knew he was wondering if their father meant to bring up a discussion about his marriage.

"There are always hidden costs in a trade. Your wife may be barren. The cattle male, and unable to reproduce. You must always beware of hidden costs in everything you do in life. Know the cost, avoid the risks."

"No one can know everything." Her eyebrows knit together as she looked at her father.

"No. But at least you have a sense of your position, and hopefully theirs."

Imani turned back to the silent trade, observing the men a moment longer. The owner hadn't spoken a word, but his scarification told her he was counted among the nomadic families in the desert. Possibly similar to the cattle herders of the Nile. Cultures such as these rarely did away with cows and even more rarely used them for their meat. "He'll take the salt. The seller is from deep in the desert. A hunter. They might be able to find freshwater in certain lakes, but salt is likely in short supply and needed to preserve their meat as they move. The buyer has plenty of salt, but likely doesn't keep as many cattle. He could be part of a salt caravan or an independent who receives salt as his wages. He sells the salt and buys the cattle to take home for slaughter," Imani said, her eyes never leaving the silent trade, her voice low.

As they watched, the owner stepped off the platform and handed the ends of the rope around the cattle to the salt merchant. The salt merchant stood immediately and walked away with the cattle, leaving the salt bars behind. The other merchants rose almost simultaneously, gathering their offerings. The hunter bundled the salt bars together and placed them in a leather bag, secured it tightly with a rope, and left with the owner.

She and Jelani followed their father, walking with Medjay close behind as the people bowed as they passed. Children waved every so often, smiles lighting their eyes. It made her smile to see them giggling as they ran from Medjay, pretend vanquishers in their games.

"Father," Jelani continued, looking straight ahead as he spoke. "Doesn't the threat posed by pawnship concern you?"

"The form of your question assumes the answer. Do you believe it does not?"

"I only meant…do you believe it threatens a return to slavery in Nudolla?" Jelani tried again.

"I do. But you already know that."

"Is there a way to prevent pawnship from taking hold in Nabara?" Jelani pressed.

"Pawnship is illegal in Nabara. Is there someone you are concerned about?" her father asked instead, his face calm.

She couldn't help sneaking glances at both of them, eyes widening as she listened to their conversation.

"Of course not," her brother said quickly.

Is he blushing? She was incredulous.

Her brother's lips pressed together as though his secret might speak for itself. After a pause he continued, "I only meant…I see the benefit of attending audience to listen to the petitions of the people and learn of the matters that affect the land and the courts. Today reminded me that debt often poses a risk for the borrower he may regret. I only hope there is a way to mitigate it. Shouldn't there be a way to keep the borrower safe?"

"One cannot prevent a fool from entering a contract he knows he ought not. Especially an oral one. Even the High Priests demand written proof in lieu of witnesses at *Kenbet*. Is it your belief that one should feel only for the borrower and not the one providing the loan who also lost a sum to support him?" Father never missed a chance to answer a question with a question.

"I never thought of it like that." Jelani crossed his arms over his chest.

"If you become High King one day, you must think of all of your people. Favoring one over the other out of pity is a dangerous thing. Your people's considerations must become your own. What effects one will affect all. It is as the concept of ma'at. Ma'at lies in everything we do. Justice and order. It is the natural order of things. It is a balance that guides our lives as people of Kush and Nubia. There can be no peace without justice." Turning slightly as they strolled, a train of young scribes approached, bowing quickly and waiting for them to pass, each holding stelae in their hands before moving on their way.

"Every leader is but a servant to the people and must act as such. As will you one day. You have always been bright and honorable. You are much smarter than I was at your age, I have no doubt." Her father's eyes shone with rare pride as he continued on. "Perhaps we should speak about pawnship together? Think about new ways to meet the threat if it concerns you?"

The surprise on Jelani's face was palpable. Straightening even more, he lifted his chin higher, shoulders rolling back as he nodded to their father. "I would like that."

"Is there anything else on your mind?" The corners of her father's mouth rose slightly as he stroked his beard.

"The High Priests," Jelani answered without hesitation. "What hidden costs do the High Priests pose, Father? What of the King's law?" Jelani stopped and turned to meet his father's eyes.

Their father's smile fell as he looked at Jelani. "We'll talk about that later. For now, let me worry about the High Priests. The court and I will work matters out on our own."

Jelani pursed his lips but said no more. Cheeks tightening as his jaw clenched, fists tightening and releasing.

Their father continued walking and they followed on either side of him, his hands crossed behind his back. "Often made, often broken. I'm stronger than rope, but I do not bend. Forget me, and you will regret my creation. What am I?"

Pondering the riddle only took her a moment. "A promise."

After a moment he turned and winked at her. "I am. And I expect both of you to keep yours," he replied, stopping a moment to look into her and Jelani's eyes. Jelani's jaw tightened, but he nodded all the same.

"Of course, Father," her brother said.

"I will." She swallowed as she wondered at his heavy words.

Walking back to the litter, she couldn't help but wonder at her brother's demeanor and the unanswered question that picked at her mind. *She knew the King's law as well as anyone; a king must provide justice and order in adherence with ma'at. A king must have an heir. If he fails in this, he may be dethroned by the High Priests, challenged by another kingdom, or forced to suicide.* Were the High Priest's planning on enforcing the King's law? Why would they? The people loved her father. Many of Nabara's ancient traditions came from the concept of ma'at. Though they followed their ancestors of the Kushite Kingdoms before them, half of Nabara's people were Christian. Just like the Christian Nubian kingdoms of Alodia and Makouria. The High Priest's would not persecute or punish simply based on one's religion. She could not imagine it under her father's rule. They lived in peace, safe from the persecutions of Christians they heard whispers of in Rome. What purpose would it serve? Jelani's eyes darkened as he looked at their father and he turned his head away. *What is bothering him?* He'd been on edge for days. She told herself not to worry; she could wheedle it out of him later. He'd never been able to keep secrets from her for long.

ASIM

"Papo, you *promised*." Azima was looking at him with what could only be described as angry reproach, not trusting him to remember. She held the hourglass out to him to emphasize her point. The sand had run out. It was time to see the *jeli.* He reached out to take it from her, the ivory handles accentuating the Nubian figures carved on each side, their hands pressed against the glass as if to keep what was inside from getting out.

"I know," he ruffled her thick curls slightly with his free hand as he stood, stretching and setting the hourglass down. Marava left their daughter's hair free for tonight.

"Mother—"

"Let her rest," he told her. "Come." Taking her hand, he led her into the courtyard and down the sandy streets of the city, the darkening sky spreading fast. He could hear the sound of lutes playing softly and continued down, Azima skipping next to him in excitement. When they neared the famed storyteller and historian, Bapa, she let go of his hands to clap her own before running to sit with the other children, her black hair silhouetted against the large fire in front of the *jeli.*

The *jeli* sat on a high seat, his long white robes flowing to the ground, a smile visible under his long beard. A shock of white against his dark skin, he stroked his beard and smiled, nodding to Asim. As commander of the High King's Medjay and adopted son of the Kingmaker, people recognized him everywhere he went. Boys and girls sat on the ground before the *jeli*, waiting patiently as the old man prepared his Nubian lyre, the *kissar,* the long strings similar to that of a comb. Light brown cedar glistened from the oil it had been recently cleaned with. A small fire lit between the jeli and his audience glowed softly, crackling as people from the city gathered close, softly whispering greetings, babies sitting on their mother's hips, fat little legs pumping back and forth as they waited.

"Tonight, I will tell you of the *Princess and the Pyramid,* but you must sing with me," he told the children. "For this story, I need your help." He plucked at his *kissar*, a three-part note that tinkled in the silence of the sunset, only half visible behind the mountains. The soft lullaby caused the children to sit up straighter, even as they looked at each other wondering how they would help.

"When I sing, you repeat it back to me; we call that reciprocity." He sang the last word in staccato fashion. The children leaned closer.

"Let's try: Ayooooo ayyyaa," he began.

"Ayaooooo ayyyaa," the children repeated it back.

"O weeee o oooooo."

"O weeee o oooooo."

"Good, Ayoooo ayaaa."

"Ayooo ayaaa,"

"O weee o ooooo."

"O weee o ooooo."

He sung a short opening in Old Nubian on the wonders of love and the desires of the heart before he began, "Deep in the desert just along the Nile, there once lived a mighty King. His land held a rich bounty of grain, masses of pure gold, and treasures untold. Little did he know, that his worst enemy, greed, had found him, in the form of a rival trickster King, whose trade was in ebony alone. The mighty king invited the Trickster King into his home, unaware that his enemy broke bread with him that day. And when the Trickster King left he formulated a plan, betraying the mighty king, murdering him on the steps of the palace, invading the gold-filled lands, and ransacking the mines filled with treasure. But there was one treasure he could not take. The heart of the mighty King's daughter, a noble princess, pure of heart, and intelligent of mind. The Trickster King tried for many moons to win her over, but the murder of her entire family by his hand and the enslavement of her people was a barrier greater than a stretch of sea. So the Trickster King built a pyramid and slaughtered four thousand cattle and five hundred servants of the mighty king's former household. He placed them in an underground chamber so that they would serve him in the next life. And he once more spoke to the princess at the opening of the Pyramid and he told her -

178

serve me or live out your days here where no one can hear your screams or the sound of your belly eating itself for want of food. But the princess refused him. So he threw her into the deepest, darkest pit of the chamber and sealed it so that no one could enter."

The children gasped in excitement and fright as they leaned forward to hear more.

"O weee o ooooo," the *jeli* returned to the chorus.

"O weee o ooooo," the children sang.

"Lovely, Ayooo ayaaa."

"Ayooo ayaaa."

"And the kingdom mourned her. But soon, the cries of the people grew too much to bear. And the beautiful sounds of their sorrow touched even the birds of the sky. And the honeyguides could no longer enjoy their honey because of the tears that mingled with their meal. And the grass no longer needed rain because the servant's spilled enough tears each day. And the lions roared in their fury at the heartlessness of the Trickster King. And so it was, that the animals took pity on the people and told their story and their song. Far in the distance, a Young King heard a strange sound and he followed it to a tree upon which sat a falcon that bid him follow. And he did. Over mountains and down valleys, over rivers and through forests, across deserts and savannah until he spied a trail of the tiniest sugar bushes he'd ever seen, one after the other, surrounded by nothing but sand. And soon he came upon the kingdom of the fallen king now ruled by the trickster. The Young King spoke with the people and learned of their loss and it made his heart heavy. But he had hope. He prayed to Apedemak who warned him to be wary before seeking an audience with the Trickster King. The Young King introduced himself as a prince and asked the Trickster King to unseal the tomb of the last princess that he might save her. "

"O weee o ooooo," he returned to the chorus.

"O weee o ooooo," the children sang.

"Lovely, Ayooo ayaaa."

"Ayooo ayaaa."

His *kissar* playing became faster now and every time he ended a portion he thumped the waist-high drum at his side. "She is dead, young Prince, said the Trickster King. It has been one full moon since I sent her there. I offered her a better life. She refused. And the Trickster King offered one of his young daughters to the Young King instead. But the Young King politely refused and again asked for the tomb to be unsealed. Now the Trickster King grew angry and banished him from his court, commanding him to return from whence he came. But instead, the people of both the mighty king who were still living, and the people of the trickster King learned of the young prince who traveled such a long way, and one by one, night after night allowed him to stay in their homes. And night after night, the Young King found a coveted item, an unknown treasure to give to the Trickster King and soon the Trickster King, swayed by his own greed and pacified by the Young King's efforts, changed his mind. What did it matter, he thought. She is but a skeleton, by now. And two moons had passed. The Trickster King gave him one day to save the princess and promised that if he did not make it out by morning, he would light the pyramid on fire and burn the young prince alive. On one condition. You, said the Trickster King, must not have any blood on your hands."

"The Young King was undeterred and he thanked the Trickster King for his kindness and he entered the tomb. Down he went into the pyramid, past swinging blades and undying fire, groups of mice and rats, over rivers of tar and pits of fire ants, and swarms of scorpions until he reached an empty chamber the size of three men with no visible door. And he pulled a mouse from his pocket and set it on the floor and the mouse ran in circles until finally it pressed its nose against the wall and disappeared through a tiny hole. The young prince followed, using his spear to chisel an opening and break through. When he did he stopped short, a deep well was before him and the princess was in the same. The Young King removed the rope that bound his shendyt and slid down it to the bottom, throwing the princess over his shoulders and climbing back up the rope. When he reached the top he set her down and stirred her awake. Chiseled cheekbones sat below her narrowed, suspicious obsidian eyes, distrust curving the planes of her full pink lips. Who are you, she asked him, her voice a whisper from lack of use. How did you survive? he responded."

"O weee o ooooo," he returned to the chorus.

"O weee o ooooo," the children sang.

"Lovely, Ayooooo o ayaaa."

"Ayoooooo o ayaaa."

"My God looked after me, she replied. 'The Trickster King left me a candle so that I might see my predicament and regret my choice until the day I died. I used it to burn the cattle he slaughtered that I may have food to eat. And the Young King smiled. It is my greatest pleasure to serve you, he told her. 'How is it that you have come here?' she asked him. 'The Trickster King lives off greed and greed alone," replied the Young King. I did not lie as he does. But I told him, truthfully, that I have many brothers, and that my father is yet alive. He believes my father to be king and believes I am only a prince, one in a long line of such he must kill if he were to take my throne. I came in rags rather than riches and so he assumed my kingdom to be a poor one rather than asking whether or not it was. In this way I keep my family safe from harm. Now princess,' the Young King continued, I have only one hour to bring you from this tomb before the Trickster King has his way. But the way we have come is no longer available, each trap has closed upon us and we must find another exit. The princess smiled. I can help you there, she said. I helped design this pyramid. Soon they reached the beginning of the second entrance and found a pit full of straw and dirt."

"The Trickster King told me when I entered, a key lay here, but he did not mention the straw or the dirt. The fire may reach us soon. How will we find it? the Princess asked beginning to dig. There is no need, the young King said. The fastest way to find the key is to burn it. And the young King walked over to the smoke wafting into the chamber and he lit a piece of cloth from the fire that blazed just there, coughing as he did. And he covered the Princess's mouth with his khat and threw the cloth torch into the pit. And it burned before them, smoke filling it larger and larger. Soon he dipped the rope back into the pit and moved it about until a clanging could be heard and jumped inside to retrieve the key. And the princess cried out in surprise as he climbed out, helping him to rise and wrapping him in the same khat he'd used on her, dousing the flames from his body as he cried out in agony. But soon he rose and handed her the key and she opened the door that set them free. Into the blinding light of the desert sun they stepped as the pyramid burned around them, flames licking the outside as it grew larger. Now the Trickster King was waiting for them believing them dead, but he hid his surprise and he smiled. I congratulate you young Prince. But I fear you have lost our wager. You…have blood on your hands."

"O weee o ooooo," he returned to the chorus.

"O weee o ooooo," the children sang.

"Lovely, Ayooo ayaaa."

"Ayooo ayaaa."

"And he was right. For the Trickster King had smeared the blood of the cattle and the blood of each servant on the walls of the pyramid so that any surface he touched was covered. And the fire caused the hardened blood to drip again. And so the Trickster King ordered the young prince taken, that his throat be slit, and his body entombed in a nearby pyramid that all the people might remember his fate and what it meant to defy a king. But the Trickster King's servants could not do it for they had heard of the Young King's bravery and so they healed his wounds and they buried him alive. But the Young King broke free and disguised himself as a servant and crept into the palace of the Trickster King. The Young King captured him and brought him to the same steps on which the mighty King was slaughtered and forced him to his knees in front of the Princess and all of the people."

"Tell me, the Young King said, Why should I spare your life, when you have denied mercy to so many through your greed? the Trickster King answered, What matters more than gold? What matters more than power? These are my people. They recognize a king when they see one," the Trickster King said."

"Well then, said the Young King, If any one of them should stand in your defense I will spare your life. And he waited. And he waited. And he waited. One day passed and no one would step forward in defense of the Trickster King. Not even his young daughters. I am immortal! The Trickster King bellowed. You cannot kill me!"

"As you say, said the prince. Then I shall grant you the same mercy you show others. And at the princess's permission, the

Young King ordered the Trickster King buried alive, deep in the desert. And he was never heard of again."

Asim smiled as the *jeli* finished. It was no wonder Azima loved for him to tell her stories so much.

"What about the prince and princess?" a young boy interrupted, his voice full of impatience to know the end of the story.

The *jeli* laughed, as did the parents around him.

"They married of course little one, and lived to a great age, with many children, and the love of their people. Their intelligence, kindness, and honesty won them the hearts of their people and made the land healthy and prosperous. What matters more than gold? What matters more than power? Love, trust, and honor. Now what do you think he learned?" the jeli asked them as he continued to beat the drum three times in succession with a slight pause in between before returning to the *lyre*. "You," he pointed to a boy before him, whose eyes were wide with surprise as he answered.

"To not be greedy!" the little boy called out.

"And?" the jeli pushed for another answer, pointing at a young girl.

"Be kind to others!"

"Very nice," he plucked at the *kissar*.

"O weee o ooooo," he returned to the chorus.

"O weee o ooooo," the children sang.

"Lovely, Ayooo ayaaa."

"Ayooo ayaaa."

"Sometimes," he told them softly as the *kissar* continued in the background, "a man will want more than you are willing to give."

"O weee o ooooo," he returned to the chorus.

"O weee o ooooo," the children sang.

"Lovely, Ayooo ayaaa."

"Ayooo ayaaa."

"Sometimes, he may try to steal it away, to cheat. But here we do not, we must not. For we know that reciprocity is important. It is fair trade."

"O weee o ooooo," he returned to the chorus.

"O weee o ooooo," the children sang.

"Ayooo ayaaa."

"Ayooo ayaaa."

The children clapped as he finished and tried to ask him for one more as the crowd laughed.

"Not tonight," he told them. "But I will come again. And you must be on your very *best* behavior. And remember, what I give you, you give me. How to thank me for this story?" He plucked at the *kissar* again. "No gold?" The children shook their heads, grinning and laughing. "A kiss or a hug then." The crowd laughed again as the children jumped up to hug him, their favorite storyteller. He laughed and pinched their cheeks as they crowded him, a mass of small arms and legs all trying to hold him at once.

Asim smiled as his daughter squeezed back through the tangle of arms and legs, running to him, breathless with excitement as she jumped into his arms. Never afraid to fall. He thought of the birds in the story and the slavers he would be searching for soon as they walked home hand in hand. She always leapt that way, certain he'd always be there to catch her. A lump formed in his throat. He hoped he always would.

JELANI

Pulling his chariot to a halt, he stepped out, nodding to the guards as he turned to watch the arriving noblemen. The sky darkened as the hooves of hundreds of horses pounded towards the palace walls, the retinue of each of the arriving kings stretching beyond the horizon. Wealthy all. Jelani sighed inwardly as he knew he'd be expected to play host for his father. *No, because of Father. You are to be the future of Nabara*, he thought bitterly. The words tasted of bitterness. He had no desire for politics, but his father expected it of him. *I'm not his only son,* he reminded himself for the fourth time today. *I'll tell him after the Festival.*

Using his forearm, he shielded his eyes from the light of the falling sun to look up at the palace. Straightening his shoulders, he fixed his *khat* and walked up the palace steps to receive their guests. Imani's face broke into a smile when she saw him. Running eagerly down to meet him, her skirts flew out behind her as she came. His sister always seemed to be in motion and full of life.

"Careful, Ami," he said softly as she kissed him. He always shortened her second name, Aminata. It was his way of calling her Little Princess since she was a head shorter than him.

Imani's black curls were adorned with a golden web of silk and gems, sparkling magnificently with the last rays of the sunset. A white leather bodice attached to a sparkling green silk skirt blew softly in the breeze. Golden bracelets decorated his sister's wrists and upper arms. Her large amber eyes were highlighted with black kohl that ran just past the crease of her eye. He wondered who forced her to wear the kohl. *Mother.* She was beautiful and fierce, and he loved her for it.

"Look how many have come." Imani turned to look at the arriving guests. Her face was unreadable. He wondered if she was nervous or simply curious. He'd told her to learn from what she would see and hear and hoped she'd taken it to heart.

"Too many to count, Ami." The beacon fires had been lit that morning, throwing the city into further frenzy as they made their last preparations. A representation of the strength and enduring

185

legacy of the Festival of Kings, they would burn until the commencement of the festival. The square in the center of Nabara had been fitted with dozens of sugar bush and lotus flowers, the pillars decorated with local beauty from the gardens. The underground steam baths had been cleaned with lye and scented with jasmine. Commoners and nobility shared separate baths, but the multitude visiting the city would require the freshest of accommodations. Local quarters were rushing to air out their chambers in anticipation of guests. Artisans could be heard practicing, music filling the city. Even the Royal Dancers were beseeched to learn new dances to perform for the festival. The market had doubled in size as merchants from villages and outlying people came to test their luck and earn what fortune they could from the Games. The smells made his mouth water. Each of the merchants had been required to pay a small tax in order to participate, and the revenue went to the treasury, carefully recorded by the scribes. Many a person was eager to visit the fortunetellers that came in abundance.

The High Priests had asked the High King to banish them from the city for their false tales of prophecy, which encouraged the wicked to ruin as a slap in the face to the Old Religion. His father had done no such thing. Every man must play a part, and even fools must try their fortune, he'd replied before dismissing them. His father adhered to the old traditions of their kingdom of ma'at, but did not enjoy the High Priests dedication to the pharaonic religion. This deity, that deity, it made no matter to him. But the zeal of some of the followers of the Christian religion was lost on him. Makourians were strong in their faith, but people were sacrificed and killed in the name of religion every single day, and he saw no reason that they were different. It was hard for his father to believe they valued love above all else. The city was alive with the sounds, sights, and smells of the occasion and all who were there to witness it.

His father beckoned to them, and they went back up the steps to wait. The soldiers that came with them were without, housing in the unused soldiers quarters outside the palace walls. Within minutes each family arrived with their retinue.

The Kibera of the forest arrived first. The queen carried a staff carved from the wood of a teak tree, and ivory teeth rattled from a necklace. Dressed in a hide of animal skin, a jaguar's head crowned the Kiberan queen. The Kiberan were fierce warriors and hunters, often wearing the colors of the jungle when tracking their prey. Their prowess with a bow and spear was legendary, as was their tendency to poison their arrows and darts if the kill was not meant to be eaten. They were dangerous, swift, and silent.

The Kandake had three children. A stillborn son had died in childbirth two years ago. She had one son of nineteen, and two twin girls of eight with long braids in their hair. They were dressed in animal skin of the same, cloaks loosely wrapped about their shoulders to guard against the night air.

"Welcome, Bamanirenas," the High King said as he embraced the Kandake. Jelani noted the familiarity with which they greeted one another, remembering stories his father had told him as a child of *King* Bakar, the Hunter of Kibera, and her adventures. Nubian and Kushite queens ruling alone were often called "king" and were well respected. It was a sign of respect by her father and others around her that they saw her no differently than a man of her status. Her cousin, a descendant of former Kandake Amanirenas of Meroë, the people recognized her lineage to the ancient queen who brokered a peace treaty with Rome in defense of Nubia though the Kibera did not pray to the Kushite gods. Her people were well protected in the forests of Kibera, retreating to their kingdoms layers of protection including massive trees, rainfall, large animals, and poisonous vines. Long spears made solely of barbed boned aided them in catching the largest of fish. They were great climbers and fisherman, which was one way to avoid being impaled by a hog or antelope on the ground. Kibera was not a place to venture without an escort.

"May I present, Bai, Banji, and my son, Bakar the Second, children of Kibera."

The twins smiled at Imani, shyly stepping forward a pace. Imani stepped closer. "What beautiful braids you wear," she replied, reaching to stroke one. "Welcome to Nabara," she said as she bent to kiss each girls cheek. Both of them blushed furiously, their delight apparent from the huge grins that appeared shortly thereafter. *They adore her already,* Jelani thought as the twins stepped closer to Imani. Their eyes looked like large saucers as they gazed at her dress and her face.

Bakar wore loose locs that framed his square jaw. The prince's eyes were filled with amusement as he watched his sisters before turning to Imani, the bow slung across his shoulder moving slightly.

"Princess Imanishakheto, Prince Jelani. Meeting you is a great honor. I hope that my presence pleases you." Bowing low before them, Jelani nodded in reply. He couldn't fail to miss Bakar's eyes as he appraised him, the Kiberan's eyes filled with barely concealed curiosity and youthful arrogance. Prince Bakar's eyes lingered on Imani as well, his eyes pleased.

"Please, refresh yourself before the rest of the guests arrive. I am at your service while you remain here. You shall want for nothing," Jelani told him solemnly, turning to his father momentarily. His father nodded, and Jelani placed a fist to his chest and inclined his head towards the Kiberan as the palace guards led them inside with a small number of their retinue.

He's grown much since the last time, Jelani thought as he watched the rulers of the Sao Kingdom step forward. Prince Komoro approached the High King. Jelani instantly disliked the look of his black eyes and lavish dress. *A whore if I've ever seen one.* He knew the look well. Polished teeth shone as Komoro licked his lips, smiling at Imani. He took his sister's hand and bent low over it, kissing it before pulling away, his bracelets tinkling softly, the sun glinting off of his bare head. Continuing to stare at Imani as their fathers spoke, his eyes lingered on her though she shielded her own eyes from the dying rays of the sun as she gazed towards the city. Komoro's eyes dropped lower, and Jelani's hand tightened on his *khopesh.* He was slim. *He's probably never done a day's labor,* Jelani thought before realizing that Komoro's eyes were suddenly preoccupied elsewhere. *Of course.* Komoro was sizing up each of the handmaidens in attendance, his eyes flicking from one to the other hungrily. Ama narrowed her eyes briefly in disgust as Komoro leaned over her own hand, turning her face slightly and raising her head in the other direction, away from his gaze as he rose. Komoro's sister, Princess Ketemin, stepped forward next, kissing his cheek, and hugging Imani tightly. The two were good friends, and he could see why. Both of them spoke their mind and their intelligence was immeasurable, as was their sense of humor. He'd always enjoyed Ketemin's company.

Turning back to his father, he watched King Kwasi whisper something conspiratorially that made his father laugh. The old man was seventy or more, though in good shape for his age. Jelani did not fail to miss the way he favored his leg. *His nephew will take his place before long. What will become of his kingdom then?*

"Just as beautiful as the last time I saw you," King Kwasi said, turning to Imani.

His sister started. "You know me?" she replied, puzzled.

"Yes. You only came to my hip, but I would remember those eyes anywhere." Imani smiled at this, blushing slightly.

"Where are the Essi, old friend? Scared to come ashore?"

His father laughed. "They'll be here soon, old man, I've had a message not an hour ago. They arrive in the morning, as will the Scorpion King and his litter. Come. You are our guests. Rest yourselves from your journey, and we will talk soon."

Jelani stood with Ama, Imani, Yemi, and Semi as their guests were led inside. His mother walked towards them, smiling.

"Go now, children. We will expect you to be ready tomorrow morning. See to your duties, but don't get lost before then," she told them, giving him a measured look.

Yemi and Semi left quickly to the garrisons to see to the guards and make final preparations for the Games. His Uncle Shaharqa was busy elsewhere. His sister kissed his mother on her cheek before doing the same to him, grabbing Ama's hand and running quickly in the other direction.

"What is it, Jelani?" his mother asked.

He turned to look at her, his jaw tightening a moment before he spoke. "Nothing, mother." He moved to go, but her hand on his shoulder stopped him.

"You're my only son. I know when you're troubled. You look as if the weight of the kingdom is on your shoulders, though you hide it well." She smiled knowingly.

"I do. I am my father's son, and I will follow in his footsteps."

His mother sighed before taking his hands. "You are the son of a High King, yes. A son you may be, but you must follow your

189

own path. There is a way to make your father proud, to be your own king without simply doing the same. In time, you'll understand why he pushes you so." She cupped his cheek. "My beautiful son. My oldest. You have been favored since the time you were born. You came into this world with a cord wrapped around your neck, black and blue and tiny, and yet you fought. Your father would sooner have a son willing to make his own way and lead than one who wasn't willing to work for all he stood to inherit." She stopped suddenly. "And if what bothers you is not the state of the kingdom, it must be a woman."

How can she know, Jelani thought alarmed. *We've been so careful,* he thought. *If Father found out...I can't let that happen.*

"Don't worry. I shall keep your secret, and soon you will tell me who has taken your mind away from the realm so easily. I would like to meet her." She smiled softly, releasing his hands and walking away, her handmaiden next to her as the guards followed.

NASTASEN

The roach crawling across the ground seemed to be enjoying his dinner better than he had. *Better him than me.* It was rumored that the food was fit to kill you faster than it would keep you alive in the Tsingy. The Tombs. So aptly named. The exiles here would never experience the luxury of being placed in one. Exile Island contained a limestone forest that rivaled the tombs and burial chambers of Nubia herself. Even if you made it past them, a salt lake with rocky white shores sat on the other side, calcifying any animal that dared to enter it, birds constant victims as they dipped inside for food before slowly turning to stone. The Tomb's sky-high trees made solely of stone towered above the ground, huddled shoulder to shoulder like vultures looking down on prey. To walk through it was to know loneliness and death. With a fortress of knife edged limestone sitting on the coast and guarding all that lay on the other side, it was inaccessible. And not a place to move through barefoot. Wet caves and fissures of giant rock made it a death trap for any who attempted the pass. Save the *sifaka*—a soot-faced lemur the size of a baboon with a tail almost three feet long and fur the color of fresh milk. As a boy he'd remembered similar animals being feared to carry the souls of the dead, a popular legend among children. A ghost with golden eyes, the *sifaka* danced with dead stone trees, leaping from the limestone structures to short fruit trees below.

Like so many rats, he was banished here and set to work mining underground from sunrise to sundown, with no way out. Mining gold, copper, rock salt, and sapphires until they fell, too weak to stand, starved, or killed themselves. And the guards preferred you get it over quickly. Betting on how quickly or in what manner one prisoner or another would die was worth a pretty prize for those who entered the pool. Most prisoners of the Empire of Nudolla were sent to the mines, forced to build, make brick, or mine salt until they dropped or finished their sentence in any one of their home kingdoms. The others, though —those too violent or convicted for committing a crime against the Gods or an

191

unforgivable crime were sent here. He touched the mark on his arm, two ovals connected at the edges—eternal service. Dead or alive, there was no leaving his prison.

His hair was matted. It hadn't seen a blade in months, and he was loath to think what may be nesting in between the black curls and dirt. His older brother Eryq had the same black curls, but used to tease him how so like a girl his were when they were younger. His older brother would laugh and say, "More girls for me, Nas, since I look like a man." He'd always been quick to laugh. And quick to charm. His brother had always gotten him into trouble. His mother would threaten to disown him, and later when Eryq confessed out of guilt, she would take a branch to his backside. She said she did it to keep them out of trouble. *Those beatings seemed like the worst pain there ever was.* He knew now that wasn't the case.

His eyes narrowed, glittering obsidian set deep in his face as he watched the roach crawling away from his dinner. It moved slowly, its legs shaking like a drunkard from a tavern. A moment later it rolled over, legs high in the air, a milky fluid leaking from it, and was still. *Who says no one escapes from prison?* Rubbing the stubble at his jaw, he paused as the slabs of concrete separating his cell from the others began to rotate. Sitting up straighter, he rested his elbows on his knees.

"Out, damn you. I don't have all day," the guard said as soon as the entrance appeared. "Or stay if it please you, Your Grace, and you can eat tomorrow."

Nas rose quickly, wiping his gritty palms against his pants as he walked out, crouching and bent at the waist to avoid the low ceiling above. Shielding his eyes with his forearm, he fell in line and up the spiraled ramp, prisoners lining up one by one.

Another guard waved them through the black gates. Sandal leather slid against stone floors as they filed out to the courtyard. The ground was strewn with rocks but not much more. The paths here were so narrow the prisoners were forced to turn sideways as they walked. Stalagmite stone swords pushed downward from the ceiling, a dangerous maze to walk through even if one needed to keep blood circulating in such cramped conditions. Sitting was preferred. Safer.

"Nas. Aren't you a ray of sunshine?" Zyqarri called to him.

"A prettier picture than you, I hope. I'm sure the women miss your pretty face."

Zyqarri laughed. Older by three years, he reminded him of his brother. With his tall, lanky frame, he stood a foot taller than most of the men and his black curls were dark and tightly cropped though his onyx skin was three shades darker than his own. He should ask Zyqarri how he managed to keep his hair short in this rabbit hole.

"The cockroaches love me better. They visit me every night when I'm lonely. They share my dinner, my bed, and they never complain."

Nas shook his head as another prisoner was led into the courtyard by a guard. Judging by his fresh garb, clean and unsoiled, he hadn't been here long. Bald, he looked to be around twelve. *How does one so young end up here?* The boy's eyes darted from crevice to corner, refusing to meet anyone's eyes. *He won't last long.* Nas told himself not to bother. The prisoners died quicker than a candle in the wind.

The other prisoners crowded the boy immediately. Zyqarri turned to watch as others rifled through his pockets, handling him as if he were nothing, searching for coin, food, or papers on his person. Anything they could trade. *What's yours is mine.* They made that clear. When they'd finished with him, most of them left while the others interrogated him for news from the Namib and King Tharbis.

"I don't know," they heard him say, cowering, as if trying to press himself inside the walls. Another stroked his hair gently, smiling as he rubbed a thumb over the boy's cheek.

Nas crossed his arms over his chest. "Leave him," he said from where he stood, eyes narrowing as he waited. The prisoners respected him enough to do as he asked. Ten years inside of the Tombs gave him seniority over many of the others, though ten years was short compared to some. "What's your name?" He stared at the boy, his gaze like burnt iron.

"Amare," he replied, looking to his left and right at the others who stood nearby.

The laughter from the prisoners echoed off the walls. "Amare, he says?"

"Are you Roman, boy?"

"It sounds pretty enough."

"Enough." Nas ignored their comments. "How did you come here, boy?"

"I...was...they brought me. I mean I—I didn't. I didn't do anything."

There was silence after he spoke. Then the peals of laughter started again, laughter echoing off the walls as the men slapped each other on the back, tears streaming down some of their faces.

"Well, we're all innocent in here, aren't we," Ismar said, shaking his head as the rest parted. Ismar was one of several who hired themselves out in order to provide for their families and relieve them of the burden of caring for them. It was a common practice and one alternative to the redistributive system of taxation used by the king. Though Tharbis used the word redistributive liberally.

"New boy!" a guard called out. "You're working today. You'll shift with mining. See that you keep up, or it will be harder for you tomorrow."

Mining involved metal works where weapons were made; men engaged in carpentry and ironwork regardless of the large population of ironsmiths in the kingdom. The underground tunnels and caves were dark, barely lit, and hot with smoke. They had sunlight and air when they worked on various architecture projects for King Tharbis, but what Nas missed most were the stars. They never knew which work duty they pulled until the guards brought them up. Being out after dark, though, was never allowed.

Today it was mining in the caves. Each of them picked up a hammer and pick, the new boy falling in with the rest though he continued looking up and around at the tunnel ceilings and floors, torches spread about to light their way. As they dug in, Zyqarri began to question him again.

"So, what have you brought us? What state would we find the kingdom in?" he asked eagerly, plunging the shovel into the soil.

"What do you want to know?" the boy asked timidly, struggling to pull his pick loose. He was small for a boy his age and had no upper body strength.

194

"Everything! Are the women still beautiful? With their dark eyes and cotton curls. Gentle lambs. Is the sun still the color of spun gold? Does High King Amkarqa Kashta still sit the throne? Or has his time come and gone?"

"They still sit the throne. They're preparing for the start of the Festival of Kings for Princess Imanishakheto's coming of age." He wiped sweat from his brow as he pulled the shovel loose, breathing heavily.

"Princess Imanishakheto. The last time I saw her she was nine or thereabouts. And a sphinx if ever there was one. She beat a farmer's boy one day after he pushed her into a pigpen. Always playing in the dirt so her clothes were a wreck. I'd never seen her in a gown. He thought she was one of the orphans from the temple. All of us moved to help her to save him from her Medjay escort, but we didn't need to. She jumped up and beat him senseless while she sat on top of him. We couldn't do anything but laugh. Afterwards his father beat him and he begged her to have mercy...she reminds me of my sister, Mara," he finished fondly.

"She's beautiful," Amare breathed solemnly, leaning into his shovel.

"I've seen plenty of women, and they all look alike to me." Nas was growing irritated with their talk.

"Says you! All the women you've seen are likely grandmothers by now anyway, so they don't count. Ten years will make you forget some things, but the beauty of a real woman isn't one of them," Zyqarri declared.

Nas shook his head, dropping to his knees as he continued digging. *Nothing but trouble.* Gritting his teeth, he remembered a beauty his brother thought no one could match. He still remembered the green of her eyes inside her dark saffron face. Eryq had been in love with her from the first time he laid eyes on her. He followed her like a cat in heat, and she knew.

"Beauty isn't everything. Beautiful women are conniving and manipulative."

"Says the pot to the kettle," Ismar laughed.

Zyqarri nodded in agreement. "A beauty like you?" Zyqarri teased. "What woman scorned you for another? I won't believe it. Eyes like muddy oil? A hole in one cheek probably as a result of

195

how many lies you tell? Not likely. That rat's nest you call a head must be hiding the smallest brain in the kingdom."

Nas ignored them. "Have you met a beautiful woman who's not manipulative? Doubtful."

Ismar laughed, "I'm sure *one* of the Scorpion King's wives is. Probably the most recent one."

"The Scorpion King's wives are just like him. All of them. He infects everything he touches." His finger's curled into fists. "Apedemak, Osiris, God…if there is *one* up there doing what they ought, he'll get his due."

"His due?" Zyqarri looked at him, incredulous. "You've got to be more specific when you pray, Nas. I pray to them all. Ra, Osiris, Anubis. I asked for a beautiful woman to fill my bed once. They sent me a woman, beautiful and lovelier than the rising sun. But she went by Tarrah by day and Tarro by night," his face darkened. "I thought it was sweet she never wanted to piss in front of me." Zyqarri shook his head as the men laughed around him, scowling when the guards joined in, holding their stomachs. "She was beautiful," he murmured regretfully.

"King Tharbis's first wife is lovely, even if she is older than me. She's like the sun and moves like the wind caressing your face," Amare replied.

"I've always hated poets and liars. Which are you?" he looked at Amare.

Amare shrank back, blushing.

"Leave him be, Nas." Zyq plunged his shovel into the ground. "He's young."

The boy doesn't know, he told himself. How could he? It'd been ten years since he'd been sent to the Tombs by Tharbis. How fitting. His brother had panicked, yelling about how he needed his help, asking him what he should do. When Eryq told him that a guard had seen the Scorpion King's concubine with him inside the temple, Nas felt fear for the first time. Corrupting the king's concubine carried a death penalty. He'd begged his brother to leave the city, but Eryq was mad with love. He wanted to go back, and steal her away. *She loves me*, he declared. *She'll go, she just needs to know how much I love her.* He had talked him out of it before leaving at the command of the Scorpion King to battle.

Nas had pushed aside the uneasy feeling in his stomach, but being called back to the city was like a sword in his heart. It all rushed back when his eyes fell upon a thick crop of curls, the head bent forward towards the ground, the man in a kneeling position on the platform. *No.* He'd listened as the king's guards declared the man a rapist, a criminal who tried to take the virgin concubine's gift from the king and defiled a temple. *He's innocent!* He'd run forward to protest his brother's innocence only to find himself held back by the king's guard. One had put a fist under his chin, forcing him to watch as his brother was castrated like an animal, his screams like that of a dying lamb. He'd screamed his name, helpless. When his brother raised his eyes towards him, he'd tried to ignore the blood pouring from his waist onto the ground in front of him. Spittle fell from his mouth from his screams, and he felt weak, drained as the guards held him there, watching. They'd tied his wrists to the crane device behind him and released his hands, the enormous sandstone boulder at least five feet thick towering twenty feet above his brother's head. The crowd had gasped, no doubt wondering how long his brother would be able to hold on. But he did. Twisting and turning and straining as they tightened and retightened the lever to release more and more of the boulder's weight. The muscles bulged on his brother's arms, but still he held on, looking out in the crowd. And then he realized he was looking for him. His brother was so close to death and still he was looking for him. The smile his brother forced just for him when his eyes found him nearly broke him. A second later the lever was released and Eryq's arms snapped up as the boulder fell, crushing him instantly. The body no longer visible to any. Spattered blood the only evidence as the observers squealed and backed away in fear while others crowded forward to see what was left of the dead man. Even the most innocent found it hard to look away from suffering. The guards declared him complicit. *Conspirer*, they kept calling him before spiriting him away to the Tombs to rot. At fourteen he'd made this place his home. To work, to rot, to die.

Shaking the sweat from his eyes, he gritted his teeth in anger, gripping the shovel tightly between his calloused hands. If he ever made it out of this place, he'd give the Scorpion King a proper gift.

Later that night in his cell, he laid upon the cold, hard floor and he dreamed. He was a soldier, trained and armed in service to King Tharbis. Dragging a bloated corpse through the sand by its feet. Flies stuck to the eyes, clustered so tightly as to appear like overgrown eyebrows, flying away each time the body jumped, caught on a rock or root, only to resettle again.

"These fucking flies. They outnumber us one hundred to one!" Mykel complained. Nas grunted as he tossed the corpse onto the growing pile of rotting bodies. *A pyramid,* he thought slowly as he stood back, gazing at the pile. *A pyramid built with rotting corpses. Countries have been built on the bodies of dead enemies for years. Why not soldiers too?*

"Our fight isn't with the flies, Mykel. It's with our enemies. The Nomadin put forward a lie and then attacked the king's caravan. Be thankful for the flies. It's the only way we're likely to know which pile to throw you in one day."

His brothers in arms laughed, but they knew he spoke the truth. "Besides," he continued, "You volunteered your services to the king," Nas finished.

"He did! Mykel, what were you thinking?" Jonus asked.

"I was thinking I'd have a roof over my head, food on my table and enough coin to support your incapable ass when you needed me to lend you money," Mykel responded.

Jonus had the grace to look embarrassed and held his tongue.

"Though none can argue it is strange that only three were able to overpower him. *This* Nomadin family had the courage of ten thousand," Jonus added.

"It's not our place to question the king. We take our orders," Mykel replied.

Nas wiped the blood from his hands, scooping handfuls of dirt from his feet to rub them together. No. Not many of them chose this life. They were born into it.

Shaking sweat from his thick curly hair he squinted as he looked towards the edge of the desert. His dark eyes narrowed as he looked up towards the sky. Service had made his body strong and muscular, but his eyes held the sharp command of a leader and he was well respected among the ranks. A rustling sound made him look down. A dark red scorpion was moving under the sand, trying to burrow itself deeper, dragging a frog behind him. Nas shook his head as he lifted his foot, stomping it twice to make sure it was dead. He might have left the poisonous creature alone, but doing that would mean he'd always be watching his step. Standing, he went back to dragging corpses. They'd need to be done by nightfall and burn the bodies. If the smell didn't kill them, the hyenas that found them would. His father taught him that. As their second-born son he'd been forced into service under the law of conscription. Survival was the most important lesson of all.

The panting made him turn around. A runner.

"The commander sends for you," he breathed, trying to catch his breath. Nas nodded once, touching his fist to his chest before following the runner to the commander's tent. The commander sat behind a makeshift desk made of wood, scrolls covering the table. A large map was pinned nearby, his assistants talking quietly.

"I am Nastasen," he announced.

The commander looked up from his work, studying him carefully before waving him closer. He picked up a scroll, reading it slowly as if to be sure.

"You're relieved of duty. You'll be paid what you've earned during your service. Pack your belongings and head back to Tharbis." The commander's face was expressionless, and that was what worried him most of all. His commander had always been generous with details, taking Nas under his wing.

"Why?"

The commander finally looked back up at him, his eyes narrowing momentarily before he clasped his hands in front of him. "Your brother has been arrested. You've been relieved from duty."

Arrested. Nas felt as if he'd been punched in the stomach. He stopped breathing momentarily as a thousand questions flew through his mind. Arrested for what? His older brother would never lie, cheat, or steal. Everyone loved him.

"Arrested for what?" he managed to grind out between his teeth, anger already taking hold.

The commander stared at him a moment before standing quickly, leaning his strong arms on the desk, towering in the tent. "Pack your things. You leave in the hour," he repeated before turning and walking out of the tent, the opening flapping in the slight breeze.

He hadn't remembered packing anything. He didn't own much anyway. When he'd arrived back in the city, his mother and father had been overwhelmed, in a state of shock trying to explain what had happened to him. This time when he looked up from his restraint by the King's guards, his brother's blood sprayed his clothes and his face. He still remembered the look on the face of the king's concubine as he'd been hauled off. His brother's screams like a faint song replaying in his head. She'd been standing next to her king. Smiling. His brother's blood and bone spread over the boulder and she was smiling. Later the rumors had surfaced that she was with child by one of the king's guards. He'd been impaled at the stake.

Nas turned his face up towards the ceiling. His parents came to him before he left for the Tomb, eyes swollen from crying. "Don't worry, the king said," his mother sobbed, "you can always have another child. I'll waive the law just this once," she cried, uncontrollably. His father rested one arm on his mother's shoulder and the other hand he reached through the bars of the cage to rest on Nas's head. "You're our only boy. We'll not replace you. Come back to us," he made him promise. And he meant to keep it.

He sat up quickly, wiping sweat from his forehead and neck, his eyes wild. His chest was slick with sweat, his clothes sticking to him like the remnants of his dream. *I won't forget. I never will.*

IMANI

Sunlight spilled through the dark tunnels as she walked with Ama through the cove. Prisms of color lit their steps before they turned down the narrow entrance, stalagmite formations on either side as they moved towards the sound of water. She'd run through these tunnels since she was a girl, escaping her lessons, rushing towards the sea, or using it to sneak into the city. Only her father knew it existed, so she never worried about being found. The entrance was too narrow to fit most, and the sharp, jutting inesite and calcite formations made it dangerous.

Her cousin stood near the entrance, not going any further in an attempt to stand her ground. "Imani, are you sure we have time for this? The rest of the families will be arriving soon. Your father expects you to be there, he asked me to—"

"I know, Ama. I promise we won't be long. I think I lost my necklace here. Jelani gave it to me. I have to find it." She stood at the edge of the pool, looking down into the clear blue water. Four large pools flowed into Torrent from here, but she'd found the pools were warm during the day.

"I won't be long," she said, diving neatly below the water. *It's so beautiful,* she thought as she opened her eyes under the water. The coral was pink below the surface and she reached out to touch it, feeling the rough texture against her fingers. Lower she went, until she touched the bottom, her hair floating around her face. Digging her fingers hurriedly into the sand she raked it back and out of her way. *Nothing but shells! Where is it? It must be here.* Bracing her hands against the pool floor, she pushed herself closer to the walls of the pool, her eyes traveling quickly up and down. If the soft current had pulled her necklace, it might be in the sea by now. Exhaling slowly, she pushed off with her feet to bring her to the surface.

She took a deep breath as she broke the surface, wiping the water from her eyes. "Ama, I'm ready," she called softly. She turned around to look behind her, the cave stones giving nothing away as her voice echoed back to her. *Where are you?* A crunching sound made her freeze as she realized someone was behind her. Reaching for the dagger at her hip, she realized she'd taken it off before going below the surface. Spinning around, she tread water to stay afloat before her eyes landed on a tall man, a *khopesh* at his hip. He was dressed in blue and black leathers, and, looking down she realized his boots made the sound.

"Looking for someone, Princess?" the intruder asked insolently.

"You know who I am," she replied. "Let her go and I'll let you live," she commanded. Staring at her a moment longer, he tipped his head slowly to the side before smiling.

"Will you?" he asked.

The sarcasm in his voice angered her. "What have you done with my cousin?" The rage in her voice masked her trepidation.

"I think we're alone you and I. Come out of the water so we can talk," he continued, leisurely stepping toward the pools.

Please be alive. Quick as a snake she dove below the surface, legs and arms pumping furiously toward the other side of the pool, under a short stone arc, and toward her dagger. The sound of boots slamming against the rock made her swim faster. *Please let me get there first.*

Reaching out to grab her dagger she broke the surface, her right hand closing around the dagger just before a hand gripped her left wrist, pulling her halfway out of the water. Imani gasped in surprise as he pulled her face close to his own.

"Release me!" she pressed the tip of her dagger against the curve of his throat. His jaw flexed at the threat, his eyes moving down rapidly before a small smile turned the corner of his mouth.

"You promised you wouldn't forget. Don't you recognize me, Aminata?" he asked softly.

Confused she felt her heart racing as the stranger's eyes stared at her. *Grey eyes. It can't be.* "Mikaili?" she whispered. He nodded, releasing her wrists to lift her by the waist, pulling her easily out of the water as if she weighed no more than a doll.

She'd met Mikaili when she was eight, their father's had been close. His, the leader of the Essi, commander of fleets. Their kingdom sat on a large group of islands known as the Floating City, water reflecting thick clouds that shrouded it like a veil. It was a thing of beauty to enter it. Some called it one of the entrances to paradise. As High King, her father had created an alliance with the Essi, agreeing to build hundreds of war galleys as well as implementing a trade agreement that would open waterways for merchants. Their alliance had fueled voyages and trade, and they'd been allies ever since. *He was much shorter then,* she thought briefly. His slate grey eyes twinkled with amusement as she realized his short crop of curls had been replaced by long, thick locs, though they still held the same dark tawny color they did when he was a boy.

He reached out to hug her, his chin brushing the top of her head and heavy with stubble tickling her ear. *He's only just arrived,* she thought. *And he smells of saltwater.* Imani pulled away slowly, realizing she'd soaked the front of his clothes, but he didn't seem to care. She blushed as she realized he was staring at her crown.

"You never take it off?" he asked.

"Yes, I do, but—"

"But your father would have a fit if he caught you without it," he finished.

A smile tugged at the corner of her mouth; he hadn't changed much. Still finishing her sentences as if he'd read her mind.

"It suits you. And it matches your eyes," he said softly, his eyes finally moving to her face.

"As a princess though, I must say I was disappointed you weren't on hand to receive me upon our arrival." He intended to mock her, crossing his arms over his chest with a lazy grin, but Imani's mouth dropped open in surprise. Ama was climbing back inside the cave, a panicked expression covering her face.

"Imani! Come quickly!" she cried. At the sight of Mikaili she stopped. "Who is *he?*" The interest in her voice was plain.

"No one."

Mikaili laughed at her reply, before nodding to Ama. "I am Mikaili, heir to the Essi Kingdom. And the pleasure is all mine, Princess Ama."

Imani grabbed her things. *The Essi arrived and I wasn't there to greet them.* The other families would be on hand as well. *Father will have my head.* Her heart squeezed as she stepped quickly into the loose silk gown, sliding it over the white, cotton dress that hugged her from chest to thigh, clutching her sandals in her hands.

"Forgetting something?" Mikaili called.

When she turned, he was holding her dagger towards her, hilt first. She pursed her lips in annoyance before taking it from him.

"I'm still faster than you," he whispered smugly, crossing his arms over his chest. Eyes narrowing, she stepped towards him. The smile was still on his face as she pushed him with her free hand, watching the surprise that replaced his smile as he lost his footing and fell backward into the pools. Ama looked at her in shock as she moved past her toward the entrance. She relished the splash she heard as she crawled through the tunnels, Ama close behind. *It's no matter*, she thought. *Swordfish know how to swim.*

Ama held a cloth to her hair as she ran, attempting to dry it before they reached the palace. "Wait!" Ama cried, stopping her. She pulled Imani's hair back, quickly making a fishtail braid over her shoulder. The ends dripped slightly, but it would serve. Ama smiled at her work in relief.

They rushed up the steps together, Medjay standing still as stone on either side of her family.

Her mother nodded briefly, signaling for her and Ama to stand beside her, and they did. From her place beside her father she could see the retinue of the burning sands; mounted upon horseback they came, filing through the gates. The queen came first, wrapped in black; veils blowing in the wind, her husband behind her. He was dressed all in black, veils covered all but his eyes and Imani saw his soldiers were much the same.

Outfitted in black, only their eyes showed as they moved as one, desert assassins, their long blades glinting in the sun. An old family in the realm. The Graveyard some called their home, while others nicknamed it the Sea of Bones. Many who entered the arid desert climate were never seen or heard from again. Others claimed that they'd died in the desert, and the fierce winds and frequent sandstorms had buried their bodies. It was common among men to joke about the hidden treasures in the sea, none of it to do with water.

"Welcome to Nabara," her father greeted them, spreading his hands as he did so. The Scorpion King bowed low before her family as he presented his sons. Terit, Tari, Takide, Teqer, and Tisaan. Boys, all. She remembered them well. The oldest had played a nasty trick on her when she was young. He'd gotten her to wait for him outside the stables before releasing one of their unbroken. The stallion would have trampled her to death had it not been for her brother and uncles. They'd beaten him senseless that night, saving his pretty face, and making sure he wouldn't tell his father by threatening him with another. *Nothing was wounded but his pride,* she thought. *And he still wears it on his sleeve like an ugly peacock.* The other four were just as bad. Tari could have passed for a girl; his beautiful black curls were well oiled and tumbled about his shoulders. Even his clothing was scented and the women threw themselves at him. Imani couldn't help staring at him in disgust as she remembered the cruelty he always showed. She'd done her best to like him, but he wanted so much to be like his brother that he was just as cruel and his temper wavered between sweet and sour. The third followed his brothers everywhere, just as the fourth did, eager to be included. The last was sweet natured, but in the shadow of his brothers it made for unexpected actions.

"Welcome to Nabara," she repeated dutifully, as each stepped forward to bow to her in turn. The oldest bent over her hand slowly, and she ripped her hand away when she felt his tongue against her skin. The back of her hand slapped his cheek so fast his mouth dropped open in surprise.

"Oh," she exclaimed. "Are you alright? I thought it was going to sting you." Jelani held back a laugh next to her and her mother's face held what could only be described as horror.

"Thank you, Princess," he replied, leering at her momentarily before bowing respectfully and rising, one hand rubbing his left cheek.

"Amkar, what are these charges that have been brought to my ears?" the Scorpion King said, his voice booming, demanding an answer. "Has the swordfish forgotten his place?"

The look on her mother's face warned her his outburst was unexpected. The Scorpion King had been accused of smuggling before by the Essi, but for the first time, the Essi had made their claims known to the realm. And the Scorpion King was furious.

"Not now. You must rest, and only then will we speak of these matters during the council meeting." His word was final.

The Scorpion King's jaw clenched in anger before he nodded his assent. "As you wish."

A moment later his son's laughter rang out as the brothers pointed at something in the distance.

"Speaking of swordfish," Terit chuckled.

"More like a drowned rat," Tari replied.

"Or a dead one," Takide muttered. Her eyes widened as Mikaili turned the corner, dripping wet. She lowered her eyes in embarrassment, slightly regretting that she'd pushed him in. He could have changed first.

"The Essi are here?" the Scorpion King asked. "All the food will be gone," he mocked.

Imani glared at him before realizing she must remain unaffected.

"Enough." her father replied. "Nabara has plenty of food and room for all of our guests."

"Did you forget how to swim, Mikaili?" The Scorpion King's sons were persistent.

Imani's eyes flicked to Mikaili, but he did not so much as glance her way. She bit her lip anxiously, waiting for him to confess all and tell them what she'd done, and where she'd been.

"No, I mistook a lion for a friend and lost my footing near Torrent."

Imani's eyes darted from him to her father. Lions had been caught near the arena for the start of the festival. If her father suspected her to be the lion, he gave no hint of it. Self-consciously she touched her hair, praying to the gods it was dry.

"I went looking for the Princess after I was told she'd been helping with preparations near the maze."

Imani blushed furiously before meeting his eyes. He'd given her an excuse for her absence. Mikaili went to greet the High King and Queen and her family then, her mother accepting a kiss on her hand, but reaching out warmly to kiss him on each cheek. He greeted Imani last, walking over to where she stood, his face betraying nothing as he stopped in front of her to kneel, his gray eyes holding her own. "Please, forgive my appearance. You may not remember me," he continued, "but we played together when we were little."

"Welcome back," she replied, holding back a smile as his clothing dripped with water. He bowed before her, taking the hand she offered.

"The pleasure is mine." His lips brushed her hand softly before he rose. He held her eyes as he straightened in front of her. He didn't let go of her hand, but instead he said, "Please excuse me, Your Grace. My father is waiting for me." A moment later he looked to her father and her father nodded to Mikaili, though she caught her father looking at her curiously. Mikaili released her hand and kissed the cheek Ama was offering with a smile before bowing to Ama, nodding to the guests, her family, and the handmaidens. Mikaili left quickly towards the guest chambers. She didn't fail to notice the blush that rose to half of the handmaiden's cheeks as he left.

"My, you are a beauty," King Tharbis said softly to a serving girl, reaching for the dates she held aloft on a golden plate. "Perfect. And so ripe." Biting into one he reached for another, leaving with his family and retinue shortly thereafter.

Turning to her, her father said softly, "I store water, but I do not need it to survive. I keep thousands of people alive. I start battles and wars, but I do not fight. I can be moved, but you cannot lift me, try as you might. What am I?"

Imani searched his face. "A *kol*. You are a well." Lifting her chin higher she met his eyes as he searched her face now.

"So? Is that what you fell into? I'm pleased to see you're taking an interest in our guests, Imani, if not the Games." Startled at her father's comment, her face betrayed her, and she blushed again.

TERIT

"Find him. We must not wait until the start of the festival. We must remain inconspicuous."

His father was furious. Dealing with a smuggler was causing more problems than he cared to admit. And now the envoy was late in delivering the message he'd promised to have to them by morning.

Father, let me track him down. I can leave by way of the river."

"No." The command made Terit wince. "You must not be gone. They will note your absence."

He bowed his head slightly in acquiescence, waiting for his father to finish.

"If he is here, find him. And don't leave Nabara. Or I will get rid of that pretty whore you keep in tow."

Terit gritted his teeth. "Yes, Father."

He watched his father's retreating steps as he made his way towards the underground steam baths. Heavy footfall marked his approach as the people gave him wary looks.

I must find him, and soon. He ran down the wide stone staircase, leading to the complex entrance, easily manageable despite throngs of people sitting and chattering away on the steps.

Just as he turned past the stone statue of the Adamantine, a small girl stepped in his path. Her sandals were well worn and her hair was unkempt. She held out a dirty hand to him, saying, "Your benevolence is well known, my Prince."

"Get out of my way." He pushed her roughly to the side with his hand.

"The master sends a message," she insisted, undeterred, her voice high and thin.

He stopped. Turning back to her, he noticed the rolled papyrus she clutched in her other hand. Without warning he snatched it from her, his backhand cracking across her right cheek. Stumbling backward, she clutched her cheek in shock.

"Next time be quick about it," he sneered, unrolling the papyrus. He didn't bother looking to see where she ran, but heard her sob as she took flight.

The fountain, two minutes. C, it read.

He looked up quickly to see what eyes may be watching before he walked away from the well and towards the fountains on the other side of the arena. The heat penetrated through his clothing, burning his skin. Even on the border of the Namib it felt like the sun was eating a hole through your very skin. This spot had been chosen for the Festival of Kings because it was a safe passageway just between Tharbis and Nabara, and home to many great hunter-gatherer nations such as the Servants of Cagn and the Sons of Prishiboro. They welcomed the trade that would stem from the Festival of Kings after receiving High King Kashta's request. *The bastard better be there.* There were too many people crowded around the fountains. Boisterous children playing at swords, soldiers, and groups of women smelling of rosewater. *Too many people, too many eyes.* He looked left and right and didn't see him.

Terit pushed closer to the edge of the fountain to take a drink. An old crone bent low for water, drinking greedily before dropping the pitcher and the cup. It bounced off the stone noisily, hitting the sand floor below. Terit cursed her silently as he retrieved it. "Others must drink as well," he started angrily as she turned around. He dusted the sand from the cup, wiping its rim with his sleeve.

After he drank he realized the crone was staring at him. Smiling at him through heavily stained and crooked teeth. The mole under her lip had hairs sprouting from it. *She's twice as ugly as I thought.* He frowned in disgust before he noticed her eyes…she was signaling to…

The smuggler? Terit almost choked on the water as he spotted the smuggler. His arms crossed about his chest as he stared at him, his eyes narrowing as he watched Terit, standing at the fountain, spilling his water. *Dressed as a Berber!* He almost didn't recognize him. Flipping the ends of his turban up and back over his mouth, he waited.

Terit straightened his back as he set the cup down and turned to walk towards the smuggler. When he did, the smuggler began to walk away from him and Terit started feeling confused, but he continued to follow, looking behind him and to his left and right as he did, his eyes moving from person to person. He gritted his teeth as his chest tightened, worry making his nostrils flare. When he rounded the corner a hand shot out and caught him by the arm, pulling him into a dark corner. He grunted as his head hit the stone behind it.

"Does the woman…?"

"No, she has no idea who I am, but she loves gold. And my employer…is not pleased."

"Well played. I didn't realize you were…in the city."

"Nonsense," the smuggler replied. "It's why you've hired me." He started pulling away, but the smuggler tightened his grip and leaned his weight into Terit's side.

"Come, my Prince. Don't be coy."

Terit relented and a few moments later replied, "How…may I assist you?"

"There's worse than me little prince. I just happen to know how to smuggle things where they're needed most. To maximize their value. Your remember that. There's worse than *me*."

The smuggler's cold eyes stared into him and for a moment Terit felt fear creep down his spine. He'd been told of a slave catcher who moved throughout the interior with a Roman merchant. Terit had been told of what he had done before his chosen profession. Killing had been easy, and expected. A triumph. The pressure of his fingers caused Terit to narrow his eyes.

"Don't forget, we have an agreement."

Terit used his hand to push the man roughly away. "Don't forget whom you speak to. I would hate to see anything happen to you." The fear that appeared in the trader's eyes was enough for Terit. He knew he had the upper hand. "I haven't forgotten. Nor has my father."

The agreement had been made almost a year ago. The smuggler in front of him was of Tharbis of course. And his trade in silk and other luxuries on the seas had lent him to come into contact with a variety of people. Terit's father had immediately agreed to a liaison with a man the smuggler only described as "the Roman merchant." Through him the silk trader made several lucrative trade deals with Tharbis. And his father wanted more. It had been an easy thing to do at first. *You give me…I give you.* Fair trade.

Furs, salt, silk, diamonds, pottery, even ivory. No matter that killing elephants for ivory was frowned upon. Anything they wanted his father had been willing to trade. It had all been in great supply, and it spurred an increase in business for the merchants in their kingdom. Their liaison had been efficient and indispensable, providing reasonable exchange rates for selling materials on a merchant's behalf. Everyone profited from the change. Among the nobles, of course. And it had made it easier to consider other offers.

His father had begun having trouble with some of the families hunting on the land. Had accused some of the hunters of stealing his cattle. In quick succession, he had allowed every miscreant, thief, and debtor to be sold off to labor mines owned by a portion of the nobility. Mines Terit looked after. He knew that some of that labor meant those sold would become slaves elsewhere. *As long as they weren't slaves while under his father's rule of law, it mattered not.* But Terit knew his father wasn't aware of the hands into which they fell. And Terit wouldn't tell him either until he was sure he could convince his father that it was right to do so. *They'll all be selling as many enemies as they can find before long. It is far too profitable a trade not to.*

Terit had met with the smuggler on his own. *No one need know,* the smuggler promised him.

"Payment has not been made. But promises have." The smuggler crossed his arms and waited.

"We paid—"

"Your *father paid.* Half. Delivery is late. Two hours I've been delayed here. The Roman merchant would sell us just to make up the difference. He and the catcher are not to be toyed with."

"We...my father sent a message that the place we would leave payment had changed. He would send his apologies as I give you mine."

"Where is it?"

"Still at the same home. The merchant has not left. You'll find it there."

"Thank you. My Prince. Don't worry. Your father does not need to know." The silk trader smiled, before turning and walking away. Terit watched him stride directly into the crowd. He squinted as he tried to follow him. But a moment later, he'd lost him among the others.

His fingers curled into his fist as he stood there. He was a *prince*. The smuggler almost acted as though *he* served him. One should be more careful of making enemies when they have no friends. And the smuggler was nothing if not the example of that. And the *catcher* he'd heard so much about for that matter. The *catcher* was in the employ of the Roman without a doubt, taking orders and kidnapping slaves at will. But the slaver couldn't do it alone. Not for long. He would need a partner soon and Terit would be there to fill his place. Terit fumed, rubbing his neck where the trader had grabbed him. *I could kill him on any road in any kingdom within the Empire of Nudolla and not one would bat an eye.* Or miss him. Or doubt Terit's version of the story. Successfully. *I've done it before.*

The look on Fera's face when it happened had given him pause. It had been hard at first, finding the courage to look his sixth mother in the face and lie. But he had. Years ago, as a child. The whole way back he made up excuses in his mind about what to tell her, wondering which lie she would believe the most, considering which ones she would dismiss the fastest. Practicing his lies word for word, revising them as he tasted them on his tongue, feeling the edges to see how well they fit into his story. Pacing at the edge of the palace, wearing his prints into the sand as he did. Droplets of sweat popped from his forehead, and he'd wiped them away with the back of his hand. It was always hot in the desert, but the heat wasn't what was making his heart race.

"Take your brother with you!" his mother called as he turned to go and play. At twelve, he resented the burden of having his six-year-old brother tagging along behind him everywhere he went. The apple of his father's eye. The love affair was like a cycle each time his father had a child from one of his new wives and Terit felt the isolation of it, especially since this love affair had lasted much longer than the others and didn't seem to be waning any time soon. With three other brothers already, he found none of them particularly interesting. They were annoyingly similar in the fragility and care with which their mother's treated them while Terit looked on with disdain.

"Stay here!" he'd commanded his little brother, like a king to his servant.

"Terit!" Fera called sternly.

His blood mother, Radhia, had yelled, "Come here!" but he'd run as fast as he could away from them both, his sandaled feet beating a path out of the palace as quickly as his legs would allow. He'd hopped over short walls and baskets of sorghum, weaving between shopkeeper's legs and heading deeper into the desert. When he reached the open sand dunes, he squatted quickly for a moment to catch his breath, smiling in his triumph, his escape. The sandstone walls of the Kingdom of Tharbis, his father's kingdom, loomed like a giant prison as he looked at it. It was one of many kingdoms in the Empire and alliance of Nudolla, ruled by the High King, Amkarqa Kashta, from his seat in Nabara, Kingdom of Gold. The High King himself had been named for the former Kushite King and Pharaoh Kashta who first united and ruled over both Kemet and Kush in a peaceful takeover amid Kemet's political disarray. *I am the Nubian who outran his captors!* he thought, nodding in satisfaction. Looking up at the sand dunes, he watched as the wind blew sand gently off the dune closest to him, the lightness of it carrying it away on the wind. And he'd never see the same grain again, he thought. It annoyed him how one grain of sand in his eye could cause so much trouble. Like a needle gouging through his skin, it stung him, blinded him, and caused his eyes to water as he tried to root it out. Picking up a gecko that had crawled into his path, he held it up to the sun, lifting it higher with his palm, its sticky skin cold and clammy against his fingers.

"Terit!" He turned quickly, closing his fingers around the gecko as it squirmed in his hand. Rising, he pursed his lips, anger building in his chest as he watched his little brother running towards him.

"What are you doing here?" he asked angrily as his brother stopped in front of him.

"What is it?" his brother asked him instead, pointing to the gecko in his hand. Jengo's small belly stuck out like the pottery he passed in the markets, no higher than his chest and round like the same.

Terit squeezed the gecko more firmly, before stepping forward and planting his right palm squarely in his brother's chest. Jengo fell from the force of the shove, sand shifting under his weight. The hurt was stark in his eyes as he looked up at him, biting his lip.

"Go home," Terit commanded.

His little brother stood, wiping the sand from his chubby thighs and adjusting his ivory skirt as he righted himself. "Mother said—"

"I don't care what she said!"

Throwing the gecko away, he walked past his little brother.

"Stop following me."

"But—"

He took off running again towards the city; he might be able to lose him in the markets. Sand flew out from under his feet as he raced through the desert, jumping over a hissing snake, the panting of his brother close behind him. Cresting small sand dunes, he slid down the opposite side, looking up to see his brother skidding down after him. *He's too fast!* Terit kept running until he heard his name called and a scream. Turning around, his brother's legs were disappearing into the sand, his hands waving as he sank, his large eyes terrified.

"Help me!"

Terit turned back, Jengo was up to his stomach by the time he reached him and Terit watched his steps, moving lightly across the sand as he crept closer.

"Terit!" his brother cried, tears forming at the corners of his eyes.

Terit moved to his stomach, reaching his hand out towards his brother, relief flooding Jengo's eyes. Terit grabbed the gold collar around his neck and pulled, once, twice, grunting with the effort. Jengo's fingers clawed at his arms in an effort to grip them and pull himself out. Terit had pulled with all his might. Finally, the collar popped free and Terit held it up to the light, studying it before looking back at his brother. He stood, staring down at him as the sand reached his chin.

"Ter…" he was gasping for breath now, the weight of the sand probably crushing his chest. "T—"

"This should have been mine," Terit told him, looking at the collar and back at his brother. "I warned you not to follow me."

He'd walked back to the palace, slipping the collar between the folds of his robes as he practiced his lies and wondered what he would tell his father's wife Fera, his third mother. But then, she wasn't really *his* mother, was she?

CASSIUS

The screaming was driving him mad. Like lambs being slaughtered it invaded his ears and made his teeth rattle. The tribune was not pleased. Cassius followed the tribune down the stairs of the god Juno's temple as he took a left down the narrowest tunnel toward the sounds. The door was open. *Little surprise we could hear them from the entrance.* Grinding his teeth together he waited for the tribune to enter and slid the stone door shut behind them, slamming the stone latch down. The noise made the physicians jump and they turned towards him in alarm.

"I thought I told you to keep this door *closed.*" Cassius growled out.

"Please, it was closed," the physicians replied.

"Not a moment ago it wasn't. Are you calling me a liar?" Cassius interrupted.

"Two of the girls tried to escape so we-"

One of the physicians screamed suddenly, his cry cutting the air as he held up his right hand towards his face, his well tanned skin turning pale as he took in the bloody stumps where his second and pinky finger used to be.

"Hold her down!" the other cried.

The third physician ran forward as the injured one dropped to the ground, crying in shock. Ignoring Cassius and the tribune, the two fought one of the girls whose movement they sought to arrest, struggling against him on the stone table. Her short hemp dress was pushed up and around her waist, her black hair in no more than five shoulder length twists that bounced left and right as she shook her head, pushing and pulling away from them like a captured animal. Blood covered her lips, staining her teeth as she bared them, threatening them with another punishment. Two fingers rolled towards his feet and he frowned as they left dark crimson tracks across the stone floor.

The tribune had until now, been standing only a few feet away, silent and watching the scene unfold. Cassius attempted to control his anger, embarrassment creeping upon him as he remembered his words to the tribune only minutes before. *You needn't worry. I have everything under control.* And here the physicians were, proving him wrong as they failed to control a slip of a girl no more than twelve. *And they weigh at least three times what she does. Fat bastards.*

Now he narrowed his eyes as the tribune walked towards the physicians, their backs turned and oblivious to his approach as the girl continued to scream. Moving closer until he was within arms reach, his arm shot out suddenly and with a dull thud and a crack the heavy stone in his hand slammed into the girl's temple, silencing her screams and knocking her backwards. Falling to the table her knees raised in front of her as the physicians held her ankles she might have only been laying in the grass outside. The physicians glanced up quickly in shock as though the next blow might be meant for them.

"She's not screaming now," the tribune said quietly. Without another word he set the stone down on the table and wiped the dirt from his hands before clasping them both at his back.

"We...we usually g-give the girls a drought so that they sleep through the procedure," the physician on the left stammered, wiping his forearm across his forehead, "but this one, she, it didn't take." He looked at his assistant expectantly, waiting for him to confirm.

"That is how it happened. It did not work on her." The second physician swallowed, standing straight as he released the girl's ankle, his toga stretched tight across his protruding belly.

"Hmm." The tribune's disapproval was written across his face. The physicians stared at him, frozen, hesitating to move.

"Get on with it," Cassius ordered.

The physicians rushed to comply, buckling leather straps across the girl's ankles and wrists quickly. Rolling out a leather pack they pulled out metal tongs, pincers, three carving knives, one pair of scissors, rolls of string and lastly, two metal clasps similar to what sat on their togas, holding their clothing closed. With all the deftness of a bull in a pen they pushed the girl's knees apart and strapped the last belts around her knees before tying the ends to the table to ensure they stayed spread and immobile. The tribune stepped closer and to the side, peering between her legs as the physicians readied for the procedure. In a moment their heads were bent, ducking in and out from between her legs. The fat one made a pleased sound as his right hand tugged at something and pulled it forward.

"That's it," the first confirmed. "Just a little further," he told the other, dipping his head further down as he reached towards her buttocks. One snipping noise later and the girl bucked underneath them, screaming murder as blood poured from between her legs and onto the table.

"I fear we have no more drought to dull the pain," the fat physician told them.

"I don't care whether she's in pain," the tribune replied. "I care that you complete the work I paid you to do.

Swallowing the physicians continued, nodding for the young assistant who until now sat motionless in the corner to come help. He ran forward stepping onto the stool at the edge of the table near the head, leaning his bulky body over the girl as he sat on her chest and gripped her knees with his hands. The girl's screams turned to wheezing gaps, the screams seeming to lodge in her throat as she struggled to breathe at the same time. Stepping closer he peered past their utensils to see a bright pink and red slip of flesh lying on the table and another in their hands as they used the pincers now, piercing it quickly. Hot from the coals next to them the flesh sizzled and smoked as the girl began to shake violently, her head slamming against the table as she tried to get away. After a moment the girl went motionless, saliva dripping from the corner of her mouth. Taking their time now the physicians pierced the clasps through the skin and closed them up. The head physician nodded to the second and waited as he rushed to bring him a small bowl filled with liquid, bloody fingerprints along the sides of the bowl and covering the sides of his cheeks. Turning it over quickly the head physician dumped the contents unceremoniously onto the flesh still clutched between his hands before releasing it. Together the physicians unstrapped the belts from her legs and ankles as they wiped the blood and flesh from the stone table to the floor in one sweep. The boy standing next to the table slipped his arms underneath the girl's armpits and dragged her backwards, her heels grazing the floor as he disappeared behind another door.

The tribune followed. Cassius moved to catch up with them, the physicians close behind. Their hurried steps and breathing filling the space at his back.

Ten rows of slave girls all in varying states of undress lay on their backs, most with their legs tied together, on the ground. Sweat poured from half of their brows, soaking the dirt underneath them and the little clothing they wore. None of them looked up or seemed to hear them enter though several mumbled incoherently in their sleep.

"What's wrong with them?" the tribune asked, his head turning from one side of the room to the other.

"Sometimes the procedure doesn't take as well, but I assure you in a day or two they shall all be fit to travel. It takes no longer than that. The *fibula* can sometimes cause fever dreams after the procedure, but they go away after a time. We give them water twice a day to make sure they have something going in. It aids in the recovery you see."

The tribune said nothing, stepping between the rows slowly as he surveyed each one, pushing aside hair here and there to better see each face. Squeezing a leg as though to test it for firmness and turning up the bottom of the feet. Pausing at the last one he stuck his finger in her mouth, pressing her lips back to get a better view of her gums and teeth as she moaned. The blood staining between her legs seemed not to bother him as he stepped over her outstretched arm on the ground.

"How many are there in total?" The tribune looked up expectantly, his hands clasped behind his back.

"Two hundred and seventy-six." The physician grinned with excitement. "The Ethiopian King was *extremely* generous. None of the girls will present a problem...or retaliation for that matter. Ezana arranged it in advance."

"And," the other physician put in, "it is better that they have the clasps to keep them from unwanted pregnancies, becoming oversexed as they grow older and to hold back any such desires. Their masters will be extremely pleased with this extra care I have no doubt. Only their owners will have the ability to remove it if they choose. It will mean they can work longer and won't lose their strength to childbirth."

The tribune held up a hand to stop the physician's rambling. "It seems our smuggler's information has paid off, and he has done his job well. He is an excellent asset to have in the south. I'm told delivery was earlier than usual. A man about his business. They'll fetch a good price. You've done well, Cassius. Making quite a good name for yourself. The Roman Merchant," the tribune finished softly.

Smiling now he nodded, pleased with the recognition from the tribune.

"Relay the message that we would like those of a higher social status as well. My customers have heard many stories they want confirmed. And their appetites are growing. See that the boys are well taken care of," the tribune ordered. "And make sure this door remains closed." Raising one eyebrow he turned towards the door, walking out quickly.

It had gone better than he could have expected and at least now he knew the tribune was pleased with the procedure and its benefits had been corroborated. *Money well spent.* Finally he turned toward the physicians and motioned towards the boy.

"I have thirty more ready for you now. All boys. I have a feeling you'll need more than one apprentice to hold them down."

SAMYA

They'd been at each other's throats for hours. The Council of Kings had begun at sunrise; each of the heads of the royal families sat around a large table in the shape of a pyramid with her husband at the peak. Amkar, the Essi, the Kiberan Queen, the Scorpion King, the King of the Sao, and the King of the Sotho. Each of the families had ruled over their kingdoms in Nudollan territory for over five hundred years. Half of them bloody and half of them peaceful. This council was no different from the others that came before it, yet as their voices rang out in the meeting hall in anger, she knew something was amiss.

"Speak in turn or you'll keep silent for the remainder of the Council," her husband commanded. The voices died at his command. The Scorpion King picked up the silence.

"The Essi accuse me of smuggling and piracy, smearing and slandering the reputation of the Scorpion Kingdom across the continent. I demand redress!"

"Slander? Quite a stretch, isn't it?" The Essi King was undeterred. Tall and lean, he had the strong arms of one used to pulling rope and manning oars in his youth. His hair was black mixed with salt, coiled in thick ropes down his back; his face held a growing beard. He leaned back in his seat, waiting, the blue cloak he wore hiding the raw leather of the sea. His hand fell casually to the hilt of his sword at his waist, a veiled threat.

The Scorpion King's face darkened, his lips becoming a thin line as he struggled to control his anger.

"One cannot accuse the kingdom of these crimes without further proof," Amkar said, looking around at them all.

When no one spoke, Samya turned to them. "Do you have evidence of this?" she asked sharply.

"Gold," the Essi King replied. "We found gold minted in the form of a snake on the body of a smuggler we killed before he could escape."

"Pity you didn't leave him alive. That could be any merchant or traveler passing through the desert. It's tenuous at best." Amkar shook his head.

"It's early yet," the Sotho King volunteered. "We've all been forced to endure smugglers and caravan raiders in the past year, and they grow less fearful of reprisal each day."

"Very true. There is one whose name has been on the lips of the masses too often. A lawless raider. A nomad. A thief. He raids any caravan he comes upon and slaughters at will." Amkar leaned forward as he finished.

"Yes. That is how we have heard it as well. He makes his home in the desert. It is no wonder he cannot be found." King Kwasi leaned back in his seat as he continued. "The people call him the Desert Falcon. Day or night he is able to track a party of gold, salt, diamonds. It makes no matter. He has no name as yet, but he wears a mask and lies in wait, ambushing all manner of caravans and taking captives too! I would not trust him with my niece. There is no way he has any honor."

"Then we will look for him too. He is believed responsible for raiding the tomb of Anubis. I want him found. Is this all?" her husband asked. When no one spoke, Amkar continued, "Nudolla will send ten Medjay out on the high seas together with ten soldiers from every family to capture and bring these smugglers to heel. They will leave before the festival. It is done," he finished, nodding to Asim.

"The festival will begin shortly," Amkar continued after Asim left. "Prepare your champions. We will begin tomorrow."

They bowed to Samya as they filed out of the Small Council. Her husband reached for her hand as she sat in the chair next to him, and they walked up to the highest tower, overlooking the city, the balcony filled with flowers on all sides. Samya loved to feed the birds from her hand whenever they landed.

"The tide is turning, Samya." Amkar's tone was thick with warning. His hands curled into a fist before he continued. "There's no proof Tharbis is behind these attacks, but it cannot be ignored."

"Many people will die if the slavers come this way in greater numbers. And if Tharbis is behind this treachery he will soon regret it."

"If we can prevent a great number of deaths, then we must try. Precautions have been taken, but it may not be enough."

"The festival—"

"Begins tomorrow. It is a distraction we cannot afford, yet we must. It is the single event that brings kingdoms together every year," he finished. "Samya-qa, if I could, I would hold off until we could ensure the safety of the city. The people need what it will do for them, especially with the drought coming. Famine is a risk we can not afford."

She understood too well. Backing out of agreements would not do and one kingdom had already felt the impact of refusing the betrothal of a daughter to the son of another. Resources were important, and friends were far more useful than enemies.

"We must assign them Adamantine after the Games."

She inhaled sharply. The Adamantine Warriors were bred from the ancestors of the Medjay. The Unbreakable. Only dead men knew the face of an Adamantine. They swore oaths to never retreat in battle unless it was to fall upon their own swords or be killed by their brothers for cowardice. As a girl, she remembered how they stood, rank upon rank, still as stone, each of their hands wrapped around a tall white spear, silver tipped and glinting in the sun. Their only armor was in the form of white leather about their torso and upper legs, falling to the knee. The same leather covered their Achilles heel, held on by the straps of their boots. She'd told her father they looked like white leaves because of their shape. Men fell like leaves before them.

"Must we use Adamantine so soon? Can't it wait?"

"It may keep. I'll send word that they be here in two weeks' time, no more." His expression was dark, and she watched his jaw flex under the weight of his decision.

After a moment, he slid one hand to the back of her neck, letting his fingers pull at the tiniest curls he found there, and lifting her cap crown from her head. Her hair was black and tinted red from the clay she used every other month. Normally her handmaids had care over it, combing it with oil until it gleamed. Other times she would rinse it herself late at night before bed. Samya knew he liked to watch her rinse the clay from her hair, her neck stretched over her favorite terracotta bowl, decorated with elephants, and steaming with water. The steam helped clean her skin at night. He would watch her, both hands engaged in running a comb through her hair, which became almost straight with the weight of the water and clay. As soon as it was dry again, the curls he loved bounced back, slightly red and full of life as she used a cloth to dry them. Now he leaned into her, releasing the pins that held up her hair and pressing his nose against her curls as they fell down her shoulders, even thicker than Imani's, and soft.

"Do you remember the first time you let me touch your hair?" he asked her.

She nodded. "The day of our engagement."

"It was the longest year of my life. Your father hated me."

Her laughter made him smile. "No father thinks any man is good enough for his daughter. Until he proves it."

"That sounded like a yes."

She laughed again. "I think he meant it to feel like the longest year of your life. And rightly so."

Suddenly he drew back, looking her in the eyes. "Why did you never write me back? I sent you a letter every single night for the month I stayed with your father."

She put the top of her fingers against his mouth. "That would have defeated the purpose."

"I wish we could go back to that day."

"We can't go back, my love. Only forward. Come what may." She paused a moment, leaning her head against his shoulder. "Do you think we can defeat them?"

"With tactics like your fathers?" he grinned. "I have no doubt. And besides, I have a weapon they don't."

"What?"

"I have you."

And he means it. The smile on his face lit his eyes like a thousand stars. Samya kissed him gently as he held her, breathing him in as she pressed her nose against his neck.

"I have to see to our guests. I have not greeted the Scorpion King's new bride."

Amkar sighed. "How many does he have now?"

"At least one for each son, but I'm sure it's at eight now. At least he spared us from having to attend his most recent wedding."

"If you must. Make sure Jelani and the rest stay away from their quarters. I want no surprises or talk. His wives are far too young. He's a jealous man, and I need none of that."

"He's famous for his jealousy. None of his subjects would attempt it." She laughed at the thought of it.

"No. He saw to that years ago."

"Do you think the boy is still alive?" Samya couldn't help wondering. *Who could survive in the mines after suffering such a loss?*

"A deserter and a murderer. Not likely."

She kissed him on the cheek and rose. "I'll see you soon." Medjay followed her as she went through the doors, and walked down the tower steps toward the east wing's guest chambers.

She heard the commotion before she reached the tall doors, twice her height. She knocked gently and entered with her handmaid, while the Scorpion King's guards stood just outside with Medjay, waiting.

"Your Grace," his oldest wife spoke first, pushing past the rest as she came forward to bow and quickly rise. Samya kissed her lightly on both cheeks.

"Radhia. It is good to see you again." The quick glance behind her and smug smile almost made Samya laugh. *She's quite satisfied at being recognized first.*

"And you. Girls, greet the queen." *Girls? Half of them are past forty.* Samya held back her astonishment as she kissed them all on each cheek. She knew it was Radhia's way of claiming authority over them all as his first wife. Radhia saw herself as their sole representative.

"May I bring you anything more to drink?" Samya asked. "Have you enough?"

One of the youngest spoke up quickly, her eyes filled with excitement, "I was told you might have some cakes that—"

"No, we are quite fine," Radhia interrupted. "More water would be nice. Some of us need more help than others controlling our figures, as you can see." Radhia glanced behind her at Kiseli, who was now biting her lip, no doubt embarrassed by the comment.

Samya only nodded, ignoring the condescending remark as she walked over to Kiseli, his eighth wife. "We'll be serving later tonight before bed if you find yourself still desiring some then." Gently squeezing Kiseli's hands, she moved away.

"Samya, Imani has grown surprisingly lovely over these past

few years." Cima smiled from where she sat near the window. *She always was quite passive aggressive.* Even when they were friends as children. And it was no surprise as she was his second wife. His second choice. Always having to prove herself and compare herself without showing she cared or even noticed the differential treatment. Samya could not blame her. Few women were relegated to being a second choice without the burden of everyone knowing it. And therein lay the problem.

"Surprising isn't the word I would use, but she is lovely; thank you for your kind words." *As backhanded as they may be.* "It's her spirit I love more." She turned to the others. "Besima, Daran, Emi? Are you comfortable?" The three of them sat silently, only their eyes giving way to the tension they felt around them, created by the older wives.

"Yes, thank you," Emi responded, a small smile on her face.

"I'm fine." Daran nodded her thanks.

"Please, don't trouble yourself," Besima pursed her lips, looking to Kiseli and then to Radhia, who was nervously folding her hands over and over again in her lap repeatedly.

"And where is Fera? Is she well?"

"Yes, Samya, she is," Cima answered this time. "She needed some fresh air, but she's quite well."

The seventh wife sat looking at the floor, having only smiled once since Samya entered the room. She was the last wife before Kiseli. *She's clearly learned the rules that Kiseli hasn't grasped yet.* Samya hadn't heard a word from her since their party arrived, though she'd kissed her on the steps upon their arrival. No doubt Cima and Radhia had put her in her place quickly enough. Looking at her face, Samya's attention moved to her belly.

"Ajna? When are you due?" she asked in surprise.

His seventh wife looked up quickly in shock at having been spoken to. "In three months or more, Your Grace," she stammered, a tight smile at the corners of her mouth.

"Congratulations, my sweet." Samya smiled at her gently. *She's no more than three years older than Imani.* "If I can make you more comfortable in the heat, please let me know. I'll send up one of my handmaids with some hot water to rub your feet. You must be tired after your journey from the Namib."

"Thank you." A slight blush rose in Ajna's cheeks.

She noticed her quick glance at Radhia and wondered how they treated her and if her new silence was the result.

"Please, don't trouble yourself, Samya. Ajna is quite active as it is. In more ways than one, as you can see. I'm sure her feet are fine," Radhia simpered, turning her head towards Ajna.

Her mouth almost dropped open in embarrassment for Ajna. *She dares make light of the intimacy Ajna and her husband might share?*

"I assure you it is no trouble." She looked encouragingly at Ajna.

"You might keep your handmaid to yourself with all of the running around I'm told you've been doing. It must be quite a challenge and a burden." Radhia wouldn't give up.

Samya finally turned her attention to Radhia, who was looking at her expectantly, a triumphant look spread across her face. *She dares intimate knowledge of my dealings with our Nomadin allies.* Radhia had overstepped her position.

"I wasn't speaking to you. When I'm speaking to you, you'll know it because I will look at you and you will have my full attention. As for the *challenges* that I may or may not face I assure you I am well equipped to handle them, and I do not see them as a burden."

Samya nodded to her handmaid, and Jala walked over to the door preparing to open it for her. "Please don't hesitate to let me know if any of you want for anything." She turned to Radhia. "And as for my feet, I don't need my handmaid to deal with such a task. My husband sees to that."

Ten young handmaids in the Scorpion King's retinue busied themselves with folding clothing in their laps, avoiding the gaze of their queens. Radhia swallowed as Samya held her gaze before bowing slowly, her eyes on the floor as Samya looked down at her. When Radhia rose, she turned on her heel and left, her handmaid closing the door behind her.

MIKAILI

"You did as I asked you?"

Mikaili looked at the Essi King a moment before responding. His father had been largely silent since coming back from the Council of Kings. Even now his father sat at the table in their guest chambers, his lower jaw clenched tightly as he looked over the messages delivered on the papyrus in front of him. His father had returned from the council frighteningly quiet. Mikaili overheard a serving girl speaking of the fury on the Scorpion King's face as he left the Council Chambers. King Tharbis had knocked her out of the way in his haste, causing the linen bedding she was carrying to fall. Mikaili stooped to help her, but when she looked up to thank him, her copper face turned almost red and her eyes became saucers in her small face before she ran to her duties.

"Yes, Father. They came afoot. Two hundred in their retinue, including one hundred foot soldiers from the Scorpion King."

His father nodded, his hands curling into fists before responding.

"They have tried too many times to take us by sea. They forget their place. The Essi have ruled Torrent and its waterways for hundreds of years." Anger burned in his eyes, his shoulders tense with fury.

"They've denied it, then?"

"With every lying breath. I can smell their lies. The stench fills my nose as the stench of rotting corpses in their sea of bones." Slamming his fist against the table, he leaned back in his seat.

"Then we must go to war," he replied, watching his father closely.

"We will speak of this later, Mikaili. The Scorpion King believes the issue at rest, but we will take him unawares, catch him in his lie, and Anubis will judge him. I know he is smuggling and pillaging from our ships. Or allowing it."

He lifted his head, turning to look at him, pride apparent in his eyes.

"You've greeted Princess Imani?"

"Yes, on the steps as the Scorpion King arrived." He couldn't help wondering what his father was up to.

"Why did you change?" his father asked suddenly. "I heard you appeared before the High King in quite a state. Though Amkar was kind enough not to mention it."

"I—" he stopped suddenly unsure what to say. Should he continue the lie? "I fell into the water near the palace. It was unintended."

"I should think so. And the princess fell into the same?"

The question startled him. Mikaili froze, his father's eyes watching him carefully, eyebrows rising as he waited, amusement beginning to play at the corners of his mouth.

"She pushed me." His father's laughter rang throughout the bedchamber. "You must have deserved it, then. See that you take care in the future. If I find you drowned in the desert, I'll be mocked for having a fool for a son—a swordfish who can't swim. That or I'll bring war to those smug-faced scorpions."

"Is she beautiful?" His father was relentless, looking up from where he sat writing on the papyrus in front of him, one eyebrow raised as he waited for an answer.

Mikaili hesitated a moment before responding, choosing his words carefully. He always chose his words carefully. "She's much the same as I remember her as a child, Father."

"As a child?" Putting the papyrus down now, his eyebrows knit as he tried to remember something. "She was wild and stubborn. Too many times I confused her for her brother, and she always gave me the same angry look. She had the look of a lion when she did, and that was often. Your mother laughed to see it. Her eyes were the color of molten gold, and her hair was the color of kohl." His father smiled at him. "Now I'm told she's wild, stubborn, and a thief." Mikaili's eyebrows rose in surprise at the accusation as his father continued. "I'm told she's well loved by the people and that she's stolen all of goddess Hathor's beauty." He continued writing again, "And despite all of this," he moved the papyrus closer to his eyes before setting it down and looking his son directly in the eyes, "that wasn't the question I asked you."

Mikaili clenched his jaw in discomfort as he reminded himself his father missed nothing. *Is she beautiful?* Thinking back to the look on her face when she'd realized who he was in the cave, her dark amber eyes were what he remembered most. They shone bright like two gold coins. Her heart-shaped face was full of shock, but not fear. Never fear. The surprise on her face reminded him of a doe he'd seen once in the savannah. When her mouth dropped open in recognition water still dripped from her lips like dew falling from two petals. "She's still wild and stubborn," he said frowning.

"To be sure. She's her father's daughter. Get to know her, but be wary, Mikaili. I don't trust the Scorpion's sons any more than I do their father.

"Why?" he asked without thinking.

"Why? Surely you're not afraid of women, Mikaili?"

He made sure his face betrayed nothing, but he did not miss the amusement in his father's voice. "No. And she's no more than a girl."

"A beautiful girl, if I'm to believe what I've heard. And *smart.*" Smiling with satisfaction, his father walked to the window with a bounce in his step as though he'd raised her himself. "From what I'm told, she's been a large contributor to the locals and her support has caused the city to flourish. She knows the land well and has a keen sense for languages and history."

He couldn't disagree or argue without his father discrediting it. It was true; she was much as he'd remembered. The way she'd ordered him to release Ama had made him smile. Her involvement with Nudolla and especially Nabara hadn't escaped his notice either. Princess Imani made it a point to know the city and invest in its success, riding with the Royal Guard until she knew every piece of the land and the independent Nomadin within it.

"The festival is to form alliances, Mikaili. I have no interest in making you miserable. You were friends once. And I expect you to honor our alliance."

"Yes, father. I will," he promised, watching his father retire to his bedchamber and closing the door behind him.

He'd met Imani when he was only seven. His father had come to explore trading options within Nabara. The day they met, she'd come running across the pavilion, a blur of white and gold as she stopped in front of him, breathless. With her father's hand atop her head, she'd inclined her head towards him and welcomed him to Nabara. She was small for her age, but fast. Always running behind her brother and sister, begging them to wait, not to leave her behind. The scowl she reserved for them would have been deadly if looks could kill. Her hair was the color of kohl and more often than not had sand in it from her constant playing outdoors. Once he'd told her she looked like a marauder when she appeared in the stables midday wearing gold harem pants and a white tunic that floated behind her when she ran.

The second time he had come to Nabara, his mother had died of red fever. It took her within a fortnight. His father grew more silent the sicker she became, and sent him away to Nabara the day after she was buried. He hadn't understood why he was being sent away, and at ten he was lonely, filled with grief and angry. Hundreds of *ushabti* figurines were made for her as a gift from Nabara, with two taller ones standing in front of them in her own likeness. Stealing one of them had been easy. He refused to forget her. High King Kashta's sons had tried to tempt him with horse rides, chariot races, and wrestling matches to no avail. Queen Samya had only filled his heart with sadness. He had wandered the palace of Nabara sullen, hiding from the curious stares of the servants and watchful eyes of the Medjay. The night before his return to the Floating Islands, he crept into a corner of his room and cried, sobbing into the pillow he clutched to his chest, wishing his mother was there. *And she heard me.*

"Why are you crying?" Imani had asked him, her slippered feet having concealed her entry into his bedchamber. Her hair was in two thick, long braids, hanging over her shoulders; the green and gold robe she wore fell to the floor, a belt knotted loosely at her waist.

Wiping his eyes with the sleeve of his tunic, he'd frowned at her. "I'm not crying," he replied, anger burning in his eyes to hide the shame.

"You were too," she countered, her voice high and confident. "I heard you from my bedchamber." She regarded him curiously before sitting down. "I know your mother died. I'm very sorry," she whispered. "She wouldn't want you to be sad all the time."

"How would you know?" he demanded, his voice angry as his tears threatened to betray him.

Imani had bitten her lip. "I don't, but you shouldn't be afraid. She's at peace now. She's with the gods."

He'd looked up at her, his grey eyes wild. "I'm not *afraid*!" He'd thrown the word back in her face like an insult. He was a prince. Princes weren't afraid, and princes didn't cry. His father taught him that.

"Then why are you crying?" she'd asked again, her voice softer this time.

Looking up at her before looking down at his hands, he balled them into fists. "My father sent me away. I—I'm worried I'll forget her."

Imani had moved closer to him, sitting at his feet and crossing her legs before him. "Your father is probably very sad. Maybe you remind him of her. Besides, that's silly," she admonished him. "You won't forget her. What did she look like?"

"She…" He'd stared at her a moment, "She had grey eyes, like mine. My father called them storm clouds when she was angry. His silver lining when she was happy. Her hair was light brown and gold, like the color of sand. She had skin the color of acacia wood. And she was mine," he finished quietly.

"See?" She was smiling now. "You won't forget her."

He smiled before adding, "She used to sing to me sometimes. Before I went to sleep, she'd sing to me."

"What did she sing?" Imani asked, curiosity on her face.

He regarded her bright amber eyes before responding, "Our Kingdom is of the Floating Islands, with rivers and waterfalls, a city in mist. But I liked to hear about the Secrets of the Pyramids."

"I know that one! Would you like me to sing it for you?" Excitement stole over her face, but he didn't share her enthusiasm.

"You?" he snorted. "You're barely half a girl! You can't sing."

But she'd ignored him, curling her legs underneath her until she was sitting on her heels, palms on her knees, and began to sing.

Now I know your secrets
When I closed my eyes
I flew across the sand

And floated in the skies
Dry your tears for me
No sadness when I'm gone
Sleep well now, my love
In your dreams, I live on
The secrets of the pyramids
Will tell you where I've gone
Sleep well now, my love
In your heart, I live on.

When she finished, he was staring at her, his grey eyes blinking back fresh tears. She'd crawled closer to him, sitting next to him on the stone floor and placing her hand inside his. They'd fallen asleep just like that. Her handmaidens had found them there, curled up on the stone floor on top of a fur coverlet, a pillow cradling their linked hands. Still sleeping at dawn, she breathed softly as her handmaiden helped him to his feet to dress him for his journey home. Her black hair spilled across the white fur coverlet, her mouth open slightly, her hand empty now, curling against the pillow with her legs tucked close to her chest.

He'd wanted to say goodbye, but the handmaidens insisted, dressing him warmly against the night air before walking him out of the chambers and handing him over to his Medjay escort. The *Sea Goddess* had been unroped from its port, pulling away from the shore when a ghost came floating over the sand. Hooves could be heard in the distance and he heard someone shout his name.

"Mikaili!" she called. Running to the edge of the deck, he leaned over the side to see her all in white, black stallion rearing up underneath her.

"You won't forget me?" he called back, his face anxious.

"Never!" The wind carried her voice to him and he watched her urge her stallion into the sea, running along the shore, hand raised high in farewell as he smiled back.

I thought she forgot. He found himself fingering the necklace he'd found in the pools. The stones glittered in his fingers as the light hit them. *She must have been looking for this.*

KETEMIN

"How dare you?" Komoro's eyes narrowed as he spoke, striding across the room with his hands curled into fists, nostrils flaring. Striding into her chamber in High King Kashta's palace of Nabara, he threw the doors open as he came.

My brother. How beautiful you are and so like father. Anguish squeezed her heart as she was reminded of her father. The similarity went no further. Panic choked her as she wondered if her brother knew she was having him followed. Commander Tesir could never fail so miserably at a task. It wasn't in his nature.

"You *dare* to speak with our uncle without consulting me?"

"*You*, are not the king," she said simply, seated on the high-backed golden chair before him.

"And you are? My sister goes before *me?*" He threw the comment in her face, mocking her as he did when she was a child.

"Your uncle sits this throne, and he will until the day he dies." Leaning forward, her hands gripped the curved edges of her seat. "You would do well to remember that."

"Remember?" Fury flashed on Komoro's face as he moved closer to her like a snake on the savannah. "Who—"

"Stop," she warned him, "before you say something you will regret."

Inhaling, his shoulders relaxed as his pointed finger and arm fell back to his side.

"How did you—?"

"The master of the treasury. When he refused to speak with me until tomorrow and then...insisted you could give me better information, I knew something was amiss." Cutting her eyes at him, she watched him pace the floor of the chamber, his black dress robe sweeping the floor as his ivory *shendyt* peeped through.

"Odwulfe was acting directly on my orders! Did you not trust that he was telling the truth?" Disbelief etched across his face. She wanted desperately to believe him.

I did not trust you. "In truth, Brother, it was much more efficient to have my questions answered by doing it myself. And I did. Are you not concerned that the guard was about to rape one of the miners?

"Of course I was, Kemi." He used his pet name for her rarely, and even now it made her heart squeeze. They'd been without a father from such a young age. It was important to her that they remained close. "I had no idea he was of such low character," he finished.

"Why trust one guard to look over the salt mines in the first place, Komoro? They are placed there for a reason. The price of salt only rises. Do you know why?" He had to listen to reason. *And stop lying.*

"Yes. I do. I'm not what you think of me, sister. I needed the extra guards for only a short while to—" he faltered.

"To what?" Raising an eyebrow, she waited for an answer, but he paused in front of her, looking at her with the same mistrust an antelope must feel around a sleeping lion. He ran one hand over his bald head slowly, raising his chin as he met her eyes.

"For my own private use," he finally replied.

"We are the Sao, and the Sao do not sit idly on this throne. We are the giants that guard our people. The fires of the Sahara warm us to the north, providing a barrier to enemies who seek our resources and for trade in human cargo. The rift to the east is a dangerous trek of mountain and rock, and to the west, our neighbors, who trade in slaves at the coast. We must defend it, Brother. I will not have it said that the Sao did not do everything in their power to conquer their enemies. I will not have us erased from history."

"Uncle knows that we have over a thousand…"

"Uncle knows that we have salt mines. And salt is white gold to our people. They must be protected. You, he put in charge. You, who removed all but one guard from our salt mines and cut the wages of the people."

"There was no need for…"

"More than one?" Ketemin interrupted him again. "One who was not watching as we rode up? One who sought to rape a woman newly married? One who allowed children yet weaned to work in

235

the mines? Our uncle values our people much more than you do, Brother." She finally turned to her right to look at him, a high chair in between them both in her chamber as the wind blew at the curtains on the balcony.

"Had you even concerned yourself with what other indecencies he might have been committing? He could have stolen salt, raped a thousand women and we might never have known!" Ketemin was exasperated at having to explain how she felt at the moment the guard had raised his hand to her. At his audacity at having put hands on a married woman. *Any* woman.

"Amun-Ra take me—of course! I love you, Kemi-qo," he said, his voice softening. "I'm glad you're safe. It is the reason I had his arm struck off. We'll continue questioning him upon our return."

"Struck off? You may have waited to ask me."

"Isn't that what you wanted?" His face spoke frustration now.

"Not while we still had yet to question him. What reason has he now to tell the truth? His own skin having already been damaged, he would say anything to save his life. Did you not think of that?" Ketemin watched him closely, wanting to beg him to be more careful and feeling like screaming at him might have more of an effect.

"I've upset you, but it wasn't my intention. I've replaced the guards at the salt mines with loyal people and a few Medjay."

"Would that you had sent the Medjay with the salt caravan to Chad. Our trade routes may become dangerous very quickly. The Niger River has cities at which it has already become customary to sell slaves. We *must* be cautious."

Komoro pursed his lips.

She leaned back now as Komoro walked towards his own seat. His anger seemed to subside as he sat, leaning back fully, his right hand stretched across his forehead as he rubbed his temples.

"Why didn't you tell our uncle about your little trip? About your meeting?" She was grasping at reeds now, trying to determine what else he was up to.

His face dropped as he realized the import of her words. "I meant to tell him about the Berber and the slavers sooner. It is the reason I traveled west. It was necessary."

The earnestness on his face gave Ketemin pause. She could normally tell when her brother was lying to her, but the first bit of information she received from Commander Tesir told another story entirely.

"Komoro. We trade in salt for the good of the kingdom. The people's will is also our own. The salt buys us grain, materials, iron. Iron makes weapons. And soldiers wield weapons. And soldiers fight wars. If we cannot pay our soldiers, how long do you think they will continue to fight? If we cannot pay our soldiers, there may be someone else who will."

Komoro's lips pursed, and she watched him closely as he regarded her in silence, his head turned her way, his beautiful light brown eyes hiding something, keeping something from her.

Footsteps sounded, and she turned her head towards the door.

Their uncle strode into her chamber, walking up towards Komoro's seat until he was directly in front of him. The rage on his face made Ketemin sit up straighter in her seat as she watched them both.

"Come with me," his words ground out carefully.

They both rose in unison as her uncle turned on his heel and walked out of the chamber, guards following them through the palace. They passed a number of handmaids and others preparing for the Festival of Kings, but Ketemin could not focus on them. Moving past decorated walls, they passed through the palace and down the steps. A Sao litter waited for them at the bottom. For the second time, Ketemin wondered at her uncle's purpose. The Medjay guards stopped at the foot of the stairs and left them with the Sao guards waiting next to the litter. The heat of the day pressed against her face as the sun beat down above her.

The three of them stepped inside, her uncle across from both of them as the ox drawn litter pulled off, the Sao guard detail in tow. Pulling the curtains closed, their uncle tilted his head, watching both of them closely as he finished adjusting the pillows to his satisfaction. A moment later he leaned forward and slapped Komoro full across the face with his backhand. Her mouth dropped open in surprise as her brother fell against the litter door, both hands pressed to his right cheek as he recoiled in shock. The litter shook heavily as it moved over rocks and pits. Her brother grasped at the door, never taking his eyes from their uncle.

"Where were you?"

Komoro edged away from him, leaning slightly and turning so his back was to the door. She was sure if they had not been moving he would have jumped from the litter to avoid another slap.

"Uncle, please," he begged.

"Where *were* you!?" their uncle barked, one fist raised and drawn up across his chest as though the wrong answer would unleash it in all fury against his nephew.

"I went west with our guards to make consult with some traders, Uncle. We must determine how to make peace with the Mandé and the Igbo. As you said, if we want to go far, we must go together." Komoro bowed his head in supplication as their uncle looked on.

Ketemin fought against the urge to shake her head. *He's lying!* And she knew it. She could always tell when he was lying. It was like an itch just under your skin that begged ones fingers to scratch. It was in the slight upward tick of his eyebrow and his quick glance down and to his left. Not as if he were really apologetic, but as though he were thinking of his next lie. His next story. The right words to receive forgiveness. When they were younger, he used to bring her treats when he'd wronged her. Sweet plantains, cinnamon cream with mangoes, yellow acacia flowers for her hair. He hadn't changed.

Their uncle seemed surprised by his answer and even Ketemin knew he would be.

"What did they say during this *meeting*?"

Komoro sat up straight again, relaxing slightly under his uncle's gaze. "The Igbo feel the sting of the Berber's press to the North as well. And they believe many of their relatives are being kidnapped by slavers."

"And the Mandé? I was told they might be trading in slaves themselves." Their uncle leaned forward.

"They can't be sure, but I think not. The Mandé are a great source of trade, water to their economy. It's best not to jump to conclusions or act rashly until we know for sure that they are." Their uncle nodded as he spoke.

"Uncle," Ketemin implored him. "The Mandé sit on the coast. Their trade is popular with the North. Trade in *slaves*. Their territory is a regular route to Roman territories, Cuicul, and others. We should not trust them."

"Ketemin. Proof is something one should always require before entering into war. And they have not declared that they are at war with us. We have more pressing things to concern ourselves with. The harvest season is almost over. If there is no water we will be at risk of drought."

"Uncle. One need not declare war on a people to have waged it. Kidnapping, enslavement, forced labor, and murder satisfy my requirements at all times. The tales are not singular. There are multiple sources. And the High King's family has already been attacked! Ama and Imanishakheto could have been killed!" Ketemin crossed her legs as she looked to her uncle and brother, hiding the frustration she felt. For Romans to enter Nabara and attempt to take the life of the High Princess was no small matter.

"Who?" her uncle asked looking at them in confusion.

She and her brother exchanged looks. "Who what, Uncle?"

"Who tried to take a life?"

"Uncle? The High Princess Imanishakheto and her cousin Princess Ama. The Romans were—"

"Yes, yes. My mind was elsewhere. Forgive me." Her uncle smiled as he looked at her. "You remind me of your father so often. So often."

"Father would have protected the people at all costs. Father would have wanted us to fight." Ketemin held his gaze as he pondered.

"I believe he would. The High King understands our position. He meets our request for soldiers with two hundred of his own. We will unite our forces, protect our borders, and determine our next move."

The shock on Komoro's face didn't go unnoticed by his sister. "So quickly? The High King has promised so many."

Her uncle stared at Komoro, the calm on his face belying the anger in his eyes. The litter rattled over rock, shaking gently.

"Custom and tradition, Komoro. Our bond is an old one and not lightly shaken. What affects one affects us all. Further. I relieve you of your duty within the salt mines. Ketemin will take command there. I have no doubt she will do an excellent job."

"You can't…"

"Can't what? Be careful of your visits to our neighbors, Komoro."

"Uncle…" Komoro could not finish his words, and he looked to her with desperation on his face, begging her to intercede. But she would not. Turning her head away, she avoided his eyes.

"And if anything should happen to the salt caravan on its journey, I will hold you personally responsible."

"Yes, Uncle."

"Everything you do reflects on this family and the rule of the Sao Kingdom. I will not have our actions nor our love for the people questioned because of your carelessness and ambition. One more mistake like that and I will put you on the front lines. By Ra, I promise you." Uncle Kwasi paused. "Without armor."

Ketemin struggled to hold back her smile as she watched her uncle lean back in his seat. Even when she believed he'd been persuaded in the other direction, he never failed to remind them he would not forget or condone. And he never failed to make clear to Komoro—he was the king.

Later that night she found herself leaving the gardens to find her uncle. He would love a short turn about the gardens before bed. The sugar bush flowers were magnificent and the lotus flowers that sat in the fountains were larger than any she had seen before.

His head bent further towards the papyrus in his hand when she entered his chambers. Scrolls of papyri were stacked on a low alabaster stand and slid into small cylindrical shelves for their storage. Her uncle always complained about the number of orders he needed to sign each day. And all of them had been brought to Nabara. The treasurer sat on the opposite side of the large, sandstone, signing table, which seemed to rise up from the ground. Embedded with gold and precious quartz, its smooth top flowed into sharp corners. The far right of the room held a long chaise decorated with pillows. A number of palm-sized bowls held a variety of meats, fruit, and sorghum. *No surprise the handmaid's walking back held empty platters returning to the kitchens.* He must have been famished. At least the view was beautiful. High

King Kashta had been very generous indeed. As soft as her steps were he still heard her approach, lifting his head slowly while squinting at her.

"Ketemin." Sounding slightly relieved as he said her name, her uncle relaxed his grip on the papyrus. Holding back the urge to laugh she shook her head. Little wonder. Her uncle hated the time spent reviewing documents for the kingdom and they always seemed to multiply. Rubbing his eyes he set down the stylus, still holding the yellowed papyrus in his right hand.

"Princess Ketemin," Odwulfe rose quickly from his seat, bowing as she nodded in reply before taking his seat again.

"Odwulfe. Uncle," she said warmly, watching his smile brighten as she came closer. "Will you be done soon? You've been in here longer than I expected," she continued, sitting carefully on the chaise in the corner of the chambers. "The hour grows late."

"Almost my dear. Just a few more items…"

"What are you looking at now?" Cocking her head to the side she waited for his answer.

"Now?" A puzzled look spread across his face as he glanced quickly at treasurer Odwulfe before looking down, grasping the papyrus in both hands. "I was just having dinner," he replied slowly, looking around the room carefully.

Ketemin laughed. "That's another way of looking at it! You do spend entirely too much time here and I hate it when you forget to eat."

Standing she walked over to him, pushing her carnelian and copper bracelets away from her wrists and up her forearms as she leaned onto the table, standing just behind his chair while peering over his shoulder. The papyrus held an official order, short but succinct. In only two paragraphs it detailed the provision of a hundred gold bars towards an increase in the military, a loan to two individuals of the nobility who traded in stones, and changed the Chief Insurer of Trade from an old, well-known family to one she'd never heard of. Frowning at the name she wondered if they were even *of* the Sao Kingdom. *And his payment for his title is almost double what was normally provided!* Tallying up the numbers quickly in her head she picked up her uncle's stylus and made a mark on the paper carefully.

"That needs fixing," she stated as firmly as she could. "I'm surprised at you, Odwulfe, you're normally so careful."

"Surely there is some mistake, Princess..." Odwulfe spread his hands in apology.

"Mistake? The consequences of implementing such an order will be attributed to more than that." Her eyes shone with reproach as she watched him carefully, her uncle still looking at the papyrus in shock.

"I would never have—"

"Who is this family?" she interrupted, taking the parchment from her uncle and setting it on the table. "I have never heard such a name before." Leaning towards the table in front of her, she put one finger under the new insurer's name on the order, her right hand sitting on her hip as she challenged him. The treasurer leaned forward squinting at the papyrus as he did.

"I cannot begin to explain it, Your Highness," he started, the look on his face earnest enough. "Dozens of requests for orders come in each day, often from the nobility. It is up to His Majesty to sign them." At this, he turned to her uncle. "Please forgive me, Your Grace. I had no idea of the change. I only review a portion of the orders. I am here only to provide you counsel as you wish." Bowing his head, he waited in silence.

Ketemin pursed her lips, doubt running through her mind, as another part of her couldn't fathom it.

"You are forgiven. Even I grow tired this afternoon." Her uncle squeezed the bridge of his nose between two fingers. "The eyes need rest."

"Princess, forgive me, I can look at it again," he said, rushing to fill the silence. The treasurer's eyebrows shot upward towards his hairline, his shrewd brown face a mask of surprise against his ivory khat.

"No, please." She moved the papyrus he reached for away quickly, smiling at the same time. "Please, refresh yourself. It's been quite a long day for you and my uncle I'm sure. I'll only be a short while and you can return."

"Of course, of course." Odwulfe rose, bowing smoothly and walking out of the chambers, shutting the door behind him.

Turning quickly, she faced her uncle. "Uncle! What on earth is this? I'm surprised you would sign such a thing." Disappointment shone in her eyes as she looked at him.

"Ketemin, I, I don't...remember..."

"We've had the same insurer for years. And an excellent job he does. Why on earth would you replace him?" Struggling to understand, she waited again for a response.

"I thought it was just the numbers..."

"Uncle, I *lied* about the numbers. Odwulfe has never made a mistake with the numbers. I just needed him to *leave.*"

"All right. All right. It has been a long day, I simply overlooked it."

"And yet you still haven't answered my question. What's going on with you lately? I'm worried about you. A *loan* to the nobility of such an exorbitant amount? Changing the insurer in the middle of a trade—"

"Ketemin ENOUGH!" Anger boiled on his face as he pounded his fist on the table in front of him.

Ketemin gasped at his tone, shifting backwards slightly. *He never yells at me!* She looked at him in shock, unable to respond. She always enjoyed their playful banter, and his love for her direct honesty was a trait that had endeared him to her at a young age. He *always* encouraged her to speak her mind. Not that she ever needed his permission. Especially as she'd grown older.

"I just...I'm sorry, Uncle..."

"Ketemin, I'm not well." The look on his face nearly stopped her heart. "I'm tired," he said quickly almost as though he was rushing to fill the silence.

Relief washed across her face as she realized he was only speaking of his day. It was natural. And he was under such a great amount of pressure.

"I understand, Uncle. Forgive me for—"

"No, no. It's not your fault. I shouldn't have yelled at you." Looking back down at the papyrus in his hands he studied it a moment. "You're entirely right. I'm glad you came in when you did. I'll have it fixed immediately. I don't usually make such mistakes," he said softly, reaching to pat her hand in assurance.

"There's a first time for everything," she replied smiling back at him as she squeezed his hand.

"Wait for me? I'll be finished shortly. I can return to this tomorrow and start again. I'd like to walk with you for a bit."

"Of course," she agreed. "Of course."

Settling back into her chaise, she watched him as he marked up the papyrus that was in his hands and set it aside for revision before picking up another. Resting her chin in her hand she couldn't help but wonder what would have happened had she not come to find him. Signing an order like *that*. It was appalling. And Odwulfe. He had seemed surprised at her reaction, but slightly disappointed too, but not in any mistake he'd made. She was sure of that. Her uncle ran a hand over his head as he picked up another order. This was far too strange for her to ignore. Perhaps his concerns about the slave trade had slipped into his mind. She couldn't blame him for being stressed.

And Komoro is no help. She doubted his oversight of the salt caravans was all her uncle's idea. Begging wasn't in Komoro's nature, but he had no problem with using a person's guilt to his advantage. It would take more than a slap to change his nature. What worried her even more was the thought of orders her uncle might have *already signed.* How on earth would she be able to fix *that?* Watching her uncle study the papyri she realized one important thing about the unknown names of the new insurer. Odwulfe hadn't answered her question.

SICARIUS

"What is it?"

Sicarius peered over the sand dune, squinting into the sun that shone in his eyes as the sand shifted underneath him. Cassius was next to him, his breathing labored in the heat. Face swollen with sweat, the slaver's handkerchief at his disposal was dripping with the same. It did him no good. They hadn't seen an animal all day, but Sicarius had assured him water was close. The trader liked hearing that word—close. It comforted him. Gave him hope. Now he looked down at the train of camels making their way across the desert. He counted fifty before he stopped. Better to count the herders. They posed the most trouble. Square and rectangular white blocks hung from both sides of each, secured together by ropes at each end. *Those aren't for riding.*

"It's a salt caravan." He could see the guards more clearly now, their *khopesh* blades swaying gently on their horses. *And only four,* he thought incredulously.

"A what?" Cassius interrupted his thoughts with the question, the curiosity in his voice plain.

"A salt caravan." Sicarius moved back behind the sand dune carefully. The last time he'd seen a salt caravan he'd been just a child. His mother had agreed to take him to market, and they'd run into a caravan on their way. The guards had been kind. He could sit, the guard told him, if he promised not to hit the camel or take the reins. Sicarius's promise had been solemn and he'd kept it, holding onto the camel's hump tightly, afraid he would fall even with his mother behind him. The guards had numbered at least twenty. And for good reason.

Now he turned to Cassius. "They mine the salt in the desert, chipping away at it to form blocks. It's wrapped, loaded and taken to the market to sell."

"Hm. Not fighters, then?"

"Not by trade," he responded, looking back down at the train of animals. A young boy skipped lightly towards the back, a staff in his right hand and another on the reins of a camel. *A son, most likely*, Sicarius thought, *learning the trade*. Every few steps the boy jumped high into the air, not a care in the world.

"That's good news. Well done." Cassius clapped him on the shoulder before moving backwards, careful not to disturb the sand and give away their position.

Sicarius watched the caravan a moment longer, using his dagger to spear the spider crawling towards him. He slipped it between his lips, crunching on the desert meat. His forest colored eyes surveyed the caravan as he wondered again at the lack of guards protecting it. Salt was a luxury. An expensive and valuable commodity for trade at any market that would as soon buy gold as it did meat and jewels. It was possible there were more at the back of the caravan, but it was hard to imagine, given that even the sides were not protected. Even in the closed Roman coliseum, gladiators protected all sides. You never knew which way the attack might come from.

Running a hand over his close-shaven head he thought a moment. Even if there were more guards, this position was to their advantage. *And we have the element of surprise.* With nothing but hills of sand surrounding the caravan, their only escape was a climb up a hill that would constantly be moving under them. The caravan had no way to outrun them. The shadow of a beard wrapped around his square jaw as he moved back carefully from the top of the hill. Black eyebrows, sharp and curveless, ran out from the bridge of his wide nose towards his temples. His hands all but disappeared in the sienna-colored sand, his skin blending well as the sun dropped from the sky. He was a chameleon here, and it served him well. Standing, he found Cassius at the bottom of the dune speaking with the other traders, excitement soaking his words.

"…only four, so this should be as easy a job as it comes. The rest, maybe twenty, all seem to be herders carrying staff and the like. Only four sitting a horse, the rest on foot. I can't imagine walking all that way." He laughed. "They must be tired."

"Such a shame," another commented, chuckling, moving his hand across his forehead as he wiped sweat away before passing it along his pants.

"Did you see anything else?" Cassius was looking at him as he slid his own short sword inside of the sheath around his waist.

"Nothing. But given the length of it, it may be best not to charge them fully. The camels might scare."

"I don't care about the bloody camels, Sicarius. I just want the people herding them." He slapped at his thighs and groaned. "Riding for so long…my muscles could use a break."

"Yes, but the salt has value." Sicarius remembered the blocks of gold that would pile up against the salt at the market.

"We can't carry salt without the camels. They'll slow us down. We came for the human cargo. Nothing more." Cassius was adamant.

Sicarius nodded his understanding.

"Do as he says," Cassius told the men after a moment. It will be better if the camels are not as spooked. If anyone runs, then at your leisure."

The men nodded as they checked their weaponry.

Sicarius walked over to one of the horses, loosening the straps on a large leather bag. It fell with a loud thud to the ground, the metal inside rattling slightly as it settled. He began to pull out the long chains wrapped inside, hand over hand as the silver links appeared. It was quite something to think that there would soon be a number of slaves carrying this jewelry through the desert. He'd seen their effect on countless numbers of raw and bleeding ankles and wrists as they dragged the chains onward, eyes vacant and resigned. Chips of dried blood clung to the crevices, but he ignored them. He was used to it. They would need these soon. He lifted the ankle weights as well, their dull and grainy appearance suited to their use. Insurance against those who decided they might still try to run, the heavy bracelets did their job well.

Next, he uncurled the large short sections of rope, as thick around as a wrist. The frayed rope would likely chafe, but that was no cause for worry, it would not break or tear easily. He moved the mouth guards to the side, their shape more suited to that of a horse or dog. The leather wound in half circles with the longest strap meant to be secured tightly behind the head, the middle metal and leather bit pressed between the teeth to separate the tongue and to keep the jaws from closing. Cassius liked to beware of biters, and even Sicarius knew the benefit of knowing he wouldn't lose an ear or a nose to one of these slaves. Many slavers had made that mistake before, one recent incident happening quite near him at the coast. A young woman standing with a young boy had suddenly snapped, moving in quickly to bite and tear the ear off of the trader attempting to uncuff her restraints for sale at the port. The buyers liked to see their cargo dance a bit, prove their agility and fitness. The ripping sound as his flesh was torn had made Sicarius turn to watch just as the slaver began to beat her, ignoring the open hole on the side of his face as he kicked her again and again while the child cried, roped to her and unable to run away. *He decreased the value of his product with every stripe.* When he saw her half an hour later, she looked too weak to stand, a mouth guard and bit now strapped around her head as the crowd laughed, pointing out that this slave may have had a bit too much wine, many of them not having witnessed the scene earlier. With her jaws open and locked in place, the drool ran freely down the sides of her mouth unchecked, the saliva wetting her chest as she stood in place.

The iron ballasts he left where they were, the rest of the number needed would be purchased at the port, right before the slaves boarded the ship. They would need them to counterbalance the weight in the ship's cargo hold for the voyage. Depending on the number of slaves they took, he knew the ballasts would steady the load. If slaves refused to eat, couldn't keep food down, or simply died from disease, it would be taxing on the crew. Fluctuating weight and offloading dead bodies into the sea meant the iron would be needed to make sure the ship remained stable during its journey. It wasn't an easy trade once you got into the details, but Sicarius was always prepared.

He moved back over to the group after securing the bags to the horses and nodded to Cassius. *Everything is ready.*

They circled around towards the front of the caravan slowly, taking their time. The deep valley they were inside would prove to be useful in containing them, and a difficult route to escape. Even camels hated to climb up mountains of sand. Some of the Berbers were pointing towards the opposite side, making sure the Roman traders could see what they did. *The caravan was trapped.*

Cassius was first, moving slowly down the sand dune. Sicarius saw the moment the head guard spotted them. They were thirty strong and coming toward them at a leisurely pace. The guard looked behind him and to his right, but quickly held up one hand so that the procession stopped. A quick glance behind him towards the tail of the caravan and he realized they were all in this deep valley, with nowhere to go and a party of thirty blocking their path.

He called out in a language Sicarius knew Cassius did not understand.

"What did he say?"

"He commands you to move aside. He says they have business waiting." Sicarius turned back to look at the four guards in front of him. The commander's head had snapped toward Sicarius when he heard him speaking. Well, *he understands Greek at least.*

"Your business," Cassius told him, "is my business."

The guard dropped the reins of his horse and laid one hand on the sickle at his side.

"You have no business here. This salt caravan is the property of Kwasi of the Sao Kingdom. Anyone who threatens or takes of it shall answer to him."

"The Sao Kingdom…" Cassius looked behind the commander. "Is it far from here? Quite inhabited would you say?" He raised his eyebrows in excitement. He was enjoying himself. "I have no intentions of answering to anyone. Nor do I have much interest in the *salt* in this caravan."

The guards began to look uneasy now. Half of them were confused by the conversation, but all three of them seemed to feel the danger in the situation having counted the party and knowing how poorly protected the caravan was. Their horses could feel it too, stamping slightly in the ensuing silence, their feet pounding in place as they shifted back and forth. The herders stood still next to their camels, heads leaning to the side as they stretched to see why the caravan had come to a standstill. Finally, the guard's eyes rested on Sicarius, upbraiding him for his participation in this before he saw the leg irons hanging from the back of his horse. *Now he understands.*

"Advance!" The guards charged the party only fifty feet away, the swords in their hands so fast Sicarius heard a gasp from behind him. The commander barreled down on Cassius, hell-bent on spilling his blood. Sand kicked up wildly as the four targeted the party in their sights.

A yelp and a squelch sounded next to Sicarius and he looked to see a dagger embedded in one Roman's neck.

"Surround!" Cassius called out, and the party branched out like a web, moving into a circular position. A Berber to his right pulled out a throwing iron, aiming at the legs of the horses as they came. Their screams of pain were almost otherworldly as they crumpled face first into the sand, sprawling onto the ground and spilling their riders. One lay trapped underneath his horse's head, struggling to pull his arm free from the heavy weight even as his leg lay at an unnatural angle below him.

Another untangled himself, rushing towards another slaver to engage him in a swordfight, circling and kicking dust up into his eyes as he fought, the metal ringing again and again in the sand dunes.

The herders had moved to action, running for the group, but the Berbers began to pick them off, and after three arrows barely grazing his arm, one finally sprouted in his chest and the others dropped to their knees, kneeling as the camels stood watching, oblivious to the blood spilling around them.

Grabbing the neck of the last guard whose breastplate was now gone he twisted it quickly, dropping him to the sand. A moment later the last guard ran towards him, a curved blade in each hand as he came at Sicarius with all his might, slamming them down against Sicarius' *gladius* sword again and again. Sicarius pressed his advantage, hands wrapped around the handle of his sword as he angled it across his body, slamming it against the guard's blade and forcing him backwards, the man's feet sliding in the sand. The party stood silent around them, everyone dead, or having surrendered. Sicarius feinted to his right and sliced his sword along the guard's back watching his arms jerk back in pain and his chest jut forward, crying out as the wound left a trail of blood down his back. Turning back around, the guard waited as Sicarius dropped his own sword, his arms out as he motioned for the guard to come. The guard did, running, slamming into his stomach, and knocking him down. Sicarius put his right fist into his left palm, covering his fist before using it as a weight to slam his elbow and back arm into the man's chest. The guard coughed up blood as he tried to roll out from under Sicarius, screaming wildly as he threw himself on top of him. Sicarius grabbed his neck as the man put his own hands around Sicarius's, holding him at arm's length as he used the *cestus* glove on his wrist and palm to squeeze the life from him, fitted iron spikes beginning to punch into the sides of the man's throat.

"Father!" a high voice sounded twice and again before the man, teeth bared, seemed to see what Sicarius already had with the corner of his own eyes.

"No!" the guard gasped. Removing one hand from Sicarius's neck he held out his palm to the child as a warning.

The force of the arrow knocked the child off his feet and slammed him onto the sand, a soft thrum sounding as the end of the arrow continued to vibrate back and forth, blood pooling under the boy's head. The scythe that was in his hand lay harmless on the ground beside him.

Sicarius released the guard and watched him run to his son. The same one he'd seen skipping and laughing towards the back of the caravan minutes ago, his bald head shining under the sun. Racing and teasing the camels under their load.

The guard's screams grew louder as he shook the boy. The party and the herders watched as he leaned a knee into his son's chest and wrapped his hands around the arrow, attempting to pull it out and grunting with the effort. His son's mouth was slack and wide in an expression of surprise.

"Round them up," Cassius ordered. "I count at least twenty-two herders, two guards. Leave the dead where they've fallen; there aren't too many of them."

The guard was still screaming, ignored as the party began to work around him, cuffing the prisoners and shackling them together. One of the Romans tried to drag the man away from his son himself, but he resisted him, struggling with his son's body. Sicarius walked over and put a hand on the man's shoulder where he knelt over his son's body, his tears falling unchecked as he grunted and strained. The arrow was an inch thick. It would not move. Finally, the guard looked at the hand on his shoulder and looked up at Sicarius, mumbling two words as he put his hands together in front of him, begging. Sicarius put both hands to the man's head and forced his head upwards. A sharp movement and a snap, and the man's body went limp. Sicarius let him fall to the ground on top of his son, almost as if he were still alive and shielding him from harm.

The Roman looked at him a moment and nodded. *Better not to have any fighters,* his eyes said.

When they were ready, they began to move again, having transferred much of the salt to a smaller number of camels. The rest they set loose after releasing the salt packages. The sand would bury all else.

At the top of the sand dune, Sicarius heard what sounded like a cacophony of screams and turned his horse around to look down into the valley. Vultures neared the bodies in mass, moving closer slowly like concerned mothers, their necks bending and ducking as they viewed the carcasses before them to check for any last signs of life. A breath here. A rising chest. A weapon. Finding none, they circled tight, covering the boy and his father like a carnivorous blanket. High above them, more vultures circled, their large wings casting shadows as they flew closer to the ground, marking the place for the others before swooping low to feed.

IMANI

The drums beat louder as the chariot neared the arena. Her skin seemed to vibrate as the sounds filled the air. The smell of roasting goat filled her nose, making her mouth water in anticipation. Smoke rose from a deep pit nearby, and from the smell she knew a pig was spinning inside of it, stretched, and pierced through to properly roast in the fire underneath it. Every time she leaned out of the litter, her mother pulled her back inside, slapping at her hands to remove them from the shade, warning her about getting dust in her hair or ruining the henna on her arms. Both of them were laughing before long. The first event of the Festival of Kings would begin shortly, and the people were hungry for a champion. Others wanted blood. Imani peered through the litter's shade again at the throng of fighters filing in through the gates. Any swordsman might enter the Games, but there could only be one champion. Soldiers were the first to sign up, eager to show their talents to their comrades in arms. Mercenaries also enlisted, coming from across the realm and selling their skills for gold. They swore no allegiance to any of the Nomadin or kingdoms but searched for what would pay the most for them to survive. Few of them had families, and fewer still lived to old age. Others were young boys, too young to become soldiers or old men, seeking a way to prove their value. Ambitious all. Yet the Games were not for the weak of heart. By the end, more than one man would be injured and broken.

The litter came to a halt as the drums beat out a steady rhythm. Her father and mother went first, waving as they greeted the crowd. Ama walked by her side as they followed behind her family towards their seats. Taking their places in the Royal skybox they stood looking out over the terrace at the thousands below. *The wind is kind today*, she reflected, as a slight breeze cooled her forehead, lifting the golden veil she wore about her head to protect her from the sands. Supple white silk covered her breast while ivory skirts of silk fell down her waist, gathering close to her feet. Golden bracelets decorated her upper arms and wrists. She wore a bright gold-and-emerald studded collar necklace. It started at her collarbone and stretched almost to the ends of her shoulders, which were bare. The front hugged the top of her chest and fell to the nape of her neck, stopping just above her gown. Black kohl ran along her eyelids and down into the creases at the edge of her eyes. Dozens of tiny twists fell past her shoulders and down her back, the golden *khat* covering her forehead loosely instead of tucked under like the nobility. The braiders had worked for hours to perfect each twist, smoothing them with rose water and coconut oil when they finished. Ama had chosen a sheer blue gown that covered only her right shoulder, falling dangerously low across her left breast, loose and trailing the ground.

"You're not cold?" Imani teased her as she watched Ama adjusting it slightly.

"Oh?" Ama said, smiling, her eyes twinkling with mischief. "Have I caught your eye?"

Imani reached out to pinch her as Ama slapped her hand away. They fell against each other laughing as they climbed the stone steps.

Each of the lower kings sat with their families on the left and right sides of the arena, her father and the rest of her family sitting at the head to form a pyramid. Their colors marked their kingdoms. White and gold for the High King Kashta, blue for the Essi, black for the Scorpion King, green for the Kibera, purple for the Sotho, and red for the Sao Kingdom. Mikaili's locs were visible from where she sat; a thick white leather shendyt tied at his narrow waist, and heavy blue-black fur hung over one shoulder and down his back. She wondered whom the Essi would champion for the Games. An elbow dug into her side, and she turned to see Ama making kissing faces at her.

"Stop it!" Imani shook her head.

"You, stop it. You didn't hear a word I said, though I'm not sure why. These princes should wear less clothing. I need a better view of their...resources. Jelani knows how it's done," Ama giggled, running a finger over her lip suggestively.

"You're too much."

All eyes turned towards her father when he rose. Even in a cacophony of chaos, he commanded attention. "The maze will be first," he commanded. "Each warrior will begin at one opening of the maze. In the middle lie two treasures, great and small. You will be tested before you reach it, so beware of its traps. Whoever reaches the treasure first may choose and choose well, for no one will leave this game unharmed," he finished.

Everyone turned toward the maze as they watched all six challengers walk to each entrance. The maze was a massive work of dry stone, built without mortar. Over fifteen feet high, it twisted this way and that with traps for the unwary. From above everyone could see the interior of the maze and what awaited the one who reached it, but the traps would not be revealed so easily. Its narrow passageways were filled with snares not visible to the naked eye.

Each of the royal families submitted one challenger for the maze, outfitting them with *shendyts* dyed to their kingdom's color. Gold, blue, red, green, purple, and black. The drums sounded once, and the challengers entered the maze, each with a *khopesh* at the ready. Some in the crowd cheered loudly for their favorites, while others waited anxiously.

The thick, black body of a rock python unrolled inside the maze, moving towards the Essian, but he dodged its strike easily, slicing its head off in one quick motion before moving forward again. To the right the Sotho moved slowly, sword at the ready, his left hand up in a defensive position. Suddenly he screamed, and the crowd gasped in unison as they watched the lower half of his body disappear, his arms and hands clawing at either side of the stone walls. *Quicksand!* Imani felt her heart beating faster. A flurry of sand rose up as he struggled, his grunts echoing across the arena as the sand sucked him down. A black khat turned down the same path, and seeing the warriors struggle he broke into a run, leaping forward to slam his right foot onto the struggling man's head, pushing off to land safely on the other side. The Sotho jammed his *khopesh* into the walls over and over again until it lodged into a crevice. With both hands, he used it to pull up as much as he could, arms straining to stay above it, but he moved no higher than his chest. He wouldn't be able to free himself, but he didn't give up trying.

"Watch the green," Ama whispered to her softly, her eyes wide. A moment later, the Kiberan warrior climbed a rope swinging in front of him, and gripping each bar above his head like a monkey, he swung himself to the other side to avoid the hot coals below. The crowd cheered in unison. The Scorpion warrior came next, pausing a moment as if to consider his chances at jumping the distance. He decided against it, climbing the rope with some effort before reaching for the bars above him. *He has no upper body strength left,* she thought, the length of time during which he paused between each bar increasing. *He should have wiped sand onto his hands as the Kiberan did for a better grip.* The crowd began to chant for the warrior even as his grunts rang out. Suddenly, his left hand slipped, and he dangled above the hot coals precariously. Reaching up again and again to no avail, he screamed as he lost his hold, dropping onto the coals beneath him, burning and twisting in agony. His screams echoed across the arena as he managed to crawl off of them, falling just at the edge, his body still. The Scorpion King muttered a curse, his disgust palpable in the silence that followed.

Three left. Imani's eyes turned towards the gold; he'd used his sword to test the sand in front of him. A warrior of the desert, he spotted the sinkhole easily, leaping across the distance. He rounded a corner as three blades fell, swinging just in front of him, their alternating patterns mesmerizing. Imani watched as he put the tip of his blade to the ground, and she realized he was tapping out the rhythm of the blades to time his movement. Finally, he sheathed the blade, dodging left, then right, pausing a moment, then right again as the blades swung. He made it look easy to the crowd's eyes, and they cheered him on as he pulled his blade back out.

As they watched, the Nabaran came upon the Kiberan, and not a heartbeat later their blades rang out, kissing repeatedly. The crowd was furious—half were on their feet, their arms waving wildly. The steel song grew faster as the gold knocked the Kiberan to the ground, his elbow meeting the green's chin. The Kibera grunted in pain as the gold's blade ripped through his forearm, sliding right to avoid another cut. His scream cut the air and the gold warrior jumped deftly out of the way, stabbing downward at the scorpion crawling from the Kibera's shoulder before wiping his blade against his leathers. The crowd drew a breath and the Kiberan stilled, the fight leaving him as his muscles froze, paralyzed with venom, the cuts leaving him bleeding in a pool of blood. He lay frozen on the sand, his shoulder against the maze's stone walls, one leg curled at an unnatural angle underneath him, his chest rising and falling slowly. The Gold warrior left him there, crouching low as he moved forward. The blue warrior began to run as he saw the glint of the large diamond before him. The gold did the same. Reaching inside, the gold pulled out a rock the size of his fist, the green lifted a heavier one with both hands, raising it high above his head. Suddenly the gold's rock came flying through the air, landing just above his brow. Blood ran swiftly over his eyes as he reached for his sword. The steel song began again and the gold fell to the ground, his calf open from knee to ankle. Rolling onto his back, he cut high and the Kiberan doubled over, grabbing his stomach as blood streamed through his fingers. The crowd roared with fury as the gold's sword sliced through the Kiberan's, leaving him screaming in pain. Cheers rose as the gold was led from the maze, and the gamekeepers ran to assist the fallen, lifting the broken bodies of each warrior. They would live. Her father was pleased. A horn sounded and she looked across at the Kibera. Bakar gave her a small nod to their victory. She smiled back in return before turning her attention back to the arena. As they watched, the arena rotated, the stone scraping against stone as the maze lowered into the ground and the next took its place. It had grown dark quickly, but the air was still warm.

As the next display started, a woman rose from beneath the ground of the arena. Fire from the torches and moonlight danced across her face. The crowd was enthralled. Imani had never heard them so quiet. Nabara's most renowned artisan rose slowly with the stone under her feet, her smile more a gentle smirk as she stepped onto the sand in front of her and took a slow turn, surveying her audience. Her close-fitting, blue sleeveless gown held a gold belt that was cinched tightly about her waist and fell behind her. Her shapely hips swayed gently, the open slits on the outer side of each leg causing her walnut brown skin to flash through as she sauntered around the arena. Her black hair was piled on top of her head, the slimmest of single braids were shaped at the top left and bottom right of her head, shining with oil. Many young girls found themselves in her service or seeking it. Mothers and fathers sent their daughters to learn the art of dance and more.

"Welcome," she said slowly, "to the Festival of Kings. It is an ancient tradition built upon unity, peace, and prosperity." The crowd cheered as they watched her. "I would celebrate the leaders of Nudolla and our tradition of Kush, with a dance." She turned and clapped her hands together rhythmically ten times in succession, and the dancers rose from the ground, all twelve sitting on their heels, palms on their knees, their skirts glowing in the torchlight. Each more lovely than the next. Their left arms rose in unison followed by their right before moving straight out in front of them as their heads turned and leaned back and to the left. Silence descended as the arena watched, riveted. Fifteen musicians were positioned to the left and right of the dancers. The dancer's shapely figures were curvaceous and elegant as they swayed in time to the music, three large fires lit behind them illuminating them even more. All wore the same skirt as their mistress, a sheer fabric that was white where it counted, and a v-shaped gold-shingled piece ran from their sternum and across their chests toward their shoulders as they spun. Their black hair swung around their shoulders in dozens of loose tiny braids as they stood, bending backwards until their tresses swept the ground before snapping up, hands on each other's shoulders and right knees raised in unison.

Male dancers walked up behind them, and the crowd cheered again, taken by the oil shining against their skin. Beside her, Ama put a hand to her heart before clasping her hands together as if in prayer as she turned her face up towards the sky to murmur a soft word of thanks. Imani laughed, throwing her head back as she clapped along with the crowd, in time with the lyre and drums. The men stood four meters behind the women, then turned to face right, their left shoulders in line with the dancers' spines. The dancers' hands rose in the air, even the tips of their fingers graceful as they waved them, reaching for the sky as though they were climbing an invisible ladder. "Oh!" the crowd gasped in unison as they suddenly fell backward towards the ground. A scream sounded as the men turned left, catching them not a foot from the ground, their hands wrapped securely around their upper arms. The slight pause left the spectators breathless as the men dragged them backwards, the dancers' toes pointed and sweeping the floor. The spectators cheered again, a yell rising as they began to clap in time with the music.

The men finally came to a stop, throwing the dancers up and forward as they twisted in the air, their backs to the crowd as they planted their feet, hips shimmying softly as they bent forward, both hands on one knee as their backs arched like a cat's, the motion sharp and quick. The men stepped forward again as they straightened, reaching for their right hands as the women pushed away from them and fell backward.

Thunderous applause broke the silence as the dancers stopped mid lean, angled like a bow and arrow as they carefully balanced on one leg, their heels raised from the ground. Ululations cut through the air as the dancers left the arena.

"Beautiful." Ama was still clapping with the rest as Imani smiled.

"It was." Her mother once told her that the art of the dance may have been for entertainment, but for men, no matter how small the movement, it was a seduction. One hand pressed against a mouth could signal embarrassment and innocence, while another might read it as being coy.

Her smile grew as her brother whispered to her, "I am a prince. But I can never be sure whether or not some beauty is batting her eyelashes at me to tempt me to speak, or whether she simply caught a bit of desert sand in her eye at an inopportune time." She turned to look at Jelani and saw his wide grin, raising his eyebrows at her quickly twice in succession, his eyes alive with excitement, and she laughed again.

She saw a movement to her left and saw Terit rise from his seat and walk away from the arena. *Where is he going?*

"Aminata." Her father looked at her with concern, interrupting her thoughts. "You have been unusually quiet since the Games began. Is something troubling you?"

"No," she responded, forcing a small smile. *Would he tell me the truth?* She wondered. She glanced quickly at the Scorpion King, his box jeering the loudest. Terit had disappeared from view.

Even from here she could tell his sons were half past drunk. "Father," she hesitated, biting her lip. "If the smugglers are found to be in league with the Scorpion King, what will you do?"

Her mother started in surprise. "Imani-qo!"

She knows I spied on the council meeting. And she had; concealing herself behind the pillars next to the servant's entrance, she'd listened to every word.

Her father leaned back in his seat, his eyes looking out over the complex. "I will do what I must," he answered, turning to her. Jelani and Nema were silent. "I will do what a High King must. As justice requires. When a king is afraid to choose the right path, he ceases to be a leader and becomes nothing more than a figurehead of power, powerless to rule his own, and he is complicit in the consequences. I will not let our people be made slaves. I do not believe Tharbis is involved in the slave trade either, no matter what people may think of his character. That will not be the fate of Nabara. Or of you." Her father's eyes were stone. He meant every word.

"Anubis will judge them," she murmured.

"I wouldn't count on any god," her father responded. "We have judged them. It is only left to see who must carry out the sentence." Her father had always been wary of religion and worship. The people's adoration for the divine amused him. Ever since her grandfather had died.

She nodded, her gaze moving across the coliseum to see Prince Mikaili signaling to her. Rising quickly, she excused herself, pulling her veil across her face as she met him above the king's pavilion.

He bowed low when she reached him.

"Enjoying the games?" he asked, rising, a smile on his face. His grey eyes moved from her to the arena as the warriors prepared for the next course.

"Some. Perhaps if I were competing," she replied, her eyes lighting on the Kiberan warriors before returning to King Tharbis. *After the attack at the market, Father would never allow it.* "Mikaili," she started, "tell me what you know of the attacks on our ships. And those of the Floating City.

His surprise was evident, but he recovered quickly, his eyes checking that they were alone. "Much and nothing," he responded. "They attack in large groups of fifty or more. They carry short swords and daggers, attacking at night under cover of darkness. Stealing spices, silks, precious metals." His hands curled into fists at his sides and his grey eyes turned dark as clouds before a storm.

"We believed they were the same group, one ship. But one night they attacked in two places at once. We don't know where they're from, who sent them. They never speak, and they die just as quietly. Any resistance by merchants or captains is repaid with blood. These men know when and where heavily loaded ships will be, waiting until merchants are too far from shore to call for help. It's the reason we believe it's the work of King Tharbis." He gripped the low stone wall of the upper pavilion, staring out past the arena to the sand beyond, the tallest tower of Nabara invisible behind Kalahari sand dunes. Mikaili turned to her. "And your father refuses to do anything about it.

His anger took her as if she'd been slapped. Mouth open in surprise, she looked at him incredulously. "My father is doing what must be done!"

"While innocent people die!"

"Innocent people always die. He can't bring justice to the people by accusing one of the largest families in the realm without proof. Our kingdom would rebel. It would only start a war."

"Wars we can win. And Tharbis's people detest him."

"A false war. You know our history. How much blood has been spilled over misinformation? How many years have people suffered the effects of famine? Plague? Death? All because of false coin?"

The look he gave her was sour. His eyes narrowed as his mouth became a grim line.

"Mikaili," she tried again, "I know you want to act quickly, but there are some things that take time. He's sent Medjay out on the high seas of Torrent to find the lost Kiberan ship, two hundred soldiers are making their way towards the Sao Kingdom as we speak, and Nabara itself is being investigated to root out any supporters of the slave traders. I do not believe it is just King Tharbis who is involved. I think this goes much further than him."

"The High King is the only king who holds the power of the

Medjay. Essi soldiers could use that support, that voice to spur the people to action. Even a princess's support would do that. The Medjay walk behind you too," he finished nodding behind him to where two stood waiting for her. "Waiting too long—"

"Will give us time to learn who is behind these attacks. Piracy and smuggling on the high seas is not our only worry. My father will do what he must," she finished stepping closer to him, defiant as she stared at him, her upturned face determined he should listen to reason. Mikaili looked down when he felt her veils touching his arm.

He lifted his hand, fingering the ends lightly, letting the wind slip them from his hands. *What will he do?* She waited as his eyes met hers, then followed his gaze to the Scorpion King. Even from here he was visibly drunk and Terit had not returned.

"Tell me you do not doubt their innocence."

"Mikaili…" She was exhausted by his relentlessness. But she couldn't. She'd heard the accusations and seen the wrecked ship with her own eyes. But even Tharbis would not deal with Rome. Would he? Even when her father held audience all the merchants sang the same song.

"At a loss for words?" He raised an eyebrow, his handsome face filled with satisfaction. "That's rare."

"The first report is always wrong. Don't do something you'll regret. It lasts a lifetime you know."

He nodded once, his grey eyes tense. "As long as I find Tharbis guilty for his treasons, I'll have no regrets."

KOMORO

The grass was so thick here he couldn't see the ground. The lush beauty of Nabara wasn't lost on him. Even if he *did* prefer the beauty of a woman to it all. Grass as tall as him dotted the savannah as he crept through it slowly, stalking his prey. It was moving towards its herd. No matter. One hit from his spear was all he needed. It was the element of surprise that excited him. Peering over the tops of the flowers in front of him he wrinkled his nose, their smell eroded by the scent of the rhinoceros. Downwind from the beast he could smell it. Drinking from the lake a short time earlier, it had urinated shortly after, its tail lifting as shit sprayed across the small marsh in a steady arc. The pungent smell permeated his nostrils like an invisible wall meant to ward off other animals and mark his territory. The rhino stopped, munching leisurely on the grass beneath it as a baby played near its feet. It was a bull, that much was clear. A pod of six females were splashing nearby, enjoying the water. After rolling in a small mud puddle, the baby moved back to the grass, its small plump body shining like a tree trunk, its belly wriggling as it moved, bright pink eyes blinking as its nostrils flared. The bull's jaws were preoccupied, but the two long curved horns just above its nose would kill him instantly, if it were able to catch him. The horns were long enough to run him through from navel to forehead and he'd seen more than one man gored in his short life. Still, he picked up speed. This was a prize he couldn't afford to let go of. He'd never taken a risk that didn't promise a big reward. His father had drilled it inside his memory long ago. And he remembered the lesson now.

It was time. Holding tightly to the spear in front of him, he brought his knees forward, planting both feet just behind it to make it easier for him to spring. With his right hand, he brought the spear back watching as the rhino turned broadside, the large illuminated profile in perfect place. *Swoosh*, he threw the spear with his whole body, a grunting alarm following the release. The rhinos dispersed, running for cover as the babies followed in confusion. Screams from monkeys sounded high above him among the acacia trees as others scrambled up trunks like ladders, swinging babies through the air to safety.

"MOVE!" Komoro was after them in a moment, briefly noting the blood-smeared grass only a few feet away. At his command his hunting party followed full tilt, chasing the rhino down the hill and over the savannah as panicked antelope wildly jumped from hiding places to escape whatever hunted them. The confusion of the females was to his advantage as some ran east and west rather than north to follow the bull before doubling back. He was on their heels, backsides knocking the reeds aside with ease. It wasn't their hides that concerned him. It was their horns. If at any moment they turned back to give chase as they were want to do, being run over by their heavy feet would be the least of his worries.

"Ughhh!" He grunted as his foot slipped over a rocky peak. Catching himself and leaping forward past the boulder just in front of him, he landed hard, rolling quickly before standing, the hides of the rhino herd in sight. Grinning, he picked up speed, arms pumping as he caught sight of his spear lying on the ground, the tip broken and black with blood. Scooping it up, he pressed on, dust flying up as the tallest grasses whipped at his face. He jumped higher and higher to keep going, to keep his prey in sight. Sweat fell from his forehead as he bent his knees over and over again, pushing stalks to the side.

"Steady!" Komoro called behind to his archer, making sure he was ready for whatever they might face, the grass and reeds whipping violently back and forth. His heart pounded in his ears as he rushed forward. He could do this in his sleep. The hunt was his favorite thing, the play, the chase, capturing the prize. He lived for it. Many preferred using the chariot for the short distance or riding a horse, but not him. Anything but his feet would soften the excitement and the rush of blood in his ears as he gave chase.

He gasped in surprise, nearly falling as he came to a halt, whispering a quick warning behind him. At the sound, the hunting party dropped to the grass like dead men, and he glanced behind him to see them creeping slowly towards him on all fours. Pointing with his right finger, they followed his direction though he needn't have bothered. Soft guttural moans sounded over the grass as the sound of ripping flesh repeated over and over. And amid it all, laughter. An excited frenzy, which he only ever heard at the market between large groups of giggling girls, some secret shared between them.

Hyenas. At least forty strong. All excitedly tearing into the rhino that was left alone, a pool of blood surrounding him as the baby he'd seen moments ago whined as three hyenas circled it. Taking turns they snapped their large jaws at him and backed away before returning again.

Their peeling laughter seemed to bounce off each other as it rang out in the night.

"Your Highness—"

One look from him silenced the coward whose voice was filled with terror. Komoro turned back now, realizing that the rhino was covered in mud from the waist down, upright and stuck in a small mud hole. Being eaten alive. *One small mistake*, he thought as the rhino's skin went from dark gray to light pink, blood smearing across him as the hyenas fought for more. *One small mistake and you'd be eaten alive.*

The feast continued, the rhino's large head still bobbed up and down, long horns useless now. The sharp edges that once commanded deference and fear were now largely ignored as the hyena's bone-crushing teeth sought the warm folds of its neck. Listening to the bones of the rhino breaking under the hyenas' jaws like snapping trees he leaned forward for a better view, head tilting to the side. The larger ones cracking every so often like the sound of an alligator's mouth snapping shut. The hyena's heads rose and fell as the smaller ones ran around the outside, waiting their turn, licking blood from another's coat or pushing their small noses past scrambling feet towards the rhinoceros as entrails spilled onto the ground.

A screech sounded from the trees, and he glanced up. The monkeys were almost hidden beneath the leafy canopy, but their tails swung down as they watched from the safety of their perch, clutching their babies to their breasts. Branches shook as some moved higher as the hyenas grew thicker. Here and there soot-colored faces peered out from ash-colored fur, through green branches, heads bobbing as though shaking them with regret. Usually the ash monkeys sounded an alarm, a warning call. But there were none back by the marsh where he'd speared the bull. And now they could only watch as their cow-eyed babies learned at a young age which predators to stay away from. Barking laughter grew louder as the hyenas piled onto the feast, using family members as stepping stones to reach the top until two stood on the rhino's head, one foreleg planted squarely inside the rhino's mouth. Safety lay in the knowledge that the rhino had not the strength left even to cry out in pain or close his jaws shut in one last act of defiance. His skin slid off in strips as the rest of the hyenas gnawed on bone, breaking it from the joint before tearing it free. The smaller ones gnawed at his forelegs, preferring to take a chunk that they could easily carry away from their pack and finish alone. Fur covered in clumps of blood.

When the head was gone, the hyenas worked together to pull it free from the mud, eating it at intervals as the torso and hind legs slid upwards and then fell to the ground, tearing at the meat as quickly as they could. When all that was left was a stump and hind legs they began to eat it from the inside out, nuzzling their faces inside the bloody bowels to gnaw meat from the remaining bone. One ran up to tear the tail free and the bowels exploded upward, feces flying and squirting from the hole as the hyenas yipped with excitement, jumping back momentarily before attacking the carcass again.

The grass was no longer green. Smeared a rust-colored red the hyenas licked the stalks to make sure nothing had been left behind before circling the death-bed and running off in the direction of the Kalahari. Nothing remained. Even the small baby had been eaten, torn apart in three quick bites after the hyenas tired of tormenting it. Komoro motioned to his men and they rose, surveying the ground. They would need to leave soon. It would be dark in an hour. It was no time to stay near blood-soaked grass when night hunters woke.

His legs were beginning to ache from the strain of squatting for so long, concealing himself from the hyenas that had grown to at least sixty by the time the feast was done. His knee would need some attention from the physician when he returned to the palace, the landing he took giving it a dull throb now as he turned back with his hunting party. It took them almost two hours to return to the palace. Having picked their way carefully through the brush to avoid snakes and sleeping lions by the smell. And he was tired. It was too late for anyone to still be up walking around, though Ketemin probably still had a book in her hand, one leg dangling off the other as she flipped through pages as she lay in her bed, dark eyes tired, but too excited to close until she learned what was on the next page. He was still furious with her, but he'd visit her later. The garden was what he wanted. He needed to feel the water over his skin before he went to sleep. The grit of the day wore on him.

An hour later he heard footsteps moving through the gardens. Peeping over the edge of the pool, he spotted a hooded figure making its way towards the garden's opening leading towards the back steps. She was walking too quickly to notice him. This despite her soft, purposely light footsteps as she looked to her left and right, as though her glance itself could ward off danger if only she saw it coming first. The cicadas helped her there, their loud buzzing permeating the night. Her black hair fell down her breasts, alternating sections of it loosely braided and the rest undone, her headband crown pushing outside of the hood of her cloak. *Who are you hiding from?* He stood, walking towards her, curious.

"Princess…"

Princess Ama froze and turned toward him with such quickness it almost made him laugh, her pink lips spread open and wide. He chuckled.

"Were you looking for me?" His eyebrows rose as he searched her face.

"Prince Komoro." His eyes fell to her throat as she swallowed, the telltale beat of a lie forming just *there.* "I didn't realize anyone would be awake at this hour."

When he stepped from the shadows, her eyes grew wider. The moonlight fell across his chest, his bare waist glimmering in the darkness, naked but for his crown.

"Forgive me for interrupting, no one is ever in the pools this late—"

"Of course not, this is your home, not mine." He smiled

apologetically, rocking back and forth on his heels with his hands set firmly on his hips.

Nodding once, she turned to take her leave.

"Were you going somewhere?" His words stopped her in her tracks.

"No, not at all. I just thought you might want…privacy for—"

"Because I thought you were attempting to be quite discreet. Dear me, have I found you out?" He moved closer to her, leaning against a pillar to her right as he smiled, close enough to touch. Warmth filled the space between them in the chill of the Nubian night.

Her eyes flashed as she pushed her hood back, annoyed and defiant.

"If such an amateur could so easily discover my secrets, I might have to come up with better ones."

Komoro laughed this time, crossing his arms and running a finger across his lips as he shook his head. *So the lady has spirit.*

"My, my. Are you calling me an amateur?" He narrowed his eyes. "I can't say that anyone has ever used that term to describe me before."

"There's a first time for everything." She raised an eyebrow as she said it, her brown skin flawless.

"Would you care to join me?" *Time for the direct approach.* "The water is quite warm. I promise there's enough heat and room for the both of us. It's…bigger than you think."

"Is it?" One eyebrow raised she shook her head. "I was told you have a large…ego. But sadly, I have no use for it. They take up entirely too much room."

"Indeed. There are other things people have no real use for, but they do enjoy them. For instance, why must one *wait* to sample certain things that seem natural? Things given to curiosity since childhood?" He stepped so close to her that his breath caused her hair to blow back from her face. "Don't you agree?"

"Some wouldn't think of it as waiting, Prince Komoro. Anticipation is something few people take the time to experience or enjoy. You've been *sampling* anything you can get your hands on since you were *born,* no doubt. Sadly for you, I rather enjoy sampling things. As long as they're not already…worn out from overuse. I should think all of your exercise has aged you somewhat. I did detect a slight limp, did I not? Shame." She was smiling now, her sharp eyes taunting him.

His smile faltered as he realized his hunt was ruining his chances for hunting of another kind. "Well. Now you've found my weakness. Why don't you tell me yours?" he finished sweetly.

"Be careful," she warned him. "It gets even colder here at night. But then," Ama looked down towards his waist before glancing up to meet his eyes, "you already know that." Turning on her heel, she walked away from him without a second glance.

"I wish my lover were a Nubian," he sang out softly, "such beauty I've never seen. I wish my lover were a Nubian, how much pleasure it would give me." She turned back once, shaking her head before continuing on.

Komoro watched her go, the frustration he felt earlier even worse than before. Groaning as the smell of her perfume lingered in his nose and made his mouth water, he walked back towards the pools. One more swim. *Then I need a drink.*

"Draw my bath," he commanded, nodding to a Sao servant girl he recognized when he entered the Nabaran palace headed for his quarters. Their retinue for the Festival of Kings included a number of their personal servants. *How would I do without them?*

She rose, bowing quickly before disappearing to see to her task. By the time he reached his chambers, the guards had already thrown the doors open for him. Two servant girls kneeled on either side of a heavy, gold tub, water steaming from the gourds as they poured the last of it into his bath. Pleased, he held his arms out, waiting as the first handmaid rose and disrobed him, carefully untying the golden belt knotted about the waist of his ivory shendyt and removing his collar, her ebony fingers sure and deft. Stepping inside of his bath he sighed with pleasure, resting his arms on either side of it as the sienna-skinned handmaid placed a mint soaked cloth over his face. The handmaids began to scrub his neck and shoulders, massaging his muscles as they went. Dropping their hands lower still they moved expertly over him, never staying in one place for too long.

"Slower," he murmured softly as they reached his waist. "There," he said, leaning his head back as they continued their work, the towel hiding the smile of pleasure spread over his face. When their gentle strokes moved to his head he yawned, knowing this perfection was coming to an end. Removing the towel from his face, the ebony handmaid smiled, smoothing her thumbs over his cheeks and up to his temples. Opening his eyes slowly, he smiled at her.

"You should see to your leg, my Prince," she said, bowing her head. Her other hand slid inside the water.

"I will call the palace physician shortly," he assured her.

"Nothing more? Your Highness?" she asked, tilting her head to the side.

"For now," he replied, drawing a finger over her lips.

Standing he allowed the handmaid to dry and robe him, the ivory habit draping over his shoulders smoothly as the sienna-toned beauty slid a golden sash around his waist. *Who would ever give this up?* he thought, smiling. Ketemin had once requested men as her royal bathers to see why he enjoyed it so much, and their uncle had nearly died from shock. It had taken Komoro nearly an hour to convince the old man his eleven-year-old sister was merely joking. As a Daughter of Ra she had given herself to purity at a young age much like the Kushite's God's Wife of Amun. But maybe it was time she had such a distraction.

JELANI

"Run away with me."

The surprise on Kachima's face wasn't new to him.

"Run away with me," he repeated.

Kachima shook her head. "I can't." The whisper was almost too soft to hear. "You shouldn't be here."

Kachima returned to her work, arms and legs covered in clay as she molded the nearly waist-high pot by hand. Its finely shaped opening rim contained her fingerprints as she pressed and kneaded it into shape. The same slender, pecan fingers that sometimes kneaded themselves into his consciousness even when she wasn't there. Nubian pottery was made by hand or not at all. The same intricate creations could be found in Makouria, a Nubian kingdom of the North. A small broom sat near her, the ends of the branch caked with goat dung, the black-brown pebbles of manure having been placed inside a sack near her feet. She used it now to mix with the red clay of the pot between her legs, a consistency needed to ensure it wouldn't shrink when it was fired to set and harden. The smell clung to his nose as he watched her amidst it all. Jelani remembered brushing dirt and sand and clay away from a rock when he was just a boy to see what was shining underneath. A diamond. His father had congratulated him on his discovery and told him to hold onto it. *Such treasures*, his father told him, *buried in the earth and protected by her, only reveal themselves to those who can look past the ugliness of the world and see her beauty. You were meant to have it.* Jelani had known from the moment he met Kachima that he'd found another as a man. Kachima's fingers continued molding the wet clay, pressing here, pushing there. Picking up a metal comb, she ran it around the base of the newly forming pot to add a pattern. She let it spin and drag, creating a lined, ring design around the bottom and neck where it fanned out like a flute, an open-mouthed lotus flower that would receive the water or wine that was poured into it.

"I need to speak with you." He refused to give up on her so easily.

271

"I'm listening," she answered, not bothering to look up.

"Run away with me."

"You've already said that," she sighed.

Setting the comb down, she used both her hands to squeeze and press the clay, adding more as her hands trailed around the pot, dragging and pinching her fingers at the mouth to make it as fine and thin as possible. It was just one of Nabara's many beautiful exports. The most beautiful pottery anywhere in the land, and a mirror of Nubian history and culture. His mother always said so.

Silence fell between them, pressing against his chest. An inhale that held the air in his lungs, waiting for her to give him permission to speak. To talk. To come closer. Her long black hair fell behind her, ten thick braids falling down her back. He longed to touch it.

"Look at me."

The words filled the silence in the room.

Kachima looked up. "Buy something or leave." She motioned to the completed jars around the edge of the room, some stored on high shelves, the noble's business a cave of sorts, with each jar containing his most valued treasure - millet and sorghum beer. Bimbola Machupa held half the city in his hand with his beer alone. Celebrations, weddings, festivals—all of them required beer and wine. Near the very back sat Kachima's jewelry. Bimbola allowed her to sell it as long as she agreed to give him half of the profits. "If he catches you here—"

"I'm the prince. If he catches me here he'll say nothing."

"I don't want to give him cause to worry. Or to doubt. Or to be concerned about anything that I do."

"I won't let him."

She shook her head, finally taking her hands away from the pot.

"Why won't you just leave me be?" Her eyes implored him to reason. But he saw sadness there, and despair.

"Because I love you," his voice trembled. "Because I love you," he repeated, walking to stand over her. Jelani reached out and pulled her towards him, pressing her head against his chest. Her heart beat, thrumming like a drum as she wrapped her slender arms around his waist. He didn't know what to tell her to change her mind. But he wished he knew what would.

"There are things that are more important than love." Her voice was muffled as she turned her face to the side, her cheek pressed against his chest. "Honor, tradition, and family."

"You think I don't know that?"

"I *know* you do. I just think you willfully choose to ignore it. I cannot."

"Kachima."

She removed his hands from her face, pushing him away. "We can't stay here. I need to take these to the river." Grabbing the pots next to her, she walked outside quickly, not waiting for him to follow. Her steps were quick and sure. He wondered if she was trying to avoid him, but ten paces later she looked back and smiled. Jelani felt his heart race as he returned her greeting. It gave him hope. Lifting the pots from her, he set them on his shoulders, ignoring her protests as he walked next to her. He watched the few shopkeepers crying the last of their wares, sweeping the sand and dust from their stores. The night wind blew gently as they reached the papyrus reeds near the River Nub.

Removing her sandals, she pulled her garment up around her knees, knotting it quickly before stepping with the pots into the river. The ends of her long braids dripping wet as they fell into the whirling black current. Shaking the water from the gourds before moving back onto the shore, she laid them down on the cloth she brought to keep them from getting caked with mud and dirt. *The old man had her emptying his pots while he used her to increase his fortune.* It drove him mad.

He waited for her. She needed time before he brought the subject up again. He owed her that much. When she finally looked at him, tears were in her eyes, falling quickly down her face. Moving towards her, he brushed the pads of his fingers over her eyelashes and down her face. Cupping her chin, he kissed her gently, wrapping his arms around her slender shoulders and letting his chin rest on top of her head, holding her there for a moment.

What should I do? What should I say? He had no answer. The rushing sounds of the River Nub continued behind the papyrus reeds as they blew like curling fingers in the wind, reaching towards the moon. The sound of the cicadas grew louder around them, filling the acacia trees and the night with a buzzing sound that invaded his ears and drowned his thoughts.

After a moment he lifted her in his arms and sat down, cradling her as her head rested against the curve of his royal collar.

"Let me pay the price for your father."

"No. It's not so simple as that."

"I'll pay it whatever the price. Bimbola will have his payment, your father will be free of the debt, and you will be free of this fool."

"Jelani,"

"I love it when you call me that." Smiling he fingered the ends of her braids.

"Jelani, please…"

"Seizure through pawnship is not allowed anywhere in Nudolla."

"I know. And I was not *seized*. Not *every* person in Nudolla sits on gold mines either. The *Nomadin* still practice it, though it is rare. And pawnship's purpose is not without some reason. A person may owe a debt and be unable to repay save with the labor of his family member, which he pledged as collateral. And its time is measured. A noble may pay for another's son to attend the temple as a scribe," she laughed. "And the noble, as debtee, may use another member of that man's family to pay the debt. It's perfect. And dangerous in the hands of dishonest men." Despite her earlier laughter, the look on her face showed no amusement.

"This is too fine a line for me. Let me help you. My father will want to know about this.

"Bimbola has done nothing wrong."

"You are his slave!" He could not control his voice any longer. It drove him mad to think of her like this.

"This is not slavery. Slavery is much worse. It is the foreigners who bastardize pawnship by selling people into slavery, stealing cattle, and only when confronted do they deign to pay. And sometimes not even then."

"He would pervert it, Kachima. I have heard stories of foreigners seizing people to sell them into slavery and offering payment to the family in return."

"Bimbola and my father are kin. Even in pawnship it is the kinship ties among families that keep a family member pledged as collateral from being sold. And love. Foreigners know nothing of that."

"He loves you *too* much," Jelani growled. "And marrying and divorcing your father's third cousin when he finds her barren is not such a strong tie, I think."

The import of his words sat on her shoulders, making them sag as worry set in the space between her eyes, tiny wrinkles appearing as he watched.

"But how will my father prove it? Shall the High King take my father's word?"

"My father may be the High King, but he is fair."

"I did not mean it the way it sounded. Only that my father's word will be against that of a noble. A noble with pockets deep enough to buy more than friends. And each one will stand for him rather than lose his support."

"Pawnship is in danger of leading us into the slave trade with the raiders of the north and the foreign invaders that take them. It is a risk Nudolla should not take. I must warn my father about Bimbola."

"Please. If you love me, say nothing. Nothing has happened yet, and your father forced his hand. High King Kashta gave us more time. My service in payment of the debt will not last forever thanks to him. Be patient or you will only make things worse."

He laughed softly in the darkness. "You've never known me to be patient. Except when it comes to you," he whispered.

Running a hand over her hair, he pressed his lips to her forehead, cupping the back of her head lightly. His hands ran down her neck, drawing his thumbs in circles over the sides, kissing the place where her heart beat a soft rhythm. Her chest rose as she took a deep breath, wrapping her arms around his neck. Removing his cloak, he let it fall behind her, pressing her back to the ground as he took in her dark eyes, her pecan skin disappearing in the darkness. But it was her heat he felt, all around him. The almond kiss of her damp skin as he rubbed her hand down his cheek, pressed his fingers against her calf.

A sigh escaped her and he moved his head from her collarbone to her mouth, running his tongue lightly over her bottom lip, tasting her sweetness. Letting the warmth of her breath envelop him. The hairs on his skin rose in the chill of the night and he slipped his arm under her head, bringing her closer as he laid on his right side, his body facing hers. His tongue invaded her mouth, testing the softness it found, heating under the texture of her own before moving to suck at her mouth. His teeth became distracted there, gently nipping at her plump lips, trying to ignore the gentle caress of her eyelashes on his cheekbones.

His left hand curious, it eagerly slipped along the smooth planes of her inner left thigh, knuckles teasing the right as it brushed along on its journey, dipping gently inside her sweetness before sliding back out. A voice murmured his name softly, and he kissed the inside of her knees, her voice a song that was pulled away by the wind. The vibration of the sounds tickled his fingers as he rested his cheek atop her knees, his right hand resting on her right leg as his thumb stroked just below her knee. Sighing he pulled her gown back down her thighs and kissed her lips as she melted against him, her skin warm.

"We can't," she whispered.

"I love you," he whispered against her ear. "I'll wait for you. As long as it takes."

Her body trembled as she nodded. Lifting her, he stood, setting her feet on the ground.

"We should go," he told her softly.

By the time they reached Bimbola's courtyard, the moon was well into the sky. Jelani had made sure to check on Bimbola's whereabouts to be cautious. He would not be home for some time. He'd made sure of it. Closing the door behind him, she set the gourds high up on the shelf, pulling out salted lamb to prepare dinner for him. Anger built in his chest and he pondered the idea of her making dinner for this man whom he hated. Who held her life in his hands.

When the door closed behind them, Kachima gasped. He hadn't even heard it open.

"Father." The surprise in her voice did little to ease the strain on her father's face as he stood at the entrance.

"Kachima, Your Grace." Akachi bowed slowly, bones creaking in protest and what Jelani felt must only be outrage as her father lowered himself towards the ground and rose again. "I merely came to visit my daughter. I hope I am welcome."

"Of course you are." Walking quickly over to meet him, she let him wrap his arms around her. Pressing her face against his neck she kissed his cheek. "The prince was just—"

"Please," he interrupted her, turning to Jelani "Your Highness I hope I am not overstepping my place, but I hope you will forgive me if I ask you not to stay long," her father said.

"I was just leaving."

"I'm sure you were. Your father, High King Kashta, has done me a great service, and I am in his debt for it. But before you leave I would ask that you not pay my daughter the discourtesy of your overtures."

"Discourtesy?" Jelani repeated, mouth ajar. *What can he mean?*

"Father, please!" Kachima's cheeks were turning red as she watched them.

"I meant no offense, Your Highness, but I hope to have my daughter married one day."

"I have no doubt she will be," Jelani answered, looking at Kachima.

"And I hope," her father continued, "that I may make a match of her, someone who would not deny her the pleasure of accompanying him in public."

Heat filled Jelani's cheeks as he closed his mouth, realizing the import of her father's words. No answer came to him. It was Kachima who refused that courtesy, fearful of Bimbola. He had asked her for her hand any number of times, but she refused. But he would not dishonor her by making light of it. He could not find his voice. Nor would he.

Kachima said not a word, her head hanging slightly towards the ground. Pecan brown skin reddening further as she finally looked up, her eyes begging him to leave.

"I meant no disrespect."

"There is none taken. But, Your Grace, the *khopesh* has two edges." He stared at him a moment before bowing again. For a man paying all due courtesy and respect to Jelani's title, her father had no trouble expressing himself. But even he had respect for elders. To a point.

Jelani nodded to Kachima before turning towards the door and

277

pushing it open, hitting something on the other side. Bimbola stood there. Eyes wide with surprise, he smiled and bowed lazily at Jelani's feet. The gesture almost seemed an afterthought.

"Your Highness. To what do I owe the pleasure? I had not thought I received a message from the palace regarding a visit. Of course...you need no invitation. What's mine is yours," he said looking quickly towards Kachima.

"I was just leaving."

"His Highness was speaking with me about our debt. The prince sends the High King's regard and wishes that we settle our matter with all urgency. I know we will. It is our honor that you paid us this visit." Kachima's father nodded to Jelani, his eyes saying what his mouth could not. Not in front of Bimbola.

"Of course." Bimbola bowed again, pausing and holding the posture, his eyes on the floor.

Jelani nodded and took his leave, hands curling as he realized he'd have to be more careful. They couldn't be discovered. A moment earlier and there would be no telling what Bimbola may have heard. Even now, he couldn't be entirely sure.

MIKAILI

Imani ran to the stables as he left his father. *She must have risen even earlier than me.* His morning ride could wait. He wanted to follow her, but there were so many eyes upon them. Fingering her necklace a moment he gripped the reins of his stallion and walked him slowly to the stable house. A stable boy ran lightly to him, smiling eagerly.

"And who might you be?" He bent to the boy's level as he posed the question.

Smiling, the boy answered, "I tend to the horses, My Prince, My Grace, my, I—" the boy stuttered, the words tripping over his tongue in his eagerness.

"Stop, stop," Mikaili laughed. "You make me sound a crowd."

"A frightening one too, by the sound of it," a voice added.

He looked up quickly to see Imani staring down at him, her golden eyes taunting him. "Come now, Hasim. Has Prince Mikaili frightened you?" Cupping his chin in her hand, she smiled gently. The smile that flew to the boy's mouth made Mikaili want to laugh again. *Is there anyone in Nabara who isn't half in love with her?*

"No, Princess," Hasim answered her, breathless. His chest rose and fell rapidly as he looked up at her, the grin on his face widening as his mouth fell open in awe, like a moth blinded before torchlight. *I should save him before he catches fire,* Mikaili thought. "His horse is here," Hasim finished.

It was Imani's turn to laugh. "Yes, I can see that, little one." She released his chin gently, tapping her finger against his nose lightly. "Be careful with him. The Essian swim extremely well, but on the earth, they need all the help they can get."

"Yes, Princess!" the boy replied, his eyes shining as he took the reins from Mikaili, leading the stallion into the stables. His stallion licked at Hasim's hair, but the boy seemed hardly to notice, turning back once or twice to gaze at Imani.

"Troublemaker," Imani accused, shaking her head.

"Me?" he snorted, affronted. "I don't recall pushing myself into

279

the cove waters," he replied drily. *Ahh, she has the grace to blush*, he noted as she bit her lip, slight fire rising in her golden-brown cheeks.

"I apologize for my behavior. I…wasn't myself."

"No? I should hate to see you when you are. I remember you being quite the same as a child, and so does my father."

Her eyes lit up and she turned to him.

"Your father? How is he?" She didn't bother to hide her excitement.

"He misses seeing you too." His father was fond of Imani, as his mother had been when she was alive. Her bubbling energy, wide eyes, and playful spirit had captured their hearts even when she threatened to be born again as a boy. His mother had convinced her otherwise. He still remembered her laughter as she sat in his mother's lap, and when he'd come near to hear better, she'd yelled at the top of her lungs, "Go away*! Women* create life and rule the world. We have no time for you!"

"Walk with me?" he asked her. He saw hesitation in her amber eyes and followed her glance up to the palace. "I'll have you back before dark," he teased.

She shook her head, pulling her veils tight across her face; her pale cream gown billowed behind her as the pants she wore underneath, molded against shapely calves, highlighting her long legs. She wrapped her arm in his, her palm tight against his bicep. The Medjay fell in line behind them, trailing in their wake, *khopesh* ready. Their white shendyts a contrast to their black skullcaps as they followed.

They were walking towards the city when one of the Medjay came running down the steps to them. He bent low before straightening.

"Princess. The High King requests that you go no farther than the palace walls."

Imani looked up towards the pyramid he'd come from, one hand raised to her brow, blocking the sun from her eyes.

"Tell my father I must go further than the palace gates if I'm to properly entertain our guests. Her eyes flashed and a moment later she sighed. "I'm sorry, Aoko." She touched his arm lightly. "I did not mean to alarm you. I won't wander far."

He smiled, pleased, and bowed again before turning back towards the palace.

"Short leash," he noted.

"Shorter temper," Imani responded.

"Well earned, I heard."

"What have you heard?" she asked drily, no trace of humor in her voice.

"That you like to leave the palace before sunrise. And before the light spilled across that pretty face of yours, blood did a fortnight ago."

He turned his head just in time to catch her jaw tightening in anger. She removed her arm from his, her eyes showed nothing kind. "You have a fast tongue."

"I don't scare easily, Princess."

"Then say what you mean."

Reaching for her arm again, he tucked it neatly against his side. "How is it that I'm always making you angry? I only meant to ask what happened. I was concerned. You mean a great deal to people," he finished quietly.

She was silent. *She can't possibly take that for an insult.*

"I should have seen them for what they were," she admitted finally.

"Foreigners multiply like dung beetles on the savannah. Not all of them are the same, but you never know who can be trusted." He continued. "I trust you've heard news of the slavers?"

"Yes."

"Have you heard that criminals from the Tombs have been involved?"

"No." She turned to him. "When did you hear this?"

"Earlier. From my father."

She was silent. The sand blew around them, settling again and again as the wind whistled in her ears.

"My father fought so long for peace. And freedom. He never wanted the trials of Meroë to follow us here."

"He did. And the price of freedom has beggared many a man."

"And made others rich. We need to follow the gold."

He smirked. *She's too smart for her own good. She's her father's daughter.*

They continued down the road, shops on either side, the path twisting and turning as sandstone buildings and homes lined their path. Entryways to courtyards knotted with small children playing in front. Men and women bowed low as they passed. "May you live a thousand years, Princess," one mother called as she picked up her son, using his hand to wave to them. The baby gurgled as his mother waved his fat little hand and Imani laughed, the sound warming him.

A little girl kicked her ball in their path, and Imani kicked it back and forth with her until a straggle of children surrounded her, screaming with delight as their elders watched from doorways and kitchen windows, *cavasse* games and fountains. Mikaili picked up the littlest boy with ease and hoisted him to his shoulders. He felt the boy's hands tangling in his locks as he squealed, part fear and part excitement at being so high. Imani fell in step with them, pinching the boy's cheeks gently.

"All of them may be slaves one day. All of them may drink from the cup of life," she said softly, staring straight ahead.

"Yes, they may. But we have a chance to save them." Setting the boy down carefully, he watched him run back to his father.

"Why else are we here, if not for that?"

"Between the piracy, the slavers, and the Scorpion King, we dare not step one foot in the wrong direction."

She looks as if the weight of the world is on her shoulders, he thought. And it was.

"Your mother believed in justice, Mikaili. She once told me that every war must only be fought for just causes. But who decides? And what of revenge?"

Mother. She would have spoken caution, he wanted to say. "Mikaili," he could hear her whisper. *"Give a man a second chance and he grows bolder. Give a man what he deserves and you will no longer need eyes to watch your rear."*

"We'll set a trap and we'll wait, and when the time is ripe we will strike."

She turned away as they continued walking without saying a word.

"I have to get back," she finally replied. "Enjoy the *tahtib* tonight." Nodding, she turned quickly as her Medjay did a swift turn, following her like a shadow. Pursing his lips, he watched her walking back up towards the palace. There had to be a way to convince her.

Later in the evening he cheered with the rest of them, on his feet as they pounded their staffs on the ground, ululating in pleasure. Mikaili cheered next to Hasani, having invited him to sit with his family on the fourth day. He knew his friend loved the art of stick fighting—the *Tahtib* or *Naboot* of Kemet and Nubia. An ancient tradition, stick fighting had been practiced for thousands of years as a method of close combat. Even the soldiers of Nabara used it to train.

"Now, there's a fighter!" Hasani yelled.

"Certainly. He's got the arms for it." Mikaili turned back to the arena to watch the fighters preparing for combat. The first champion was engaged in a traditional song that sounded more like it was meant to lull the crowd to sleep. His voice deep and the notes long and soft, his audience listened as a soft drum tapped out the rhythm as he sang of his lands and his home. Singing of his family and the cattle that raised *him*. Their horns teaching him to stand tall, their size giving him courage as their milk kept him strong. And he sang of the Nile. His longing for the beautiful waters of the Nile from whence his ancestors came. Rapt in attention, even Mikaili felt the beauty of his words.

Over five thousand sat below on the stone seats, watching. Another two thousand stood, circling the edge of the arena, peering over the dry stone wall to get a better glimpse ten feet below.

Most of the warriors were well trained and strong. Every now and then some young contestant would step forward, goat's milk still on his breath, for a chance at a black eye. Or the purse that came with it. Some of the nobles would bet on their prizefighters, others on their family members, and others against them. One thing was certain—they always put on a show.

"Drink?" Hasani leaned toward him, motioning out of the arena. There was plenty of wine around them as the Essi were well provisioned by their host, the High King. He'd spared no expense to keep his guests at ease. Mikaili nodded and rose, placing one hand on his father's shoulder as he passed. Walking together down the wide ramp that spiraled around the whole arena, they passed a number of open passages allowing access to the seating areas. When they reached the bottom, Hasani nudged him slightly and Mikaili turned to where he motioned. Five women stood talking near a fountain, their hair covered by beautifully decorated khats that wound around their hair or covered it entirely, falling past their shoulders or defying gravity as it sat upon their heads, showing off the gracefulness of their long necks. Each wore identical gold necklaces around the base of their throat and varying colored gowns shaped like tubes that hugged their curves. *They must be sisters.* All of them favored one another in shape and features, lean shoulders touching as their wide lips opened and closed, speaking fast. One caught Mikaili's eye and tried to hide her smile. He turned away, not missing how she pulled at her sister's skirt to get her attention.

"Beautiful distractions, no?" Hasani was saying.

Mikaili punched his arm, pushing him towards the merchant they needed. His millet beer was the best at the festival, and the people knew it. Despite the line, the people moved at their approach, nodding slightly as the two came.

"Your Grace," the merchant bowed to Mikaili and nodded at Hasani just behind him.

Hasani held up two fingers to the merchant, and the old man reached down before scooping millet beer for them. Handing them over he thanked them as Mikaili dropped the offered gold as payment into a bowl nearby.

"That's more like it." Hasani was smiling as they drank, walking down the path of the festival market. "Now you can experience a little bit of the fun of my kind."

"Your kind?" Mikaili hooted. "And here I thought we were all human, made from the same gods."

Hasani snorted, "Your gods put more gold in your pocket."

"My father's pocket."

"Oh—have the inheritance laws changed?"

He sighed, defeated. Hasani was good at winning arguments.

Hasani laughed, clapping a hand on his shoulder. "It's been too long, old friend. You gave up too easy. Which girl has made you soft this time?"

"No one has made me soft," Mikaili scoffed.

"No? Well, hard then."

Mikaili scowled.

"Hard-headed!!" Hasani emphasized before laughing wildly, holding his stomach at Mikaili's expression.

"You're no funnier than the last time I saw you." He pushed Hasani away roughly, still laughing.

Stopping at the next merchant, Hasani flipped him a coin, which the man took, passing him two more portions of millet beer.

"Drink," Hasani said seriously, handing Mikaili a beer.

Mikaili took it without question, raising it to his lips. It was even more bitter than the last, but he didn't mind, tipping it back slowly. As he did, Hasani tipped the bottom forward, spilling half of it on Mikaili's chest before dashing off quickly.

"It was a joke!" he called back as he fled. Mikaili had him in a headlock in ten paces and the people laughed, pointing as they watched, "The ring is the other way, Highness!" an old man called.

Hasani looped an arm over Mikaili's shoulder as they caught their breaths. "Come on, you're missing it. You can tell me about her later."

"Who?"

"The Princess Imanishakheto," Hasani said casually. "They tell me she has saltwater in her veins."

"More like fire."

"I love a bit of fire. Keeps me warm." He was smiling and Mikaili couldn't help but roll his eyes. "And I could drown in those eyes if she'd let me." He looked up to the stars in mock worship, darkness falling quickly.

"You're in love," he stated, shaking his head. It wasn't a question. *He's always in love.* He'd been introduced to a number of pretty girls, farmers' daughters, artisans, scribes, and even a High Priest's granddaughter. Hasani had always begged for an introduction to those he had no interest in. And had courted a few of them.

"Of course I am. Half the city is in love with her, and that includes the women. And seeing her at the Games, lovely as an oasis in the Kalahari."

"Oh. Does she know you?" Mikaili teased him.

"Don't mock me. Of course she does. She's heard of the second captain of the *Desert Arrow*. The High King's used our galley!"

"You are losing your mind." Mikaili tipped his head slightly as he turned to look at his friend.

"Possibly. She distracts me unfairly. Those eyes…"

Hasani missed Mikaili's scowl as he turned to smile at a girl passing by them, her long hair in one thick braid. She lowered her eyes mischievously, and Hasani turned to speak to her until she stopped at a meat stand and he realized it must be the merchant's daughter. The scowl the man gave his friend in return for his glances confirmed it.

"Better luck next time, Hasani." Mikaili was glad he could have a bit of fun at his expense.

"Next time," he agreed. "Come! The whole city has turned out to see the event, and you have me here."

They walked past the merchants' stalls as other traders cried their wares. Sweet fig cakes were being sold to their right, bite-sized dates that were sweet and smooth to their left. Roasted duck was being served with bread at the corner for those with a few coins to spare and no woman to cook for them. An olive oil-smoked wildebeest had been buried in a great pit, and the smell of the smoke wafting towards them made Mikaili's mouth water, but they'd miss the *tahtib*. The favorite of fortunetellers was at it again, he saw, the palm of another young girl in his hand as he sprinkled it with oil.

The crowd parted in excitement as Mikaili and Hasani walked back up to their seats. He spotted Imani and Ama from a distance and dipped his head in greeting as they smiled in return.

"Ladies, gentlemen, or a little of both," the announcer started, grinning to his left at a group of perfumed nobles, bringing the crowd to laughter, "Welcome to the bullfight of the century." The crowd roared with delight, stamping their feet where they stood and waving.

"On our left, we have the reigning champion of Nabara, born near Torrent's shore, a farmer's pride and joy. On our right, a newcomer, laden with plenty of gold. Please give your hands to our champions for the evening." Screaming, the crowd roared their approval, mad with excitement. "And last, but never least, the gods have honored us with a token, a favor of their good will, by bringing Prince Mikaili the first, Son of Makalo and Heir to the Essi Kingdom. A great fighter in his own right, we welcome him today."

He blushed as Hasani elbowed him in the ribs. Mikaili stood, his hand gripping the hilt of his *khopesh* and extending a nod to the announcer. The crowd roared with delight, yelling blessings upon him before he took his seat again.

"Champions," the announcer continued, "you may use any of your wits at your disposal, but keep in mind the crowd prefers *physical* contact." The audience laughed as he finished. Should you find yourself unable to rise or flat on your back…to the victor go the spoils. Take your places."

The crowd's talk quieted to whispers as the contestants took their places on opposite sides of the arena. The Nabaran wore no breastplate, and neither did the Essi. The Nabaran's hair was shaved close, only a simple short shendyt covering his thighs and wrapped around his waist. Oil shone on his skin in the heat of the night. His dark skin looked as smooth as ink. His opponent wore long linen pants, but he soon took them off, revealing a shendyt of the same as the Nabaran's and muscles that challenged the others. The women hooted their approval as he disrobed.

At the sound of the drum, the fighters took stance, picking up their acacia bars as they began circling one another like prey.

The acacia wood was strong and in great supply. Some used palm, but acacia trees surrounded them on all sides and were known for their sharp thorns, which made the strongest of climbers wary. Elephants would tear them down in a heartbeat, standing on their hind legs to push the tree down with their front. Giraffes used their strong teeth to bite at the leafy treat that was too tall for most and challenged the hungriest of animals to reach. It was the acacia's ability to survive in places where water was scarce that gave it its value. Each of the fighters held two bars that had been cut and carved by Nabara's most famous carpenter into a cylindrical weapon just three inches thick and four feet long. The finish was smooth as marble and would soon hold a number of nicks and cuts as the combat began. Fighters kept their wrists strong and flexible in order to keep a firm grip around the base of the bars, holding them with one hand and later two in case one broke or was cut in half during combat. Mikaili himself had trained with acacia bars, though his time pulling rope on his father's war galleys made it less of a necessity to strengthen his arms. Each champion would need both his strength and body to properly use the bars as a weapon, throwing their weight into each blow. If they were brought down hard enough, the bars could do irreversible damage. Even to the untrained eye, an organ or two might suffer from having been slammed by an acacia bar as an elephant stomped the snake.

The Nabaran lunged at the Essi, left and right before drawing back quickly and circling again.

"Tell me we don't have a coward in the ring," Hasani scoffed.

"Not a coward," he replied. "He feints to draw his opponent's weaknesses. To see which leg or arm he favors most."

The Essi preferred to drag right, using his right leg as his foundation and bringing the bars down towards the Nabaran's shoulders. He connected hard, smashing the Nabaran's bar as it snapped up to block him. The Nabaran didn't waste time repositioning. As soon as his bar slammed to block the Essi's, he drew it down with the other, slamming them hard into the Essi's thighs before he had a chance to step backward. The crowd went wild as the Essi fell to his knees, balancing on his bars, the base in the sand as he rose to his feet. The Nabaran stepped back, watching the Essi rise. He swung his bars slowly as he waited, his wrists easily switching back and forth. Suddenly the Nabaran rushed forward, his left holding the acacia bar in the middle, his right holding one at the very bottom with it raised high in the air in attack position. The Essi countered, meeting it and thrusting his right acacia bar in an undercut that was knocked away. Back and forth they landed a series of blows, the acacia bars making a series of *click-clack* noises as they met. The audience was engrossed in the dance. Suddenly the Essi's acacia bar dragged right and slammed into the right side of the Nabaran's face, leaving him reeling in the sand, his cheek split open and one eye hit from the cut above it and the lid drooping fast.

"He's lost an eye. And depth perception. There's no way he'll recover. I'm going to lose this bet," Hasani moaned.

"You bet against us?" Mikaili was incredulous.

"It's not personal, brother." Hasani didn't take his eyes from the arena.

"He's lost an eye, not his will to fight. A blind man can still have courage even when he can't see his enemy," his father interrupted.

"You're rooting for the Nabaran then, as King of the Essi?" Hasani finally turned to look at him, doubt in his eyes.

"I'm stating a fact. One the two of you should learn in case you ever find yourselves in such a position. The bat does not fear the spider." Mikaili watched his father turn back to the arena and wondered what was going through his mind.

The Nabaran fought from the ground, one knee still planted as the Essi attacked. The crowd gasped in shock as the sound of splitting wood cut the air. Only one acacia bar remained per champion now, and each sensed the last leg of the fight.

The champions wrapped both hands around their acacia bars, circling slowly as they sized each other up. The Essi favored his leg like an injured penguin, no doubt still in pain from the acacia bar having slammed into it. The Nabaran's eye was now closed, blood dripping from the right side of his head to his shoulder.

"That's what you get for betting against Nabara!" Hasani yelled, watching the enraged fans whine as their debts were collected.

As the next fight was prepared, Hasani rounded on him. "Now, tell me who she is."

He shook his head, watching Hasani's eyes narrow. "Is she Nudollan?"

Mikaili looked at him a long time before answering. "That's not what's bothering me."

"You'll tell me after, yes?" Hasani looked at his friend, leveling his eyes at him. Mikaili nodded briefly and they turned back to watch the next match.

The drums beat again and again and the crowd whispered excitedly.

"This is what everyone waits for, brother."

They watched as both competitors moved left. Slowly the fighter from Nabara raised his acacia bar and pointed it at the Essi. *A challenge.* The arena cheered with excitement at the challenge and began to chant. "Answer! Answer! Answer! Answer!" over and over.

The drums began to beat as the two circled each other slowly. When the Essi's acacia lashed out, the drums stopped, freezing the air with tension as the battle began. The Nabaran was quick, but slightly off balance as he put on a dizzying display of dangerous moves that left the crowd alternating between abusing him and cheering as they leaned in closer. It would be blood or injury for him, and they wanted to see it either way. Mikaili watched as he realized he was compensating to make up for his loss of depth perception. Opting for horizontal moves rather than vertical ones to increase his chances of hitting his target. Getting closer to make sure his acacia reached far enough, knowing his target now appeared closer than it really was.

A moment later the crowd screamed as the Essi drove the smaller back, a series of blows that put dents in the Nabaran's acacia bar and tested the strength of his shoulders to meet the weight of his opponent as he slammed him repeatedly. Mikaili and the others were on their feet as they watched the Nabaran's arm rise and slam into the stomach of the Essi; a lower hit his only option. But a moment later his leg moved up, his knee pounding in between the Essi's legs, and he screamed, falling to his side. The smaller was standing over the larger now, but instead of beating him while he was down the smaller stood back and waited, circling the Essi before standing a ways off, watching. The Essi yelled suddenly, his arms outstretched and his acacia drawn as he ran towards the smaller. Mikaili's mouth dropped open in shock. The smaller had not moved; he'd waited as the larger ran towards him. Then with a movement quicker than the crowd could perceive he ran forward at the last minute, ducking under the Essi's arm until he stood behind him. Raising his arms, both hands wrapped around the acacia bar he brought them down sharply, slamming them into the back of the larger's head twice before the larger grunted, dropping to his knees, and falling forward face first to the ground. Silence fell on the night as the onlookers watched. A moment later piercing screams hit the air as the crowd cheered, screaming for the champion. The women began to sing the victory song, their arms raised to the sky as they expressed their delight, ululations rising.

"You were never that fast." Hasani grinned as he looked from the champion back to Mikaili. The champion moved to exit the ring as women threw necklaces made of sugar bushes and lotus flowers to him, but the commentator stopped him, forcing the Nabaran to stand and wait until the crowd finished cheering.

"He was *excellent.*"

"He was *well trained.*"

"Jealousy does not become you, friend."

"Never that." Mikaili stroked his chin momentarily as he watched the champion walk off, his shoulders back, his head high.

"Tell me, Mikaili…" Hasani's voice dropped to a whisper, drowned by the crowd. Mikaili rose and moved with Hasani to the highest part of the stone complex, walking around the top of the arena slowly.

"My father wants to move on them, but we need the entire alliance of Nudolla behind us and only the High King can provide that. He alone commands the Medjay and Adamantine as well as making decisions on foreign threats and matters. We don't want to turn this into a war if we don't have to, especially if we know the source of the crime. It need not be so difficult."

He'd known it had to be the work of King Tharbis. His reputation was growing fast, and not in a good way. The captains and traders had been talking about the raids, and how piracy on Torrent, interior waterways, and soon *land* may affect their trade. *There's no way they'll stop that easily.* He'd felt compelled to warn his friend. Theirs was an old friendship, and he trusted Hasani with his life.

"The High King must have proof then?" Hasani's eyebrows were narrowed as he waited for his answer. After a moment Hasani's eyebrows rose in surprise. "Your father would move without him?"

"We can't let our people be slaughtered while we wait for an ally."

"The Kiberan ship has not been found, no one knows what happened to it. And an ally? Mikaili. The High King is more than an ally, he is the *law.* I am in your debt for warning us of what is to come. The high seas come with many a danger, but knowing what we may find is to our advantage. We'll have to hire fighters to protect our cargo, at once."

"Then you'll stand and fight with us?"

"Fight? High King Kashta has not declared war. He bought us years of peace. It's easy for you to sit there, begging for a war from your throne, but it's the people who suffer the most. It's our villages that will burn, our children who will be carried away and no one to mourn or avenge us."

"It won't be like that. We do it for the people."

"It's always like that. We fight for you; yes, we die for you. The people respect him because he understands the needs of the many and desires to build them into something greater. War would change all of that. I'm not saying that justice shouldn't be done. I know our words. But going into a war blindly could mean disaster. We should hold onto peace while we can."

His jaw clenched in anger. *He doesn't understand.* "Peace? You want peace? There's only war and everything leading up to it. Poverty, hunger, crime. If you want freedom, then the cost is blood. What do you think the price of peace is, friend? You don't have to call it a war for there to be one. So when you're sitting there, watching Torrent run red, and your farms dry up, and nothing comes down from the north except corpses and blood, and you wonder what will come down next, you tell me if you'd rather fight now so you don't have to die later, or sit and wait for death when you could have decided your fate."

"Mikaili—" Hasani tried to grab his shoulder as he turned away, but he wrenched away from him.

"I never guessed I could not count you among my allies," he finished quietly.

"I *am* your ally. But you are the fighter in the ring. You just cannot see it. You've lost an eye, *yes.* You're angry. As you should be. But just as he took the time to recover and create a strategy, so must you! You are trying to fight without knowing how close or how far or which *direction* your enemy comes from. Is it so hard to see? Is it?" Hasani pressed.

Mikaili rose abruptly from his seat, shouldering through the crowded arena, ignoring the curious stares as he passed.

"Mikaili!" The crowd turned to look at Hasani, curious, but he ignored them all as he watched his friend leave.

Mikaili strode away in his anger. *Peace.* He'd been born on the water, just like Hasani; it was his home, his birthright. Like the Nile, the River Nub was life. War would change all that, yes, and for some disproportionately. *Everyone wanted peace, but no one wanted to fight for it.*

IMANI

Ama walked beside her, arm in arm down the roads of Nabara. Medjay followed closely behind. What was there to fear on such a night as this? It seemed the gods had brightened the stars, pulling them closer to shine upon the city. Everywhere the city was abuzz, children laughing and running, their parents sitting outside, merchants continuing to scream their wares. The festival kept them up well past midnight. Each and every Nabaran loved the prosperity, the change, and the relaxation the Festival of Kings brought them. They were drunk with love for the city, her people, and her leaders. One of the most famous *jeli* sat behind a large fire. Crackling and spitting, the embers burned and rose towards the sky like fireflies as children began to crowd closer and closer to the storyteller. Crossing their legs in front of them, kneeling near their brothers and sisters, they sshh'd one another excitedly as they waited for his story.

"Look, Imani," Ama whispered softly, tightening her fingers on her arm slightly, pulling her in the opposite direction. "Just there. The *Iyalawo* of the Yoruba."

Imani followed her gaze slowly, glancing up the narrow street to a hooded silk tent not far away. A figure sat at a table just outside of it. A black robe concealed the wearer's face, but the moon reflected beautifully off the colored glass ball sitting in front of them.

"The Yoruba of the Kingdom of Ife?" The tent was so black it might not have been there at all. No crowd surrounded it as it did the others. "Ife means expansion in their language. I wonder if she's trying to expand her trade. She's travelled quite a distance for it. Every merchant is welcome."

"She's not just a merchant, Cousin. She's a fortune-teller."

"A fortune-teller? The High Priest wants them all banished for their lies."

"A High *Priestess*. The city has been talking of her. Three days she has been here, and for three days she has only given three prophecies. Each of them has come true. They call her the Mother of Mysteries," Ama finished gravely.

"Mother of Mysteries?" Imani repeated, narrowing her eyes at the tent in front of her. The Temple of Mysteries sat on the outskirts of the city, a sandstone-stepped pyramid that was the pride of Nabara. Unlike the other pyramids in the Kingdom of Nabara, this one held Meroitic inscriptions both inside and *out.* Posing riddles, questions, mysteries to any who ventured upon it. It was the only pyramid that stood unguarded in all of Nabara. *And no need.* Who had ever been seen to enter? None that Imani could tell. The inscriptions provided answers to how to enter the Temple of Mysteries and were not easily discovered. The neophyte initiates who trained under the Mystery System were sworn to secrecy when they pledged, and few were selected. All of their training and education was delivered orally to protect the secrets of Kush's rule over Kemet and the thousands of years of reign of the black kings of Nubia. Writing was forbidden. Hypnosis, prophecy, power over nature, the study of mathematics, astronomy, philosophy, metallurgy, and more were only a few of the subjects studied in the Temple of Mysteries. Her father was well versed in asking her questions and riddles when she wanted answers from him, forcing her to reach the answers and conclusions she sought on her own. One day, he'd told her, you will enter the Temple of Mysteries on your own. Yet here Ama was, whispering in her ear that another mystery sat right in front of her. Her curiosity might get the better of her here.

"Only three? A line of people stand in front of *that* famed fortuneteller's tent each day, paying a pound of gold for his prophesies. He owes half the people in Nabara for his own fortune." *What was so special about this one?*

"Half the people in Nabara stand in line to hear tales of butterflies and beauty. Have you ever known someone to go seeking something other than a good fortune?" Ama looked at her expectantly before rolling her eyes. "If they knew they would be penniless tomorrow or dead the day after, would they want to hear it?" When she didn't answer, her cousin continued. "He tells them they will meet their lover in a week or in a month. That they will grow rich if they learn to understand the ant. That the nobles will reward them for their service if they prove their worth. It means nothing, but fools will always pay for good news and lies rather than accept the truth for free."

"And this High Priestess? How is she different?" she asked cautiously.

"*Her* prophecies have come *true*."

"Which ones?"

"All of them. The seamstress's husband was told his wife had cuckolded him. More than once. He did not believe her. She told him to take a spool of thread from his wife and tie it across the front door at bedtime for three nights. She bid him to look out his window on the third night, and he would find the bird that stole his wife away from him every night. The first two mornings after he found the thread broken he realized his wife had risen in the night, though she lay next to him then. On the third night, he rose after her and went to his window. He saw the raven trainer kissing his wife, and the same day, he requested a divorce from the nine High Priests of the *Kenbet*." Ama raised an eyebrow at her. "Shall I continue?"

Her eyes were wide as she nodded to her cousin. "And the second?"

"A noble. The fortune maker told him his business would flourish due to his philanthropy and kindness, but to be wary of false friends. When he asked who was a false friend she told him that envy is green. He didn't understand. The same night another noble offered him an investment he dared not refuse. Malachite. His friend offered to sell his malachite across Torrent for him. But he refused and the same night, moved the stones for safekeeping, replacing them with colored glass. One of the captains refused to let the noble onto his boat and he threatened him, demanding that he leave in the dead of night for Rhapta. The city soldiers were called, and they detained him. They found the glass stones on his person, but he claimed they were his own. They arrested him and found he'd stolen from other nobles in the city. He's been sent to a quarry near Tharbis."

"Do you want to know the third, Imani?" Ama asked.

"Tell me."

"A young girl. She asked the High Priestess whether she would be rich like her grandfather when she was older. She told her she would be just as rich as he, but not nearly as happy with her riches for to gain them she would suffer. The next day, her grandfather's heart gave out as he walked to the river. He left all his wealth to her, his favorite grandchild. They say she has not stopped crying since she learned of it."

She glanced toward the fortune maker's tent furtively, biting her lip to mask her fear. *What would she tell me? If she really saw the future, could she tell me what I want to know? Do I want to know?*

When she looked up this time, she could almost feel eyes upon her, though she could not see them.

"Come, dear heart. Sometimes, it's best if we don't know the future." Ama took her hand.

"No. She's been waiting for me," she replied softly.

Imani thought back to her dreams. She dreamt a girl, riding lightning, touching it, letting it strike her, her hair aflame, yet she seemed to feel nothing. Later she dreamt that same girl falling headlong over a cliff to her death. The next night she watched from behind huge black stones as red vultures ate the eyes from large dead worms. Green worms.

When they reached the tent, a figure came out without saying a word and moved inside the tent. Curiously small. Imani thought it must be the fortuneteller's child. *How not?*

"Wait for us," she told Medjay, taking Ama's arm and pushing the heavy black curtains aside.

Five torches burned inside, but still the center of the tent remained dark, dim light flickering in the corners. In the middle of the tent stood a tall cylinder-shaped structure. Soon it began to glow. The child beckoned her closer before sitting opposite, her knees near the mouth of the cylinder. *This is some trick,* she thought leaning over and peering into the cylinder. There was water inside, and it churned furiously as if Torrent were beneath it.

"How—" Imani stopped short as the child raised a hand towards her, palm up.

Where is her mother? Imani looked around, suddenly thinking that perhaps only a fool would seek his fortune like this. When she turned back, the child held out a small jar, filled with coins, cowrie shells, ivory, silver, and gold. A pile of palm nuts sat behind her.

Reaching carefully into her belt, she pulled out a single gold coin, dropping it carefully inside. The child stretched a hand toward her own and Imani complied, refusing to let this child see her trepidation.

"What will you give up, child?" she asked slowly. Her voice was surprisingly soothing. She sounded much older than she looked.

"Give up? I—I paid you for—"

"Yes. But the world asks for more than gold from us. No one passes through life without suffering. How else would we know peace?"

"There is no such thing as peace."

"So wise for one so young," the child replied, smiling.

"Not as young as you." Imani couldn't believe the irony in this conversation.

"Your eyes will only ever tell you half of the story. Remember that." The child held her eyes, tilting her head slightly, watching her.

"The others," Imani asked slowly, "what did they give up?"

"What is truth worth to you? Would you kill for it? Die for it?"

For a moment, Imani was silent. Was she asking her to give her life to know, to answer a question, for truth?

"Yes."

"Blood then," the child replied swiftly, pulling a blade from her sleeve.

The child pricked her finger so quickly it was over before she could react. She didn't flinch. Nor did she flinch when the child squeezed it between her own fingers. Three drops of her blood fell into the water. Immediately, the water stilled, turning a dark red, almost black. When the child raised her head, she realized she'd been holding her breath. As she watched, the smooth, unlined face of a child with long silver hair and brown eyes that seemed to glow red gazed back at her. Imani could not hide her surprise. The *Iyalawo* took no notice.

"You dream, Daughter of the Desert."

"Everyone dreams." She couldn't hide her suspicion. Nor would she.

"Of death and lightning?" When Imani didn't respond, she

continued. "But you do not fear them. Vultures eat what remains of your allies, but more abound. When the eye falls in the sky in three days, look to the south. Listen to your dreams. Do not turn them away. Soldiers are not enough to stop what comes this way. You've tasted their blood already. It's bitter and full of greed. All children must grow up. Let us hope your training was not wasted." Her red eyes flashed as she finished, unblinking.

Imani's heart beat wildly in her chest. *Our allies are dwindling? What could be falling from the sky? Did she mean the moon? The sun? My dreams. Whose blood have I tasted?*

The *Iyalawo* watched her carefully. "Questions need answers. Soon. Beware the enemy at your table. A hidden knife is the most dangerous of all."

Of course it was! Why was she speaking in riddles? There were at least a hundred royal guests to entertain for the Games. How could she watch them all?

"Tell me their names," she said instead.

"They are of no value to you. Every man has a master in this world. Even kings are slaves. And some men deserve a second chance."

Her red eyes rolled back, revealing the whites of her eyes before returning again, soft and brown, but still glowing, it seemed.

"Listen to your dreams. Go now. Your cousin fears for you."

Imani turned to see Ama standing still as stone inside the entrance to the tent. As she neared her, she realized her cousin's eyes were like marble. They did not move. Touching her arm, she shook her cousin gently. "Ama?"

Her cousin blinked once, eyes dazed. "Are you so scared? You've always been hard to convince. We can leave, Imani. I do not trust this one."

Imani's mouth dropped open and she turned quickly around towards the High Priestess again. The robe covered all again, and she nodded slightly. She pulled Ama outside. "I did, weren't you listening?" She was confused. *She'd been standing right there.*

"You never left my side, Imani. Don't be silly. You are scared to enter, aren't you?"

"You didn't hear…" Ama shook her head, giving Imani a

concerned look. Medjay fell in behind them as they exited the tent. *It was real*, she told herself. *I did not dream it.* But when she looked back down the street, the tent was gone.

SICARIUS

"Come now, Sicarius. It is wonderful to have you returned and in such good health. I knew you would keep our dear Cassius safe."

He moved a step to his right, carefully stacking the paintings he'd been asked to see to in an attempt to avoid her curious fingers. The large gourds of mixed paint were under the table, and he'd see to them next, lifting them for storage so the old man wouldn't need to suffer from the strain.

"You are so *strong*," she whispered softly, placing her right hand on his wrist, holding him there. Removing her palm from his wrist to flick her flaxen curls over her bare shoulder, she let her *palla* fall to her elbow, the top of her left breast exposed. Arching her back as she perched on the table she tipped her head to her left, narrowing her eyes at him. When he didn't answer, she leaned towards him, her long hair brushing against his arm as she moved her lips closer to his ear. "Freedom looks quite good on you, you know. Don't you agree?"

"Sicarius!"

She jumped at the sound of the voice, turning quickly, but not quick enough. The flash of surprise on the young apprentice's face was the only sign that he'd seen anything. It came as quickly as it went. He was an artist training under the famed Grecian painter of Italy, brought to Cuicul to study landscapes and to learn. But he was still a slave.

"I apologize, mistress, I did not mean to interrupt."

"Of course not, Liber." She walked closer, placing one hand on the young apprentice's cheek, smiling lightly as she slid the sleeve of her gown back up on her shoulder from where she'd let it fall. "I was just leaving. I meant to leave word with the Grecian. He is to paint me soon."

"And a lovely work it will be, though I doubt he could do you justice," Liber replied. The slave had a gift for words, he would give the boy that. Though Liber preferred to use his gifts for

301

making pictures. It mattered little to him.

"Oh, stop," she simpered, both rows of teeth showing as she grinned at him. "You ought not to tease me, you bad thing. Sometimes I have to remember you're just a boy." Her hand trailed slowly down his chest before she pulled it away. "I'll return tomorrow before I leave for Constantinople. Cuicul is growing quite boring. Tell him as soon as he returns." Without even glancing behind her for confirmation, she strutted from the room, her backside swaying in the folds of her robe as she left. She didn't need to. Knowing she was giving a command to a slave was enough. It made her a dangerous person to cross.

"Hm...*you're* in trouble, aren't you?" Liber looked at Sicarius and back at the doorway to make sure she was gone. "She wants more than a painting I would say."

He said nothing. And didn't need to. She was like all the rest of the women who lusted after the steel and blood and violence of the life of a gladiator. The ones who sat as close to the center of the coliseum as possible so they were able to see each battle. Holding their hands to their breasts in fear and anticipation. Clutching their gowns at the knees and gathering the folds inside their palms as they caught their breaths in excitement. Augustus knew what he was doing when he commanded women be given certain seating much higher and further from the gladiators they came to see. Only the Vestal Virgins were permitted to sit at the closest edges, renowned as they were for their chastity. But Sicarius had seen the open mouths and quickly rising breasts, the teeth that bit at their bottom lips, the fingers stroking at the same. The Vestals were, after all, only women. And no magic spell could prevent one from feeling something as powerful as lust.

Only he was no longer a gladiator. He was *rudiarii.* A gladiator who had won his freedom through hundreds of gladiator fights and the love of the mob. The coveted *rudis,* an honor that slaves of the coliseum prayed for every time their name was called and they won a victory for their master, had become his reward. And it was rare. Sicarius had political freedom now and at his earliest manumission was paraded about at celebrations and dinners around Rome. Feasting with prostitutes, artists, farmers, moneylenders, traders, senators, and priests had become a weekly occurrence. All eager to meet the former gladiator who'd killed a mountain of men. Important men. Well-connected men.

"It's my fault, you know," Liber interrupted his thoughts apologetically. "I told her you were here. I should have known she was...well...she—"

"You are not to blame," Sicarius told him.

Liber's surprise that he'd spoken at all showed, but he nodded, his earnest brown eyes thanking him. After a moment he began organizing the paints and canvas that the Grecian would use as quickly as he could. His smooth black hair was slightly ruffled. He was a Syrian. Despite the young apprentice's love for art, he too had heroes among the gladiators. Flamma, the Syrian gladiator who refused the *rudi,* was his. Slim like a reed and always talking, Sicarius didn't mind his company. The boy was sharp, and always respectful. As was the Grecian who once advocated for Sicarius's release from the gladiator games. And to whom he owed a debt far larger than he could ever repay. He finished storing the items he needed to and moved towards the door.

"You're leaving? Already?" Liber wiped his hand across his forehead, smearing paint over it.

Sicarius turned back and nodded.

"Well...I'll tell him you came, shall I?" Liber replied hopefully.

Nodding again, Sicarius turned and walked out the door, his heavy *gladius* swinging gently at his waist. He'd have a drink before they left for the interior again. And he knew just the place.

The first thing he noticed was the stench of vomit in the air, and he recoiled from it. His stomach heaved even as he tried to hold his breath, his eyes opening slightly to ascertain where he was, the source of the smell, the source of the darkness. His chin was wet, and he soon realized the vomit was his own.

It had been hours since he'd left the Grecian's shop. Attempting to sit up in the darkness was difficult, the table in front of him covered in his own filth and his last portion of beer with it. Recoiling from the mess, he wiped his sleeve down his chin and rose on shaky legs, which steadied after a moment. Walking over to the trough, he pushed his face under the water, bending at the waist to push himself further under. He needed to drown out the voices. He needed to drown out the screams. His head swam, pounding with pain. He and the other slavers had come here immediately after their arrival in Cuicul, a former Berber town. It was now home to a Roman garrison. Hatred followed him everywhere, eyes scathingly penetrated the Roman numbers fixed on his skin. Even here, in a *ganea.* A brothel. Or *home*, as many of his Roman brothers called it affectionately.

"Master…?"

He turned as he pulled his head from the water, wiping his eyes dry.

The girl was only a child. He noted her wide eyes, how she stayed on the last step rather than come into the room with him. Laughter and voices drifted down the stairs and she didn't move, standing still as if frozen as she looked at him.

"I…I came for…my mother told me to…she needs water…" Her words came to a halt just as suddenly as they started. The sheerness of her clothing was evidence enough of her profession. Mother, she called her. How very unlikely they were related by blood. The girl was a Berber, and by the look of her slight frame had been forced into the brothel if she wanted to eat. No doubt her *mater* had recently finished off one of her customers upstairs and desired water for cleaning herself. If only to service the next.

"I'm not your master. Bring me fresh clothes. Tell your *mater* I am leaving."

The girl nodded, her head bobbing up and down rapidly as she backed slowly up the stairs before spinning quickly around to take them two at a time. As soon as she left he stripped down, pulling the thick leather vest over his head and sliding his top shirt over broad shoulders, his pants still hugging his narrow waist. Within ten seconds he stood naked in the corner of the *ganea* as he turned sideways to look at the wound on his right side just near his back. A long, jagged red cut stood out against his light brown skin, joining dozens more. Most of them had been put there by gladiators he'd killed or the slaves he'd been sent to capture. One of the slaves he'd captured had sliced him when he'd tried to escape with his family. The wound was shallow. It should heal quickly. The others always did.

The squareness of his jaw and his dark brows made him forever angry in the eyes of many, and his pale eyes turned now to the girl as she crept slowly back down the stairs. Stopping suddenly, she gasped when she saw his naked body, eyes wide in shock as the fingers of her right hand clutched the wall in trepidation. The fear in her eyes made him grit his teeth. Some of the businesses had been spared when they'd run the Berbers out and raised Rome as the new mother of Cuicul. The slavers valued the prostitutes they frequented. It eased the pressure of the trade. Turning towards the girl now, he appraised her features once more. He'd been far too generous with her age earlier. If he'd been honest with himself, ten was a much closer guess. There was no slight sag to her skin like many of the prostitutes he'd seen. As though their skin became looser and looser each day, shedding it like a coat of arms before donning it again the next. Wide eyes stared out from between feathered lashes. Nut-colored cheeks smooth and round, as full as any fig he'd find in the market.

"You know what I am?" he asked softly, turning from the mirror to face her.

She didn't answer but merely nodded, attempting to back up a step before realizing she still stood on the stairs. Her heel slammed into the back of the lowest one, arresting her movement.

"Are you going to take me away?" she whispered, her voice softer than a breeze.

"Have you seen my face?" he asked her, stepping closer. "Will you tell them who I am?"

She was shaking now, crossing her arms about her waist as if to protect herself. "No," she whispered.

"Leave her be."

Sicarius looked up at the woman descending the stairs, her shoulder-length straight dark hair covering one side of her face like a window. She put one hand on the girl's shoulder and the girl jumped, unable to take her eyes off of Sicarius. The woman ran her eyes over him insolently, teasing, the slack smile knowing.

"I could cut your throat for that. Or send you across the sea."

"Only if you're immune to flattery," she replied, dropping her gaze to the middle of his waist before drawing it back up. Her eyes lingered on his scars and she swallowed carefully, her chest rising and falling slowly.

Sicarius tipped his head slightly, watching her. "Are you protecting her? And if so...from whom?" He looked around the front room as a series of moans punctuated the silence, a rhythmic slapping following close behind them. "Clearly, not yourself."

Her lips pursed in anger as he gestured to the girl's flimsy clothing.

"Do you want to come with me?" he asked the girl, holding his hand out gently. She seemed to stop breathing in front of him, her mouth dropping open in horror.

The woman's hand tightened on the girl's shoulder, and even she could not speak. Sicarius grinned, his white teeth shining in the dark as his eyes lingered on the woman's breast for a moment. That would teach her not to bargain with him. The slavers paid far too well.

"Do you want to know a secret?" He turned to the girl now, kneeling in front of her and taking one of her hands in his. "Something even your *mater* doesn't realize." He tucked her raven-colored hair behind her left ear and leaned close, whispering softly. After a moment he pulled away, looking into her dark eyes, much less wide now, narrowed, wary. Running his thumb over the back of her hand a moment, he bent forward, touching his lips briefly to it and moving forward slowly to kiss her cheek. "Remember that." Her nod was slight, but it was enough.

Rising, he released her hand and took the clothing the girl held from her hand, sliding into the pants and shirt slowly, his muscles sore. He kept his eyes on them as he slid his clothes on, past his hips and over his shoulders. The laces on his pants he took his time with, slowly sliding them through and through, his eyes on the *meretrix*, considering. The woman shifted slightly as he looked at her, her hands tightening on the girl's shoulders. She was afraid now, and that was just how he wanted her. His vest came last. Securing it tightly to his chest, keeping the two of them in front of him as he dressed, silence in the lower rooms save the occasional laughter and grunts coming from above. He looked like them, but he was no longer one of them. That bond had been broken long ago and he needed to remain vigilant. At any moment, someone may try to put a sword through him.

When he looked back at the woman, he saw the desire hidden

in her eyes, but there was more besides. That look he knew too well. Many slaves had tried to bargain with it, convinced it might work. Desire and disgust just barely concealed. He could spot it even in the dark and a mile into the desert.

"You'll catch plenty of women for us if your face is to judge," Cassius had told him once, cuffing him on the cheek gently the first night he'd come into his service. "You'll do perfectly."

And he was right. It was as he told the girl. *Neither of us has a conscience. She'll use you again and again while convincing you she's saving your life.* Walking towards the door he turned suddenly, eyes catching the girl as he put one finger to his lips, his face expressionless. When he left the brothel, the light hit his eyes and he embraced the pain. Even in the blinding sun the sight of all of those slaves jumping from the ship had been etched in his mind, deeper than the ones he'd tracked down, deeper than the ones he'd slaughtered. Pushing away the images, he looked towards the edges of the mountainous ravines stretching towards the moon like robed monsters, Cuicul sitting between them like an animal caught in a trap. Lowering his chin again, he moved towards the main basilica to find Cassius. He still had more slaves to catch.

ADURA

"**I've seen her,**" Zaxasha said. "**Hair like black gold, skin like rich earth, and eyes like the burning sun.**"

"But does she bear the mark, Zaxasha?"

"She has the sight. She doesn't know it yet, but she does. And she dreams," she whispered. "She dreams of Adura. And more."

"Without proof we can't—"

"The truth is there. I've seen it," she finished, looking down into the center of the pool.

Water bubbled like boiling goat's milk, smoke rising from it every few moments, hissing like some great snake. Adura crouched behind the precipice of rock, watching the meeting take place. *Why would the princess dream of me?* Her excitement obliged her to lean down, watching the boiling water until her eyes grew tired.

"…She could save us all, Aiona. As her mother, you have to face this reality before it breaks you," Zaxasha said.

"She's just a child."

"And so were we all." Zaxasha's voice grew impatient.

They sat on flat stone, their seats large, strong, and unmoving. None of them seemed to want her present, though it was her name on their tongues loudly and often. Her sisters and brothers were hunting near the edge of the forest. They would come back soon, long spears red and slick with blood, their kill swinging on their shoulders as they marched back inside the safety of the mountain.

They lived off the bounty of the mountains and crags. Valleys. They never ventured too far north or east towards the sea. They always stayed on the edge. And Zaxasha had warned them that something was coming. She kept speaking of a key, the mark, the sight, and slaves. None of it made sense.

"I've seen them." Zaxasha was unrelenting. "My dreams may change, but they're never wrong. The slaves flee this way in droves. Famine will bring many to their knees. And trade routes will be as honey to a bee."

Slaves. Adura's ears caught onto the only word she didn't

know. *Were they animals, like the antelope that flocked in herds? They must be to run in such large numbers. But what were they fleeing?* Her foot slipped in her excitement and rocks shifted under her, crashing to the floor near the walls of the cave. Wincing at the sound, she froze in place.

"Adura," Zaxasha spoke. "Come down and speak with us. It's time for your lesson, child."

Adura poked her head out first, her dark brown hair bouncing as she emerged from her hiding place. Hanging her head guiltily, she climbed down the wall to stand in front of Zaxasha as her mother looked on anxiously.

Zaxasha's eyes glowed like two rubies packed in the earth. Adura raised her chin higher to seem taller as she stood still. A smile broke over Zaxasha's face, and she took her by the hand, leading her towards a tunnel and outside the mountain. When she turned to look back, all of them were smiling encouragingly at her.

Zaxasha led her from the cave, climbing slowly. *How many seasons does she truly have?* Adura thought, her eyes glued to the witch's gnarled fingers, her black nails curving over her toes like talons. The sky was a bright blue. A flock of ravens stood near the watering pool. Antelope grazed quietly in the valley. The view was beautiful. Zaxasha's presence made her hesitant though, and she kept her eyes on her, lest she try some trick.

"Still you fear me?" Amusement played across Zaxasha's face like a lyre.

"No...I—,"

"*Liar,*" Zaxasha whispered, like it was some secret she could betray her with. Adura bit her lip and was silent.

She took her far from the base of the mountain. Adura followed close behind, before she turned towards her.

"Can you swim, child?" she asked, her red eyes calm.

Or maybe they were brown. She didn't answer. She couldn't. Her throat had closed shut like the mouth of an alligator around its meal.

"Good." Zaxasha turned back around, picking up her pace. The sun was low in the sky, leaving a path of orange and purple clouds behind.

She's taking me to the cliffs, she realized. She loved standing at the edge to watch the green and black hues of the land—the view like nothing she'd ever seen. Zaxasha was climbing up the cliff now, and she struggled to keep up with her. She'd climbed the cliff a hundred times. One of her older brothers had jumped from the edge and broken his neck. His mother had never been the same. She'd wandered the mountain a shadow of her former self. The cliff was remote and surrounded by rocks on either side; no one survived the fall. Sometimes the others claimed to hear the voices of the dead calling to them if they stood close enough to the edge. Breathing heavily as she reached the top, her tiny fingers gripped the edge tightly as she heaved her body up. Zaxasha waited for her near the edge, looking down into the abyss below.

"Do you know how baby seals learn to swim?"

"No." *Why does she ask me such strange questions?*

"A mother seal grips her baby by the neck and throws him in head first. And he swims."

Adura's head snapped towards her, eyes widening. "Why would she do that?"

"It's how they learn. It's how many of us are forced to learn. When I was young, I was a curious child. I picked up everything I touched, everything I could hold in my hand. One day I sat near the fire and it excited me. So I reached for it. To see if I could hold it too."

Adura's mouth hung open as Zaxasha turned to her, her red eyes glowing bright against the growing darkness.

"My hand burned and burned and burned. My skin puckered like rotten grapes. But I learned that fire is hot, and if you touch it you will be burned. Do you understand?"

Adura nodded, though her eyes spoke her confusion. Why should she care if Zaxasha had been a stupid child? It was nothing to her. She must think Adura would make the same mistakes.

Zaxasha stepped closer to her, putting a hand on her shoulder before stroking her brown curls gently, "Soon, you will. And if you live, much will change for all of us. Not all sacrifices are voluntary," she whispered softly. "Do you trust me?" Without an answer, she placed a palm in the center of Adura's chest and shoved her from the top of the cliff.

Screaming once, sharply, she fell, reaching for Zaxasha's hand even as she realized what she'd done. The air pushed against her face like a hurricane, the air sucked from her body from the pressure. Hair whipped around her face as she flipped again, and again, and again. A moment later she hit the surface, water sucking her further down under she struggled to swim towards the light. Her eyes wide she looked up to see Zaxasha walking towards her.

"The water..." she murmured, her voice trailing off as she glanced at the walls of water.

"A fish if I've ever seen one," Zaxasha replied, her red eyes glowing bright.

"This valley floods with the storm," she told her, smiling, even though she could have killed her. *What if there hadn't been any water at the bottom? She could have killed me.* "It is what God asks of us. To trust Him. With our faith, He shows us wondrous things."

Adura woke to a number of voices. The elders' excitement had not waned since her fall. Adura didn't feel the same. She was excited, yes, but her head hurt. A thousand butterflies fluttered in her stomach. The feel of the wind against her face as she fell haunted her. Just as the sudden loss of balance haunted her, the memory of the earth tilting made her stomach dance every time her feet left the ground. *Is this what special means?* It was only a matter of time before they turned their attention back to her again. Her mother made small glances toward her like she was afraid she'd try and run again. *They'd just catch me and bring me back.* It was the reason the lambs they slaughtered so rarely ran when they came for them. They knew it was only a matter of time too.

"Sit, Adura. You must not tire yourself so quickly." She didn't fail to notice the glances they gave her. *They're scared of me.*

"You have a gift, little mouse. You'll have to trust me if you are to use it." Zaxasha's smile was warm and sincere. "We will teach you everything you need to harness your power."

Adura was quiet. "You tried to kill me."

The audible gasps from the elders echoed softly in the cave, as if the ghosts of their ancestors were also in shock and denial as they listened from their graves.

"You pushed me off and watched me fall." Adura turned her eyes towards the mouth of the cave, the mountains looming.

"Only an Iyalawo can see. Only a High Priestess knows what to look for, how to interpret. I saw you, little mouse. It's your destiny. It's your *ori*. We live in two worlds, not one. Only fools hold on to dreams rather than face reality. Light and dark are in all of us, and man yearns for the bounty of the earth, that which gives us life and sustains it, as well as bringing great wealth and power. Love is powerful, yes, but so is hate. What is happiness without grief? Generosity without greed? We are the mountains. The rock that holds flood waters at bay, that borders the great valley and shields it from the harshness of the sun so that life may grow, that promises water and safety to travelers in the desert. We are the promise of hope, faith, and life. We walk with God."

"We'll teach you," her mother whispered gently.

Adura's eyes flew from one elder to the other and panic rose in her throat like the tide. The same waters from earlier seemed to crush her chest as she watched them.

"Your very name means 'my prayer has been answered'. Don't worry, little mouse," Zaxasha said. "The future scares us all."

TERIT

"Your Grace." Their chief advisor bowed before his father.
"It is with great pleasure that I bring you news from the North."

His father shifted in his seat, reclining as he waved one hand towards the advisor. "Continue."

"Your...allies have won you a fair bit of trade. With the best Kiberan ship lost, the prices of ivory, palm oil, and sorghum have risen considerably in certain cities," he replied smiling slowly. "It's only right that we aid them by selling them what we have aplenty. As it's been recovered, we might put it to good use."

According to plan. "Good. Separate and dye the fabric and any silks. Make sure there can be no trace. Then take the value at market and double it." His father's satisfaction was undeniable. Stroking the short beard at his chin, his father raised one eyebrow at him. *See?*

The advisor nodded. "Yes, Your Grace." He penned a note on his papyrus before adding, "We've had word that the deserter still lives. I'm told he will be used to assist with the construction of High King Kashta's relief in Nabara. Ten years have passed since the boy earned his place in the Tomb."

Inhaling sharply, Terit cut his eyes to his father, wondering how he might react. It was forbidden to speak of the deserter, Nastasen. A fallen soldier and leader of his father's armies, Nastasen deserted and returned to Tharbis, cutting down two guards of the Scorpion Kingdom in an attempt to save his older brother. Both of them shameless. The oldest had tried to rape his mother and received execution as his sentence. He'd been told the story many times.

His father's eyes narrowed. The soldiers had grown increasingly unsettled of late. And the noble and his wife visited audience once a year asking for their son's release. There were rumors that Rhadia had horned his father before the guards informed him. Instead of ordering the boy executed his father sent his best to learn who the boy was and to what family he belonged. An old family, the Zanga. And wealthy. With two boys, the second-born became a soldier under conscription and grew to be well respected. His men came from similar families, and his father could not risk letting him go free.

"He's a liability, Your Grace," the advisor continued. "His former brothers in arms may take up his cause. Perceived or not. With the festival so close, it is a risk we should not take."

Terit couldn't understand why he wasn't dead yet. They'd assured him it would be better to let him die in the Tombs rather than create a martyr. And yet he was still alive. *After trying to corrupt his mother.*

"Send our best after the Zanga son. The Tombs make too much noise. I want them quiet. See that it is done."

"As Your Grace commands." The advisor bowed low before departing.

The Zanga boy would be one less worry. His mother and father could continue bringing gifts and offerings for his release. He quite enjoyed the sweet treats and homemade wine from his mother. Looking over at the life-sized sculpture of himself he smiled. *The carpenter father wasn't bad either.* Even if he was a weak fool. Terit took leave of his father and mother, quickly walking towards the High Priest's temple, watching as the people of Tharbis went about their business.

He hated waiting for the old man. The High Priest had never been on time a day in his life, it seemed. Irritation bubbled just under his skin, making him itch. Making him angry. It helped that he had the advantage over the old man. The more he thought about it, the more it made him smile.

"Nephew!"

Looking up at the greeting, he turned about at the fountain where he stood, using his hand to shield his eyes from the sun.

"Uncle!" He forced excitement into his voice, reaching out for the High Priest's hand to kiss his ring momentarily. "Thank you for coming."

"Please, please. Do not trouble yourself," the High Priest waved his hand dismissively, green and blue rings on each forefinger and pinkie shining in the sunlight. "And as for your brother, it is no inconvenience. I am happy to do it." The High Priest had been asked to tutor his father's youngest in legal policies of the transfer of property. Tissan intended to be married soon and needed information about the brideprice, among other things.

"You realize we are greatly in your debt. Your experience far exceeds the other High Priest's, though they are exceptional." Terit smiled.

The High Priest couldn't help smiling despite the fact that his voice was only a portion of the nine votes needed to make decisions, transfer land. Or order the king to suicide under the old tradition of ma'at. Though all of the nine must agree in order to carry out *that* order. As one of four children, the High Priest sympathized with the desire to set oneself apart. To prove worthy of your station. Your life. And the man had no sons. It made it a great deal easier to gain his confidence.

"Marriage is a difficult thing. Especially for a husband. Training a new wife. Making sure she gets along with your family. Hoping she's fertile. It can get quite complicated when one gets married. Not to mention that agreeing upon inheritance and brideprice is quite a difficult task." The High Priest shook his head as though the simple thought made him wary.

Terit took the opportunity the pause gave him. "Imagine if the High King were deposed for failing to rule as he should. What would become of High King Kashta's kingdom?" he mused, eyebrows knit in a veil of curiosity, doing his best to ignore the plump behind of the woman walking past them to lean over the fountain. Folds of blue fabric clung to her ample curves, bunching at the waist as she stretched her gourd towards the water. The water splashed into the pool below, wetting her dress slightly at the waist.

"What indeed?" The High Priest's words caused him to snap his head towards him. The High Priest tilted his head to the side as they began walking around the perimeter of the High Court, having missed his wandering eyes. "What indeed?" The excitement in his eye revealed more than he intended, and Terit knew he would answer. The sand at their feet blew around them gently as the winds picked up. Even with the cool breeze drying the sweat on his forehead, the Nabaran sun still beat down on him like a hammer.

"It depends on the method of deposition first. Rival kings may lay claim to any property, handmaids, or *slaves* if you are in another land as in the old days of Kemet or even the current climate of Meroë. Meroë has no problem trading in slaves. Even wives and daughters. Forced deposition by the High Priests is another matter. The court would be entitled to a share before apportionment to any remaining family."

"And forced suicide? What of that? Is this the same if the High Priests did not order it?"

"What other type of forced suicide would there be?" Confusion wrought over the High Priest's face as he turned to Terit, his thick bushy eyebrows rising in alarm. "Well this is just the sort of exception that can come into the laws...but..." His face fell momentarily as he turned to look at Terit.

"We are speaking hypothetically? Surely...?" The doubt in his eyes turned to fear. Glancing about, the High Priest checked that no one was in earshot or privy to their conversation.

He knows he's said too much. "Of course, Uncle. I love listening to stories of your work. It's difficult not to want to learn more of the knowledge you possess."

The High Priest pursed his lips, still unsure of whether he should continue.

"You know you're like a father to me." *Best to lay it on thickly.* "I just enjoy our conversations and the nuances of the law. Please, don't trouble yourself if I am taking you away from your duties." Terit knit his eyebrows as he spoke; the feigned hurt in his own voice almost made him smile at his ability to fool the old man. Touching his *khat,* he put a hand to it as though to apologize for his thoughtlessness.

"No, no, you are no trouble. It is just. In times like these, the High Priests must be very careful. Our legal decisions and rules can matter just as much as someone hearing our opinions on certain matters. I want no parts of impropriety." The smile returned to the old lawmaker's face. "You understand?" Putting a hand on Terit's shoulder, he looked at him closely, his voice grave.

"Yes, yes I do."

"Good. Good." The High Priest squeezed his shoulder affectionately.

They continued around the High Court, passing a train of maidservants carrying huge stacks from the market on their heads.

Their loads stretched the width of a watusi's horns and were piled at least three heads taller than their own. Of the three, only the third struggled. The first wore black harem pants and a top, covering her from chest to navel. The fingers on her right hand were delicately touching the top of the load to hold it steady, the bread piled upon the fish as the lighter of the two. The second wore an outfit of the same, her hair woven into one long braid down her back. What appeared to be half sorghum and half cinnamon rested on her head, both arms swaying slightly as she walked. The third's arms stretched towards her head, her teeth biting her lip in concern as her eyebrows knit in determination. Clearly the youngest of the three, she was also a head shorter. Terit smiled as he realized the salt she carried had sprung a leak, bits of white sprinkling down upon her nose as she struggled to keep the moving parcel upright. Loaves of bread, fish, salt, cinnamon, sorghum. Their master must be very rich indeed. And expecting company. *She'd best pray she doesn't sneeze.*

Young scribes passed by and stopped, bowing to the High Priest briefly and to Terit, soft greetings on their lips. They nodded in acknowledgment and watched them rise, going quickly about their business.

"Now, Uncle," Terit continued when no one was within earshot. "The possibility of instability continues to worry me."

"As it should," the High Priest sighed. "As it should. Though instability may be a stronger word than I might use. Every kingdom has its incursions. Kush and Nubia have faced down more than a couple of poor mercenaries. And the princess is unharmed, may she live a thousand years. Poor, sweet child she must have been terrified."

"I live for my family. All I want is that they're safe. I hear rumors of uprisings, slave trading, and...well...I should not speak of it; you never know who may be listening."

"You have no cause to fear me. What rumors? Tell me what troubles you." The High Priest had slowed considerably, leaning closer to hear what Terit feared to say. *He always was one for secrets. There's no hiding that.*

"Overthrowing the High King." The best way was to be direct, and he ignored the High Priest's shocked expression as they continued towards the pavilion at the back of the High Court. "I don't want to see him killed any more than his own family would. His reign, that stability, is a marker of unity and strength. If we have challenges to it, it would only deepen our internal wars with each other and neighboring families. It would be better if he were forced to suicide than that. It is difficult, and the people would be hard-pressed to revenge themselves upon a dead man's own decision."

"Forced suicide by a king is hardly his *own* decision," the High Priest cut in at a pause, mouth wide open in shock. "The High Court *orders it* with or without his consent. As is our right under the law."

"But if a king carries through, it would be less divisive, no? I feel terrible thinking of a situation like this, Uncle. But my family? What of them? And if the people no longer trust their king."

"No longer trust? Who makes these claims? Kashta is of a finer breed than any. Not to mention the peace he brought. Surely—"

"I've said too much, Uncle," he cut in quickly before the old man became too distressed over thoughts of insurrection. "I should never—"

"No. I will...I will keep your confidence. It's just taken me quite by surprise is all."

"But, I have no desire for you to be even partially mired in treasonous accusations. It is difficult to have discussions of opinion and politics without them."

"Well...it is not something done...regularly. Merely hypothetical. Please continue."

"If the people no longer trust Kashta or even if they love him and he was killed, others may revolt, seek revenge on the purported responsible. Suicide however cannot be contested or blamed on anyone. Even the High Priests. Forced suicide, if carried out, shows that the king involved understood his actions were the best thing for the people. And any new king would be welcome and supported for the sake of unity and leadership. I worry sometimes. The people are at a loss, and if they were to riot..."

The High Priest's face was a beacon of worry. He stroked his beard as he looked into the distance.

"Yes, I understand your concerns, but you need not worry. Continue to make sure your family supports the High King. All will come out well. Right now, his focus is on protecting the people and his own family."

"But a king must have an heir. There has been one attempt on the High King's family so far. And we live in precarious times."

The High Priest nodded, his frown deepening, the heavy lines around his forehead and mouth like grooves in wood.

"Uncle please, please. I fear I've caused you too much pain for one night."

"No, no," laughed the High Priest turning to Terit and sitting on the stone seats behind the High Court, shaded from the fading sunlight. "You keep my mind sharp." He put one finger to his temple.

"Well...if you can spare me a few more pieces of advice, I would be in your debt."

"Please." Nodding encouragingly for him to continue, the High Priest looked up expectantly.

"It concerns...the fairer race of humans..." He smiled broadly and the High Priest began to laugh, holding his belly as he did, his robes shaking.

"So, you've found a girl to take your mind off politics. That is all the distraction you need!"

"She does that. A beautiful creature, and young. Sometimes I put my nose to her hair just to smell the scent of coconut lingering there."

"Good for you! In my day I had a litter of them all running after me, eyes following me everywhere I went. It was like a dream." His eyes became distant as he recalled the memories, his smile faint.

"Speaking of running, I can't seem to run from her. 'No,' I tell her. 'Your father would forbid it, and your uncle would break the law to see me killed.'"

The High Priest clapped a hand on Terit's back. "You stayed strong, did you?" the look in the High Priest's eye told him the old man hoped he hadn't. The lawmaker lived for forbidden stories and gossip. *And I won't disappoint.*

"I tried, but she sings to me sometimes, and it pains me to tell her no. By then she was eating out of the palm of my hand, father and uncle be damned by Anubis."

"Make sure they don't find out about you," the High Priest warned. Family is a precious thing. No one wants to find out their own daughter or niece is a plaything for some young schemer such as you!" Smiling as he finished, he continued, "We're all allowed a little bit of fun though, are we not?"

"Well, by law, I thought?" Terit responded, laughing as he leaned back. "She does this...this thing with her tongue...when she wants me. It's maddening," he sighed as he thought of her, making sure he kept a watchful side eye on the old man.

"Experienced, is she?"

"No, no, Uncle. Not her. She is sweet and lovely. I'm her first, there was no doubt of that. When I ask her where she's learned some new thing, she says she only wants to please me so I've been...giving her instructions and...she is a model apprentice."

The High Priest began to laugh uproariously at that. "Corrupting the youth. I had no idea you were such a sly one."

"Oh...I mean her no real harm. I am wanting for places to take her, though. Her father and uncle scare her so much sometimes she shakes as a leaf."

"I see...have you thought of taking her out towards the mountains? A short hike, but not very many people. And the baths can be a very good place as well. Plenty of steam to disguise a hand or two, and if she wears the same robes as the handmaids there, no one would suspect a thing."

"You *do* have good advice, don't you, Uncle?"

The High Priest chuckled, "In my day I didn't need any advice. Girls like that. Young and sweet. Naïve. It is a wonderful sort of distraction. And no real harm being done." The High Priest shook his head. "My word, Nephew. Remind me to keep my own nieces away from *you!*" he said, laughing uproariously at the thought.

"Of course, Uncle. Perish the thought. There's no real harm being done."

NASTASEN

Tiny rocks fell on him from above, scattered gravel and dust flying up like a cloud, surrounding him. Over one hundred feet up Ismar was waving down at him, smiling. He was but a dark brown speck among the layers and layers of hand-built wooden floors, a precarious staircase leading to the top of what would be a monument of King Amkarqa, draped in armor with his *khepresh* crown on top of his head and his right arm throwing a spear. From such a height it was a wonder Ismar could even make them out clearly, surrounded as they were by a vast sea of sand near the walls of the entrance to Nabara.

Next to him, Zyqarri shook his head and wiped sweat from his brow, grumbling as he worked. Shielding his eyes from the sun, Nas looked up once again. The shendyt below the king's armor above him provided little shade. His fellow brothers in bondage likely regretted whatever crime had landed them here, burning under the sun as the sand chafed at their skin. Dozens of bodies shone with sweat, sand caked at their ankles and the backs of their legs, as their axes and picks chiseled away at the statue, a light rhythm.

The guards had tried to force him to create a smaller replica of the High King's face before they'd started work, but he'd been adamant. He didn't need one. His memory suited him fine. *Father taught me well.* The mallet and chisel they brought were inadequate for the work they expected, and he'd indicated as much. Pointing required a proper mallet and chisel to carve out and remove the amount of stone required. As a child he'd sit and watch his father working for hours on some replica for the nobles of Nabara, ambassadors of Sao, and any number of citizens from Tharbis. They came from all over to see his work and often requested the honor of watching him as he did. His father had never attempted anything as large as this before though. It was rare they'd let someone from the Tombs have the honor of creating this sculpture, especially during the Festival of Kings. Most of the sculpture workers had hired themselves out or were regulars.

Desirous of the honor and willing to follow orders. But for Nas they made an exception. If he was as good as his father, they told him, his crime could be overlooked for one day. And they'd allowed him any assistants he needed to finish the job before placing a hood over his head and transporting him to the ship that would take him to Nabara. He would receive no credit or recognition, but this was enough. Smiling, he nodded to Zyq, Amare, and Ismar, who worked nearby.

His eyes began to burn from the strain of looking up, and he returned to his work before the guard to his left decided he was the problem today. The guard was young, but ruthless. In his efforts to prove himself, the guard had been unnecessarily cruel. Landing a blow on one for taking too many water breaks, another for sitting briefly when his head began to swim. And yet another for the rocks that fell on his feet as the men chiseled from above. Still, they were treated a deal better than the four from the Kingdom of Tharbis who worked alongside them. All of the men traded stories. And what tales they told.

Scraping away at the stone in front of him, Nas continued refining the edges of the toes. Over five times his size, it had taken a deal of work to get it right. Nas had come close to finishing his sculpture of the face hours earlier until he noticed the young guard walking back and forth behind him every so often. Pacing like a lion, his eyes narrowed as he observed Nas's work. After a while he strode past and raised his arms above Nas's head while the other prisoners gasped in shock, a warning shout sounding just before the guard's hammer slammed against the side of High King Kashta's nose, shattering the work Nas had already completed. "Do better," the guard had told him, walking swiftly away, the hammer slung over his right shoulder.

"I think he likes you," Zyq had replied, winking at him. Nas had gritted his teeth and gone back to work.

An hour later the feet were nearly refined. "You're finished," another guard near him said. "I need you to go below and make sure there are enough supplies. Let the workers finish the rest. Store the gold bars. If any of them are missing," he pointed at Nas with his *khopesh*, "I'll know."

The guard motioned to the gold bars behind him. He nodded,

quickly stepping forward to pick up two in each hand. The bars glowed under the sun, like a newly forged *khopesh* hot from the fire. Placing them in the linen lined bag next to them he stood and walked towards the feet of the replica. The *shaduf*, a crane used for lifting water from wells and transporting stone, moved up and down slowly like a heron searching for food in shallow waters.

"You do excellent work, Nas." The guard's words stopped him. "If it were my call, I would have you employed as a city architect." The guard didn't smile, but he nodded. He was a far cry from the younger guard who'd smashed the king's nose earlier. An older sort who rarely lashed out at a prisoner over small things. He knew as Nas did that respect was earned. The look of disappointment mixed with apology as the guard's eyebrows furrowed together in the middle of his head, lips pursed with regret. Nodding once in reply, Nas turned, walking towards the opening of the underground chamber below the statue.

It was well situated. Directly below the High King's crown jewels and hidden between his ankles lay the entrance. *Which does he favor more?* Nodding to the engineer, he turned his back to wait for the man to open it. The entrance may not be as secret as hoped given the amount of people working on the effigy, but *how* to gain entrance would always be. He was sure the trick to it was hidden on one of the massive calves or feet, but he didn't care enough to concern himself with it. Most people longed for fortune. He thought only of freedom. Of home.

Stone scraped against stone, and he turned at the sound in time to watch a small portal opening in the left heel. Looking down into narrow stone steps that seemed to descend into the darkest pits of the earth, he stepped down carefully, taking the steps one at a time, using the bars to maintain his balance. Slowly feeling for the next step, his eyes adjusted to the darkness as the entrance became a round yellow moon above him. When his feet reached even ground, he lit the torch with the flint he found at the bottom, its light cascading over the walls around him. They were decorated with every color imaginable; the epigraphs on the walls were made of delicately carved inscriptions and prayers, some darkened with black stain. A sun followed by a spear was carved to his left. *Amun will fight this war.* A scarab beetle appeared on his right. In Nubia and Kemet, it was a symbol of transformation. All of these gods and goddesses amused him. Zealots were always trying to sell you something. Even the Christians murdered in the name of their faith, and it would happen again. Some of the peaceful ones had run with tails between their legs after the Roman Emperor Diocletian had culled them by the thousands. Doubtless still that the Ethiopian King Ezana still sold slaves, Christian king that he was. Now, he was told, deep caverns in the desert were their homes, or so the tale of the desert hermits went. Faith, peace, abundance, fortune, health. All lies. Even with all of that, a king who saw you as his enemy could fell you with a slight shake of his hand, or a nod, and bring your world crashing down like waves around your ears.

Even back down here, underground, he was reminded of the cool cloak of darkness in the Tombs where he would soon return. His prison for the last ten years. And likely where he would die.

Nas grimaced as he was reminded he might have a new prisoner to share his hollow quarters carved into the pit of the prison. Everything was shared if you were sentenced to the Tombs as punishment. Prisoners were required to mine gold, serve as labor in quarries, and more. And his service was eternal. He'd had bad luck with the prisoners he'd shared a cell with since he first came to the Tombs. The first was a foreigner who'd been arrested for selling himself for coin and later stealing from the homes of his patrons. He died with large sores peppering his face. The guards disposed of his body quickly, burning him before he died to make sure the sickness did not spread. The smell permeated the tunnels for weeks, as though the man still clung to life through the mold and fungus on the walls. The second had been twice Nas's age and three times as mean. He'd bloodied Nas's face without cause, "to see how pretty you look with a bit of rouge," he'd sneered, smearing blood across Nas's face. Even in the tombs, fighting was only permitted at the guards' leave. The third had been mad. Nas woke one night to the feel of cold stone pressed against his throat and the man babbling about rats the size of grown men nibbling at his feet and stealing his gold. A sharpened stone was slowly piercing his neck, and he'd frozen for a moment as he assessed the situation. When he looked down to see what gold the old man spoke about, the old tomb raider shook the remnants of his broken teeth in his hand. "Gold is hard to come by, boy," he'd said, holding three rotten teeth tight. He'd convinced him to drop the stone weapon, and the man had been transferred elsewhere a week later. It had been the longest Nas had ever gone without sleep.

For ten years he'd not caused trouble and worked in the mines, trading what he could to the guards. They wouldn't give you freedom, but it was worth the loss to sleep in comfort rather than in the cellar where groundwater pooled. Men woke wet and shivering or half drowned. Or being the last to bathe on bath days. The guards were all pocketing what they could. Some of them were former soldiers, and the pay was significantly less. Cringing at the possibilities, he pushed the thoughts from his mind, stacking the supplies just inside the underground chamber. The engineers and architects would retrieve them later. Far be it for them to allow a prisoner to know the actual location of such luxuries.

Moving the gold carefully, he walked back up the steps into the light before returning to darkness, much like each day of his life since he was imprisoned. Perhaps the man would be amiable. It was only a matter of time before he found out. *If I had good iron.* His brother would tell him an iron sword or other weapon often wouldn't make a difference. "There's more than one way to kill a man, little brother. Don't think that because you have iron in your hand and so does he that that's the only way you'll die." And he was right. During the war he saw plenty of soldiers die from sword wounds, but it was the other wounds that hurt soldiers the most. Some men died from stupidity, some from bad luck. Some died from poor hygiene and others from disease. Some lost their will to live, while others were killed as deserters, and some just went mad. But they all died. You could only cheat death so many times before he came to collect. And so he waited in his cell, keeping his body strong and his mind alert. Keeping clean and dry despite weekly baths. He learned which guards were smart and which were cruel or cowardly. Which would report you and which would trade with you. It all depended on what they valued, and such a weakness was never hard to find. As the stone door rotated shut, Nas looked up in surprise, his eyes narrowing as he wondered what was going on above him. *Do they mean to bury me here?*

A soft slap met his ears, and the soft crunching of small pebbles under sandals grew louder. Someone was making their way down towards the underground chambers. *Towards me.* Straightening from where he crouched, his own breathing in his ears, he stood, arms at his side, waiting to see what would emerge from the darkness in front of him. And finally, it did. The man standing there looked like he'd been carved from stone, his shoulders and chest like fused rock as he ducked his head into the chamber.

Nas waited a moment, watching the man's eyes briefly check behind him with curiosity before returning to look at him.

"Are they looking for me?" Nas asked.

"Someone is," came the man's reply.

"What was the message?" he replied.

"First a name. You are the boy they call Nas, aren't you?"

"And you are?"

"You can call me Anubis, boy."

"I'm not a boy." Narrowing his eyes at the man's tone, he crossed his arms about his chest.

The man frowned. "No? Well, I'll make sure they know I never touched a hair on any boy's head. The king wants me to ease your load. In any way I can." Smile deepening, the man stepped forward, eyes taunting him.

A moment later he rushed forward, but Nas was too fast. Leaning backward to avoid the swing and crouching quickly, he grabbed at the man's legs as he fell, pitching him over his shoulder. As soon as the man tried to rise, Nas punched him hard, watching blood spray from his nose to the floor. The man planted both hands on either side of his nose, giving a sharp tug. He didn't flinch at all as his nose locked back into place.

Smiling through his bloodstained teeth, he pointed at Nas. "You've got nowhere to go, *boy.*" He emphasized the word, throwing it like an insult in Nas's face. "This," he spread his arms wide, "is your new home. It is more than you could ever dream of is it not? Now come. Greet death like a man."

This time when the man came Nas was ready; feinting sideways, he pushed one foot in the man's back, slamming him into one of the walls on the left head first. Nas stood, waiting as the man recovered, lips pulled back in a snarl as the torchlight fell across the man's chiseled face. Stepping forward slowly, the man stretched his arms out on either side of him like a bull's horns, making himself bigger, challenging Nastasen. "Don't make this hard," he told Nastasen, his chest heaving rapidly.

"You don't have to do this," Nas replied, standing his ground.

Ignoring his words, the man ran forward, throwing the bulk of his weight and his head into Nas like a ram, arms locking around Nas's back. Nas grunted at the impact, struggling to free himself from the viselike grip he'd been ensnared in. Inhaling quickly as he felt the pressing weight of the man's arms and shoulders squeezing the life from him, he tried to ease the pressure of the man's grip on him. Something in his back cracked, and Nas cried out in pain. *I am the prey.* The image of his older brother holding out a stick before a rock python wrapped itself around it, squeezing and breaking it in three pieces, floated across his memory. This man would break his back if he didn't free himself. Nas inhaled as much as he could with the force around him, placing his right fist inside of his left palm before bringing his arms down with as much force as possible against the man's temple twice. The muffled grunt near his torso and the loosened hold allowed him to take in a deep breath, his feet now on the ground as Nas raised his right leg and brought his knee up sharply, using the man's shoulders for leverage. The impact caused the man to fall backwards, clutching at his stomach as his nostrils flared, his mouth dropping open in surprise for air as he caught his breath. The torch was burning low now. The man turned to it as he rose, wrapping thick fingers around the base to lift it from its place on the wall, panting shallow breaths. Nas could feel a sharp pain in his back, but he ignored it, his ribs still feeling the pressure exerted upon them. He let the man come. As the man lashed out with the torch to light him on fire and burn him down here in the darkness, Nas jumped back, avoiding the flames. The man rushed towards Nas again. Arms pummeling him as he pressed the torch to Nas's left shoulder, causing him to scream from the sizzling sound of his flesh and the burning heat. Lifting him from the ground, the man brought his forearm up, pinning Nas by the neck against the painted rock walls as the fallen torch rolled away on the ground. Slamming Nas's head a second time, he punched him in the face for good measure. Nas's blood mingled with the engraved prayers on the walls he'd observed minutes ago.

Grabbing the man's neck, Nas squeezed, but the man only slammed Nas's head again, causing him to squeeze his eyes in pain before bringing his left elbow up and ramming it against the man's shoulder. When the man growled in reply, he punched his fist inside of the man's mouth, grabbing his bottom jaw and pulling downward, but the man was quicker, tripping Nas with his foot to pull him down too. They rolled across the sandstone floors, slowly at first, one atop the other as they fought, picking up speed. Suddenly, the ground under them disappeared and Nas felt himself falling downwards even as he grabbed for the man's neck. Hitting the ground three seconds later, the wind was knocked from him as they met solid ground. The man rolled over quickly, jamming his knee into Nas's stomach, a soft chittering sound reverberating in his ears. When the man looked up quickly, Nas grabbed the back of the man's neck and threw him down on the ground face first, digging his knee into his back and pulling his head back, avoiding the man's arms as he struggled to regain control. When Nas's grip slipped, the man reached up and grabbed his arm, twisting his right arm roughly and breaking it from its socket. Nas screamed in agony before gritting his teeth and locking his left arm around the man's neck, pulling him close to his chest as his teeth gritted with the effort. An arrow shot out of nowhere and Nas ducked, gripping the man tighter. Two dangers didn't mean he could ignore the first. Three more arrows followed and Nas ducked low. When the man kicked, he didn't let go but held him closer still. When the man went limp, he continued to hold on. As his body grew rigid, he tightened his grip further, sweat pouring from his brow, arm shaking as he held the man tighter. Closer. His head pressed against the man's like a lover. And he held him tighter still. Looking up, he saw a black mass moving towards him and his eyes widened in time to see driver ants rushing towards them both, quickly moving insects that would graze over a hippopotamus and leave nothing but bones behind. Nas pulled the man's head back, quickly slamming it into the stone as blood splattered under him. He stood quickly, placing his feet on the man's back as the ants covered the dead man's legs. Nas popped his right shoulder blade back in place, gritting his teeth as the bone cracked. Jumping upwards he caught the short rope hanging in the middle of the chamber and climbed towards the ceiling, shoulder protesting at the weight it carried. When he got high enough, he began to swing himself slowly at first and then faster, blood dripping from his broken nose as he let go, propelling himself towards the edge they'd fallen from moments before. When he landed and rolled, he looked back over the edge and saw nothing but a shifting mass of ants covering the ground. *It's as close to mummification as he's like to get.* He rose and lifted the torch from the ground where it still burned, having never gone out during the struggle.

Nas quickly kicked sand over the blood on the ground to cover the trail, placed the torch back, and stopped to put his nose back into place. Hurriedly, he sprinkled dirt across the burn on his shoulder and gritted his teeth against the pain before turning towards the yellow moon that was slowly opening to allow him to exit. Stumbling, he used his shift to wipe the blood from his face and his hands, spreading more sand across his clothes.

When he reached the top, the guard looked at him in shock, the smile falling as he took in Nas's disheveled appearance. Behind him, the gravedigger's face was a mask of fury and disbelief as he uncrossed his arms from where he leaned and straightened, looking behind Nas in confusion.

"What happened to you?" the guard questioned him.

Nas looked towards the gravedigger and back at the guard.

"I fell. It's a death trap down there," he told him as the other guard laughed.

The guard motioned towards the other prisoners with his head to let Nas know to get back to work. Not daring to look at the gravedigger as he passed, he joined the others, knowing he would return to the Tombs before darkness fell. He hoped to live long enough to repay him in kind.

KETEMIN

Bending her knees slightly, she dipped her shoulders and chin underneath the water with the rest of her body, turning her head upwards to look at the moon. It seemed she could almost touch it from here. Penguins played on the shore and in the water near it, waddling to and fro, moving behind the mountainous boulders that peppered the sand. *Water is life*, her uncle always told her and Komoro. *Water is life.* He wasn't wrong. She turned her eyes toward the Kingdom of Nabara, alive with the sounds of music, dancing, and wrestling. The Nudollan Empire celebrated. From the fisherman to the High King, water was the center of their prosperity. The fisherman used his nets to catch what lived deep in the shimmering silver-blue waters of the River Nub and sold it at market or fed his family. The High King employed reservoirs of water and underground sanitation systems, flushed the gold mines, and supported irrigation methods for sorghum farmers throughout his empire. Water was life. Ketemin loved it for a different reason. She stretched her arms out and closed her eyes, water running from her naked body as she broke the surface, floating. In the water she felt free. In the water she surrendered control, free from the pressures of the kingdom, the expectations of her uncle, the love her brother took for granted, the people she was responsible for. She turned her head to the side and sat up quickly, her body moving back underneath the water. Someone was watching her. Ketemin swallowed, unable to move as the figure came closer, past the boulders and the penguins, never bothering to look down to ensure they weren't in his path. She wrapped her arms around her waist as she realized the danger of her situation.

"Princess!"

Relief flooded through her as she recognized Tesir's voice; the commander had stepped into the water after her despite being fully clothed, his voice full of alarm.

"Stop. I'm fine. Don't worry I won't have your eyes cut out." She waved a hand at him to repel the concern she heard. She swam until the sand was under her feet, stepping out of the water, bathed in nothing but moonlight and darkness. The commander removed his cloak for her, looking away as he held it out. Being the Daughter of Ra had its advantages. Ignoring the offering, she bent instead to pick up her gown. Sliding into it quickly, she clasped the ends together at each shoulder and snatched her crown from the ground at her feet, now caked with wet sand.

"What are you doing here?" she asked him, trying to hold back the annoyance rising in her breast as she squeezed water from her hair, running her palm over the tiny blanket of curls popping from her scalp. The chill of the air made the hair rise on her arms and neck, and she gritted her teeth against it.

"You told me to come and find you if I had any news." The commander quickened his step to keep up with her.

"It might have waited until morning. I thought you would be taking part in the celebrations, Tesir."

"I thought you were more important." He turned to look at her without breaking stride, not a trace of amusement to be found. She studied his dark brown eyes, wondering. "And you shouldn't be here alone," he told her as they neared the edge of the city. When she stopped to slide into her shoes, he placed his arm out to steady her and she leaned against him briefly before rising again.

"What news of Komoro?" There was no time for pleasantries. She'd known by the look on his face it was important and she needed to know what he'd found.

"The prince has been allowing some of the soldiers to work as mercenaries outside of your uncle's kingdom."

"For?"

"I don't have a name yet, Princess, but they provide protection on some of the trade routes south of the Sahara. Many of the men he removed from the salt mines are a part of this venture."

"Is he...is he selling slaves, Tesir?" Dealing in slaves carried a death sentence she cared not to think about. Even a royal could be held responsible for such a transgression. And the High King was notoriously unwavering in his commitment to keep it from invading his empire. It was the reason he always donned a *khepresh* as a symbol of his reign. It was a war crown. Void of the snake figure present on the crowns of the Pharaohs of Kemet and Nubia, and gold to represent the numerous gold mines and treasures of the Nubian lands of Kush. The *khepresh* represented the High King's warring values, rejecting Roman and Assyrian domination and trade in slaves to reinforce the independence of Nubian kingdoms. His empire had long fallen out of favor with Meroë, their connection not forgotten, but broken because of Meroë's continued trade in slaves with Rome and others. Including Makouria and Alodia. They looked down upon his refusal to engage in the slave trade, and the High King had stood fast, building his empire in the south, protecting those within his reach. Many kingdoms such as hers had followed him in his resistance, paid tribute, and built an alliance for protection and the independence he'd fought to give them. Even though the Sao were sun worshippers and held to their own gods as sons of Ra, it made no difference where the lives of their people were concerned. They had a common enemy.

"Not that I can tell, Princess. I can find out more, but you should know that at least one of the ports on their trade route has sold slaves before. A Nomadin gave me the information. He indicates the trade may be spreading further south with the help of the Berbers." When he finished, he held out his arm and gripped her fingers, helping her step up onto the last of the boulders before jumping down the other side and turning to lift her by the waist and to the ground.

"I knew he was lying about something; I just didn't know what." Ketemin had no words. *He lied to me.* "How could he hide this for so long? The salt miners…" Her voice trailed off as anger overtook her.

"I believe the treasurer may be assisting him in his efforts, Princess. He can always be replaced," the commander offered.

Execution would certainly send a message, but whether it would eradicate the problem she was not so sure.

"A half measure and no more," Ketemin dismissed the idea. "What he's done would amount to treason had my brother not known of his actions. But my brother…he's put us all at *risk.*"

"There's more. We've had word from Chad that our salt caravan never reached the trading city. Berbers spoke of skeletons being found in a valley two days' ride from Gao. It is likely vultures and hyenas. Both animals are known to eat the bones as well. And the sand hides most sins as always."

Ketemin felt sick, but she knew she needed to keep her composure. The great lake. Chad had been named by the local people. Something growing in the pit of her stomach told her her own people were dead. It twisted and curled inside her like a worm inside spoiled fruit. And Komoro was responsible. *I told him not to send them near Gao.*

"How many traveled?"

"Two hundred camels, Your Grace, and at least fifty men. Only five skeletons were found. The salt and the people have both gone missing."

"How many guards?"

His hesitation told her more than she needed to know. "Four, Your Highness."

Her jaw tightened in anger as she continued toward the palace with Commander Tesir following at a quick pace to keep up.

Four. Her mind was spinning with unanswered questions and the audacity of her brother. The carelessness with which he held his position.

"I must speak with my uncle."

"Yes, Princess. I'll inform him right away."

"No need, Tesir. I will go to him myself." Turning to him suddenly before they reached the walls of the palace where the guards could hear, she lowered her voice in warning.

"Speak of this to no one. I realize the news of the caravan will be difficult to contain, but we must for as long as we can. We must notify the families first thing, but first, do everything you can to get the name of every man who traveled in the caravan. They won't be expecting news for some time, but as there will be no return trip…" She shook her head as she thought a moment.

"If my brother asks you for more men, deny him."

"Your Grace, he will not allow it. Who am I to—?"

"Deny him. Tell him his sister requests his ear and that they have been allotted for other purposes, which I would not give you intelligence of."

A slight smile came to the commander's face. "Yes, Your Grace."

She smiled after a moment, putting one hand on his shoulder. "You're a good man. You've never let me down, Commander. I don't expect you to start now."

"Nor will I." His eyes exuded strength and confidence. Your father held fast to his convictions as you do. Even as a boy I remembered how well his orders sprang from his plans. It appears you share the same shrewdness of strategy as he did."

She felt the pride building in her chest but declined to answer the compliment.

"See me if you learn anything more, Commander, or have more news." She nodded once and he returned it.

"Whatever you require." He signaled to two of the Sao's royal guards and they fell in line behind her, walking with her through the High King's palace and towards the guest wing set specifically for their use.

It was an enormous palace. Truly magnificent in all of its glory. The walls were imbued with protective symbols, hieroglyphs, Meroitic script, and beautifully intricate carvings depicting Nubian scenes and gift processions to the High King's family. Portions of it celebrated Nubian rule over Kemet, telling stories of the twenty-fifth dynasty of Kushite pharaohs who united Upper and Lower Kemet with Nubia, creating a lasting tie that could not be erased from history. From their burial rituals to their pyramids, Kemet and Nubia had traded, shared, and taken on each other's culture, becoming better for it. The ceiling towered high above her as they finally rounded the next corner. When they did, the guards at her uncle's door bowed briefly to her, and she knocked quickly on the door while one of them pressed it open for her to enter.

"Uncle?" The door closed behind her, leaving the guards outside. "Uncle?"

The silk sheets on the bed were strewn about and falling over the edge in disarray. The sheer hanging curtains were parted just so, blowing in the gentle breeze that caressed her face. A cup on the dresser was overturned, the wine having spilled onto the polished stone floors, the fish and sorghum half eaten. Ketemin picked up the cup, turning it over gently as she looked towards the open balcony.

"Uncle," she sighed as she saw him leaning over the edge of the balcony. "You scared me terribly. Why didn't you answer?"

"I thought you weren't coming back." Her uncle smiled as he stood.

"What do you mean?" Ketemin laughed. "Did you miss me for my hour long journey?"

"I'll always miss you, my darling. Sit, sit." Waving at the chaise on the balcony, he adjusted a cushion for her as she sat.

"You've always been beautiful," he told her. She smiled back, shaking her head. *He could be so sentimental at times.* Even so, this news could not wait.

"Komoro hasn't been honest with us," she started, her eyes serious as she moved straight to the point. She'd never been one for banter.

"Is that what's troubling you? I knew something was wrong the moment I looked at you. He's just a boy. You must allow him room to grow."

"You don't understand, it's different this time. He's put us all in danger." *Why wouldn't he listen to reason?* One could only make so many excuses.

"I thought he was your favorite. What kind of danger could my nephew get into? He's only six!" Her uncle stared at her perplexed, a look of astonishment on his face.

Confused, she couldn't hide her frustration. "In his mind! I'm talking about Komoro, he's out of control!"

"You can't be serious?" He looked at her with a hint of smile on his face. "When Komoro is older, then I'll worry. Whose skirt has he been lifting now? It's only natural the boy should be curious even at so young an age, but he's a child. The women will forgive his curiousness—he barely reaches the height of their knees. I wondered what was under your gown at one time too." At that he patted her hand and looked out towards the city.

The shock on her face stopped her words momentarily.

"Uncle..." She could only manage a whisper as she watched him. Sitting there, his head began bobbing gently from side to side as though some music only he could hear played inside his head. He looked out at Nabara's center and sometimes towards the River Nub. *This cannot be.*

"You know, his sister is becoming as smart as a priest. I'm convinced Ketemin knows more than the scribes." He chuckled softly. "And the way she wrote my brother's message in Meroitic script, Latin, and hieroglyphics quick as a whip!"

"She takes after me," he nodded, smiling at her as he wiggled his eyebrows.

Ketemin swallowed. *Who does he think I am? He must be joking...isn't he?* Touching his arm gently, she hoped he would turn and laugh at her naïveté, the ease with which he'd beguiled her into believing he didn't recognize her. When he felt her touch, he turned.

"Dina, what's wrong? If it concerns you so, I'll have a talk with him tomorrow." He cupped her face gently before taking her hand. His fingers moved away before he could feel the tears running fast down her dark brown cheeks like rain.

Leaning her head against the back of her seat so that he wouldn't see, a wave of memories swept her back in time. Her Aunt Dina had passed away over five years ago in her sleep. Her name meant 'life' in the language of the Toubou people who inhabited the mountains near their kingdom. Her uncle used to tease her that she was the reason he kept on living. That she gave him life. Converting her upon their marriage, she came to understand their love for the sun. Their love for Ra.

Biting her lip as she pressed her free hand to her mouth to keep from sobbing aloud. The message he'd mentioned Ketemin translating had been sent when she was only five. When her father had still been alive. And her aunt. And somehow her uncle had returned to that time in his mind and no longer recognized his only niece. *He thinks I'm his dead wife.* She had never felt so alone.

CASSIUS

He'd paid dearly to transport each slave. The Berbers had kept a tight pace as they trekked towards Cuicul. He couldn't wipe the sweat from his face fast enough before it returned, sand clinging to him like flies to dung as his face and neck burned in the heat. The nights brought little relief. No one had warned him that the weather became so cold he would need to huddle around a fire. And each morning as the sun began to rise and waves of heat became visible just above the sand, he would long for the night. Each time he'd heard a howling he'd woken with a start, clutching his sword, his shoulders hunched around his neck. Looking about him quickly, he frowned, determined not to let his men see any hint of fear. The sand moved without cause, rock-shaped tunnels moving away from him wherever he planted his feet. He never could have made this journey alone. Even with the Berber's attempts to explain it, he still had no understanding of how they navigated the Sahara. The wide stretch of desert was little more than a graveyard waiting for fools to cross it. He'd constantly had to ask them for water or when their next stop for it might be, though they'd cautioned him to preserve his water. He and his companions couldn't help panicking the first time they ran out and despite being reassured had mercilessly berated the Berbers for having gotten them lost. And suddenly, like some miracle in this hell, they'd crossed a sand dune and the oasis they'd described had been there. The Berbers had looked at the men without emotion, but Cassius knew it was an attempt to conceal their disgust and amusement, sitting on their camels, high above them as his own men threw themselves towards the water, kneeling at the edge as though paying worship to Dionysus himself. That he paid them at all was a mercy. The Roman garrison had taken over Cuicul and run the Berbers out, sold some, used others. Though there were still a number of them who refused to submit, they were of no consequence. It didn't matter how they treated the nomads. *That's why the Berbers were paid upon delivery.* Any hint of foul play and his men at the various trading ports would know which family to kill, who to come looking for. Not that they'd find them. But sometimes, threats were enough when fear took over courage. *Amaziɣ,* they called themselves. Free people. Quite a name for what they were now. Berber is what the Romans preferred. Barbarians were what they were. The rest would never outlive the weight of Rome.

The ship could sail any number of days *before* it reached Byzantium. Or, as citizens were want to call it, Constantinople. The captain was promised half now, half payment upon its arrival. He'd made sure to capture more than he needed. Even if half failed to survive the journey, his pockets wouldn't suffer. Stacked as they were like logs for a fire there was no need to concern himself with want of space. For now, he was surrounded by mountains, pressing in on either side of him.

"You there!" he called to a young Berber boy squatting on the ground. He was using a stick to draw figures in the dirt in front of him. "Come here for a moment!" He would need to have more chains before he left. Better to have the blacksmith make additional ones for Sicarius as well.

The boy looked at him curiously as Cassius came closer, his eyes like two eggs inside a nest of thick, wild brown hair. Suddenly he jumped up, standing frozen to watch his approach, his skin appearing as though it had been stained with berries.

"Don't be afraid," Cassius called as he came closer. "Tell me—"

The boy turned and took off running in the other direction, fleeing him like he'd seen a ghost, and never once looked back. He cursed the boy as he watched him run. *Roasting in my own sweat.* Lifting his shirt slightly, he relished the breeze that traveled inside. Just as suddenly as it came, it went. Kicking at the ground in disgust he walked towards the *cordo*, hoping the road would still be lined with a few vendors eager to sell who could point him in the right direction. Running his fingers through his dark hair, he looked across at the tall stone columns rooted in the ground. Not two hours ago, it held hundreds, all crying the last of the days catch, some roasting clams, shelling oysters or pulling bones from fish. Soldiers had marched towards the military camp in training.

Now those same ones hung from brothel doors retching up their day's meal. It was likely there would be more than one bastard conceived tonight.

His employer had told him no children at first, but had quickly changed his mind. The man hadn't been hard to convince. And the mob loved them in the gladiator games. It was hard to break tradition. Surviving the journey was a difficult thing, and feeding them was often a problem as well. "If I want them, I'll breed them," he'd told him. The tribune made his eagerness for the shipment clear. The slaveholding class of Rome waited eagerly for the delivery. Many of the Ethiopians and people south of the Sahara were useful for their skills in farming, husbandry, and the raising of cattle. Far be it for their future masters to do it themselves.

He looked past the *cordo's* columns to the homes and buildings on either side. Stacked layer upon layer, each level contained homes, glassmakers, seam shops, and bakeries. Steam rose from the thermal baths like a fog, enveloping the stone structure like a shroud. The baptistery was easily marked, even in the distance. Diocletian's legacy meant nothing with Constantanius II now on the throne, and completely at ease with allowing temples dedicated to animal sacrifices and sun worship to continue while practicing Christianity. As he perceived it anyway. In name alone.

The inn he'd slept in would have plenty of beer for supper. *And the catcher will be there.* The slave catcher had been of great value thus far. With their footprint, Sicarius easily served them both as a guide and in making sure they picked off the right groups at the proper times. The salt caravan had been an excellent call. And knowing whether or not the salt caravan had fighters had made it easier to plan their attack. The element of surprise had dealt them a greater chance of success. He had never been able to read the *catcher's* face, stuck as it was in a permanent scowl, his dark eyes penetrating no matter what he was looking at. A killer's eyes. It wasn't lost on him that Sicarius might be dangerous to have on such an expedition. But he'd proven himself, and his skills would be needed again. He was *rudiarii*, loved by the mob, by the women. And even the nobility. For reasons which would likely never come to light. There was no reason for him to give that up.

He showed no emotion for the lives they took, nor the cries of the slaves as they were chained. Apathy. It was his greatest quality.

Pushing the door to the inn open, he found the air as hot inside as out. A large fire spit embers towards the back. The innkeeper had cleared it for their private use.

The mercenaries he'd hired looked up at his approach. Sitting around the table, they each nodded to him and he came to sit, taking the beer offered as he did. Many of them were extremely young, and at least half of the group had not yet reached the age of thirty. But some of them were his former naval crew. The company had promised each their own slaves, gold, and land if they served. It wasn't a hard decision to make.

The patrician sat at the head of the table. And next to him was his second, Marcus. As a patrician, he held high social status in Constantinople and was visiting Cuicul at the behest of a portion of the ruling class to make sure their gold was performing its function as well as doing what they thought it ought. Increasing. Marcus needed investors after all. His commanders were in conversation even now. Altogether this group formed what Marcus thought of as his company. A well-funded group of slave traders and catchers that traveled as a caravan, moving through the northern territories of the continent to gather slaves for export to Rome and trade with the east.

Their voices were low and hushed, but the excitement and greed filled their voices like maggots on a carcass. They'd be rich men just like the patrician very soon.

"The savages' hold on their land is weak. Our company can take their forces in a day. The element of surprise is with us," Antonius was saying, leaning back with a smug confidence on his face.

"I agree. The Berbers have given us a great advantage to reaching the interior. Making it through the Sahara will take less time with them as our guides. And according to them, we'll find more than enough slaves and more gold than we can carry. Meroë can't be the only place we'll get it. And from what I hear from Ezana's court, we won't have to worry about the Kushites much longer."

"It would be good to know the climate before we go." Marcus

looked around the table. "I've heard the eastern tribes have been at war with the desert and valley cannibals for centuries. Why not give them some new grievance to argue about? What do they fight over down there? Gold? There's nothing but darkness below the Sahara. Better to let them kill each other."

"No. They'll be wary now. Fear of the slave trade is spreading. The black rulers just south of the Sahara are far from welcoming to foreigners, even if they bear gifts," he warned. The commanders nodded in agreement around the large table. A crude map was spread to each corner, their beers pinning it in place. "But they may act on the wrong information. Whether it is a lie or not, they may want to know of it. And we have the Berbers and the *catcher* on our sides. Who better to spread discord than one of their own?"

Marcus raised an eyebrow, considering what Cassius said as he stroked his chin, thinking, the group quiet as they waited his instruction.

"Cassius." The tribune turned to him. The tribune's short hair grew in thick and black with shades of silver at his temples. Pale green eyes bore through him, and Cassius drew himself up to full height, squaring his shoulders. "You know the terrain, and the people. Which kingdom is likely to give us the most trouble? Which the least?"

The mercenaries turned to him, waiting for his response.

"The Sao, Nubian, the tribes of the forest territory, and the remaining Kush, though King Ezana will help us there. The farmers and herders, even the hunters further south, we can easily take. The Nubians have proved the tales of their skill to be true. The mercenaries who weren't slaughtered on our last caravan told us their number was no match. The Kushite archers need not stand still when they shoot their arrows. They rode away, turning back towards them to shoot from on top of the horses. The bastards might as well have had *wings*! And we still have no word of the slave ship bound for Rhapta and Opone. Two hundred men, gone just like that." He paused a moment, thinking. "But there is opportunity over land. If we can convince more of the Nomadin or even a kingdom, we may gain access to their trade routes. As long as we have the right gifts to trade."

"So, we only need offer them a few women? Is that the way of it?" a young commander suggested lewdly, laughing and gesturing crudely with his hands.

"Some lust for power. Power that this Nubian *Empire* seems to hold over quite a wide swath of southern territory. We can trade with them, make them believe it is gold and salt we seek. And find a way to gain access. We can start with the Sao. No one can refuse a messenger or a request for a meeting."

The tribune rarely smiled, but the pleased look in his pale eyes was unmistakable. "See that the *Forgotten* moves south. I'm pleased with her captain. His knowledge of Torrent is excellent."

Cassius nodded; the compliment to himself was well deserved.

The *Forgotten* had finally returned after sailing north. The ship could carry five hundred slaves comfortably, but it was better to attempt twice as many to make up for those who weren't able to survive the voyage. It would need to be scoured before they took it anywhere. He'd surveyed the ship for repairs when it docked. The smell of shit and blood had been repulsive. He'd ordered the ship scoured with lye and water twice over. It had been battered by the seas and winds, but was otherwise unharmed. They'd replaced the barrels of water and sand kept in cases of fire and filled them with as many weapons as possible. The gods favored the prepared.

"It's dangerous to move south so quickly," Marcus spoke up. "The kingdoms will have sent search parties out looking for mercenaries and slavers to protect their people. The seas may have patrols. And our ship *never* returned."

"They can't patrol it all. Stick to unguarded territory as much as you can and send word when you reach any one of our allies."

"Will we move further south after?" Cassius inquired.

"I'm working on that…in the jungle. More of a swamp as I understand it. But if it offers cover and a land route that we can exploit, then I aim to do just that. I will keep you informed. See that you provide me the same courtesy."

"At your command." Cassius nodded briefly, watching the tribune exit the inn quietly, his fingers linked at his back as he strolled through the door, his robe blowing in the strong night wind, though he didn't seem to feel it. He moved as if he controlled the wind itself.

He knew what was at stake if he failed to provide the cargo the tribune requested. His powerful employer would quickly turn into his enemy.

Five days later he found himself aboard the *Forgotten*, having left Cuicul. His brother Nicolae was with him. A fast learner, he'd been a great help during the journey. Five of his men had fallen sick at sea, and they'd kept nothing down. One had stupidly drunk seawater on a dare from the deckhands. When Nicolae finally saw to him, he'd been drinking from one of the barrels of fresh water a full day with only bread as a supplement. He'd been too scared to tell him why. The boy couldn't stop licking his lips either and was vomiting uncontrollably. The second had a bout of vomiting the crew thought to be food poisoning and swore off food, until Nicolae had given him something to settle his stomach. *Should have continued with that line of reasoning and there would be more food for me.* The third's hand had swollen to twice its size. When the thumb split and began to ooze pus, even his strongest men could not stay to watch. Nicolae was tending to him now. The fourth died on the third day of their journey. Homesick, the crew told him. The fifth had a bad case of diarrhea and had been scratching at his skin all day, sun-beaten and sick; they were all contemplating throwing him over board. He thought he might allow it. *If only to stop his moaning.*

"How is he?" Cassius looked down at the man as he walked into the room. The man's hand seemed to have doubled since he'd last looked at it. And now his *arm* seemed to be getting bigger *too*.

"I can't say." Nicolae looked up, wiping the sweat from his temples with his forearm before dipping them back inside the bucket of warm water at his feet. He had to keep his hands clean. "But if he keeps swelling up like this, his other fingers will burst too."

"All of them?"

Nicolae sighed and held out his hand, palm up. "You've seen sausages?"

"Of course I've—"

"Well then, a sausage can only take so much heat. The minute you put a little heat on a sausage, it begins to swell, nice and juicy. And sometimes you can see the skin. If it doesn't peel, it pops." He made a popping sound with his mouth that startled Cassius. "It won't be pretty." He looked back at the man, his forehead soaked in sweat as he struggled under the covers, his head turning this way and that.

"Is there nothing you can do?" He couldn't afford to lose any more of this crew.

"I can take his arm."

"His arm? What will I do with a rower who only has one good arm?" He scoffed, scowling at his brother.

Nicolae shrugged. "One arm or another body overboard. You can always ask him to serve the food."

"And pay his way too," he spit back. *Useless. The man goes and does this, probably just to torment me.*

"Have to clean up the rats when you see them, Brother. They spread disease. And I have it he was bitten on the hand about a week ago."

"Bitten." He finally looked up. "Do what you need to do."

Nicolae nodded. "It's alright. I'm here." He gave the man some water and waited. After a moment he pulled back the sheet on the arm, rolling up the sleeve to the shoulder.

"I need five more men here. Five," he called out.

Cassius stepped out of the cabin and pointed at some of the rowers. "You three. Come. You. And you as well. Quickly."

The men walked in, stooping under the low entryway, broad-shouldered and confused as they packed into the cabin. A few held their noses in revulsion as they took in the sick man's swollen arm.

"I need you to hold him down." Nicolae looked at each of them in turn. The men looked at each other quickly, their confusion and wariness apparent.

"I said hold him down!" Nicolae yelled. "You grab his ankles. You, hold his knees. You, arms; you, left shoulder. And right shoulder," he shouted, pushing the other man into position.

"Cassius, I need water and beer."

"Beer?"

"Beer. Hurry. We need to do this quickly." The man moaned in response as if he too realized the severity of the situation.

Cassius nodded and left, returning with beer and a bucket of water, which he splashed down at Nicolae's feet. Warm as it lapped the sides, it had been heated already, and he knew it was just the right side of burning.

"Shouldn't we tell him what we're doing first?" one of the men asked.

"I don't like this; it's not right," another responded, shaking his head as though he were the one lying on the bed with his shirt off.

"We have no choice. It's infected." Nicolae's voice was firm.

"Yes, but he does. He should know."

"Either hold him down or I'll throw *you* overboard." Nicolae fixed him with a steely blue-eyed stare and Cassius held back a proud smile. *So. He did inherit a thing or two from me.*

Nicolae picked up the saw to his right and took a deep breath, letting it out in a rush. No sooner had the saw bitten through the man's skin than his eyes flew open and he began to scream. For his part, Nicolae ignored the sounds and continued on, the saw grating back and forth as the strangled cries dragged on. Cassius shook his head and pulled his handkerchief free as bits of flesh plopped onto the floor.

"Thank you, Brother," Nicolae said, his expression changing to shock as Nicolae watched him stuff the cloth into the man's open mouth, his screams muffled but not abated. A moment later he took a swig of the beer, ignoring Nicolae's indignation. *Why waste good beer?*

"Carry on," he told him. And Nicolae did. When the blood spurted onto his feet, Cassius looked down and bent to wipe them clean before turning and leaving the room. He walked up to the deck to breathe in fresh air. The sun was about to set, and it was marvelous. The water sparkled as the light reflected on it, moving and lapping at the sides of the ship. Black waters hiding who knows what under the protective cloak of the sea. Unknown treasures. For him to find. A falcon swooped low, skimming the water before opening its beak and closing it around a fish, leveling out to secure his mouth around it when suddenly a shark jumped slightly from the surface, closing around the gull, feathers and wings snapping wildly back and forth as the shark's mouth closed around it. Staring in awe, he watched droplets of blood on the water. *Nature takes its course.*

An hour later he was in the captain's cabin, his shoes by the door. His dark brownish-red hair was slicked back from his bath. He'd rolled his sleeves up his forearms, the cream shirt dry and clean. Two torches lit his cabin as much as he needed while a third candle sat on his writing desk with blank papyrus and quill. Sitting at his desk chair, he leaned his arms on the table and began to read.

> *Greetings, Cassius,*
>
> *May this letter find you well and in good company. I have secured your next rations at the coming trading post. Ask after Crispus and you will find you have all you need. I realize your work takes you on quite a journey, and I have been instructed to give this message to you.*
>
> *As you should be aware, our Great Constantine issued the Edict of 325 years ago, banning the gladiator munera in protest from our Christian and newly welcomed members of Roman society. Please understand that the souls of the dead are no longer to be paid tribute using gladiator munera and will cease to be used at all costs."*

Edict of 325? The man was twenty-five years too late. Cassius shook his head and continued reading.

> *The timing does not escape me, but I write because I implore you yet to continue to treat child snatchers as a plague. Constantius has sanctioned a munus for the great benefit of the public. They are all that matters. Their thirst for blood shall not be satisfied nor abated. Do everything in your power to continue to round up those we deem criminals in defiance of Roman law.*
>
> *The praetorian express their thanks as the magistrate's administrative duties are costly and you and your work are able to expense it.*

You will be hailed a hero when you return. I
look forward to your next report.
Long live Augustus Constantius II."

Cassius moved towards the desk as he read the words a second and a third time. After the fourth, he held the letter to the fire, watching as the flames took hold, turning the parchment a bright yellow and then orange before it browned at the edges and the flames licked it, growing larger the more they consumed. The door opened, and he didn't bother to look back as the hinges on his bed creaked softly, groaning under the new weight.

"More news?" Nicolae asked.

Cassius nodded as he turned behind him to see his little brother wiping the blood from his arms, soaked up to the elbow. A partial bloody fingerprint sat on his right cheek as he spoke. He seemed not to be aware of it.

"Valerius Petronianus asks for more slaves and sends his regard."

Surprise flew to his brother's face. "Ignoring an edict of the emperor? They fly in the face—"

"They fly in the face of nothing. The emperor is the one who asked for more slaves. The edict means nothing if he does not enforce it. He may be leading us as a Christian empire now, but the pagan temples still stand, and the games continue. And he awaits more slaves, for more games. The *munera* to be exact. A hero, is to be celebrated."

"So it is to be just as the edict of Milan ending persecution of Christians. How many more escapees will we send running for the safety of the desert? A farce. Who is to be celebrated?"

"They did not say. I told you before, Nicolae, the emperor is subject to the will of the people. And the people want blood. They do not care where it comes from."

"We're pulling children from their homes. It doesn't seem right, or fair—"

"Men would find a great deal more happiness in this life if they were to strike the word *fair* from their vocabulary, Brother. They are barbarians-uncivilized. Some sell each other. Just as we do."

"Criminals, war captives, just as Rome does, but—"

347

"But what? You begin to sound more and more like a Christian. I will have none of that talk on my ship while I am in command. Don't forget that Christians are still forced to compete in the games, Brother. Best pray to Neptune for a safe voyage. Family or not, you are here because I allow it."

Nicolae seemed to freeze in front of him; only the rise and fall of his chest told Cassius he was yet still breathing.

"Brother, please!" Cassius laughed. "You look as if I might actually give you over *ad bestias*. Fighting beasts as a gladiator is no station for a brother of mine." Nicolae began to smile softly at that, his smile slightly unsure. "I swore I would look after you until you became a man, and I will."

Nicolae seemed to breathe easier, and his shoulders relaxed as he threw the rag he was using to wipe his face into the bucket near the door. His dark blue eyes searched Cassius's and seemed properly reassured as he nodded and closed his eyes a moment, raking a hand through his dark red hair. It had none of the brown that Cassius's did. And the blue eyes Nicolae held alone, while Cassius's were brown. The color of their father.

"Now come, I need you to pen a letter in response to Petronianus for me. Your writing is much better than mine. One of these Nubian *kingdoms* has signed their names to an agreement with the tribune, and I mean to make sure they keep it. It is too excellent an offer not to."

ASIM

The sound of his daughter's cries rang in his ears as the deck swayed beneath him. Azima had cried when he told her he would be leaving for such a long time. *Look for me at the next full moon,* he had told her. Brushing back her tears with the ball of his thumb he had squeezed her tightly. Her sniffling sounds had made his heart ache while he held her in his arms, watching her large, bright eyes fill with tears. He'd hugged his son and reminded him he was head of their house while he was away. When he'd left their courtyard, Azima had watched him, briefly looking up at the moon every few moments. The salt spray reminded him of the taste of her tears as he'd kissed her cheek.

Five days they'd been gone, searching ships on the River Nub before traveling west, then south and east on Torrent towards a channel of waters that sat between Exile Island and the eastern shore of the Sotho Kingdom. The Essi Kingdom built all of the High King's war galleys. They were born on the water and knew no other home. Flying Nabara's symbols, they stopped at various harbors to question local villagers. They had few answers, and their investigation only tripled the amount of questions they needed answered.

"Pull it down, we'll have easier sailing that way!" Runi called.

Hasad growled back, "We sail with Nabara's sigil or we don't sail at all." Hasad was the shipmaster, and what he said was law.

Hasad's first mate, Heron, nodded in agreement, turning to hoist the sail. His eyes narrowed as he watched the scowl on Runi's face deepen, the sail unfurling, Nabara's white and gold khepresh symbol dancing in the wind.

Nabarans had been requesting passage on the *Desert Arrow* constantly since the festival began. Other cities had much to trade and eager passengers were willing to spend more for passage aboard the *Arrow* than any of the other galleys. The *Desert Arrow* wasn't as much a beauty as the rest and held no luxuries. But she was swift, her captain was honest, and he knew the seas better than anyone. *Too many captains with goat's milk still on their breath might think like Runi. But not Hasad.* He'd spent his life on this ship, and owned ten others. Taking risks on Torrent was stupid and reckless. He was neither.

"Are you going deaf on me, old man?" Hasani asked.

Asim watched Hasad turn, his salt-and-pepper hair blowing gently, loose locs falling to his shoulders as his eyes fell on Hasani, his second mate. Hasad's son. Hasani's hair fell in his eyes, long, thick, and black. The well-shaped beard at his chin was growing in strong now as well. Like Marava, Hasani's mother would call him unfit and refuse to allow him out to sea again. She'd want him home. She'd want him safe. But Hasani had no mother. And Hasani craved just the opposite, but the gods had blessed him with common sense if nothing else.

They were a pair to watch. And the pride on Hasad's face was unmistakable.

"Quit worrying about my ears and worry about your ship. With any luck, you'll fall on a blade and come out with a proper shave," Hasad growled back.

The crew joined Asim as he laughed. Hasani had been found when he was barely five years old. Naked and shivering, he clung to a rotted log in Torrent, looking for all the world like a rat clinging to his last morsel of cheese. *Who could blame him?* Half drowned, Hasad told him how Runi had poked at him with a long spear, laughing, "Let Torrent have the little monster; we don't need any more mouths to feed," attempting to push the boy back.

Hasad had stopped him. Children were a blessing from the gods. Hasad had refused to let Torrent have him.

"Daydreaming, old man?" Hasani clapped him on the back, and Asim winced. *He still doesn't know his own strength.*

"Come. The Scorpion King will be waiting for us." Asim motioned for them to follow. "He's commissioned this galley for a shipment after the festival."

"Let him wait!" an oarsman yelled.

"Yes, the way he makes fathers and mothers wait for their daughters to return," sneered another.

Both oarsmen were old and had not forgotten the stories of the lost daughters. Asim didn't believe it was true. Children were sacred, and these still so young. Even he had heard the tales of the Scorpion King and his tributes to the High Priestesses. Every year, King Tharbis picked the loveliest girls to serve. Many believed it to be a great honor, as each girl's family was showered with gifts, titles, and sometimes land. Neighboring kingdoms were not so easily placated, and a number of stories sprang from them. Each varied in time. Some believed a boy was taken, some said a girl. Some said the girls weren't lovely, or that the Red King sent the families away. One thing they all agreed upon was that the girl was never seen again.

Asim watched as Hasani tied back his locs. There were as many inches as he had years, and they gleamed black in the sun.

"We'll board them soon and make for the channel between Exile Island and the coast, then back to Nabara. Better we have more Medjay, if what they say is true." Asim preferred caution over chance. He didn't want to risk his men's lives if he could avoid it. He could still remember the Deffufa as it disappeared from view on their departure. He turned away, doing his best not to think of his daughter. He'd be home soon enough.

"It's true enough. People don't disappear willingly," an oarsman grunted.

"Men disappear easily enough when they're running from their wives," Hasani quipped. Laughter rang out across the ship.

"True. But ships with cargo that disappear? It's a bad sign. Better they're found wrecked than that." He shook his head as he shared a knowing glance with the shipmaster. He and Hasad had been through countless battles, but the men who disappeared never came home. Their wives had felt the gravity of it even more than their crew. And the Kiberan Queen was out for blood knowing that the risk she'd taken in allowing a trading ship to move Kiberan goods had been lost. She was like to never resurface from her lands again.

"Mikaili will find out, the Essi know Torrent better than any fish," Hasani declared.

Hasani and Mikaili were fast friends. Having grown up on the sea, they moved from port to harbor, and the young prince would always call upon Hasani and Hasad if trade brought him to Nabara.

"The young prince may, but not if they find him first." Runi responded, not bothering to look up as he tied knots.

"I'll have no more talk of this," Hasad cut through the silence. "We're amply provisioned, and all of us know how to wield a blade. It won't come to that."

A silence fell and Asim felt the crew's eyes upon him, heavy and questioning. He hadn't been entirely honest with what he expected to find, though he'd shared his thoughts with Hasad.

If the slavers and pirates come for this ship, they can have her. But not before they pry her from our cold, dead hands.

"It will be dark soon, Asim," Master Hasad said from his position beside him, shifting uneasily. He'd been wary from the start, his black hair just graying at his temples. The scar across Hasad's cheek moved with each word, running towards his mouth and stopping just at the outside of his cheek. The admiral claimed to have won it at a game of *senet* at a local tavern. He refused to be cheated.

"The winds have picked up," Hasad continued. "A storm is growing. It's best we turn into a harbor tonight," he warned, crossing his arms over his chest. The admiral wore a knee-length shendyt, gold in color, as well as a vest of white leather and a gold amulet around his neck.

"I know," Asim responded, turning to his brother in arms. Even he could see the storm building from miles away; the thick blue-black clouds seemed to reach from the sky all the way to the water in a wall of rain. "But something tells me we'll find what we're looking for if we stay on Torrent tonight." *Or perhaps try a parallel channel. Maybe then we will find what we are looking for. Or they'll find us.*

"Stay on Torrent?" the admiral echoed. "It's not sound. It's not safe. With the winds at our back we could outrun the storm, but at our front," he pointed north, "the clouds are black, and the storm will fall on us like hyenas on a carcass. We'll have no chance. If we're lucky, we'll be taken by the same raiders we're looking for and thus succeed in our mission. If we're luckier still, we'll be smashed between those rocks."

"We'll not go back to the High King empty-handed, Hasad. Trust you to be more concerned with a storm than slavers." His voice was firm. The High King had given him his orders. *And I always deliver.*

"Empty-handed? We'll go back without hands if we do it your way. The vultures fly over the water too," the admiral growled back.

"Still. We continue north." His tone left no room for argument. He sensed Hasad's anger but said nothing. *He knows there is no other way.*

"Well, then. You're either very brave or very stupid. And none of it will help us much without a little planning. And I was never one to turn my back on a little adventure. There's still some youth in me yet," he responded grudgingly.

Asim turned to him, the grin on his face widening as he did so. Hasad's smile gleamed back at him as he clapped him on the back.

Yelling to the oarsmen to keep them steady and stay alert, Admiral Hasad ordered the archers off the rails, making sure the port and stern were clear for what was about to come. The sea began rocking the galley as if it heard Asim's thoughts. The wind grew as Hasad commanded the crew to reef the sail to avoid being battered and moving too quickly across the water. If a storm came, the wind in the sails could smash them towards the rocks. It was best to use the oarsmen and the rudder for close quarters.

We're too close to the rock walls. Asim moved to port, wondering if they were as close as they were starboard. *We've got to drop anchor or we'll be smashed.* The storm had come upon them so suddenly they weren't prepared for it. Lightning struck above the cliff in front of them as darkness fell.

"I thought we'd have more time..." a deckhand gasped, his mouth ajar as he gaped at the sky above.

"Quickly now, or there won't be time!" Asim yelled to him. "The anchor!" The wind had picked up so quickly his voiced was drowned in the storm. The water rained down on the ship like rocks, causing the crew to slip across the deck. Running to the anchor, he used the rail to brace himself, untying it from the rope. The ship heaved suddenly and a deckhand pitched across the wooden deck, flying like a rock before landing, his head splitting on the wood before disappearing into the sea. Asim clung to the pillar in front of him before reaching back for the short rope to hold onto, not resisting the boat's movement as it threw him forward, waves crashing down over his head as he held fast.

"Anchor, now!" Hasad commanded, his last word drowning out by the waves falling around them.

Grabbing on with Asim and three more deckhands, they smashed at the metal ring attached to the anchor, before the wind caught it and it fell heavily down into the water, disappearing beneath the waves, white caps growing larger before them. Hasad nodded to him quickly before they made their way back towards the mast. Suddenly, the boat rocked forward with the waves and the crew shouted commands as they held tight. Asim looked up as the rock walls drew closer, menacing with edges as sharp as lion's teeth on either side. They held fast. *The anchor's found the bottom,* he thought, relieved. Hasad may not forgive him for not turning back if he lost his ship.

As suddenly as the storm came, it went. Breaking like the sun over the mountains, the rain slowed and the winds became like lambs in the darkness.

"By the gods..." an oarsman whispered. Unbelting himself, he leaned over the edge.

"What's that smell?" asked another, his nose crinkling slightly.

Asim moved to port, the stench strengthening with each step he took. The boat was crammed between two rock walls thrice the height of the pyramids in Nabara. At first, he didn't understand what he was seeing. *Seals. Dead seals.* Dozens of them seemed to be littered along the edge of the thin, narrow strip of land that ran from sea to rock. He surveyed the black rocks near the wall. *No.* They were more bodies, bloated, battered, and black. *They must have been here for at least a week.* Dead men lined the shore, the bodies lying at unnatural angles against the rocks, water lapping at their arms and legs. *The storm must have washed them ashore before sharks made a meal of them.* They were buried well. Hasad dropped a skiff over the port side, lowering it slowly before crewmen stepped in.

"With me." Asim gestured to three of his soldiers to follow him. Climbing over the side of the ship, they rowed toward shore, keeping careful watch of the rock walls for any signs of danger. The high-walled ravine remained eerily quiet despite the recent passing of the storm. They heard the sound of rocks falling and turned towards it, their archer at the ready, only to find a vulture sitting on a ledge, watching them, a stark white eyeball dangling from its flesh and out of the bird's mouth. Flaps of ripped skin hung just above the ground.

"They say there's no rest for the weary," Kelmar said, the back of his hand pressed against his mouth and nose.

"It's true. Burn me so I can make sure I'm resting," Moreq replied.

They stepped out of the reed boat carefully, walking among the bodies in turn. They were Kiberan men. That much was clear. What ripped and shredded green clothing they still wore marked them as Kiberan, the dense forest and jungle kingdom ruled by the Queen Bamanirenas. But the others. *Merchants and traders.* Asim lifted the cloak of one of the Kibera and found a wound just below his chest. *He died slow, this one.* Moving on to the second, he kicked at the vultures making a meal of his stomach and crouched low to sift through his robes to find what he was looking for. He pulled the pouch out slowly, loosening the drawstring. Pouring the coins into his hand, he flipped them over. One of them showed a coin of Meroë and another of Aksum. The note detailed a shipment of cloth, palm oil, ivory, and bamboo. *Bodies and no ship and no cargo.*

The skiff crew looked at him, nervously holding their hands to the *khopesh* at their hips as his soldiers stood at attention, on alert as they watched each dark crevice in the rock walls around them. Balling the note into his fist, he poured the coins and other contents back into the pouch.

"Remove what you can from their persons so that I can comb through it."

Asim turned to look at the group of vultures landing on the ledge above, others creeping ever closer to the nearest of the dead, their quick steps giving voice to their eagerness to feed.

"Burn the bodies. We're done here."

Nodding, they set to work. It took a full hour to pile the bodies and move them for the funeral pyre. The stench and rot filled their noses as they rowed back to the ship. Hasad extended his hand to him as he climbed aboard.

"We'll hug the coast as best we can," he told him as he watched the fires burning, smoke curling towards the rock wall in thick black clumps. "We need to return as soon as we can to inform the High King. He'll want to inform the Kiberan."

They had easy sailing the first two days. The third was harder. Just after midday on the fourth, Asim found himself breathing a sigh of relief. They'd been gone almost half a month and he'd known the reports to the High King would require more explanation. They'd burned the bodies out of respect for the Kiberan, but not before bringing two aboard to examine them further. Master Hasad had cursed him for a fool and refused to bring the corpse onto the ship, but he had insisted. Even now the physician was finishing his examination. A physician was always on hand to assist with the crew in case of lesions, cuts, and diseases caught from other cities. A knock at his door caused him to sit up, wondering if they'd learned something new. The admiral stood there, a grimace on his face.

"The physician wants to see you. At your leisure."

When they arrived, the physician stood over one of the dead men, his long thin knife stuck halfway inside of the man's mouth, his left hand holding the thick purple tongue to one side. Dry and rotted, it sprang from the corner of the dead man's mouth like a worm.

"This one is not of Kibera, he said aloud, not bothering to look up, his head moving from side to side as he brought his face closer to the dead man's before stepping back to speak to them.

Master Hasad stood at the door to the physician's quarters.

"How do you know?" Asim asked.

The physician inclined his head, and he turned from the rail to follow the admiral down the steps to the hold. The smell met his nose before the corpses came into view, filling his nose like some rotten perfume. The physician had wrapped the body in linen soaked with palm wine to guard against the smell, but it had only helped a little. It kept the rats at bay, but the body had been too long in the sun, rotting as the carrion ate away at its entrails. Candles burning incense were heavy in the air. Stepping closer, he steeled himself against the smell.

"Well?"

"Show him," the admiral signaled to the physician.

The old man stepped back to the table, his hands lined and weathered, but not shaking as men his age so often did. His thick grey hair was cut close. Choosing a metal instrument from the table, he inserted it inside the corpse's mouth. Using both hands he pried the mouth open, stretching the instrument wider until the corpse gaped at them like some unnatural dead, the smell seeping from its body as though they stood knee deep in a swamp. The physician gestured to the corpse, and Asim leaned closer along with Hasad to peer into the mouth.

"I see nothing," he stated, raising his gaze back to the physician.

The physician sighed, cutting his eyes at them both as if to make sure they knew he found teaching them what he had learned insufficient for his station. "The body is rotten, but the teeth are not." The physician used his hand to pull back the lips of the corpse, pulling down the chin with his right, exposing the dead man's upper teeth. Something shone in the lamp light, winking at them softly.

"Is that…"

"Gold," the physician cut Hasad off. "Untreated, raw gold. I thought it was a rotten tooth at first, until I began to scrape at it. I told you what; I can't tell you why."

"I've seen this before," Asim responded. "In the Tombs."

"And I," Hasad sighed. "There's no telling if he's a prisoner or a guard. No one leaves that place, and here he is, with no papers and dressed in the way of a noble. Only his teeth gave him away."

There were many places to send criminals of the Kingdoms in Nudolla, but the Tombs were different. The Tombs were a punishment that lasted forever. And were only for those who had committed a crime against the gods or unforgiveable crimes.

"The High King will want to know of this." Looking back at the man, Asim wondered what else it meant and how many more there were.

"Complete your examination," he told the physician. "I want a full report by tomorrow night. Tell no one but the admiral and myself about your findings."

"There's something else." The physician paused uncertainly.

"Please," Asim motioned for him to continue.

"I didn't know what to make of it, but the second body. A letter in Latin and some Greek." He turned to pick it up from the table. "It holds the symbol of the High King— his *khepresh*—and…"

Asim snatched it from him, reading quickly. "Latin for murder."

The physician nodded as Hasad took the letter from Asim. "It can't…"

Asim walked over to look at the body quickly, recognizing a mark on his neck, less bloated than the rest. *The fourth man.* He was with the others from the shipwreck from weeks past. What if it wasn't a wreck? What if they were there on purpose? Who could have showed them towards the edge of Nabara?

Grabbing the physician's arm, he made his voice hard. "Tell no one of this, do you understand? I will arrange a meeting with the High King, but until this no one must know. Especially the other families. We don't know who can be trusted."

Asim turned to Hasad, whose eyes had grown to twice their size. "Old friend, I need you to make this galley fly. And quickly. The High King is in danger—we need to return now."

"I've had wings since I was a child. We'll be there by tomorrow night." The admiral took his leave quickly. Asim could hear the sound of his feet landing as he took the steps to the upper deck two at a time.

The High King was surrounded by friends and any number of enemies at the Festival of Kings with no knowledge of the danger. *As fast as you can, old friend. Or I fear we may be too late.*

AMKAR

Damn the High Priests and their refusal to see what was right in front of their faces. That he must address their concerns at all was an annoyance far greater than he had the time for. Climbing the sandstone steps to the temple, he looked out towards the edge of the city. Soon the statue would be finished. And what a relief it would be. He had no interest in seeing a monstrous-sized replica of himself standing guard at the entrance of Nabara's high walls. But the people had insisted.

"Your Grace."

"Your Majesty."

The temple guards greeted him as he strode inside, flanked by Medjay on either side, his shoulders covered by a long golden cloak, the head of a lion hanging behind at the nape of his neck. His *khepresh* sat low on his forehead as Medjay threw open the tall doors. The surprise on their faces gave him small pleasure.

"Your Grace!"

All nine rose at once.

"Be seated."

Looking up again at the stone statues of the gods Anubis and Re lining opposite sides of the high ceiling chamber, their eyes lifelike, alive, he hoped he achieved his purpose in coming here. The command plain on their frozen expressions had inspired fear, forced confessions, and rooted liars. Their fingers pointed to a lone chair in the middle of the room. It was meant for the accused. Or anyone who wished an audience and presented himself before the High Court.

Lowering themselves, confusion writ across their features as they doubtless wondered at the reason for his visit.

"I'm told you think sending Medjay across the High Seas...unwise."

They fidgeted in their seats, as though the hot coals they often doomed others to walk across were under their own chairs. Discomfort showed on their faces in the deepening silence.

"And that you also think it unwise to send Medjay towards the Sao Kingdom."

High Priest Dahket spoke first, eagerness to please decorating his long face. "It is so *very* far, Your Grace. And unwise is not quite the word we would use. It is a decision which may be made without so much...haste."

"Haste?"

High Priest Enu spoke this time, rushing to fill the growing silence. "We had thought to speak with you about our wishes before the decision was made. Together." The other High Priests were nodding now, heads vigorously bobbing up and down in agreement like fish in one of the palace ponds. "Jointly. As one."

Amkar nodded. "I can see how you would think so. Power, such as it is, so often goes hand in hand with entitlement."

High Priest Enu gasped.

"Your Grace. I fear you mistake the *Kenbet* court. I find their explanation lacking in their efforts to define the cause for our concern. Something like this is torturous." High Priest Dahket smiled amicably.

"You mean tortuous."

"Excuse me, Your Grace?"

"You said, 'Something like this is torturous.' You meant to say...tortuous."

"I don't understand..." The High Priest blinked rapidly as he looked to his colleagues for assistance, but none came to his rescue. Their tightly held lips held in air as though to speak was to breathe in a poison.

"I'll explain. Torturous indicates a pain or suffering. Tortuous implies that something is complex. Full of twists and turns. Now. High Priests. I did not come here to quibble over words though sometimes words can do more harm than our actions. Our original conversation yielded a great amount of information, including the fact that you seem to much prefer it if decisions where Medjay are involved are made jointly."

"That is...true," High Priest Enu replied.

"How many of you were elected?" he questioned them.

"Your Grace, none of us were."

"Exactly. You all would do well to remember that." He ignored the shock on their faces as he continued. "As the Nine High Priests, you are tasked with hearing cases among the people of Nabara. *You are* required to recuse yourselves from matters involving your family or your own interests. In the event that the defendant has committed an unforgivable crime, you are to refer the matter to the vizier and to *me*. You may call witnesses, require an investigation, use legal documents and written deeds. In the event that a majority do not agree, I, as High King, rule on the matter after a public hearing. These are your duties and your responsibility in maintaining law and order in Nabara under ma'at. For *minor offenses*. The armies remain my purview alone. I will do with them as I wish. I'm sure your families would not quibble over their use for the protection of your children."

"Your Grace, we meant merely to assist in any way we can." High Priest Enu was contrite. "And we noticed that a private council may have been called, and we hope only to be of service."

Amkar stared them down. "Well then, would that not defeat the purpose of calling it a *private* council? That I pay you the courtesy of having the vizier notify you of its taking place does not mean you will suddenly be privy to the conversation."

They were looking at him now with varying degrees of humiliation, acceptance, and defeat. Much like his children when they were given an order by him or Samya. And none of them could counter the fact that his words held truth.

"Your Grace," one of the senior High Priests said. "Please. Do not remain affected by the impertinence of some on the High Court. Not all of us feel this way. We were wrong to question the harvest tax with the ensuing drought. You made a wise decision. And many of us are still aware of your expertise in warfare. We have every confidence that where Medjay go, your ability to broker peace by word or sword will follow."

Amkar nodded first to High Priest Harem for his sage words and then to the rest in turn. "Your request is no hardship. It is done." Relief flooded the faces of the few High Priests who had not spoken at all.

"High Priests. I understand your concern for the business of the kingdom and appreciate your love for Nudolla and the safety of all in Nabara. You *must know*. The attack on the Princess will not go unpunished. I intend to root out the problem and bring it forth from the darkness into the light. This is not the time for half measures. Gird your loins. Each of us may pay a price when this is over. Our enemy is near." Looking at them all once more, he hoped they would understand. He hoped they would listen.

"High Priests." Amkar turned swiftly, and the chairs scraped the floor as they hurried to rise as he took his leave.

"Your Grace." He left them in his wake. Striding back across his land with Medjay close behind, he put the High Court from his mind. There was more pressing business to attend to.

An hour later he sat in his receiving hall with the Kiberan Kandake, the sun already gone from the sky. Merchants continued to cry for customers down near the market, and the flames that lit either side of Nabara's walls shone bright in the distance. Turning to her, he took stock of her calm face, which did nothing to diminish the worried look in her eyes. She cared much for her people. And had lost family before for them. He knew how much it pained her to think of it again. There was a reason to remain as secluded as she did, protected in the forest.

"We are still awaiting news from the high seas," he told the Kiberan queen.

"The Kiberan crew still has not sent word of their arrival. Neither the goods nor the ships have reached their destination." The Kandake leaned forward in her seat, fire burning in her eyes. "If they are dead, we will repay those responsible in blood." She slammed her closed fist down on the table, eyes flashing.

"Asim is a good man. He always delivers. He will return soon with news. It will give us the time we need to plan."

"Old friend, fatherhood has made you soft. We will be cargo soon should we not act."

Never. Not again. Not while I reign.

"We need proof. Proof we do not have. In a day Asim will return." *I need more time*, he stopped short of saying.

His *khepresh* weighed heavily on his head, and he needed to think. His lovely wife. His children. His people. They were counting on him.

"And I agree with you, Amkar," she replied. "I will wait for proof before I enter into a war with ghosts who have no master. Or a scorpion disguised as a lamb."

Amkar chuckled. "You were never one to mince words, Bamanirenas. Speak your mind if it please you." Picking up the gourd on the table, he realized it was nearly empty. Raising an eyebrow at her in inquiry, she shook her head in amusement before nodding once to accept his offer. He never kept the handmaids and cupbearers around when he needed to speak about matters in the kingdom, news of intelligence, or other sensitive matters. Nor would he. He knew curiosity was like a dog that would only stop pestering you for food if you satisfied it. When he finished pouring he set the gourd back down and waited as she took a deep breath.

Leaning forward in her seat, she tilted her head slightly. "I know what they say, Amkar. So he was a soldier." She shrugged. "Many of us were. My own husband, may he rest well with the gods, even if he watched your back as you did his before you became High King. Tharbis saved your life. Not your soul. You owe him nothing. The penalty for engaging in the slave trade is death. I don't care if a thousand of our northern allies engage in the trade. Nudolla is ours and ours alone. An alliance built by free, independent, resource-rich kingdoms of varying cultures. Don't underestimate him."

Amkar sighed. "I underestimate no one, Kandake. As always, I appreciate your council. It is well advised. Do you take your own advice?"

"What? I do not understand your meaning." She sat up straighter in her seat, leaning back now as though someone had pressed her there.

"Bamanirenas. Do you take your own advice? You once told me you questioned the manner of your husband's death. Later still, you told me your caution was only the delusion of a grieving queen. And yet still, at times, the glimmer in your eyes when you look at Tharbis is as a pool in the desert that incites thirst the nearer you get to it, only to find nothing the closer you get. A trick of the mind." Now he leaned forward, intent on getting an answer from her. "Now tell me. Did you once underestimate him?"

A slight motion of her jaw occurred before her face went still, calm as lake water. "No. My people spur me on. I want none of them dead or facing death."

One day he would find out why Bamanirenas had no such love for the Scorpion King. Her lies grated on his patience, but he could not force the truth from her as one might a criminal on a rack. Tharbis had been well loved years ago, but he feared his kingship had made him suspicious and hardened him to the plights of others. Still, he had been a strong ally in eradicating the slave trade throughout the coasts on the south and making sure it didn't spread into Nudolla via the nomadic families. Sending Tharbis throughout Nudolla to ensure that it was done had endeared him to many. Almost thirty years later, his hold on the people's love seemed to be fraying at the edges. Amkar stared into her eyes. Calm though they were, he didn't believe her. *What did you do, old friend?* He would find out. Soon. Secrets never stayed that way for long.

When the Kandake left, he called for his vizier to provide him with more papyrus maps of their waterways and land routes as well as every last known location of the nomadic families. Their alliance would be invaluable. And he needed to know which would need his protection. His own spy was almost in place, gathering intelligence where he needed it most. The spy had put their safety at risk to carry out his orders. A bravery that couldn't be bought. He poured over the maps at length, moving armies over the stone like a game of *senet*. When he could not find a farming nation, he called for his vizier again to commission another map immediately, to be prepared before the end of the night, as well as to update any changes to the routes to their gold quarries. Samya came to check on him from time to time but left him unbothered, making sure his dinner was delivered even though he told her he had no plans to eat it. Smiling knowingly, she had kissed him on the forehead and stolen one of the mangoes on his plate. She had her own matters to attend to, including overseeing the festival activities and the collection of taxes within the kingdom. He finished the entire plate soon after she left. Hours passed before he paused to look up from his work and walk into the adjoining bedchamber. The sky was beautiful, even with the soft rain. He knew from his hunts that the animals would be taking shelter beneath the trees while the elephants bathed in the puddles made afterwards, soaking their hot skin in the mud and reveling in the cool treat. It would not last long.

Samya stood at the balcony, looking out towards the city, her long black braids underneath her golden crown. Arms crossed as she leaned in the entryway, her head rested against the wall. Amkar walked over to her, wrapping his arms around her waist and pressing his lips against the back of her neck as he held her. The sigh that greeted him in reward made him smile. He looked down and saw their youngest daughter and niece step from their litter. Imani kissed Ama lightly before running towards the Unbroken. Imani likely meant to calm the horses; thunder rumbled gently as the winds picked up, whipping the veils behind him. From high atop the palace, their daughter looked not a day over ten, so small amidst the sand. His heart squeezed in his chest. He knew it wasn't so. They stayed like that until the rain stopped and let the thunder have its time.

Samya turned to him, tilting her head upwards as she said, "Thunder and no rain. God must be angry."

That made him smile. *She puts so much faith in her God.* Would that he could. He did not respond immediately, thinking quietly about Asim and his return.

"Why so tense, my love?" she asked him, leaning her head against his chest, her arms resting against his while they held her waist. "Is King Tharbis making more trouble for you?"

"Always," he answered, stroking her arms gently.

"Have the Essi demanded blood?"

"Not yet. But the Kandake may when she learns the fate of her ship. You know our words. The Essi will not leave here without justice."

"Nor should they." Pulling away, she turned to face him. "Sometimes wars are necessary." Her eyes did not waver as she spoke.

A smile touched his lips before he responded, "Since when does my wife thirst for blood? Is this the same sweet-tempered bride I married? Have I rubbed off on you, beloved?" he teased, his hands cupping her chin.

"Marriage changes everyone. And victims will always seek justice for a wrong," she replied, moving back to the balcony. The city was lit up at every manse.

"Samya…" His voice was heavy.

"My sister knew what he was. She warned me. It was why she would not accept his hand, and he still throws her death in my face at every chance."

"You told me he asked after you and gave you his regrets."

"He gave me nothing. His words were a reminder of her death and nothing more than salt on an old wound that he wanted to make worse.

"Wounds always take time to heal."

"Time heals nothing. Wounds burn, wounds fester, wounds rot. "His wife knows. They're an old family. I will have my answer one day."

The Scorpion King's wife had been a playmate of Samya's, he knew. They'd been close once. It was rumored that the Red King sought Samya's hand. Her beauty, artistry, and intelligence had been well known throughout the kingdoms. None could hold a candle to his wife or her sister Salara. Salara had been younger, bright, and fair to look upon. Her dark brown eyes sat wide apart in her cinnamon-colored face, like some beautiful bird. Salara refused him. It was rumored that he might make an offer for Samya, but Samya was sent to the temples for education and thus was unavailable for marriage until her completion. The better for him. A harem was no place for his wife. Kushites were known for their powerful lines of ruling queens. No ordinary woman could have become the Great Wife of Nabara.

"Samya," he started softly. "Things are changing, and quickly."

"I know," she breathed softly. "And I can't save them from it."

"You won't have to. I'll fight for you."

"The High Priests may see fit to have us all slaughtered to a man if they believe we can not keep order or keep the empire safe."

"They won't. We have plenty of heirs, and the High Priests have never forced a king to suicide in years. And the vote for that must be unanimous. Ma'at governs under our laws and the people may still worship as they please, to God and his Son, to Ra, to Amun, but these practices are rare."

"Rare, but still in place. I wonder about the High Court at times. Their rulings make too much mention of the old religion of Meroë's ancient Pharaohs. They won't *now*—"

"But they are men. And men scare easily," he interrupted her.

"Yes," she whispered.

It pained him to see her carry his worries. He had refused to speak them to her out loud before now, but given the threats they faced—the slave trade, the incursions, the piracy, and the drought to the north—they needed to be prepared.

"And women do not?" He was smiling now despite the gravity of their conversation, wanting to see her smile again.

"I never did," she cupped his face. "I wish you would take more care with your life than you do now, my love. If only for my sake."

"All I do is for your sake. I would give my life to make you happy."

"A life without you would be anything but."

He moved his hand to one of her braids, undoing it slowly. "Asim should be arriving soon, and I expect better news. I sent him to root out the pirates and who may be paying them so that we can protect the high seas. Keep them safe. Danger on our trade routes will make us all vulnerable. And I fear that the men who attacked Imani at the market were only a shadow of those we slaughtered at the coast. I fear more are coming. And we must be prepared."

Samya's eyes closed as she pressed her face to his chest. "I know." She stepped back, taking his hand to pull him inside.

"Can we send scouts north to learn more information? Without them getting caught or sold as slaves in the trade?"

"It would be quite a risk," he told her thoughtfully, as he paced across the large expanse of the room, its high, decorated walls alone hearing their secret thoughts. "But not if we made sure no one would question their motives. Give them no cause for concern as they moved towards Rhapta and through the Sahara."

Samya's eyes narrowed, "You're not suggesting—"

"Have them pose as slave traders. Or something similar to it. It is the fastest way. No one is ever more comfortable with another person unless they believe them to be of the same mind. Alike. Perception is reality."

"Amkar..." her voice trailed off as she took in his words.

"You know it is the best way. If we could find out how they

know and who may be working with them, it would give us the advantage. Information is the greatest asset in *any war.* Your father knew that."

"Amkar, who would agree to this?" Smiling now, he could tell from her question his words had convinced her.

"I am a king, Samya. I can never guarantee anyone's safety. Even my own. But while men are willing to protect those they love and their land that gives them life, I would have their service again and again and again. And respect them for it."

Samya finally sat down in the high chair closest to the balcony, silhouetted by the soft glow of the moon behind her.

"You are a dangerous man," she told him slowly, shaking her head while her eyes traveled from his feet to his face.

"That's why you married me."

She laughed, throwing her head back as she did, the sweet notes caressing his ears and warming his heart.

"I won't *take* this insubordination from you." Her eyes narrowed as she rose from her seat.

"That's why I married you."

A smile lit up her face as he drew closer. He felt her lips before her hands drew a path up his chest and he wrapped his own around them, kissing her lightly, before placing both hands at the nape of her neck to pull her into him, deepening the kiss. When he pulled back, her face was flushed slightly, her eyes dazed as she kissed his chin.

Samya used her hands to undo the gold clasp at his shoulder, carefully removing his *khepresh* and setting it behind them on the table. He dipped his head to suck at her collarbone as she put one hand to the back of his head, a sigh escaping her softly.

Amkar slowly undid each of her braids as he kissed her. Filling his hands with her black hair, the ends soft as cotton. It was one of the things that enchanted him about her besides her mind. Her spirit. It was the reason she was his greatest confidant.

Nipping at his lip with her teeth, she moved closer. Sliding his tongue inside of her mouth, he sucked the sweetness of her gently, finding no defiance there.

His hands moved to her left shoulder, gleaming brown and bare and smooth against her golden gown. Sliding his right hand inside the opening at her waist, he let his fingers trail across her stomach, kindling a fire just there as his lips moved to her throat. Her sighs filled his ears and stayed there.

"Ssshhh…" he whispered against her ear before kissing it gently.

Coconut and mint filled his nose, and he slid his tongue back inside her mouth, loving the feel of her soft lips as she trembled against him, warm and inviting.

Samya's hands left his chest to lift the crown from her hair, but he stopped her, putting one hand on hers.

"Leave it."

She swallowed before answering him, her voice thick and soft. "But—"

"Leave it. I like reminding myself of my greatest treasure.

"Your crown?" A smiled played on her face.

He kissed her again, placing his forehead against her own as he gazed into her eyes. "You."

IMANI

Her father was worried. That was plain. He hid it well, but never from her. He'd never been one for religion. It was the reason he allowed the fortunetellers and others at the Festival of Kings. She'd watched him walk towards the temple in the direction of the Deffufa from her window just before sunrise, turning around just before he reached the entrance. He'd never forgiven the gods for how her grandfather died. She'd contemplated walking out onto the veranda but stopped, knowing he went when he needed time to think, before he gave judgment when the High Court was deadlocked. *He doesn't want to bring his people into war. If not for the Festival, he might have more time.*

The council had met at length to discuss the news of the missing Kiberan ship. Queen Bamanirenas was not taking this lightly. Her father had ordered the Medjay to watch for large shipments of goods being sold by merchants. She knew none would be found. But perhaps the Adamantine he sent for would fare better in their search. Asim's came from the Meded nation, the origin of the fierce Medjay warriors, but the Adamantine were unbreakable. She'd never seen them, but her father spoke of them at length and her grandmother, the Kingmaker, had told her tales since she was a little girl no higher than her knees.

"Imani-ka?" Ama called to her from the door, "It's the last day of the Games. You should rejoice."

She turned to look at her cousin. Her large trusting eyes reminded her of the little boy Mikaili had lifted onto his shoulders. The people they were sworn to protect. Ama's golden crown circled her forehead, falling low on her brow. Her ivory sheath overlaid with a sheer emerald cover. Bright and playful, just like her.

"I will. When the slavers are caught."

"Imani, you mustn't—"

"I know." She lifted her veil from the floor where she'd dropped it. "The charade is almost over, Cousin."

Ama sighed, shaking her head before falling in step beside her.

The *Desert Arrow* hadn't returned as yet. *Father must be worried.*

Her mother waited at the steps for her and so did their litter, drawn by ten of their finest stallions. "Your father will join us later." She seemed to read her thoughts easily. "Come."

Stepping into the litter, she drew back the curtains to view the market and dancers as they passed. When they reached the arena, they were borne to their seats in the stone arena, accented by an open balustrade. There was no danger of falling. Their seats were further from the edge, and Medjay took their places behind them, still as stone. The stone that lowered into the vaults under the arena floor had been covered today. *The gifts.* She couldn't conceal her excitement. A large golden canvas covered it in equal parts silk and linen. Ten Medjay soldiers stood on opposite sides, the sunlight glinting off their gold-rimmed shields, spears in hand, their *khopesh* sheathed. The crowd was larger today than any other, she noticed. *Of course. They are eager to see what gifts come too. And some have made these themselves.* She smiled. She'd had a chance to visit some of the orphans at the temple who were housed there the day before, and they had asked a thousand questions during her stay. A few hinted at what was to come, bouncing up and down in their excitement as they asked her for kisses. Smiling, she turned her attention towards her mother.

"Each year the most talented artisans compete for the chance to make the gift given to the High King's children who come of age during the Festival of Kings. It is an honor above all others," her mother explained. "Notoriety, patronage, and fortune. This promises all. You have the power to change someone's fortune for the better. A simple act, a simple courtesy, can affect ten thousand in so little time."

Imani thought of Ama's whispers of tigers, brilliant gemstones, and rock water. She hoped it was all true. Lifting the veils about her head, she allowed them to hang down her shoulders, like bright sleeves against her long ivory gown, the bodice an intricate detail of gold and crystals. Each of the families were taking their places, and soon, so would her father. From the litter she could just make out the long train of pilgrims who came to pay homage to Amun and Apedemak at the Great Temples of Nabara. Built deep into the mountain just inside the city walls and opposite the palace, it was a sight to behold. Most Kushites believed life started at the mountain at Jebel Barkal in Napata. Here, in Nabara, the Kingdom of Gold, they sought to pay homage not just to their love for Kush, but the life, beauty, genius, and creativity of Nubians. The steep angles of the temples along with the elaborate decorations of the painted rock art were like none in this world.

As one, the arena rose, and she turned to see where her father came. She spotted him at the base of the arena, slowly climbing the stone steps. When he reached the top she rushed into his arms, embracing him tightly. She felt his hand grasp her curls momentarily, and a rush of affection swelled in her heart.

"My Little Princess," he whispered.

It was what he would always say when he called to her when she was younger rather than use her name. Come here, Princess. Princess, what are you reading? Princess, why are your dress robes covered in mud? He loved her no matter what. He kissed her forehead before he released her, bidding her to take her place. He'd never been one to show much affection in public. Even now he wore the face of the Ruler of Nabara, Pursuer of Justice, High King of the Nudollan Empire. Still, she didn't miss him placing a quick hand under her mother's chin in affection before greeting each of his other children in turn.

Finally, he turned to the arena standing over the balustrade to look down at the audience below him, excited whispers dying as he did. "As we near the end of the Games, it is with solidarity that the Kingdom of Nabara welcomes gifts from across the realm in tribute to our empire and Daughter of the Desert, High Princess Imanishakheto Aminata Kashta, as she comes of age." At this, Imani rose from her seat, her hair billowing behind her in the breeze.

"May she live a thousand years!" the crowd chanted, replying as one.

"Bring forward your gifts. We accept them with appreciation as we serve you in the years to come."

The crowd roared with delight as the stone vault began to rotate in place.

A man stepped forward, covered head to toe in black garments of the Kingdom of Tharbis, his head bald and glowing softly in the sun. A handmaiden followed him. "No desert flower shines so brightly as one grown without water, born in the midst of sand, which melts as glass. Thus, we gift from the Burning Sands a looking glass in the shape of a lion and remember and celebrate the beauty of Princess Imanishakheto."

"May she live a thousand years!" the crowd chanted.

Do they think I'm as vain as their sons? She looked across at the Scorpion Family as King Tharbis raised a single hand towards her and his retinue bowed low. She inclined her head in approval as they took their seats.

Four dozen black-robed men soon appeared, carrying large earthen jars filled with what Imani knew were diamonds. The Namib Desert surrounding Tharbis was filled with them. The crowd cheered at the favor.

Next came the Kiberan's gift. Ivory, cloth, palm oil, and medicine. The Kiberan only sacrificed elephants for ivory when they were found dead or sick. Hunting them in Kiberan territory was illegal, and they dealt severely with poachers. Their prowess had earned them a reputation that kept the animals safe from harm. The medicine yielded from the many plants found in their forests and, mixed with various herbs, healed even the most afflicted. Many believed them immortal, and though the kingdom was known for its isolation, many attempted the journey out of desperation, seeking whatever cure they could find. If the journey itself beyond the Bridge of Martyrs did not kill them, a lucky few might have a chance.

The Sotho King and his retinue offered beautiful black stones speckled the color of the tree frogs in Nabara. Their greenish-yellow luster stood out even from a distance. Rare and beautiful. The families of the Sotho people were numerous but well connected across their vast swaths of diverse territory including snow-capped mountains, rock pools, waterfalls, and large cave networks containing art from the hunter-gatherer families that spanned the ages.

The Nabarans' gift was brought by the vizier and a retinue of scribes, apprentices, and orphans from the temples and pyramids where they prayed, submitted offerings, recorded judgments and building projects onto papyrus scrolls, and prepared the dead. She'd seen for herself how the priests supervised the cutting of the bodies and the removal of the brains and other organs before cleansing the body with fragrant oils and applying its final linen wrappings for burial. It was a ghastly task, but necessary. The boys and girls were dressed all in white. Gold jewels and painted *khats* decorated the High Priests. Next came beautiful crowns made with the greatest care and emeralds sewn into a wonderful tapestry of a map of the Nudollan Empire and its heart, the Kingdom of Nabara. Looking closer, she gasped. When seen from afar it yielded into her very own face—brown forests of earth became her skin; the sand became her golden eyes, made from gold and amber; blue and red waters formed from lapis and garnet represented the tiniest highlights in her cheekbones; and black mountains made of oil and iron were her ebony-colored hair, long and wild and flowing down her shoulders, guarding the kingdom on all sides like a lion's mane. It was breathtaking, and the crowd cheered as the tapestry was turned towards them. Even her father rose in appreciation of the intricate details. *It's my own likeness.* Her breath caught in her throat, and she dipped her hand in the gold dust at her side and threw it forward, letting it fall. A sign of her appreciation. The crowd roared with delight.

The Sao brought salt. Imani rose and walked over to Komoro and Ketemin to thank them, as they were seated closest to her family. She kissed Princess Ketemin on each cheek, hugging her tightly in appreciation. Princess Ketemin was as a mentor to her.

Last, the Essi stepped forward on the sand, proud and regal, their blue and white robes blowing softly about them.

"We make a gift of salt. What we have in abundance we would share with you. Take this salt as a gift from the Essi." Fifty stone jars containing salt were brought forward, and the crowd cheered with delight. Salt was used in preserving meats, flavoring dishes, and as a scrub for the body. It was highly favored, and Nudolla shared equally in such luxuries.

"Sugar." The Essi King raised his hand, and a team of handmaidens and apprentices ran forward from the canvas, each carrying woven baskets filled with sugar along with a number of brightly colored objects. "Once," the Essi king began, "my wife enjoyed sweet riches made from the saltwater, and we enjoyed them in abundance. Her generosity, strength, and sweetness were unmatched. After her death, I forbid the treat as a delicacy should ever be made again." Imani could hear the winds whispering to her as she listened, the crowd silent below even as she leaned forward at the edge of her seat. "My son convinced me otherwise. Your spirit is much like hers, and it would honor us, should you accept them. We hope you remain unyielding like the acacia tree, which survives through the harsh starvation of water and the bitter lash of winter frost. May your generosity never wane, as the sun will surely rise. May you live a thousand years!"

Imani held back her tears. She remembered his wife well. She had been her mother's closest confidante and treated Imani as her own.

"I do," she responded, the words echoing across the coliseum as she rose from her seat and walked down the pavilion towards the Essi King. When she reached him their retinue bowed low, bending their knees before her in the sand. She bowed before him, ignoring the gasps of the crowd, and took both his hands in her own before softly kissing his left and right cheeks in affection. "I remember. I loved her too."

His eyes shone bright with unspent tears, and she held his hand tightly in her own as he turned to Mikaili, nodding slightly.

"We have fought many great battles together," Mikaili began stepping forward. "And there may be more to come. We pray that the Nabaran and Essi remain fast friends. Just as a ship needs a captain, so too a Daughter of the Desert and warrior of Nabara needs a weapon."

The crowd quieted in confusion.

"Iron. In the Floating City, we have many treasures from such a simple thing. And here is one fit for a princess." The waters on which his kingdom sat were filled with mist. Many of the people in Nudolla visited it simply to see the large ships float along as though carried by the clouds themselves. He held out his palm slowly and the metal glinted in the sunlight, reflecting the light easily and winking in his hand as if he held glass. The crowd was silent. It was the smallest gift that had been given. Something every villager owned. *This gift was surely meant for my brother.*

She released the king's hand, stepping forward as Mikaili kneeled before her, the knife in his outstretched hand. She took it gently, the weight of it surprisingly light in her hand. Rolling her thumb over it, she found an inscription so tiny she could not read it. *What words are these?* She held it up to the light, squinting at the cylinder-shaped handles. A slight ridge gave under her thumb, and she applied pressure lightly at first before allowing her thumb to slip into its pocket. With a sharp sound of drawn metal, the cylinder came to life in her hand, a sharp spear like metal opening on either side, nearly three feet long on each end. She removed her thumb in surprise, holding it away from her body as the spear points disappeared and folded out, twin blades slicing through the air, as if twin axes had been fitted on opposite sides and paired against one another. More gasps of shock rose from the crowd as she replaced her thumb, spinning the blades above her hand and slashing down abruptly in front of her. A *khopesh*. Sharp and smooth, the blade appeared before her eyes and she grinned in delight, not noticing that Mikaili had moved swiftly to her right. She moved her fingers across the handle, rolling it as the blade was replaced by a forked instrument, thick, and bulky as her mouth dropped open. She rolled her thumb again. *A hammer!* She held it high as the swell of the crowd rose, using her thumb to apply pressure to the same ridge and the blade folded and disappeared in her hand, a cylinder again, small, unassuming, and disarming, frighteningly unalarming. *Like me.* She let her breath out, her chest rising and falling rapidly as she looked up and the audience erupted in applause, booming with cheers and yells at the unexpected display, hooting with pleasure.

Heat warmed her cheeks as she blushed, turning back to the Essi. "Thank you for this gift. It is an honor to wield it."

"The honor is ours," Mikaili replied. He stepped forward with a small leather box and inserted the blade inside before handing it back to her. His grey eyes were solemn but warm as he reached for her hand, holding her there. When she turned back in confusion, a small amber and diamond necklace lay in his hand, glittering against the sunlight. Reaching for it in surprise, she enclosed it in her palm as he rose.

"I meant to return it sooner," he said. Her amber eyes danced as she looked at the necklace again before reaching for both of his hands. She rose quickly on her tiptoes before him, leaning closer, her black curls brushing his shoulder. "Thank you," she whispered softly against his ear. Releasing his hands, she smiled at him as his iron eyes met hers. She turned back to her seat to the cheers of all of Nudolla.

The stone vaults were being opened again, and the arena was alive with murmurs as they watched the great canvas billowing in the breeze, wondering what wonder would come forth. She heard them before she saw them, chains dragging against the stone. Her heart skipped as she turned to see her father looking down at her. She smiled at him, unable to contain her excitement as she turned back towards the vaults.

Excited whispers filled the arena as half the audience saw four manes rising from the ground. All four had legs that rose past her own shoulders. Two males and two females roared as their shoulders appeared and then their thick trunk-sized legs. Suddenly their heads dipped down, and the sound of ripping flesh rang out in the silence, their bloodied mouths devouring whatever lay between their legs as they rose higher. *In the name of Amun, why would they feed them during the ceremony?* Suddenly the crowd's applause of pleasure gave way to screams of terror. An arm dangled from the mouth of one of the males, the forearm and bicep visibly swollen from the clamped grip of the lion's teeth, the fingers dangling towards the ground. Blood ran freely to the ground. Gasping, Imani stepped back, and Mikaili's arm stretched out behind him, forcing her backwards.

"What is this?" Her chest rose and fell rapidly as Medjay approached the beasts carefully moving toward whatever carcass lay at their feet, spears drawn.

"Who..." She couldn't finish her sentence as she watched the other lions tearing at similar pieces, one body torn at the waist, a gaping wound at his throat, his leg torn off, and his entrails being devoured greedily. Two seemed to realize they had an audience, looking around the arena.

"They're not..." *They're not chained.* She did not hear the words her father shouted, but the crowd erupted all at once. "Move!" Medjay shouted, running towards her. Men she did not recognize appeared as if from nowhere, cutting down one Medjay and the next as she spun about, Mikaili next to her.

"Back!"

The beasts roared behind her, the earth seemed to shake beneath her feet, and the hair rose on her arms at the sound that penetrated her bones. Imani watched as two sprang from the stone pavilion towards the closest in the crowd, their warning growls like claps of thunder.

She gasped as Medjay near the stands rushed toward her, watching in horror as the crowd swarmed them like ants, crushing some underfoot in their panic.

Turning back towards the lions as the lighter male moved towards her, his eyes burned into hers. She found herself unable to take her gaze away as his strong shoulders moved forward, alternating with each step even as she moved backwards. *He's hunting me.* She stopped moving and so did the beast, slowly lowering into a crouching position, his tail flicking back and forth like a reed on the banks of the River Nub. She blinked and suddenly he was airborne, blocking her eyes from the sun as he fell toward the earth, towards her.

Remembering the gift, her grip tightened as she swung the blade in a tight arc towards its chest and stepped sideways. When his teeth sank into her, she saw another blade swinging towards her own face, and she saw no more.

AMKAR

"Your Grace!" The messenger flew up the steps, his hands outstretched as he came. Shocked murmurs came from the audience as they took in his appearance. Sweat poured from his brow as he climbed up the stone steps, Medjay holding people in place as they allowed him to pass. Clutching a small glass container, he came, leather sandals separating at the mouth. His tongue repeatedly ran over cracked lips that would not moistened. His eyes were bloodshot.

When the messenger finally stood in front of him, he began to bow before his knees buckled under him. Stepping forward in shock, Medjay grabbed him to hold him up.

"Please..." he begged weakly. The Medjay to his right took the parchment he pulled from the container and handed it to him. Samya touched his arm as Amkar took it, and she went to put a hand to the messenger's forehead.

"A physician, quickly!" Samya commanded, watching as other Medjay ran to find him. Pouring water from a vase, she held it to the man's lips, one hand under his chin as he drank. Samya wet her hands and rubbed them over his neck.

"Please...you must read it. I come from Meroë." His head lolled slightly as he struggled to stay upright, knees shaking every time he tried to stand unassisted.

Amkar had not moved. "What is it?" she asked him, her face filling with dread as she watched him.

The message was written in Meroitic script, the uncial letters growing fainter, smaller, and increasingly rushed as he moved down the page. Dark red-brown smudges were a decoration that forced him to grit his teeth as he read from the papyrus:

"We are overcome. Ezana has set us aflame. Meroë can not stand against him. Look for friends elsewhere, Brother. There is a traitor among you. Find him before he destroys your world as he has ours...Find the king. Kill him. Isinja."

"The Aksumite king? What is this? Who is Isinja?!" he

379

demanded, staring at the messenger as he waited for answers.

"I…" the messenger muttered softly before Samya tilted his head back to give him water, the physician arriving to quickly wrap cool linen compresses against his neck and arms.

"The heat, Your Grace," the physician said apologetically. "No doubt the journey and heat addled his brain. It is a wonder he lives!"

Amkar fingered the bloody fingerprints at the top and sides of the parchment. A cold began to whisper at his neck, a cold the sun would not warm.

"Who is Isinja? Why is the hand written not equal?"

This time the messenger shook his head, inhaling a shaky breath. "His fingers," he gasped, "they were too badly burned to write. It was the last word he spoke. He could not write it but asked me to. Isinja…Isinja. He said it twice. I wrote his words as he lay dying. I left nothing out. 'Find the king,' he told me. My duty is done."

"Who is Isinja? Is this a Nomadin name?" The messenger grasped his arm tightly.

"You must…Isinja…He's *here*."

Amkar looked at the man, his mouth gaping wide as Samya and the physician leaned over his tattered skin and bones.

Amkar walked quickly to the edge of the balustrade, his eyes finding his daughter. Imani looked up at him, her golden-brown skin sparkling in the sunlight as her black curls fell behind her like a cloak, tiny wisps surrounding her neck and face as the wind played in it. And her smile. Her smile was glorious.

Amkar saw the men rising the same time as she. The smile faded from her lips, confusion taking over. At least ten stood in each section of the complex. Four golden manes rose on either side of the sand, the bodies of four magnificent man killers attached to them. A mangled body lay next to one beast as he ripped flesh away from bone as the stone rose higher. *Chainless!* Soon they would be free.

"Medjay! Protect the Princess!" he bellowed.

Screams and grunts met his ears as he turned and pulled his *khopesh* from its sheath, shedding his heavy cloak in one fluid motion.

"Return to the palace!" he commanded. Medjay wasted no time, forming a human shield around Jelani and his siblings as Tamayis began to cry. Pushing Samya back and into the protective circle of the Medjay, he forced her away from the lifeless body of the messenger. The Medjay bore them down the stone steps, sweeping not past the crowd but through it, using their spears to rake people back. They moved so quickly they seemed to float. They'd been trained for this.

Amkar fought beside the remaining contingent, knowing more had been warned from the sound that pierced the air next. Drums, a hard, steady rhythm, loud and chilling, as it seemed to make the very air around him vibrate. Blood spilled onto the dry stone as he cut his first enemy down and wondered where they would find this Isinja. And what had become of Imani.

MIKAILI

He slapped her again. Softly at first, and then harder when she wouldn't wake. The blood seeped through her dress like spilled wine, darkening every moment against the ivory silk. He dared not pull it back to see where she'd been hurt. Her chest was so still. *Please.* Mikaili pulled her head over the side of the fountain letting the water hit her full in the face; water ran over her eyes and mouth. Filling his hands with water, he moved over her neck and chest, gently running water over them, his hands shaking.

A drum sounded, and he froze. Long, and loud, and chilling. The Drums of War.

"They're coming this way!" Villagers ran past him, clutching their children to their chests, screaming in fear.

He could see the tower at the top of the pyramid in the distance. If they moved to a villager's house, they'd likely be found and killed, along with the owners. *We hesitated. And now we can only retreat with a wall at our backs.*

Imani seemed to grow heavier every minute, and Mikaili gripped her about her waist to keep her from falling. Her skin almost looked…looked…*She's losing too much blood.* The palace was too far. They'd never make it.

The ship. Slipping his hands underneath her, he lifted her into his arms like a child, breaking into a run, his sword swinging at his side. Sweat ran down his back as he jumped a low stone wall with her, the sand sucking at his feet. When he spied the gold and white sails of the *Desert Arrow,* he moved faster, gripping Imani tighter in his arms. They will have heard the horn too. Sure enough, panting he looked up towards the sail to see one of the deck crew, his legs tight about the mast, one hand to his forehead to block out the sun as he called out to those below. The masses of Nabara were on his heels.

He tripped over something and went down on his knees hard on stone, never letting her go. Rising again, he kept running. "Hasad!" he called out. "Hasani! Let her down!" His breath was stolen away behind him with the wind, sand getting inside of his mouth. "Hasani!" His desperation was apparent as the sand stung at his eyes, rising about him he ran, watching the sail billow out. *They're leaving.* Ignoring the cramp in his legs he moved faster, Imani limp and bloody in his arms.

"Faster, Mikaili!" Hasani had seen him. The dock began to break away under his feet as the ship moved swiftly away without pulling lines to escape the soldiers. A moment later he heard them snap, one by one, as it pulled away.

"We can't stop her! Faster, Mikaili, damn you!" Hasad yelled to him.

Amun help us. Jumping into the water before the dock could swallow them he kept one arm around Imani as he pushed towards the ship, reaching for the broken lines. The smell of smoke reached his nose, mingling with the screams of Nudollan's as the horn sounded, blaring through the cries of desperation behind him. Imani's head was dangerously limp, her mouth and nose dragging underneath the waves.

"*Stop!*" His enemies had reached them. "I command you in the name of the High King Kashta. *Stop!*" Nabaran soldiers. He turned around to yell to them and watched as an arrow pierced through the first's eye with a spurt of blood, dropping him like an anchor. The others turned, drawing their *khopesh* as more arrows rained and the rest were cut down.

"Stop!" This time it was another, armed and clad in pale robes, covering all but his eyes. *A mercenary.*

Mikaili ignored him, his grey eyes focused, swimming towards the ship with all his might before something sharp entered his left shoulder and his hand, and he began to sink with Imani below the deep blue of the River Nub.

ASIM

Something was wrong. Thick, black smoke rose from the far edges of the city. It blotted out the sun. Today was the last day of the Festival of Kings. Surely this wasn't some type of display taking place. The vizier had made sure he'd been privy to the schedule prior to his departure. As the commander of High King Kashta's Medjay, he'd made sure to take several precautions, including increasing the detail on the royal family. Each of them had four Medjay no matter where they went. They'd been informed not to skirt their protection for any reason. *What can this be?* Suddenly the drums began to sound and he flew into action, jumping from the *Desert Arrow* before Hasad could stop him. Sliding down the rope as the sound of screaming reached his ears, he yelled back to his Medjay. "With me!" Twenty of his warriors poured from the ship, breaking into a run.

"Asim!" the admiral bellowed behind him.

"Mikaili!" another voice cried out as he ran.

Running as quickly as his feet would carry him, he leapt over low walls, cutting across landowners' estates. Goat and cattle meandered slowly across the streets, ignoring him and bleating softly as he ran past. Asim jumped, pushing off from a large pot to propel himself onto the brown horse sitting in a courtyard nearby, his men taking the other horses in the stable. Kicking his feet into its hide, the horse broke through the courtyard doors, beating a path towards the arena at the edge of the city. They flew past fleeing masses of Nabara, pressing towards him like a herd of antelope.

Faces frozen in terror, they came screaming and falling in their desperation. Tripping over other fallen bodies as the crowd thickened, widening in a mass of rushing bodies down narrow passages, searching for safety. Some ran into nearby homes.

Others had come out from their shops, the few who hadn't attended the games. They stared open-mouthed at the people pressing towards them in shock.

"Move!" he yelled at them, shaking some from their positions in the middle of the streets. "Go back to your homes! Get inside now!"

The wind beat at his face as he pressed the stallion faster, the edge of the arena built for the Festival of Kings coming into sight as bush turned to savannah and then to sand. The sound of hooves filled his ears and when he looked back he saw that his men followed close on his heels, their faces as determined as his own.

He pulled the arrows from his pack at the first sight of a swordsman with his blade high in the air, preparing to cut down a woman cowering on her knees. Her hair was scattered across her face as she looked up at him, one hand raised in defense as she tried to ward the blow that was sure to come. The arrow punched through his chest and the sword fell harmlessly to the sand as the woman jumped up, running first backwards, and then turning to get away. Asim spurred the horse faster. *I must find the High King.*

Reaching at his waist, he retrieved his *mambele*. Shaped like a bird with wings outspread, the sharpened edges would slice through flesh as clean as any knife. Grasping at the ridged handle of one, he narrowed his eyes at his target. He only had ten. His aim had to be sure. *Pfft.* The four-edged pronged throwing knife spun through the air. It found its mark, spiking through the forehead of a thick-bodied, bald man wielding a hammer. *Pffft Pffft.* Two more cut into the shoulder and planted in the throat of a tall invader, but not before the man's blade ripped through the arm of a young boy, cutting him at the shoulder. Scooping him from the ground as he cried, Asim handed him to a woman allowing people into her home.

"Take him!" Asim commanded, dropping him into her arms before turning his horse back around and into the thick of the swarm, his Medjay ahead and behind as the Drums of War began to sound. The little ones' screams rang in his ears as he pressed forward. Kicking his heels to urge his horse forward as a ram, he barreled through a group of the assailants, screaming as he ran them down. One thrust a sword into the horse's neck and Asim was thrown forward, slamming into the ground and rolling to avoid the weight of his horse as it dropped to the sand with a braying scream. His *khopesh* was in his hand before he rose.

"Press forward!" Asim yelled to Medjay as his own men began to outnumber those who surrounded him.

He drew his sword diagonally from left to right. The belly of his opponent spilled onto the sand as he grunted and keeled forward, clutching his belly, rivers of blood spilling from his mouth. Asim pushed him aside.

Wwwhhh. Wind whipped past his face and he quickly dived to the left as a second arrow just missed his right eye. Behind a sandstone statue of a lion, he searched for the archer.

"Asim!" someone called, a broken sound. Peeking out from behind the statue he searched and found a Medjay warrior lying in a puddle of his own blood, his right leg missing as he raised his hand upwards and to his left. Before Asim could turn to look, an arrow sprouted from the man's chest, punching through his palm and pinning it to his chest. His head falling to the left, the warrior looked at him, his eyes wide with surprise.

Gritting his teeth, he lowered his head slightly as he looked for his mark. Arrow after arrow rained down as men, women, and children were cut down around him. There was only one archer. *I see you.* He pulled out two more *mambele* and stepped from behind the statue. *Pfft pfft.* The dead man fell over fifty feet to the ground, breaking clay pottery beneath him as he landed. Running over to him, Asim pulled his sword on the man, pointing it below his chin as he lay dying.

"Who sent you?" he demanded.

"You're too late," the man replied, inhaling a shaky breath as he coughed blood, the arrow having done more than its job. "You're too late." The man began to laugh, choking blood and laughing before gasping, the death rattle wheezing from between his lips. He lay still.

"WHERE IS THE HIGH KING?" Asim turned towards his Medjay. His question went unanswered as he ran, cutting a swath into the large arena. What he saw was chaos. Plumes of smoke wafted out of the arena, largely emptied now save for the remaining fighters and Medjay. His men formed into the shape of a buffalo's horns and pressed forward into the arena, cutting down invader after invader as they tried to take them.

A lion fed on two Medjay soldiers, his teeth clamped firmly

around the dismembered head of one as he lay midway up the sitting portion on the stone steps of the arena.

Asim spotted the High King whose own *khopesh* was landing blow after blow. Running towards Kashta, Medjay followed, metal clanging against metal as they fought side by side, moving closer to Amkar with every swing of their blades. Ripping through the invaders one by one. Retrieving a long narrow spear from a dead body near his feet, he pulled it free, spun around and hefted it upwards quickly at the swordsmen charging behind him. It punched through his flesh and the man grunted in surprise as Asim pulled it free with a squelch.

Turning without a beat, he launched the spear forward again, running as soon as it left his hand, not waiting for it to pierce the chest of the attacker directly in front of him. *A swordsman.* He ducked and rolled as his next opponent's thrust almost took his right shoulder. Thrusting his *khopesh* into the man's groin from his crouched position, the scream gave him satisfaction as he pressed it deeper. The man screamed and his legs gave way under him. Asim rose and drove his *khopesh* down, slicing his head in half. Blood sprayed across his face as the man's head became two. There was no need to wipe it off. More would follow.

Like the sound of sharpening blades, the weapons around him rang out as Medjay fought for the High King and his family. For Nabara. For Nudolla. Two lions lay dead on the ground, but when the others rose, Asim cut his man down quickly, running towards the beast without delay. He launched himself forward as the lion did and drove his spear into its chest as its weight fell against him. Asim grunted with the effort as the beast's bloodstained upper teeth sank into his left wrist before he pushed the beast off of him.

Where are you, Azima? Please be safe. He fought to quell the desperation filling his chest as flames licked at the arena's walls, rising higher with every moment. Chaos reigned around him as remaining villagers and townsmen ran from the complex in droves. He could hear some screaming for help, but he ignored them as he threw himself into the crowd, pushing people out of the way.

The Scorpion King pushed a mercenary's body over roughly, lifting the bloody body underneath.

"Takide," he repeated over and over again. "Takide." Blood

covered his hands and arms as he shook the boy's shoulders, trying to bring his son back to life.

When he turned back, the High King was gone, but there were trails of blood on the sand and among the stone seats. Blood covered the steps, and his head pounded as he wondered who might have been hurt.

Asim gritted his teeth as he turned around again and again, the Medjay guards now circling around the High King. He ran swiftly towards the stone vault, his *khopesh* drawn. *Had the Medjay taken all back to the safety of the palace?*

Tripping over something he looked down, his eyes falling over Rhaka, the young archer he'd helped Shaharqa train not long ago. Rhaka's fist curled around his bow as blood trickled over his lips. A sword had caught him just under his chin, thrusting out through his cheek like some ill-fitting jewelry. Shaking his head, Asim knelt to close his eyes, that he may see the beauty waiting for him on the other side rather than the hell that had found him here.

Kwasi was walking back into the arena with his guards, his own *khopesh* held in front of him, black with blood. Kandake Bamanirenas pulled a barbed spear made entirely from bone from one mercenary's throat, wiping it on her clothing. Catching Asim's eye she nodded quickly, before moving towards the edge of the arena with her escorts, making sure their enemies were dead.

When he looked back up he spotted something, the bright green of it bordered by white. Walking over to it slowly, a dread filled his heart as he realized the paw was covering something brown, something limb like, something human. *No.* His hands shook as he lifted the paw, staring into the eyes of Princess Ama, so like a niece to him. Her cheek half eaten, jaw wide as though she had screamed as she died, neck mangled and ripped from her body. Horror filled him as he struggled to draw breath, dropping to his knees as the pain filled him, burning his eyes. Only one eye remained of the two that were always so cautious around Amkar, her uncle and ward, but so playful at all other times. Following behind Prince Jelani like a shadow as soon as she learned to walk. Begging Imani to wear jewels and buy kohl and gowns for every celebration. Teasing the stable boys. *I've failed you. Apedemak forgive me.*

"Asim, where is she?" the High King screamed wildly as he caught his eye, piercing Asim's gaze as he demanded an answer.

"Your Grace...I..." Unable to speak he turned towards Amkar, helpless in his reply as he put a palm to Ama's remaining cheek, looking up to the sky in anguish.

Shaharqa's eyes met his as they struggled to find the words, neither of them wanting to utter the answer.

Swords were sheathed behind him as the High King stood in the middle of the arena, blood dripping from the end of his *khopesh* as he finally reached Asim. Looking down at what lay before him, Amkar stopped short, nostrils flaring as he swallowed, shaking his head in disbelief. Asim could not bring himself to look up at his High King. His brother, whom he'd failed.

"I thought...I tried..."

Amkar's words were more a demand than a question as they echoed throughout the near-empty arena, chilling Asim to the bone.

"WHERE IS MY DAUGHTER!"

EPILOGUE

Cupping his right hand to his forehead, Chukwu shielded his eyes from the harsh glare of the sun as he watched them, his painted ivory and acacia mask covering the rest of his face. They didn't know who he was, but soon they would. His peregrine falcon dove low before rising back up, sounding a low call as it circled the top of the caravan, black and white patterned wings spread wide. After tracking them for so long, he knew they numbered no more than what he saw before him. No follow party trailed them as with normal caravans worth this much. And it had not always been a slave caravan. Nodding to his cousin on his left, he pointed to the last of the captured slaves. From his vantage point, one could make out the large gold bricks they carried. *And they even have some camels.* It was a pleasant surprise. The smile on his face grew wider as he counted the value in his head. Even the Silk Road wasn't always this kind.

"Take out the four Berbers on the side," he told his men. "Aim lower than you normally would. The turban conceals more than you think."

Moving swiftly, they thundered towards the party full speed. Gliding over the sand his camel ran smoothly, its feet used to the terrain and built to travel for long periods without water. The animal was meant for long journeys and built for the heat of the desert.

By the time they saw him, it was too late. A warning call rang out as the slaver turned towards him. Two dull thuds sounded in his ear, followed by screaming. The Berbers toppled from their camels onto the ground as his party advanced. Pulling out his mace, he stopped his camel, the sand blowing around them like a storm, settling quietly as the slavers looked from him to his family. Quiet defiance shone in the slaver's eyes, a desperate calculation playing in them as they tried to determine the greater threat. Him or the arrows now trained on them. Pointing his mace at their leader, he looked down at the man as rage played over his red face.

"Tch, tch, tch, tch. You're not from around here are you?" He shook his head as he looked at them. "My, my. Have I spoiled your party?" he asked the slaver.

"How dare you! These slaves are *my* property! Release us or you will pay for this." The slaver was furious.

"I understand. Truly. I do. But if you cannot protect your own property, then of what use is the demand?"

The slaver swallowed, lips pursing as he took a step backwards. His men circled the slavers slowly as he urged his camel forward, forcing the slaver backwards. Suddenly, a ragged sob came from his left, and he turned towards the sound.

"Help me! Please…" One of the slavers had been caught with an arrow in his stomach. Writhing on the ground, he held his side as blood trickled from between his fingers, spreading onto the sand. Looking down at the slaver, he sighed, jumping down from his camel to walk closer to the man. Shaking his head, he walked nearer, kicking the man's dagger away before squatting slowly.

"Please…I…I don't want to die here," the man begged, groaning as he pressed his hands to his side.

"Let me see." Chukwu tried to pull the slaver's hands away from his wound.

"No, no, please!" The man was sweating profusely now. Spittle ran from his mouth as he groaned in agony.

Ignoring him, he pulled the man's hands away, sighing. Pushing his shirt up, he wiped the blood away from his wound. *Ridiculous.* It was only a flesh wound.

"You're fine. We haven't killed you. It's only a flesh wound," he told him, irritation rising in his chest.

"No, I'm dying…" The man was delirious.

"I promise. You'll be fine. I'm giving you a second chance. But I need you to do one thing for me. Be quiet. I need to have a conversation with your leader. Can you do that for me?" He pulled his hands away, standing up.

"But I'm dying! You can't do this! I have children, a wife——"

Suddenly the man reached for a second dagger and with one swift move, he brought his mace forward, raising it high above his head before slamming it down on the man's head. The cracking sound it made was followed by gasps behind him. He didn't need all of his strength for this job. He'd been swinging his mace for

391

years. He could hear someone vomiting behind him, shallow breaths telling him others were trying not to. The slaver's brains had sprayed across the sand and over his feet, sticking to his mace as he looked at the pieces of flesh now sticking to the ends of it like bloodied pig's meat. *Children? A wife? Did he think he was the only one suffering right now? The only one with a family to think of?* Slaving was a strange thing. No matter how many men and women they tore from their own families, no matter how many children were killed or injured because of their efforts, they never saw any of them as human. And never would. Frowning in disgust, he stood back up slowly, wiping the mace as best he could before turning back to face the slaving party, the slaves, and his men. The surprise and shock on their faces made him sigh again.

"I was *trying* to have a conversation!" he said incredulously before laughing softly.

"Come now. I'm a reasonable man," he began again. "I'll give you a chance to claim your property before I take it." He turned his mace towards the slaves. "Is this man your master? Are you his property?"

None of them spoke. Emboldened by the silence, the slaver finally smiled.

"You see?" The slaver took two steps forward. "They are *mine*."

Chukwu turned to the slaves once more. "Fear sleeps even in the bravest of men. Until he douses it like a flame with water. Like a snake beneath his feet. I ask you again," he challenged them. "Are you his property?" he bellowed.

"No!" a voice cried out. The slave's voices rang out in the desert together.

"We are not!" another said.

"He lies!" said another. "He stole us!"

"Stole you?" He held up a hand to silence them. "A thief?" Feigning surprise, he walked towards the slaver. "Well. Common ground. So you understand me?" Striding back to his camel, he jumped up onto it quickly. Circling the slaver on his camel he noted how the slaver's men shifted uncertainly, looking towards their leader for their next move. Suddenly, a slave woman turned and spit on one of the dead Berbers at her feet, the chains on her wrists ignored as she kicked at the *takoba* sword the dead man once held. The *takoba* was an extremely long and narrow sword made with a brass or copper hilt and iron down its length. Many of the Berbers believed them to be imbued with magical powers by the metallurgist caste that created them. *Not so magical after all.* Face down in a pool of blood, the arrow had pierced the Berber's left temple and gone straight through to the other side. He had trained his men well.

"Tch, tch, tch, tch, tch. They don't seem to like you very much," he laughed. "I don't blame them. You Romans. You turned a Berber mountain village into what *you* decided to name Cuicul. Turned Cuicul into a garrison. Stole their grain and cattle. Forced the Berbers out and killed whomever resisted. Raped their women. Enslaved their sons. And now look at them. Half of them are serving you."

His eyes fell back to one of the dead Berbers as he looked up apologetically. "Well, *were* serving you."

The slaver's leader was growing bold again. "You have no right to—"

"To what?" he challenged him. "I was born on this land. This land is mine. And so is everything on it. You see, I asked about you. I met…some people you knew. The Whore of Rome! The Slave's Nightmare! They called you a great number of different names."

"I will make sure Rome burns you and your family if—"

"But they never said you were smart."

The Roman's mouth slammed shut as if he were pondering his next move. The precariousness of his situation seemed to dawn on him.

"You see," he continued. "I just killed every one of your guides, I think." Smiling at the remaining Berber, he held up a single finger. "But one. And yet here you are more concerned for your cargo than your own life. How thoughtful."

Nervousness broke out like hives on the slaver's face. He doubted he would make that mistake again.

Circling the slaver slowly he began again. "I am searching for someone. Perhaps, if you tell me what I want to hear, I'll leave you a camel, yes?"

The slaver gritted his teeth, jaw flexing as he turned again, and again in an attempt to follow the camel as it circled him. The slaver's eyes were wary. *I cannot blame him.*

"I'm looking for a man," he continued. "You may have come across him in your *business* dealings. Your...trade. They call him The Zanj's Master. The Enslaver. Among other things. They say he is well known to another trader known as The Roman Merchant. I need to find him."

"I have no knowledge of either man. I would tell you if—"

"Yes, I'm sure you would," he responded drily.

"I have gold." The slaver tried another tack. "I'll give it all to you and half the slaves if you take me to the next city. My arm—"

"Slaves." Stroking his beard, he pondered a moment, swinging his mace gently from the camel. "You mistake me. I am a thief. Not a slave trader. I have no interest in slaves. But your gold I will take."

Nodding once, he signaled to his men and waited as they relieved the slavers of their weapons. He could feel the anger drifting off them in waves, directed at him like a thousand bee stings. When they were well and finished, one of the slaves dropped to his knees and clasped his hands together.

"Thank you, brother. For freeing us!" Tears ran unchecked down his face.

"Freeing you? There aren't enough camels for that. Brother. Besides. I need someone to carry what the camels cannot." He turned to the other slaves, nodding to the gold bars they had dropped. "If you please," he said encouragingly.

The shock on their faces amused him. Most of them looked at him like a deer that had walked into a trap. Once the chains were removed they slowly began to gather the remainder of the gold that had been strapped to the camels. One by one, his cousins slammed the butt of their weapons into the back of the slavers' heads. All but the slaver and the last Berber remained standing.

"Who are you?" The slaver had been relieved of his weapons, but his hands still curled into fists at his sides. *He's a proud fool,* he thought, shaking his head.

"Who am I?" Adjusting the painted wood and ivory mask covering his face he picked up the reins of his camel. Narrow slits for his eyes carved inside of it allowed him to see. The round shape of the forehead slanted into a narrow pointed chin. The white and black markings of the Igbo became the source of stories men would tell their children to strike fear or give courage. Many paid homage to the spirits of beautiful women, some long passed. "You're asking the wrong question."

Nodding to his men, he spun his camel about as they started their journey. "Kill these two if they begin moving before we can no longer see them." His cousin nodded, spinning around on his camel to ride backwards, his bow and arrow trained on the kneeling men. *If he lives another day, I will congratulate him on his victory.* He smirked. It was a long way to their next destination, and it couldn't be found on any map.

Nearly two days later, he called to one of the slavers' former captives to walk by his side, handing him a skin filled with water.

"How did you come to be in his service?" He couldn't hide his curiosity.

"He was like you," the man told him, sneering as he answered. "He stole us. He ran my family down."

"Tch, tch, tch, tch. Next time, run faster." Motioning with his chin, he signaled to the man to fall back in line.

An hour later his falcon sounded another call, higher this time. Landing on his shoulder, its bright yellow beak nipped at his ear. Petting its head gently he slowed, whistling softly as the crimson sand blew about the ivory-streaked mountain passes. Two tall, tree-shaped sand stone markers stood on each side. Battered by the rough lashing of the desert sand and winds, they stood over fifty feet tall. A sharper whistle greeted him, and a man stepped out from behind one of them.

"You have no shame, my son," the old priest greeted him. "First salt, sorghum, and gold. And now this." Disappointment was etched into his heavily lined brown face as he looked at the caravan of slaves.

Turning around he frowned at them. *They could at least look happy.*

"I have no interest in slaves, old man. But a man cannot live on bread alone." With that, he jumped from his camel, leaving his family and the slaves at a distance as he walked beside the old man. The priest's long, white robes swept the ground. A long rope wound itself around his narrow waist. Salted hair reached his ears, and his long beard was as white as the clouds above and slightly disheveled by the wind. But his appearance was of no concern to the priest.

"The fathers have heard tell that it's not just the Sahel that is at risk from the trade in slaves. Arabian traders on the eastern coast are growing bolder as well, coming into the interior as far as they can to sell what slaves they find."

"What you here is true. The *Zanj* is what the Arabians call these slaves. The men are made eunuchs and personal butlers meant to wipe the asses of their masters. The women caretakers, gifts, and concubines. They sell them even to Asia and widely for labor because of the Nubian's knowledge of salt and sugar mining for Arabian elites with too much land and no idea how to make it productive. Mesopotamia, the Greeks call it. A land between two rivers. I would see them drown in a sea of tears as they begged for their lives."

"You must be *careful,* my son."

"I am not your son. And I never would have imagined you would use the word *careful* when speaking to me." Raising an eyebrow he looked at the old man in surprise.

"Of course not. But the people who come here tell me stories of you. They don't know your name. But they know your words and your actions. Your character they describe well enough. *Legend,* they call you."

He laughed at the old priest's words. "Then I am in good company."

"Truth now." The old priest looked at him gravely, eyes narrowed as he put one hand on his shoulder. "This is no way to live."

"In truth, old man, I know no other way."

The priest sighed. "How long will you live like this? Riding, stealing, killing?"

"As long as I can," he replied, looking away. "Perhaps when I am old and gray like you I will come here and settle. I like the desert. It *suits* me."

"I became old and gray *here*." The priest was unrelenting.

"Each man has his own path," Chukwu quoted the priest's words back at him.

The father laughed, "As you say. As you say. Though I do believe some of the men you have brought me who would have become slaves would look kindly upon you for the pains you took to save them."

"There was no pain involved. I care only for the gold."

"As you say. As you say. I only mean to make an honest man out of you."

Now it was he who laughed, throwing back his head as he held tightly to the mask in his hand. "Now you sound like my wife."

"Ahh, so there is someone you care about? Someone who cares about you?" The priest's voice was curious. *I can't blame him for prying.* The priest had always been good to him. And he was set in his ways.

The desert grew darker as he stopped walking, looking out into the pressing darkness, the heat of the sun and her orange hue almost fading behind sand-covered mountains and stone figures that loomed as though the dead rose from their dusty graves.

"Once," he replied. "Once."

The father nodded, and he knew he was accepting his answer. For now. Replacing his mask, he turned with the priest back towards the caravan.

"I've tarried too long. Unload your gold onto the camels. Quickly," he commanded the slaves. They followed his instructions without question. Their newfound captivity had humbled them. A resignation settled over their actions and movements. Their bowed heads a testament to the impact of even a short period of enslavement.

"When shall I see you again?" The father looked at him with a sadness that Chukwu could not place.

"Soon, I should think." His brothers nodded to the priest as they leapt back onto their horses and camels, waiting for him. "The desert has more animals than one would guess. And I seem to be running into more and more each day."

"You see more than your falcon, I think."

"No." He shook his head. "He sees for me."

The father nodded. "May God protect you."

397

He smiled. "Your God is busy doing more important work, I should think."

At that he turned his camel, his brothers following him as he continued making his way through the desert. Popping two kola nuts into his mouth to quell his thirst for a time, he tapped the camel gently. He didn't look back as he continued through the stone pass. Shadows fell on them as they continued into the darkness, the gold bars winking softly in the dying light from the backs of the long train of camels.

....

Shaking his head, Abba Moses watched him go. The thief was a troubled soul. *God be with you, my son.* He was a raider, a thief, and a murderer with a taste for trouble. But he had a good heart. He just didn't know it, yet. He shooed the men and women towards the narrow rock-face opening, their tired eyes vacant and unquestioning as they did, once again, what they were told. Heads bowed in resignation they crowded, waiting for him to enter last, unable to forge their own path forward even out of curiosity. Their short stint in slavery forcing them to treat each new person as their new master.

Abba Moses pulled a torch off the wall as he closed the entryway back into place, hiding it from outside travelers and those who searched. They would not find it on any map.

"Please, follow me," he said. Shuffling along behind him slowly, they felt their way along in the dark. Their soft breaths were hesitant and filled with trepidation as they ducked under the low walls. He could smell them. Sweat clung to them like mud on a hippo and permeated the air, but he did not cover his nose. It was not his first time smelling such as these. No doubt they had been refused a bath time and again. When rocks fell from the low ceiling, some of them cried out in fear, but he reassured them softly, telling them not to worry and assuring them they were almost there.

Twenty feet later they reached a wide, circular opening where one of his brothers stood, dress robes hanging loosely on his lean frame. A short black beard adorned his pale jawline. In his hands were a number of black robes that he held tightly, one large piece of soap sitting on top of the pile. Just behind him, the rushing sounds of water grew louder as it cascaded into the black pool below, gurgling and splashing as it fell.

"Use it sparingly," Abba Moses told the group, handing the first slave the large piece of soap and motioning him towards the pools. The women he handed another. For a moment the man stood there, as though unsure of what was being asked of him.

"Please. You will come to no harm. Go. Clean yourselves." Abba Moses pushed him gently, guiding him towards the waters. The man put his feet in slowly, standing ankle deep before suddenly his body began to shake, trembling as he added his own tears to the pool. But he began to bathe. One by one the others followed him until all of them were standing naked in the pools, their clothes discarded as they washed themselves. Passing the soap from one to the other, they cleaned themselves, unconcerned for their nakedness in the dim light, which gave them some semblance of privacy. The men turned their backs to the women out of respect even as they passed the soap. Moses knew with the auction block and branding, this lot might have already experienced the indignity of baring their nakedness for slavers. *And still they hold on to their humanity.*

As each finished, his brother held out the fresh black robes for them to put on and they did so without hesitation, securing them tightly with a bit of twine. This time when Moses and his brother continued on, the men and women followed without question or delay. They passed a number of rooms carved into the walls, consisting of only a slab shaved into the shape of a bed. Many of his brothers were at their daily prayers, knees bent in supplication, hands raised as they prayed to God silently.

Turning to his wards, he addressed them softly, "You find yourself among the refuge of the Desert Fathers, Christian followers of the one and only God and his son, Jesus Christ, the only righteous man to have walked the earth and an example to us all. You may stay as long as your body and soul require. There are only two meals each day. Breakfast and dinner. I hope you are all early risers. We ask of you three things and three things only while you stay here. You must not give into temptations nor encourage others to do so. You must find yourself in service for at least three hours of the day. And, when you leave here, you must not communicate the whereabouts of this sanctuary nor the identity of its residents or tasks you may see to anyone. It is for our safety as well as yours. If you agree, you will accept this token, and you may follow my brother to your quarters."

"What happens if we don't agree to this?" a woman asked, mistrust in her wary eyes as she peered at the papyrus in his hand.

"No one has ever failed to agree." Abba Moses smiled kindly at her. "But I am sure we can find a place for you instead."

The woman swallowed and looked slowly up towards the ceiling, crossing her arms about her chest before stepping forward quickly behind the others and thanking them as they passed. Abba Moses left them, assured they were in good hands. Walking quickly down one of the eight pathways that branched off from the circular opening, he walked quickly towards another chamber, his dress robes sweeping the floor as his hands stroked his white beard, concern wrinkling his forehead. *Two girls this time.* His brother had warned him there would be more, but asked Moses to speak with them as they refused to speak with anyone. How they came to know this place was a mystery, but even he knew that God worked in mysterious ways. If He wanted to reveal this path in the desert to these girls, far be it for anyone to get in the way of His plans.

When he reached the last steps, he took his time, moving carefully downwards, his hand brushing against the sandstone walls built by the first refugees of the Great Persecution by Diocletian. His was a lasting legacy of murder, grief, and pain. He himself had sought refuge from Egypt for things that still tormented him. Despite the Edict of Milan, many of his brothers and sisters remained under the watchful and vengeful eyes of Roman magistrates who refused to recognize the Christian religion. *One day, we will hide no more.*

The girls cowered in a corner of the chamber, an amma trying to tend to them but failing miserably. The mother's unused bucket of water no longer steamed with the heat it had when Moses left to receive his most recent wards. The wet rag in her hand was received by the girls as though she wielded a sword. Letting her touch them was the last thing on their minds.

"There now, daughters, what is this?" he asked of them. "Have you come so long a way only to sit in silence? Will you not eat? See now, did your mother teach you to let hot water run cold?" he scolded them gently. "What would your father say?"

The oldest looked at him with her large moonlike eyes, her dark pupils wide with mistrust.

"Our father is dead." Cutting her eyes at him, she clutched her sister tighter.

The amma gasped next to him, covering her mouth with her free hand.

Moses came closer. "Who killed him?" he asked her.

"The slavers. Our neighbor. We don't know," the younger whispered, as though they might punish her for her treachery in revealing them. Swallowing, she looked towards the entrance from which he came.

"We saw them. They killed our neighbor, but *he* may have killed our father...they weren't monsters. They were men. We didn't know who to trust." She shivered, tightening her hold on her little sister.

"And how did you come to be here?" he asked gently, seating himself a short distance away. When she began to speak, he nodded once at the amma and she began wiping the dirt from the youngest's face. Allowing her to remain tethered to her sister like an anchor, the amma slowly scrubbed the sand caked on her legs away.

"My father...my mother..." Tears fell fast from her face. "They told me of a sanctuary no man would find on a map. Where anyone who found it would be safe." Her cracked lips stopped moving, and he stood.

"You are two very brave little girls. Grown men fear the journey you made. And your father...taught you to read the stars, did he?" When she nodded, he was satisfied.

"I am Abba Moses the Black, and this is Amma Sarah. And of course, you have already met God. He brought you through the *Šihēt*." He smiled. "Some call it the Scetes, the pronunciation and variations change depending on the city. It all means the same thing, daughters. *Measure of the Hearts*. And yours are strong. Once you have changed, I will return to take you to eat." The littlest one licked her lips as he finished.

"When I come back, whom shall I ask for?" he asked. He looked at both girls and they turned to each other, their faces unsure. The oldest eyed the amma warily, sizing her up carefully before turning back to him.

"This is Naima. And I am Nekili. We are from Meroë."

CHARACTER INDEX

EMPIRE & ALLIANCE OF NUDOLLA

1. KINGDOM OF NABARA (GOLD)

a. High King Amkarqa Arkamani-qo Kashta, King of Nabara, High King of Nudolla

b. High Queen Samya Nasala Kashta, Queen of Nabara, High Queen of Nudolla

c. Prince Yemi Kashta, Prince Semi Kashta, twin brothers of Amkar Kashta

d. Prince Jelani Kashta - son

e. Princess Nema Tabiry Kashta, daughter

f. Princess Imanishakheto Aminata Kashta - daughter

g. Princess Ama Kashta, cousin of Imanishakheto

h. Queen Arami Kashta - High King's mother, Kingmaker

i. King Aman Kashta – High King's father, deceased

j. Prince Shaharqa Kashta – High King's brother, military commander

k. Asim Kashta– Medjay Commander, adopted son of Arami

l. Ram- Medjay, cousin of Asim

m. Adum – High King's Vizier

2. SCORPION KINGDOM (CENTER: THARBIS)

a. King Tuma Talib Tharbis, King

b. Queen Radhia Tharbis, 1st wife of King Tuma

c. Queen Cima Tharbis, 2nd wife of King Tuma

d. Queen Fera Tharbis, 3rd wife of King Tuma

e. Queen Besima Tharbis, 4th wife of King Tuma

f. Queen Daran Tharbis, 5th wife of King Tuma

g. Queen Emi Tharbis, 6th wife of King Tuma

h. Queen Ajna Tharbis, 7th wife of King Tuma

i. Queen Kiseli Tharbis, 8th wife of King Tuma

j. Terit, 1st son of Tuma and Radhia

k. Jengo, 2nd son of Tuma and Fera, deceased

l. Tari, 3rd son of Tuma and Cima

m. Takide, 4th son of Tuma and Besima

n. Teqer, 5th son of Tuma and Daran

o. Tisaan, 6th son of Tuma and Emi

3.KIBERA KINGDOM (CENTER: KIBERA)

   a. Queen Jara Bamanirenas, the Hunter of Kibera
   b. Prince Bakar Bamanirenas II, son
   c. Princess Bai Bamanirenas, daughter, twin
   d. Princess Banji Bamanirenas, daughter, twin
   e. Late King Bakar Bamanirenas, husband, deceased

4.SAO KINGDOM (CENTER: KINGDOM OF THE SUN)

   a. King Kwasi Sora, King
      1. Prince Komoro Sora, nephew
      2. Princess Ketemin Sora, niece
      3. Late King Kemaris Sora, brother, deceased
   b. Chief Treasurer, Odwulfe
   c. Noble Domin
      1. Desa, leader of Noble Domin's harem
      2. Saai, wife of Noble Domin and Prince Komoro's lover
   d. Essivi, young handmaid
   e. Hasea, young handmaid
   f. Commander Tesir, leader of King's armies
   g. Father Komil, Temple Priest
   h. Deemat, Salt miner
     i. Deema, daughter
     ii. Duumel, son

5.ESSI KINGDOM (CENTER: FLOATING ISLANDS)

   a. King Makalo Mansa, King of Essi
   b. Prince Mikaili Mansa, son
   c. Queen Makeda Mansa, deceased wife

6.SOTHO KINGDOM (CENTER: HIGHLANDS)

   a. King Yuri, the first, King of the Sotho
   b. Prince Yuri, the second- son in law of High King Kashta,
   c. Princess Nema, wife of Prince Yuri, daughter of High King Kashta
   d. Prince Tamayis, son of Prince Yuri and Princess Nema

HIGH PRIESTS OF NABARA (Only those that appeared)

1. High Priest Hameht
2. High Priest Dahket
3. High Priest Enu
4. High Priest Harem

NOMADS & DESERT DWELLERS

1. Nomadin
2. Berbers
3. Tuareg
4. Bedouin

HUNTER-GATHERERS

1. !Kung (Sons of Prishiboro)
   a. Chief Kumsa
2. Sons of Cagn

FARMING & HERDING KINGDOMS

1. Luba
   a. Chief Nkole
   b. Elder Andikan
2. Goko
3. Kalanga
4. Zulu
   a. Luba
   b. Goko
   c. Kalanga
   d. Zulu

PASTORALISTS & CATTLE RAISERS

1. Khoekhoe
   a. Damara (People of IIGamab)
   b. Namaqua

SLAVE CATCHERS

1. Cassius
2. Nicolae
3. Sicarius
4. Berbers
5. Tribune
6. Physicians

EXILES

1. Nastasen Zanga
2. Ismar
3. Amare
4. Zyqarri

SEERS

1. Zaxasha, High Priestess of Yoruba
2. Adura, Daughter of Aiona
3. Aiona, Mother of Adura

PROLOGUE CHARACTERS

1. Nekili, daughter, citizen of Meroë (Kingdom of Kush)
2. Naima, daughter, citizen of Meroë (Kingdom of Kush)
3. Naqyrin, father of Nekili, Naima and Neka and farmer of Meroë
4. Neka, son of Naqyrin
5. Kedjeh, neighbor of Naqyrin

MARKET CHARACTERS

1. Sanaa, artisan's daughter, friend of Imani
2. Karim, scroll maker
3. Bapa, Storyteller, Historian, Jeli

EPILOGUE CHARACTERS

1. Chukwu, Igbo Caravan Raider
2. Slave Trader, Slave's Nightmare
3. Abba Moses the Black, Desert Father, Christian hermit
4. Amma Sarah, Desert Mother, Christian hermit mother

ACKNOWLEDGMENTS

Thank you to everyone who supported this endeavor! Thank you to the representatives of the National Museum of African American History and Culture, the National Museum of African Art, the National Museum of Natural History, the Warren M. Robbins Library, the Library of Congress, and Sankofa Video Books & Café. A special thank you to those who encouraged me, gave me advice on how to move forward with publishing, and answered my calls and emails. Thank you for listening as I explained this story and many of my first descriptions of characters as I brought them to life. Your support and excitement meant so much and I appreciated every single minute of it. Mom, Dad, Mylene, Jeannine, Crystal, Victoria, I remain forever grateful.

Finally, a huge thank you to my readers! I hope you enjoyed this book and plan on reading the second book in the series! Feel free to leave a review on my Amazon page. Please feel free to contact me through my website contact form at www.ofcaptivityandkings.com!

ABOUT THE AUTHOR

E.Y. Laster is the author of the book *Of Captivity & Kings.* She majored in English literature and enjoys a variety of works. This is the first installment in her series *Of Captivity & Kings,* a work created from her curiosity and love for history, travel, film, and literature. This book began in 2013 on the back of old receipts and continued being written during commutes, in waiting rooms, during lunch hours and even while running to train for the Rock N' Roll Half Marathon and The Color Run. In the spring of 2016 she decided to publish. When you decide to chase your dreams it's better to wear sneakers! For any questions regarding this book please contact her via her website or by email at info@ofcaptivityandkings.com.

Book Website: For more information, to subscribe to our mailing list, or read samples of the next book in the series, please visit www.ofcaptivityandkings.com.

Beta Readers: E.Y. Laster is searching for and welcomes beta readers for Book Two in the *Of Captivity & Kings* series, which is already in draft form! This includes historians and others who have backgrounds in 4th century history, trade, religion, and travel. Please send an email with your information directly to info@ofcaptivityandkings.com if you are interested in this opportunity.